THE
FRONTIERS SAGA
PART 2: ROGUE CASTES
EPISODE 6

FOR THE
TRIUMPH OF EVIL
RYK BROWN

CHAPTER ONE

Ensign Aiden Walsh had spent hours in the Cobra simulator during his training back on Kohara. Some of his sessions had been so long that he was certain he had broken some previous record. Flying a Cobra gunship was all he could think about. All he had ever wanted was to be a pilot, but he hadn't the money to pay for flight school. The Alliance had been his only way to achieve his dream.

Originally, he had wanted to fly the famed Super Eagle jump fighters. Sleek, fast, single-seat; they were the ship of heroes; jumping in and out of combat, always keeping the enemy guessing. But he lacked the discipline required of such pilots. Discipline *and* connections. And so, the Cobra gunship had become his billet. They were not as fast, nor as sleek, and flying them did not hold the mystique and respect that Eagle pilots carried. Even worse, they were flown in packs, using auto-flight algorithms designed by tacticians back at Alliance Fleet Command at Port Terra. Few tales spoke of heroes flying Cobra gunships, other than that of Captains Robert Nash and Gil Roselle, both of whom he and the other Cobra pilots were currently following back to the Pentaurus sector.

It could be worse, Aiden thought. *I could be flying a shuttle.* Aiden smiled. Now, he was not only flying a Cobra gunship, he was following the legendary Captain Nathan Scott. He was going to join the Karuzari. He was going to fight alongside the Ghatazhak, the greatest warriors known.

Of course, to do so had not only required him to go AWOL—either that or defect, he had yet to decide which it was—but he had dragged his crew and his friends along, as well, nearly getting them killed in the process. It was a fact that had bothered him for the last two and a half days, and he suspected it would bother him for some time to come.

"How many more jumps?" a voice called from behind.

Aiden glanced over his shoulder, immediately straightening up in his seat when he realized who was asking. "Uh," he said, glancing at the auto-jump sequencer display on the center of his console, "two hundred and eighty-seven...make that two hundred and eighty-six. So, about fourteen and a half hours to go."

"Fourteen point three, I believe," Corporal Chesen corrected as he moved toward the copilot's seat. "May I?"

"Of course."

The Ghatazhak corporal stepped over the center console, making the necessary contortions to slip into the seat. He looked over the console. "It is definitely not the same one that we studied in the VR sim."

"Yeah, I heard about that," Aiden replied. "Seems like a pretty bad oversight on the planning side."

"We had insufficient intelligence, which is often the case in war. That is why we are trained to adapt."

"You were going to fly one?"

"If necessary, yes."

"Then you're a pilot?"

"In the sense that I know *how* to pilot a spacecraft, yes. All Ghatazhak are trained to do so. Although, admittedly, I have not done so in many years."

Aiden looked at him. "But you could have? Flown one of these gunships?"

2

"Yes," the corporal replied. "Not as well as you, I suspect, but I could have gotten it launched and back to the rendezvous point." Corporal Chesen smiled, looking at Aiden. "I doubt I would have tried to bounce it off the surface of Kohara, though. *That* was an impressive feat. I am curious how you calculated your angle of incidence, kinetic energy loss during impact, and all the other variables involved, prior to committing to that particular maneuver."

Now, Aiden smiled. "I got lucky."

"Ah, then it was instinct. A very valuable talent, to be sure."

"Actually, I thought I'd have enough thrust to pull up to a clear jump line," Aiden admitted. "When I realized we didn't, I was pretty sure we were all going to die."

"Then why did you attempt the maneuver?" Corporal Chesen wondered.

Aiden shrugged his shoulders. "It seemed like a good idea at the time."

"Had that slight downhill grade not been there to lessen your impact, and the tall, wet grass not been there, had the slope not angled quickly upward again..."

"...Like I said, I got lucky," Aiden repeated.

"I was there. Yes, you were lucky that all those elements were present. The slopes, the wet grass... But *you* slightly altered course just before impact, causing us to clear the crest and strike the surface at a less dangerous angle. That was not luck, that was *skill* and *instinct*."

"Yeah, I guess."

"However, in the future, it might be better if you were to consider your actions a bit more carefully in the heat of battle, and avoid unnecessary risks," the corporal advised.

Aiden looked surprised. "I thought the Ghatazhak were all about risk. I mean, you guys are the greatest soldiers ever known, right?"

"We are, because the risks we take are carefully calculated in order to ensure our success," the corporal explained.

"You're saying you would have *calculated* all that stuff? The angle of impact, the drag of the surface, the transfer of kinetic energy during impact and sliding down, and then back up the grade...*all* of it? In the *middle* of *battle*?"

"Yes."

"All of it?"

"All of it," the corporal replied confidently. "Possibly more than once," he added, a wry smile on his face.

"I don't see how that's even possible," Aiden insisted, shaking his head.

"It is all part of a Ghatazhak's training."

"They taught you to do such equations in your head?"

"There are no calculators on the battlefield," the corporal replied. "Nor time to use them if there were."

"What else did they teach you?" Aiden asked.

"Many things: science, philosophy, economics, psychology, religion, physics, astrophysics—many, *many* things. And of course, all things combat-related."

"I had no idea," Aiden admitted. "I always thought..."

"That the Ghatazhak were just highly-trained killers," Corporal Chesen said, finishing Aiden's sentence for him.

"Sorry, I meant no disrespect."

"None was taken," the Ghatazhak corporal assured him. "Such misconceptions were the result of the Ybaran Legions, *and* the rule of Caius Ta'Akar."

"The *Ybaran Legions*?" Aiden wondered.

"Brutal, bloodthirsty men, made that way by difficult and torturous living conditions on a harsh world not originally of their choosing. They were trained in none of the disciplines I listed. Only in the art of combat, and they were *quite* adept at it, to be sure."

"Why them?"

"The empire of Caius grew quickly. It is a mistake made often by those seeking power. Be it in power or business; they were seeking to grow beyond their means of logistics and support," Corporal Chesen explained. "The original Karuzari recognized this and took advantage, taking down Caius's forces, bit by bit. The Ybarans were a marginalized segment of Takaran society. Caius recognized their strength, and made them into a new form of Ghatazhak."

"Sort of a *Ghatazhak-light*?"

Corporal Chesen looked confused. "If by that you mean not as completely trained as the real Ghatazhak, then yes. The Ybaran Legions possessed only the combat training and hardware of the Ghatazhak, but none of the knowledge and intellectual ability needed to use them. They were men willing to kill in the name of Caius, in order to gain the people their rightful status in Takaran society."

"And did they?" Aiden wondered.

"For a time, yes. But they backed the wrong noblemen, and that was their undoing."

"What happened to them?"

"Their entire world was destroyed only a few weeks

5

ago by the Dusahn," Corporal Chesen replied, "for refusing to pay proper respect to their conquerors."

"The Dusahn wiped out their entire world?" Aiden questioned in disbelief.

"From orbit. Men, women, children, the elderly; Ybara is now a complete wasteland, as is Burgess."

"Burgess?"

"The world that was *our* home," Corporal Chesen replied, his voice taking on a somber tone, "until recently."

"They destroyed *your* homeworld, as well?"

"Our *adopted* homeworld, yes."

Aiden suddenly felt ashamed. "I didn't know."

"How could you?" Corporal Chesen said, hoping to assuage Aiden's guilt.

"I guess we all assumed the Ghatazhak returned to Takara. Isn't that where you're all from?"

"Yes, but we could not in good conscience align ourselves with men who claimed noble title, yet did little to deserve it."

"But aren't you fighting to *free* Takara?"

"For her people... *our* people, yes... Freedom for those calling themselves nobles will be an unfortunate side effect," the corporal explained. "We fight for those who cannot fight for themselves. We fight those who believe they can lay claim to whatever they wish, simply because they have the power to do so. That is why the Ghatazhak were created centuries ago."

"I thought you were all programmed," Aiden said, still appearing confused. "Some sort of brainwashing to make you all obedient."

"In a way, yes, but only for a time," the corporal replied. "You see, the Ghatazhak are trained equally. Every man, from trooper to general, is just as capable. Each would come to the same decision, given the same situation and intelligence. It was necessary, since a battlefield could easily be separated from command by time and space. But it is also what makes us so lethal. No order is unsuspected; no order is met with hesitation or uncertainty because each man would give the same order, were the responsibility to fall on his shoulders. When Caius rose to power, this worried him. He wanted the Ghatazhak to be feared, not respected."

"So, they programmed you to be more brutal?"

"They tried, but it did not work. Our training and mental discipline was too great. Hence, the need for the Ybaran Legions. The best they could achieve was to ensure each Ghatazhak's loyalty to his commander, and he to his, and so on up the line. *This* edict was counter to neither our training, *nor* our oath. But even *that* did not hold."

"What do you mean?" Aiden asked.

"The programming had to be refreshed too frequently, which made the Ghatazhak difficult to deploy," Corporal Chesen explained. "Once the ranks of the Ybaran Legions had grown to sufficient size, the *true* Ghatazhak were put into stasis, with only a few hundred kept awake, mostly acting as either palace guards or to serve as instructors for the Ybaran Legions."

"Weren't some of you programmed to protect Captain Scott?" Aiden asked.

"After Caius was assassinated, yes. One hundred of us were given to the captain as a gift from Prince Casimir, and were programmed to protect him and assist him in his quest to liberate Earth, just as he had liberated the Pentaurus cluster, and the Ghatazhak."

7

"Then you're still programmed to serve him?" Aiden asked. "Captain Scott?"

"I was not among the first Ghatazhak assigned to Captain Scott. However, their programming wore off long ago, *before* he surrendered to the Jung. Those of us who followed had no programming at all."

"Yet, you are still willing to follow him into battle?"

"In a manner of speaking, yes," the corporal replied. "Our commander believes that Captain Scott has the instincts and leadership abilities to unite humanity."

"And you agree with him?"

"I know of no Ghatazhak who *disagrees* with the general's assessment." Corporal Chesen looked quizzically at Aiden. "What about you?"

"What *about* me?"

"As I understand it, you made a rather sudden choice to follow Captain Scott, as well. I suspect this choice, much like your choice to jump in and defend the last few departing gunships, was made *purely* on instinct. Am I wrong?"

"No, I suppose you're right," Aiden admitted. "I hadn't really thought about it."

"I suspect that statement is inaccurate," the corporal said, trying not to sound like he was making an accusation.

"I meant at the time," Aiden added.

"Ah, I see. Another human male who takes action without forethought. This tendency fascinates me."

"There is such a thing as thinking *too* much," Aiden said in his defense.

"A more accurate statement would be that it is possible to take too *long* to make a decision."

"You know what I meant."

Corporal Chesen smiled. "I am having fun with you, Ensign."

"Ghatazhak have fun?"

Corporal Chesen recognized that Ensign Walsh was having *fun* with him, as well. "If I might ask, why *did* you choose to abandon your life on a whim, and follow Captain Scott?"

"It seemed like the right thing to do at the moment," Aiden replied.

"Without any evidence to support your decision?"

"Yup," Aiden replied as he checked the auto-jump sequencer display again.

"The Ghatazhak would consider your actions foolhardy, at best," Corporal Chesen said as he rose from his seat.

"Kinda my style," Aiden muttered, more to himself than to the corporal.

Corporal Chesen climbed back over the center console, moving behind Aiden and patting him on the shoulder as he passed. "You and Captain Scott will get along quite well."

Aiden stared at his console, pretending to be monitoring his gunship's status displays, unsure of how to respond. So many thoughts were racing through his mind, the most important of which was: if his perception of the Ghatazhak had been so wrong, perhaps his perception of Captain Scott was questionable, as well.

* * *

"I don't think I've gotten a single question that *wasn't* about the Ghatazhak attack on Kohara since it happened!" President Scott declared, throwing his hands up in frustration as he stormed through the doors of his office. "Has the entire sector forgotten we're still only a stone's throw away from an all-out war with the Jung? Have they forgotten that most of us are still recovering from the *last* war with the Jung?"

"Kata Mun's latest broadcast isn't helping matters as much as we'd hoped," Miri stated as she followed her father through the double doors.

"If anyone, I thought she would be more objective," Mister Daley stated as he too entered the office, directly on their heels.

"I think she was," Miri insisted. "At least, in comparison with all the others."

"Because she didn't come right out and accuse the president of collusion?" Mister Daley said.

"No one has accused us of collusion, John," President Scott insisted.

"Not in so many words, no, but the public will interpret it that way. That's *why* they phrase things the way they do."

"Nevertheless, there *was* no collusion, so there is nothing to worry about."

"Respectfully, Mister President, I disagree. False evidence has been used throughout the digital age... much of it difficult to disprove. The old position of *knowing* oneself to be innocent is no longer enough."

Miri looked at her father. "He *is* right about *that*, I'm afraid."

"Draft up a counterstatement to Miss Mun's piece for me to review," President Scott instructed his press secretary. "Quick as you can. The faster we reply, the more 'off the cuff' it will appear, and hopefully the more credible."

"Yes, Mister President," Mister Daley replied.

"And key points only," the president added. "Let's not give the press anything *else* to spin."

"Of course," Mister Daley replied, turning to exit.

Miri stood quietly, waiting for Mister Daley to close the door on his way out, and then a few extra seconds for the sound suppression fields to kick in. "If the press discovers Nathan was *here* on Earth, and that you *spoke* with him *before* the attack..."

"I know..."

"There will be no stopping them. No statement from you, or anyone else, will dissuade the public..."

"And it will give Galiardi even more leverage," the president added with a sigh as he plopped down in the chair behind his desk. "As happy as I am that my son is still alive, I fear his actions have put us in a difficult situation."

"It was not his intent," Miri defended.

"Intentions are irrelevant in politics. Actions and results are all that matters. The public learned long ago that words are meaningless..."

"Except when they're being spewed from the mouths of their favorite broadcasters," Miri corrected.

"Unfortunately, you are correct."

"You reviewed all the security camera files from the arena?" the president asked.

"Yes," Miri replied. "Personally. Luckily, both Nathan and Jessica had the foresight to keep their heads down and look away from every camera they encountered. The most anyone could claim is that a man and woman, each in their mid-thirties, were escorted from the public seating areas to the presidential suite complex for unknown reasons."

"I'm more concerned about the possibility that one of the cameras on Kohara might have captured an image of Nathan," the president said.

"We don't even know that he was *there*," Miri insisted. "For all we know, he was long gone by then. It did happen nearly two days *after* he was here. He

11

could have been halfway to the Pentaurus sector by then."

President Scott cast a skeptical look at his daughter.

"Yeah, wishful thinking, I know. But still..."

President Scott turned slowly in his chair, his hands in his lap, thinking as he came to face the big picture window behind him. "We must publicly state our disapproval of this attack," he finally admitted.

"But, if we had honored the terms of our alliance with the worlds of the Pentaurus cluster..."

"It doesn't matter," President Scott insisted. "The people of Earth will only care about *this* planet."

"Not everyone," Miri argued.

"No, but the majority will, and they are who we must play to."

"*Play to*?" Miri wondered. "I thought we were supposed to represent everyone, not just the vocal majority."

"It is that vocal majority who Galiardi will be calling to arms, once he learns Nathan is alive and that we knew about it."

"But we didn't."

"Unfortunately, no one will *believe* that we didn't." The president looked at his daughter. "Politics is not about truth, it's about perceptions."

* * *

"Rainey is a good man," Cameron insisted as she and Commander Kaplan walked down the corridor of the Aurora's command deck.

"Without a doubt," the commander agreed. "But he's a crappy captain."

Cameron cast a doubtful glance Commander Kaplan's way.

"He looks good in a uniform, and he's probably

quite adept at engaging Takaran nobility at the captain's table over dollag steaks and greisha. But his XO ran the ship, and he's dead...along with the Mystic's department heads."

"So, what are you saying?" Cameron asked as they rounded the corner. "You think he's not qualified?"

"He's in over his head," Commander Kaplan stated plainly.

"But he's got you to help him."

"Part-time, sure," the commander said. "But that's not enough. Rainey needs a *full-time* executive officer, not one who's jumping back and forth between two ships."

Cameron stopped just outside the command briefing room and sighed. "Adjust the split as needed," she finally decided. "Spend more time on board the Mystic, at least until things settle down and we can find a permanent XO for him."

"What about the Aurora?" the commander asked. "We're not exactly fully crewed here, you know."

"Maybe, but we do have all our department heads, and I can handle things when you're not around."

"And if you go to general quarters while I'm not aboard?"

"If that happens, then it means the fleet itself is under attack," Cameron pointed out. "In which case, it would be better if you *were* aboard the Mystic...for the sake of all the civilians."

"Of course," Commander Kaplan agreed, nodding as she followed Cameron into the command briefing room.

"As you were," Cameron ordered before her staff could rise to their feet. She moved to the head of the conference table, taking her seat. "What's the latest count?" she asked Lieutenant Commander Shinoda.

Ryk Brown

"With the addition of the Manamu and the Innison, we're up to eight ships, including the Aurora."

"The Innison?" Cameron wondered.

"Another medium cargo ship, like the Manamu. Corinairan registry, commanded by an ex-Corinari by the name of Coran Goggins. I checked with Mister Montrose, who vouched for the captain's character. My people are currently interviewing his crew. Of course, we can't really do a background check on any of them. Not without contacts on Corinair."

"We're working on that," Cameron replied. "Anything useful aboard either of those ships?"

"The Manamu was carrying miscellaneous cargo. Not of much use for anything other than raw materials to feed our fabricators," the lieutenant commander said. "But the Innison is carrying a variety of textiles, and quite a bit of clothing, all of which should come in handy."

"But no consumables," Commander Kaplan stated with disappointment.

"Speaking of which, how are we holding out?" Cameron asked.

"The Mystic was well-stocked in that department," Commander Kaplan assured them, "just in case something happened that delayed their return to port," she added with a wry smile. "I don't have a tally from the two ships that just joined us, but what I do have indicates that we're good for a few months, longer if we start rationing."

"That may be true for food, but not for medical supplies," Doctor Chen added.

"I thought medical was fully stocked," Cameron said.

"It was," Doctor Chen agreed, "but we've treated a lot of wounded, military and civilian alike. If this

14

were peacetime, I wouldn't be concerned, but since it appears that this conflict is just beginning, well..."

"Make a list and give it to the quartermaster's office," Cameron instructed. She turned to her CAG, Commander Verbeek. "Any progress filling out your deck crews, Verbeek?"

"We picked up about a dozen people from the Lawrence refugees, most of whom have at least turned a wrench in their lives. We're teaching them basic, routine maintenance tasks, freeing up the mechanics we do have to do the more specialized tasks. Unfortunately, we're still spread pretty thin. We've got about one full maintenance crew for every four fighters. If we get into any real combat, it won't be long until we're unable to keep more than a handful of ships in action at a time."

"Any chance we can start training complete novices to work on Super Eagles?" Commander Kaplan wondered.

"Super Eagles are fairly complex ships," Commander Verbeek replied. "Our techs spend two years learning to work on them."

"We'll operate twenty-four fighters," Cameron decided. "Rotate them, with one flight of eight down at a time. And tell your pilots to start getting their hands dirty and help work on their own birds."

"They already are," Commander Verbeek assured her. "It would be easier if we only operated two flights instead of three."

"As long as we're not in any firefights, you should be able to keep three flights in service at all times," Cameron insisted. "In the meantime, I'll make sure recruiting keeps an eye out for people with spacecraft maintenance skills."

"Captain, we're a thousand light years from

15

Earth," Commander Verbeek said. "Super Eagles are *Earth* ships. Even if you found an expert spacecraft mechanic, they wouldn't be qualified to work on our fighters. Not without significant training."

"I understand your concerns, Commander," Cameron replied. "But I urge you to keep an open mind. Based on past experience, I expect the people out here to surprise us; perhaps even teach us a thing or two."

"I hope you're right, sir," the commander replied. "Especially if we *do* end up in regular firefights."

"Are we anticipating combat?" the chief of the boat wondered.

"Sooner or later, it seems inevitable," Cameron replied. "Even if they come back with a dozen gunships, eventually we're going to have to go up against the Dusahn's battleships ourselves. Hopefully, not for some time, however."

The intercom beeped. *"Captain, Bridge. The Seiiki just jumped in. She's squawking proper codes, sir."*

Cameron pressed the intercom button on the conference table in front of her. "Very well, clear them in. I'll meet them myself."

"Aye, sir."

"Commander, finish up this briefing, and then check in with me later, before you return to the Mystic."

"Aye, sir," Commander Kaplan replied.

"Oh, and I want you to teach Lieutenant Commander Shinoda how to run combat, in case we have to go to general quarters while you're off ship."

"Sir?" the lieutenant commander said, both surprised and concerned.

"Your service record says you've had tactical

training and that you're combat qualified," Cameron said as she rose.

"Yes, sir."

"Then what's the problem?"

"No problem, sir," the lieutenant commander assured his captain. "Just a little surprised, I guess."

"We've got to improvise," Cameron said as she headed out.

"Yes, sir," Lieutenant Commander Shinoda replied.

"Don't worry, Kenichi," Commander Kaplan said. "I'll go easy on you."

* * *

Nathan stared out the forward window of the Cobra gunship as he waited for the next jump in the final leg of their three-day journey to auto-sequence. With each jump, he would momentarily turn his attention to the navigation displays, ensuring the gunship's computers had determined their new position in space before calculating the next jump in the series.

It was a mundane way to travel, but it was one he was quite familiar with from his years as Connor Tuplo. The Seiiki's systems functioned in the same way, completely automated for ninety-nine percent of their journey. If it hadn't been for the occasional flights into uncharted space, he and Josh would never have gotten to *actually* fly.

Of course, all of that had changed since the Dusahn had arrived. *Everything* had changed, even Nathan himself. He had spent the last five years *being* Connor Tuplo, unaware of his true identity; unaware of the meaning of the images that occasionally flashed into his mind.

"I do not know how much longer I can eat this

stuff," Vladimir said as he entered the gunship's flight deck. "Whoever decided that *this* was *food* should be *shot.*"

"Stop it, you're making me hungry," Nathan joked, accepting the plate of food from Vladimir.

"I tried mixing a few things together, and then burying it all in sauce, to try to make it more palatable," Vladimir explained as he climbed into the copilot's seat, being careful not to spill his own plate of food. Once seated, he scooped up a spoonful and put it into his mouth. His face soured as he chewed, finally swallowing hard. "I believe I have failed...*miserably.*"

"I've eaten worse," Nathan assured his friend as he too forced himself to consume the unappetizing meal.

"Impossible," Vladimir replied.

"Try eating Jung prison food sometime."

Vladimir did not respond, his mouth full of food despite its lack of appeal.

Nathan stopped chewing for a moment, his face taking on a curious expression. "Except for that one time."

Vladimir looked at him, waiting for him to continue, but his friend just stared straight ahead as if waiting for the memory to fully form in his mind.

Nathan shook his spoon several times as the memory became clearer. "The night before my execution... Someone brought me... It was a guard..." He looked at Vladimir. "A Jung guard. The same one who had treated me with contempt and hatred throughout my trial. He brought me the most amazing final meal."

"The guard did?"

"Trever...something," Nathan said. "He asked me

what I wanted for my last meal, and I didn't know what they had other than the crap they had been feeding me."

"What did he bring you?"

Nathan smiled, remembering. "Corintakhat and ergin tota," he said fondly.

"What is that?"

"The best way to describe it would be very tender beef, with a tangy fruit glaze, and cheesy-spicy mashed potatoes in a caramelized crust."

"Sounds delicious," Vladimir said.

"It was, and unexpectedly so." Nathan thought for a moment as he suffered another mouthful of Vladimir's modest attempt at making their emergency rations bearable. "But that's not what struck me the most about that meal," he continued. "It was the guard... Soray," he finally remembered. "Trever Soray. That was his name. Married, with three kids." Nathan looked at Vladimir, smiling. "The same man who would have been just as likely to slit my throat earlier that day, sat down and shared a magnificent meal with me, as if we were old friends." Nathan looked down at his plate, thinking to himself as he scooped up another spoonful. "For an hour, I almost forgot he was my enemy."

"The *man* was not your enemy," Vladimir said. "It was the uniform he wore."

Nathan looked at Vladimir. "And for a person's choice of clothing, it is okay for us to kill them?"

"It is not their choice of clothing," Vladimir explained, "it is the responsibility the person accepts when they agree to wear it. They accept that the *enemies* of their uniform will try to kill *them*, and that *they* will try to kill the enemies of *their* uniform."

19

"And if they had no *choice* but to wear that uniform?" Nathan asked.

"Everyone has a choice, Nathan."

"Earth history is replete with governments that *required* military service of their citizens."

"And the citizens of those governments had the choice to oppose such requirements."

"I can cite numerous examples from the past where such opposition would have been impossible," Nathan argued.

"Difficult, yes, but *never* impossible," Vladimir countered. "If the people refuse to rise in opposition to governments and policies they oppose, then they must accept the responsibilities of their failures to do so," Vladimir insisted.

Nathan smiled. "When did *you* become so philosophical?"

"I am a complicated man," Vladimir replied as he wolfed down another spoonful of his meal. "This is really bad."

Nathan continued to ponder Vladimir's point. "So, you believe that those marines on Kohara *deserved* to die?"

"No one *deserves* to die," Vladimir said. "With the possible exception of some very bad criminals, I suppose. But those men chose to serve *knowing* death was a real possibility." Vladimir looked at his friend. "You are not responsible for their deaths, Nathan; nor are the Ghatazhak who ended their lives. If anyone is responsible, it is the Dusahn. Or perhaps even the leaders who failed to honor the original Alliance charter."

"Like my father?"

"I suspect, given a choice, your father would have sent as many gunships as possible," Vladimir insisted. "Unfortunately, leadership is never that simple, especially at the top." Vladimir took another spoonful of food. "But you already know this."

Nathan poked at his food, pensively. "I still can't help but wonder... If we had been better prepared; if we had better intel..." He looked at Vladimir. "Those men did not *need* to die."

"You cannot know this," Vladimir insisted.

"How do you mean?"

Vladimir stopped eating for a moment, sighing. "What if the deaths of those marines make the people of the Sol sector realize their leaders' mistakes? What if it makes them force their leaders to send the support we need to defeat the Dusahn? Would their deaths then have a purpose?"

"Perhaps," Nathan admitted. "But we can't know that."

"Which is exactly my point," Vladimir insisted. "Surely, when you *agreed* to the Kohara mission, you *knew* that some of those marines might die?"

"Yes, but I also believed it was possible they might *not* die."

"That was wishful thinking," Vladimir dismissed with a wave of his hand. "You and I both know this to be true."

"But it was never my *intention*..."

"Of course not," Vladimir agreed, attacking his food once again. "Few intend for bad to happen. You were merely doing what you felt was necessary to accomplish your ultimate goal. And *that* goal, *without question*, is a righteous one."

"As was their defense of the assets we stole."

"Correct."

"You're not making me feel any better."

"I was not trying to," Vladimir replied.

21

"You are not the same Vladimir I knew," Nathan admitted.

"I am older now...wiser." Vladimir smiled. "I know it is difficult to believe that I could be even wiser than I was before, but it is true. Age and experience bring wisdom, whether we like it or not." Vladimir looked at Nathan. "You were wise beyond your years when I first met you. Although you still look as young as the day I met you, you too have gained wisdom through experience." Vladimir took another scoop of his meal and shoveled it into his mouth, continuing to speak with his mouth full. "Just do us all a favor and don't act like you did last time."

"How did I act last time?" Nathan wondered.

"Like a whiny, little boy who thought he was being treated unfairly."

"That's a bit harsh, don't you think?"

"*Da*. But you were. It was understandable, at first. It was a lot of responsibility...for all of us. But even after you stepped up and took command, every once in a while, you slipped back into that, 'Why me? Why is it all on me? I'm not qualified.' *Blech*! It was nauseating."

"Seriously?"

"Okay, maybe I exaggerate a bit," Vladimir admitted. "Just don't be that guy again, alright? Accept your role as leader, and we will all be much happier, believe me."

"I thought that I was," Nathan defended.

"Yes, you have," Vladimir replied. "But this... 'Did they need to die?' stuff... It serves no purpose, and it is very much what the *old* Nathan would do, not the Nathan who sacrificed himself to save his world."

"So, I'm not allowed to feel guilt for the lives my decisions cost?"

"Not if it prevents you from *making* those decisions."

"And has it?"

"Not yet, no."

"Then why the concern?" Nathan wondered.

"Because of who you were as Connor Tuplo," Vladimir explained.

"You didn't even *know* me as Connor Tuplo," Nathan pointed out.

"No, but Marcus and Josh did. And it worried *them* enough that they told *me*."

"Since when did Marcus and Josh become experts in the personality traits of effective leaders?" Nathan wondered.

"Jessica also expressed concern that the Connor side of you might be a problem, as did General Telles."

"What about Cameron?" Nathan asked halfheartedly.

"Cameron is still not convinced that you are the same Nathan she once knew."

"Yet, she was willing to risk her career, and possibly her very life...correction; the lives of her crew, in the hopes that I *am* the same man?"

"I suspect she did so because she felt it was the right thing to do, despite her doubts, which is exactly what you would do. And, because she knew if she didn't, that I would," Vladimir added with a grin. "Do not misunderstand, Nathan. *I* believe you are the same man, and I suspect the others do, as well."

Nathan sighed, looking away.

"What is it?" Vladimir wondered, noticing the concerned look on his friend's face.

Nathan looked at his friend for what seemed an

eternity. "I'm *not* the same man, Vlad," he finally said.

"We know, Nathan. Your experiences as Connor Tuplo have undoubtedly changed you a little..."

"It's not that," Nathan interrupted. "I mean, yes, those experiences have changed me somewhat, but that's not what I'm talking about. I'm talking about what the cloning process has done to me."

"What do you mean?" Vladimir asked. For the first time since he had sat down, he actually stopped eating.

"They did something to my mind. At first, it was just that I could remember everything with great clarity."

"You mean your memories...of before?"

"No. I first noticed it when I started studying the Aurora's specs from her last overhaul. The one that occurred *after* my death. Every page I looked at, every word I read, I'm able to recall it all in *complete* detail, without even trying."

"And you attribute this to the cloning process?"

"I spoke to Doctor Sato about it. The Nifelmians had to genetically modify their brains over generations in order to make them work properly with their technology. Photographic memory is a side effect of that genetic restructuring."

"That sounds like a *good* thing," Vladimir said.

"Yeah, you'd think so. But it takes some getting used to. But there's more. I've always been able to size things up quicker than others. I've always been able to see 'the big picture' in my head, but my own sense of ethics and morality was quite often in opposition to the things I *knew* I had to do. *That's* why I was—how did you put it—*whiny?* My intellect was at odds with my sense of right and wrong...or at least what *I* thought others *expected* me to consider right and wrong. Now, I find myself having to make an *effort* to factor those *same* ethics and morality *into* my decisions."

"And that bothers you?" Vladimir asked.

"In a way, yes. Should it *be* an effort? Should I have to *remind* myself to do so? And what happens if I forget to?"

"Do not worry, I will be the first to remind you if you forget. And if I do not, I am *quite* sure that Cameron will," Vladimir promised as he continued eating.

"Yeah, I'm sure you're right," Nathan agreed. As he continued with his meal, he wondered how Vladimir would react if he told him about the other things that were different about him now.

* * *

"I take it you have read the reports from our operatives on Kohara?" Lord Dusahn asked his trusted military advisor.

"I have," General Hesson confirmed as he strolled through the garden with his leader.

"Does this news concern you?"

"It is but a handful of gunships, my lord. They pose little threat."

"Except that their presence will require steps to protect our frigates," Lord Dusahn pointed out. "That will limit our area of control."

"Marginally, at best," the general insisted. "We can still manage the entire Pentaurus cluster quite easily, and the cluster is the only thing that matters at this point. That is where the industrial and technological infrastructure lies. Expansion will come, in time."

"The reason we took the Pentaurus cluster was to

25

expand the Dusahn Empire," Lord Dusahn reminded the general. "Those gunships will give the rebels the ability to hide out of our immediate reach, and to strike at will."

"They lack the firepower to take down our larger ships."

"But their attacks will embolden the populations, inspiring them to resist Dusahn rule."

"I think you are overestimating their influence, my lord."

"To do otherwise invites failure," Lord Dusahn warned.

"It is unlikely they have the manpower to crew and maintain the stolen gunships," General Hesson pointed out. "It will take them some time to train crews to operate and support their new assets. In the meantime, we can take steps to protect ourselves against them."

"What do you have in mind?"

"We must send more operatives out to surrounding systems," the general recommended. "Not only those of the Pentaurus sector, but to all neighboring sectors, as well. These rebels cannot operate without support. They need people, food, medical supplies, raw materials, equipment... They will seek help from worlds *beyond* what they consider to be our threat reach, yet close enough that those they seek help *from* will feel compelled to do so for their own sakes. We may not currently be able to reach these worlds with our warships, but we *can* reach them with one of the jump-capable cargo ships we have captured, since many of them have multi-jump capabilities."

"And what will these operatives do?" Lord Dusahn wondered.

"Form alliances, assassinate those who support

the rebels in order to spread fear, whatever is necessary," General Hesson explained. "Our operatives are quite adept at such things. We risk no assets in doing so, *and* we keep our warships here, in the cluster, protecting our new industrial base."

Lord Dusahn continued to stroll through the garden, considering the general's words. "The Dusahn have always been known as legendary warriors...the fiercest of all the Jung castes. The other castes all paled by comparison." He turned to look at the general beside him. "Did you know at the battle of Dormahgees, not a single caste was willing to commit to the battle until *our* ships had arrived?" He looked to the sky, as if he could see the ships above him. "Massive warships, with dark gray hulls trimmed with blood red and gold." Lord Dusahn stopped walking for a moment, closing his eyes and breathing in deeply.

"I am aware of our legacy," General Hesson reminded his leader.

Lord Dusahn opened his eyes again, looking around at the gardens and at the distant mountain ranges beyond the palace grounds. "I can see why they chose to settle this world. It has a unique beauty. Stark; unforgiving. The addition of such landscaping as this, of their architecture... A beautiful contrast, don't you think?"

"Indeed."

"The Dusahn have never been ones to resort to subterfuge, General," Lord Dusahn stated. "Such is the way of lesser warriors."

"Perhaps *that* is why the Dusahn were exiled," General Hesson suggested.

Lord Dusahn looked at the general with

disapproval. "I can always count on your honesty, can't I."

"Always, my lord."

Lord Dusahn smiled. "I suppose even the fiercest warrior must know when subterfuge is a better option than brute force."

"Battles are won by those who fight," the general said. "Wars are won by those who think."

"Esian Dusahn?"

"One of the greatest leaders our clan has ever known. Someday, I expect you shall outshine him in the eyes of our descendants."

Lord Dusahn sighed, continuing his stroll. "Expand the scope of our covert operatives. I want them on every industrialized world within five hundred light years of Takara, no matter how small."

"What actions would you like them to take, my lord?" the general wondered.

"Intelligence gathering and establishing contacts. No aggressive actions are yet to be taken. We need to be sure of what we are doing."

"As you wish, my lord."

"Meanwhile, we must strengthen our defenses, so that our warships are free to move about," Lord Dusahn said. "When will the Teyentah be ready?"

"If all our resources are dedicated to her completion, perhaps...thirty days," the general replied.

"How many large, jump-capable cargo ships have we captured?"

"Six, my lord," the general replied.

"And how long would it take to convert them into warships? Nothing fancy; just basic point-defenses, long-range missile launchers, and heavy shielding, of course."

"If work on the Teyentah is suspended, perhaps the same. But they will not have as much firepower as the Teyentah."

"Heavy fighter production is highly automated, requiring limited personnel."

"But considerable raw materials," the general warned.

"Which are abundant in the cluster," Lord Dusahn added. "We will build more heavy fighters to fill their decks. Perhaps as many as fifty per vessel. *That* will make them quite formidable, will it not?"

"Indeed, it shall, my lord," the general agreed. "Six instead of one. A wise trade."

"I am pleased you approve," Lord Dusahn replied.

"I shall make the arrangements immediately." General Hesson bowed respectfully, turning and departing the way they had come. Lord Dusahn looked up at the brilliant sky, taking in another deep breath. "Yes, *this* is the world from which the Dusahn will return to glory."

* * *

Cameron stood just outside the starboard large-transfer airlock, which had become the Seiiki's parking spot when aboard the Aurora. As the doors opened, she could see Abby and her family being escorted down the Seiiki's aft cargo ramp by Dalen Voss. Cameron had seen Abby a few months ago, but had not seen her children in more than seven years, and the difference was surprising.

The captain put on her best smile. It wasn't an expression that she wore often, but she genuinely liked and respected Abigail Sorenson. Abby, on the other hand, did not appear as pleased. Cameron had no doubt the unexpected journey had been a difficult one for Abby and her family. Once again, they had been asked to leave everything they knew, quite possibly for a purpose they didn't fully understand.

"Abby," Cameron greeted.

"Captain Taylor," Abby replied as she led her family away from the Seiiki's cargo ramp. "It is good to see you again."

"I only wish it were under better circumstances."

"Of course." Abby turned toward her family. "You remember my husband, Erik, and our children, Nikolas and Kirsten."

"A pleasure to see you all again," Cameron said. "I'm sure you have a lot of questions."

"Not really," Abby replied. "Marcus and Neli filled us in on the way here. A heck of a story."

"Yes, it is," Cameron agreed.

"Sir, I have orders to escort the Sorensons to medical," a med-tech announced from behind.

"Of course," Cameron said. "If you will all follow this man to medical, so Doctor Chen can clear you."

"Melei is on board?"

"Yes," Cameron replied. "Another long story." Cameron turned back to Abby's family. "We appreciate the sacrifice you are all making, and I promise we will do everything possible to keep you all safe and comfortable."

"Not like we had a choice," Erik said as he led his children past the captain.

Cameron looked at Abby. "What was that about?"

"Jessica threatened to knock him out and drag him here, if he didn't come voluntarily."

"Oh. I'm so sorry."

"That's alright," Abby assured her. "I understand why she did it. Unfortunately, Erik doesn't. And it will take some time for Nikolas and Kirsten to come around. They were all quite happy where we were."

"I take it you weren't," Cameron said, noticing her tone.

"I enjoyed my work," Abby explained. "I just didn't care for the people I was working for, or their agenda." She looked at Cameron. "Are you guys sure about all of this?"

"As sure as we can be, considering. But I know how you feel. Believe me, it wasn't easy for me to throw away my career, hijack my own ship, and fly off to the PC. But, it was Nathan..."

Abby finally smiled in agreement. "I'd better join them."

"We'll catch up later," Cameron said. "Before you transfer to the Mystic."

"The Mystic?"

"The ship where you and your family will be living."

"I'm not going to be working here, aboard the Aurora?"

"Actually, *where* you'll be working has yet to be determined," Cameron admitted. "However, you and your family will *live* aboard the Mystic Empress. Trust me, you all will be a lot more comfortable there, and likely safer."

"Of course," Abby said. "Until later."

Cameron watched Abby follow her family toward the forward exit from the main hangar bay.

"He is not too keen on all of this," Marcus said as he stepped off the cargo ramp.

"So I heard," Cameron replied, turning back around to face him. "How was the flight back?"

"Easy, but long and boring. I like being able to move about the ship a lot better. Being cooped up in that flight deck for three days sucked. Josh and Loki can have it."

"Well, you all deserve some downtime," Cameron told him.

"Have you heard from any of them?" Neli asked, after coming down the ramp behind Marcus.

"No, but I didn't expect to, either," Cameron replied. "Assuming they managed to pull it off, they should be here in about ten hours."

"Guess there's not much to do but wait, then," Marcus grumbled.

"And eat," Dalen added, coming down the ramp behind them.

The three of them looked at him.

"What? We've been eating the same crap for nearly a week, now."

"Take them to the mess hall, and then get some rest," Cameron instructed. "Once you're rested, get the Seiiki ready for her next mission."

"Any idea what that's going to be?" Marcus asked.

"I have no idea," Cameron admitted. "But I'm sure Nathan and Jessica have something already in mind."

"That's what I'm afraid of," Marcus grumbled.

* * *

Sergeant Krispin Bornet sat in the small, windowless room, his hands secured to the metal table at which he sat. He was relaxed, focused, and without fear. It was not his first time in this type of room, and undoubtedly, it would not be his last.

The sergeant had been incarcerated for nearly four years. In that time, he had been transferred six times, for fear that he might find a way to escape. Military prisons had not been a priority for the rebuilding efforts of Earth, and those facilities that had survived the Jung bombardments were outdated and, in many cases, still suffering their original damage. With the people of Earth in full support of the buildup of their military defenses, there simply weren't that many military prisoners to house. The Jung officers who had been captured during the war had long been returned to Nor-Patri, and the few who had chosen to stay on Earth had become willing collaborators with the Alliance. Closely watched collaborators, yes, but collaborators, nonetheless.

The few hundred total prisoners who were housed in the handful of military prisons scattered about the planet were generally nothing more than soldiers who were unable to follow orders, or had committed crimes while in the service of the Earth Defense Force, and the Alliance.

And then there was Sergeant Bornet, whose only crime was love. Love of the wrong person.

Krispin Bornet had suffered endless interrogations during his incarceration. Countless men and women, each of them seeking some crack, some chink, some foothold that would lead them to the information they sought. What they did not realize, or simply refused to admit, was that the young sergeant had no information to give them; for he had done nothing wrong. He had not shared any secrets, not committed any crimes, not disobeyed a single order, save for the one, which he had no ability to do otherwise. In four long years, he had seen every angle used to try to pry nonexistent information from him. No tact surprised him these days.

Until now.

There was a buzzing sound, followed by a clank, and then the metal door before him swung open. An elderly man, confident and fit looking, entered the room. Unlike most the sergeant met with in such

33

rooms, this man was not wearing a uniform. Instead, he was wearing a business suit.

"Are you supposed to be my lawyer, or something?" the sergeant inquired in a sarcastic drawl.

The elderly man in the suit said nothing as he took a seat across the table from Sergeant Bornet. The metal door behind him closed and locked as the man placed his briefcase on the table and opened it. He pulled out a small electronic device and set it on the table before them. He pressed a button on the center of the device, causing a green light to appear.

"Who are you?" the sergeant asked, becoming a tad impatient.

The elderly man looked at the sergeant, and took a breath. "My name is unimportant," the elderly man replied as he pulled a data pad out of his briefcase. He activated the pad, then placed it on the table, sliding it under the sergeant's shackled right hand. "Please place your hand on the data pad."

"Why?"

"So I can verify your identity."

Sergeant Bornet laughed. "Seriously?" When the elderly man did not respond, the sergeant shrugged and did as instructed.

The elderly man pulled the data pad away, checking its results before putting it away. Finally, he looked at the sergeant. "Sergeant Krispin Bornet, you have been charged with fraternization with a known Jung spy. Do you deny this charge?"

"I do not deny having an affair with her," the sergeant replied, annoyance in his tone. "I only deny ever knowing that she was a Jung spy."

"Do you still love her?" the man asked plainly.

The question caught the sergeant off guard. After a moment, he replied, "Yes."

"You hesitated."

"You surprised me."

"Would you do anything to be with her?"

"What is this about?" the sergeant wondered.

"Please answer the question, Sergeant."

"Why? It doesn't matter, anyway. I'm never getting out of this place. And even if I do, I'm sure she's either locked up somewhere just like me, or shipped back to Nor-Patri, or..."

"You are correct," the man replied. "Miss Jassa *is* still being detained, just as you are. What *becomes* of her, however, is up to *you*."

"This one has already been played," the sergeant said, leaning back in his chair, his curiosity all but gone. "It failed. And you know why? Because I don't know anything. I never did."

"I am here to make you an offer, Sergeant."

Sergeant Bornet sighed, rolling his eyes and leaning his head back. If he had anything else to do, he would have been annoyed at this waste of his time. "I know, I know. Tell you what I know, and you'll let her live. Or you'll let us both live, on some farm out in the middle of nowhere, where we can raise goats and kids, and live happily ever after." The sergeant looked at the elderly man in the suit. "Like I said, I've heard this all before."

"You are half-right, Sergeant," the man explained. "However, I seek no information...only your services."

Sergeant Bornet's curiosity returned.

"I ask you again, would you do anything to be with Miss Jassa again? To live out your lives together, perhaps even on that out-of-the-way goat farm you spoke of."

Krispin was suddenly quite unsure of himself,

which was a feeling he hadn't experienced in some time. "What kind of *service*?"

"I need you to kill someone."

The sergeant stared at the elderly man sitting across from him, suddenly realizing the electronic device on the table was a sound-cloaking field. "I'm not an assassin."

"You are a highly trained EDF Marine. I have studied your service record. Killing is your specialty."

"Killing the *enemy* is my specialty," Sergeant Bornet replied.

"The *enemy* comes in many forms," the elderly man countered. "Not all of whom wear uniforms."

"Who are you?" the sergeant asked again.

"I am merely a representative, a middleman, so to speak."

"Then who sent you?" the sergeant wondered. "It has to be someone pretty high up, if you can get me out of here, not to mention get Sara out, as well. Assuming you're not full of shit, that is."

"I assure you that I am not."

"Then who sent you?"

"Michael Galiardi."

The sergeant's eyes widened. "*Admiral* Galiardi?"

"One and the same."

The sergeant laughed. "Right. Okay, I'll bite. Who does he want me to kill?"

"You still haven't answered the question, Sergeant," the man reminded him. "Would you do *anything* to be with Sara Jassa again?"

Sergeant Bornet studied the man, long and hard. The old guy had a stone-cold expression that had not changed one iota since he had entered the room. Krispin imagined the man was quite good at his job, whatever that was. He certainly wouldn't want to be sitting across a poker table from him. "Yes, I would do anything to be with Sara again," Krispin finally replied. "Even if just for a moment," he added, looking down in shame. She was his only weakness. She was the chink in his armor. Finally, he looked up at the elderly man sitting across from him. "Who do I have to kill?"

With the same emotionless expression he had worn throughout their brief conversation, the elderly man replied, "President Dayton Scott."

CHAPTER TWO

"Report!" Cameron barked as she entered the bridge from her ready room.

"Single jump flash!" Lieutenant Commander Kono reported from the sensor station. "One point five million kilometers out."

"Identity?"

"Unknown," the lieutenant commander replied. "It jumped in cold. Whatever it is, it doesn't want to be seen. It's not emitting anything. Should we go active?"

"Negative," Cameron ordered as she stood in front of her command chair. "Position?"

"The jump flash was detected at one five seven by two two five," Lieutenant Commander Kono reported.

"That's in the expected arrival sector," Lieutenant Commander Vidmar stated from the tactical station behind Cameron. "But why would they be running cold?"

"In case the fleet had been captured by the Dusahn," Cameron said. "At least, that's what I would do."

"Shouldn't there be more of them?" Lieutenant Commander Kono wondered. "If it *is* them, I mean."

"Should we vector the patrol Eagles to intercept?" Lieutenant Commander Vidmar suggested.

"Not yet," Cameron insisted. "Comms, transmit an escape jump warning to all ships."

"Aye, sir," Ensign deBanco acknowledged.

"Are we emitting?" Cameron asked.

"Very little," Lieutenant Commander Kono replied. "Ship-to-ship comms and data exchange is all via laser link. Other than occasional station-keeping thrusters, the fleet is running cold, as well."

"Then they can't see us, either," Cameron surmised.

"Well, they can't see *us*, but they can see most of the other ships, if they look long enough. Most of those cargo ships leak emissions like crazy, and with all those windows, the Mystic emits a lot of visible light. They can see the fleet, they just can't hear what we're saying to each other."

"All ships report ready to jump, Captain," the comms officer reported.

"Very well."

"If it is one of ours, shouldn't they be contacting us?"

"They will," Cameron insisted. "Just as soon as they're sure it's us."

"Captain," Ensign deBanco said, "I'm receiving a data transmission on a Ghatazhak frequency."

"Direction?" Cameron asked.

"Same as the jump flash," the ensign replied. "One five seven by two two five. It's a text message, sir. Message reads: *'Don't shoot, it's Jess and Bobert.'*"

Cameron smiled. "Try to hail them via laser comms."

"Yes, sir."

"Why only one?" Lieutenant Commander Vidmar wondered.

"We're about to find out," Cameron replied, not revealing that she was just as anxious to know as the rest of them.

"Contact!" Lieutenant Commander Kono announced. "They just lit up. One Cobra gunship, squawking Ghatazhak transponder codes. Range is seven hundred thousand kilometers and closing fast. Target is decelerating."

"Laser comm-link established, Captain."

"*Aurora, Cobra One*," Jessica's voice called over the loudspeakers. "*Request permission to join the fleet.*"

"Cobra One, Aurora Actual," Cameron replied. "Permission granted. Good to see you, again. How many parking spaces are you going to need?"

"*Good to see you, too*," Jessica replied. "*Eight more on the way, so nine total.*"

"*Nine*? You managed to snag *nine* gunships?" Cameron replied, surprised.

"*Yes, but the price was high*," Jessica replied, her voice turning a bit solemn. "*Twenty KIA, half as many wounded. And we lost all the Rakers, Cam, ships and pilots.*"

The bridge fell silent for several moments. Finally, Cameron replied, "Understood."

"*Most of us are a bit shot up, but Cobras Three and Ten are worse off than the rest.*"

"I thought you said you took nine ships."

"*We tried to take twelve*," Jessica explained. "*Only nine made it out alive.*"

"We'll get Three and Ten down first. How far out are they?"

"*They should be jumping in momentarily*," Jessica replied. "*See you soon.*"

"Actual, out." Cameron turned aft. "Alert flight ops," she instructed her comms officer. She looked over at her tactical officer. "Nine gunships."

"In exchange for twenty lives and six Rakers," he reminded her. "Was it worth it?"

"Let's hope so," she replied. What she really

wondered, was if Nathan was among those who had lost their lives.

* * *

Once their gunship was secure on the external flight deck, aft of the Aurora's main hangar deck, Nathan and Vladimir grabbed their gear and exited the cramped vessel that had been their home for the last three days. After passing through the narrow boarding tunnel connecting their ship to the Aurora, they stepped through the airlock and into the aft end of the main hangar bay.

Nathan breathed a sigh of relief as his feet touched the hangar deck. It was good to be back, although he still didn't feel like the Aurora was his home...not like before. Not like he remembered from years ago. In his mind, the Seiiki was still his home, just as it had been for the last five years as Connor Tuplo.

With each passing day, it seemed like more of Connor was giving way to Nathan, and it bothered him somewhat. He had liked his life jumping around the Pentaurus sector. It had been difficult at times, often becoming stranded on a less-than-desirable world for lack of paying runs. He had long ago lost count of how many times he nearly had his ship impounded because he couldn't pay his berthing fees. But despite all that, it had still been a good life. Success, or failure, had been his to make. He had been in control of his own destiny.

Or at least, he had thought so.

He breathed another sigh of relief when he spotted the Seiiki, safely berthed in the starboard large-transfer airlock, with Marcus and Dalen busy inspecting the exterior of the ship.

"I'm going to check on the Seiiki," Vladimir said. "Want me to take your gear?"

"Thanks," Nathan replied, handing his two bags to Vladimir. "Just toss them in my cabin, will ya?"

Vladimir took Nathan's bags and headed starboard to join Dalen and Marcus, while Nathan continued forward.

Nathan looked to his left, spotting the two most heavily damaged Cobra gunships in the port large-transfer airlock. The two ships, piloted by General Telles and Josh, would need extensive repairs before becoming operational again. Both ships had been lucky just to have escaped Kohara, let alone make it back to the Aurora.

Although he had seen the damage during the occasional glimpses of the other ships during their transit, this was the first time he was able to get a good look at them. Nathan paused, watching as the Aurora's mechanics and engineers swarmed about the ships, preparing to move them into the main hangar bay for the duration of their repairs.

General Telles stood next to one of the line chiefs, pointing out the damage that he was aware of. The general noticed Nathan, and turned to head toward him.

Nathan had been thinking about what to say to the general all the way home. He had not liked his decision to use deadly force against Alliance Marines back on Kohara. In fact, three days ago, he had been quite angry about it. However, time to reflect, as well as numerous conversations about it with Vladimir during their long journey, had caused his anger to subside, becoming more of a concern.

"General," Nathan greeted as General Telles approached.

"Captain," the general replied.

"Impressive that you made it back in one piece."

"It looks far worse than it is. Josh is the one to be congratulated, if anyone. His damage is far more extensive. Were you aware that his auto-jump sequencer failed halfway through the journey?"

"I was not."

"He had to calculate each jump, and get his ship on course and speed manually before jumping. Yet, he still managed to keep up with the pack."

"Why didn't we just slow down for him?" Nathan wondered.

"Captain Nash offered to do so, but Josh insisted they maintain their pace."

"For a day and a half?" Nathan exclaimed. "When did he sleep?"

"I don't believe he has," the general replied. "At least, not in the last two days. Loki offered to change ships with him, so he could get some rest, but Josh refused that, as well."

"That kid constantly amazes me," Nathan admitted.

"He is no longer a child," the general proclaimed. "In fact, he has grown into an impressive, young man. A bit reckless, perhaps, but his natural skill and determination more than make up for it." The general looked at Nathan. "Reminds me of someone."

Nathan understood the reference, as well as the compliment contained within it, which made what he wanted to say that much more difficult.

General Telles sensed this. "You wish to voice your concerns over my decision to use deadly force back on Kohara," he said, inviting the discourse.

"I don't *wish* to," Nathan corrected.

"Rest assured that the decision was not taken lightly."

"Of course." Nathan turned to continue walking

43

toward the forward exit. "My concern is not with the decision you made, but, rather, that it does not seem to bother you."

"On what do you base that assumption?" the general asked as he walked alongside.

Nathan thought for a moment. "Good point," he finally admitted. "Does it bother you?"

"No, but not for the reasons you might expect," the general explained. "I take no pleasure in the taking of lives...not even those of legitimate enemy combatants. And for the record, I did not consider the Alliance Marines to be so. However, by the same token, I do not feel any regret in taking lives, if doing so is necessary."

"And you feel that taking the lives of those marines *was* necessary?" Nathan asked.

"Would you have preferred that my men and I lay down our own lives in order to avoid taking theirs?"

"Of course not," Nathan insisted. "I only wish it had not been necessary."

"As do I. Unfortunately, it was. Would it make you feel better if I were to run down the thought process behind that decision?"

"I don't know. It might."

"Primarily, it was for the sake of the mission. Had we not acquired at least four gunships, the mission would have been a complete waste of time and resources. Even with eight, one could argue that it was still not worth it."

"Nine," Nathan corrected.

"Eight," the general stood firm. "Josh's gunship is too badly damaged to repair, but we *can* salvage many usable parts which will help us repair the others and keep them operating."

"I don't see the point."

"The point is, I had to decide if we could achieve a satisfactory mission outcome without taking the lives of those marines. I concluded that we could not."

"You said primarily," Nathan pointed out.

"Indeed. The second reason, and it was a close second, our numbers are limited."

"But we haven't even begun our recruitment drive," Nathan countered.

"I speak of the Ghatazhak," the general corrected. "It takes at least a decade to properly train a Ghatazhak. Longer, if the process is not started in adolescence. That makes the lives of my men even more valuable to the cause than those gunships."

Nathan was taken aback, stopping in his tracks.

"Something troubles you?" the general asked.

"It's just that I don't ever remember you being concerned about the loss of your men."

"There is still much you do not understand about the Ghatazhak," the general replied.

"I suppose you're right," Nathan agreed, continuing to walk. "There is one more thing that concerns me."

"And that is?"

"Which one of us is going to be in charge of this rebellion?" Nathan asked. "Am I to be a figurehead; a poster boy to inspire the masses? Or am I to actually *lead* them?"

"Captain, if all we needed was a face to make speeches, we could have used your clone without your consciousness. We could have programmed it be loyal to the Ghatazhak, in order to make it do as we wished."

"Then I am to lead the rebellion."

"That was the idea."

"And if I had countermanded your order to use deadly force against those marines?"

"I would have instructed my men to ignore your order...and they would have. Furthermore, should you have given such an order, it would have brought serious doubt into your qualifications to lead this rebellion," the general explained further. "You see, I expect many such decisions will need to be made before this war is over. We will be forced to do things that would normally appear horrendous. Some will call us terrorists, brutes with no emotion..."

"Like the people of Earth did after the massacre at the evacuation compound," Nathan reminded him.

"An excellent example. One that makes my point quite nicely, in fact..."

"Look," Nathan interrupted, stopping again and turning toward the general. "I understand what you're saying. And for the most part, I agree with you. Sometimes, good men must do bad things for the greater good. But sometimes, good men have to refuse to do such things, in order to remain worthy of their positions of leadership. You see, the ends *don't* always justify the means. For if we must become as evil as those we fight, we win nothing. We simply replace one evil with another."

"On this, we are in complete agreement," the general assured him.

"Are your men in agreement, as well?" Nathan asked.

General Telles paused a moment before responding. "*My* assurances could prove meaningless. I would suggest that you review the helmet-cam recordings from the battle. *There* you will find your assurances."

* * *

"The Cetian Leadership Council is demanding

that only *Cetian* officers are put in command of the Benakh," Admiral Cheggis said. "In fact, half of them are demanding that her *entire crew* be of Cetian citizenship."

"Can you blame them?" Commander Macklay declared. "It was *their* world that was attacked, and it was a Terran who made it possible."

"Gil Roselle has always been a wild card," Admiral Galiardi admitted. "That's why he was given a scout ship instead of a warship. I should have replaced him the moment I was reinstated. I should have replaced all of them on day one."

Admiral Cheggis looked confused.

"Robert Nash is missing," Commander Macklay added, for Admiral Cheggis's benefit.

"What?"

"He left his ship five days ago," the commander continued.

"Why the hell didn't his XO report it?" Admiral Cheggis wondered.

"Nash gave his XO some bullshit about being on a top-secret assignment," Admiral Galiardi explained. "Ordered him to go dark, like he was chasing a sensor contact."

"You think he was in on the Kohara raid, as well?" Admiral Cheggis asked.

"He and Roselle go way back," Commander Macklay told the admiral. "And he made several trips to Kohara, at the same time that Roselle was there visiting his girlfriend."

Admiral Galiardi sighed in resignation. "We'll give the Cetians what they want," he decided. "The whole crew."

"Half the Benakh's crew is Terran, Gil," Admiral Cheggis reminded him. "That's going to put the

Benakh at a pretty steep operational disadvantage for at least a few weeks."

"It can't be helped," Admiral Galiardi said. "All of our destroyers are built in the Cetian system, and the Trinidad is still four months from trials. *Three* destroyers will come out of the Cetian shipyards by then. The last thing we need is a work slowdown at that shipyard. If anything, we need them to speed up production."

"I *may* have a better idea," Commander Macklay said rather sheepishly.

Both admirals looked at the commander.

"Send the Cape Town to the Tau Ceti system, and move the Benakh here."

"Are you crazy?" Admiral Cheggis wondered.

"It makes sense," Commander Macklay defended. "After all, Stettner *is* their golden boy."

"That doesn't solve the crew problem," Cheggis argued.

"Actually, it does. Move all the Cetians from the Benakh to the Cape Town, and all the Terrans from the Cape Town to the Benakh. The Cape Town is far more automated and can operate quite well with only two shifts. So, she won't suffer operationally while she's retraining her new crew. And just think how happy the Cetians will be with a Protector-class ship parked in their system. One commanded *and* crewed by nothing but their own people."

"He's got a point," Admiral Galiardi admitted.

"But the Cetians don't have the facilities to service the Cape Town," Admiral Cheggis reminded them.

"She's brand new," Commander Macklay replied. "By the time she needs servicing, they likely will."

"And if the Jung attack Earth?" Admiral Cheggis asked.

"Tau Ceti is a single jump away," Commander Macklay pointed out. "And we've got a boatload of jump missiles here to hold the Jung at bay until the Cape Town arrives."

Admiral Galiardi looked at Admiral Cheggis. "I kind of like the idea," he admitted. "It would make the Cetians awfully happy, and we need them more than any other system right now."

"It's going to piss off our people, though," Admiral Cheggis argued. "And you're going to lose support if you give up such a big asset."

"I'll lose even more support if we lose our Cetian allies," Admiral Galiardi retorted. He turned to look at Commander Macklay. "Any progress on those battle-cam videos?"

"Roselle knew what he was doing," the commander replied. "He disabled every camera on the base. The only recordings we got from them were about the last five minutes of the battle. And most of the helmet-cam videos were from too far away to ID anyone. However, we were able to confirm the attackers were wearing, what appeared to be, Ghatazhak body armor."

"Are you sure about that?" Admiral Galiardi asked.

"There were some differences, possibly some upgrades, or something, but they were Ghatazhak. They were terribly precise and extremely well trained. The only reason we were able to keep them from stealing every damned gunship on the line was because our marines had overwhelming numbers on their side."

Admiral Galiardi did not appear pleased. "The president is going to play this for all it's worth. He's going to call for a public outcry to support the

Karuzari in the Pentaurus sector, even if it means stripping our own defenses to do so."

"Your supporters won't stand for it," Admiral Cheggis insisted.

"No, they won't," Admiral Galiardi agreed. "And neither will I."

"It's going to get ugly," Commander Macklay warned. "If you oppose President Scott publicly, there's going to be fallout."

"It will be a lot worse if I don't oppose him," the admiral insisted. "Have you forgotten that we had Jung ships just outside our own system just a few weeks ago? Does anyone really think that *won't* happen again?" The admiral thought for a moment. "No, *this* is when we must stand strong. We *must* show the people we will *not* yield to political pressure when the safety and security of our world hangs in the balance."

"The media is going to accuse you of being too aggressive," Admiral Cheggis warned.

"It won't be the first time."

"Scott will publicly admonish you," Commander Macklay said.

"He can admonish me all he wants," Admiral Galiardi said dismissively. "I'm not going to let another stuffed shirt prevent me from doing my job. Not again."

* * *

Jessica and Robert strode toward Nathan from the starboard side, just forward of the Seiiki's airlock berth.

"What was that all about?" Jessica asked, noticing both the look on Nathan's face and General Telles walking away.

50

"I don't think he liked me questioning his order to use deadly force," Nathan replied.

"Can you blame him?"

Nathan looked at Jessica, confused.

"The guy has been through ten years of highly specialized, extremely intense training, spent five years in service of that nutball Caius, a year helping us liberate Earth and the core, and then the last seven years keeping his people alive, so he could be there to protect *you* when needed." Jessica shook her head in disbelief. "If I were him, I would have knocked your ass out," she added, continuing past Nathan in an attempt to catch up to the general.

Nathan looked at Robert. "I've been back for five minutes, and I've already pissed off two of my favorite people."

"Wanna try for three?" Robert joked.

"No, thanks." Nathan sighed. "I guess I'm still trying to figure out where I fit into all of this."

"What do you mean?" Robert wondered.

"At first, I thought I would be more of a recruitment tool. You know, using the whole *Na-Tan* thing to convince people to join the cause. I fully expected to be doing my part, and fighting alongside everyone else. I just didn't really expect to be in *command* of all this again."

"Seriously?"

Nathan looked at Robert, confused again.

"Come on, Nathan. *Leading* is what you do. It's what everyone in your family does. It's what *you* are good at. Please, tell me this isn't going to take you as long to accept as it did last time." Robert walked away, also shaking his head.

Nathan sighed. *That's three*, he thought.

"Glad to see you made it back alive," Cameron

commented as she walked past Robert, heading for Nathan. "Based on the amount of damage some of your gunships have sustained, I'm guessing it wasn't a cakewalk."

"Not in the slightest."

"How bad?"

"Ghatazhak had fourteen KIA and four wounded."

"That would explain the look on Telles's face."

"We lost all six Rakers, as well," Nathan added.

"Any of the pilots make it?"

"None that we know of."

A concerned look came over Cameron's face. "Who are those people?" she asked, pointing behind Nathan.

Nathan turned around and spotted Aiden and his crew walking toward them, along with the two pilots from the other gunship who had agreed to join them. "Volunteers from Kohara."

"What?"

"We should probably detain them for now," Nathan said.

Cameron turned toward the nearest senior chief working the hangar deck. "Senior Chief!" she called out.

The senior chief turned to make eye contact with his captain, immediately recognizing her hand signals.

Cameron tapped her comm-set. "Security, Captain. I need an armed escort team to the hangar deck...*now*."

"*On the way, Captain.*"

Nathan began walking toward the approaching group, which was being followed by the two Ghatazhak soldiers who had ridden with the two gunships on the way back. "Why don't you all hold up right here for a moment," he suggested, raising his hands to signal them to stop. He nodded to the two Ghatazhak soldiers following behind the group, both of whom immediately stepped back, spreading to either side behind the group, raising their weapons in readiness.

"Is something wrong?" Aiden asked, noticing the look on Nathan's face. He then noticed Cameron, and snapped to attention. "Captain," he said, raising his hand in salute. "Ensign Aiden Walsh, commanding officer of Cobra Three Eight Three, requesting permission to come aboard."

Cameron returned the ensign's salute as she spoke to Nathan. "What the hell is going on, Nathan?"

"My crew and I wish to join your ranks, sir," Aiden continued. "As do Ensigns Tegg and Wabash of Cobra Three Eight Two," he added, gesturing toward Charnelle and Sari to his right.

"Nathan?" Cameron repeated, seeking an explanation.

"Like I said, these people volunteered to add their gunships to our forces," Nathan explained. "In fact, this young man saved our asses, with a slightly psychotic maneuver."

A team of four security officers, each of them armed with energy rifles, came jogging across the hangar deck, surrounding the group of Koharans.

"What's going on, sir?" Aiden asked Nathan. "Are we under arrest, or something?"

"We need to detain all of you for a while," Nathan explained. "Until we can be certain of your intentions."

"I assure you, sir, we have no ill intentions. We just want to help...to follow *you*."

"I appreciate that," Nathan replied. "But you

53

must understand that we cannot be too careful. Any one of you could be a spy, yourself included. And the rather abrupt way you volunteered your services, I'm not so sure your crew agreed with your decision."

"We talked it out on the way back, sir. They're with me on this."

"I'm not," Chief Benetti mumbled. She suddenly realized she had spoken too loudly. "Well, I wasn't, at first... Hell, I don't know. I still think this is all crazy, but it's not like I have much choice."

"I have no control over the matter," Nathan insisted. "You will all have to go through medical and security screening before we can allow you to join our ranks. Until that time, you will be detained."

"You just said we saved your ass, sir," Aiden began to protest.

"And I greatly appreciate it," Nathan assured him. "But I would be remiss were I not to follow procedure here. You will all be made comfortable during your confinement, I assure you. The process should not take more than..." Nathan turned, looking to Cameron for an answer.

"A day or two, at the most," Cameron said.

"You see? No time at all." Nathan offered them a reassuring smile as he continued. "Just follow these gentlemen to your quarters. I'm sure you'd all like to get cleaned up, change your clothes, and get some real food."

"I just want a real bed," Ali muttered.

"That, too," Nathan said.

"As you wish, sir," Aiden said, resigning them to the inevitable.

"Lieutenant," Cameron said to the officer leading the security team. "Escort these people to section one four, deck E. There should be enough empty cabins there to house them. Get them whatever they need, but restrict them to their quarters until Lieutenant Commander Shinoda clears them."

"Understood, sir," the lieutenant replied smartly. He turned to Aiden and his group. "If you'll please follow me."

Aiden looked at the lieutenant, then Cameron and Nathan.

"I'll be down to speak to you myself in a few hours," Nathan assured Aiden. "And thank you."

Aiden nodded respectfully, then turned to his crew. "You heard the man, people. Follow the lieutenant."

Nathan watched as the lieutenant and his security team led the group of young Koharans forward.

"I told you this was a bad idea," Chief Benetti muttered as they walked away.

The two Ghatazhak followed the Koharans, nodding respectfully to Nathan and Cameron as they passed.

Cameron watched them walk past, then turned to Nathan. "I can't wait to hear all about *this*."

* * *

The door to the room Birk and Cuddy had spent the past week working in opened, revealing the smiling face of their leader, Michael Willard.

Cuddy looked at Michael, then at Birk.

"Why are you smiling?" Birk asked Michael. "You never smile."

"It worked?" Cuddy asked.

"It did indeed," Michael replied.

"Are you sure?" Birk wondered.

"We had people place calls from multiple locations, using suspicious dialogs designed to pique the Dusahn's interest, if they *were* able to

55

intercept. If the Dusahn heard the calls, they would have responded to the fake intelligence," Michael explained. "We also noticed no discernible changes in network traffic patterns that might indicate an intercept. Thanks to you two, I believe we now have a secure method by which our resistance cells may communicate."

"Great," Cuddy replied, feeling somewhat relieved.

"Especially since we've been cobbling together all these comm-units for the last five days," Birk added.

"What about secure to unsecure?" Cuddy asked.

"We tested that, as well," Michael assured him. "As long as a secure communications device is initiating the call, the routing codes will be scrambled, so they are untraceable. However, the conversation will not be encrypted."

"Does this mean we can call home now?" Cuddy asked.

"Indeed, it does," Michael replied. "However, you cannot tell anyone what you are doing, or where you are."

Cuddy looked at Birk.

"What are we supposed to tell our families?" Birk asked.

"We have prepared a cover story for you both," Michael explained as he handed his data pad to Birk. "One that will not raise any suspicions and should put your parents at ease."

Birk looked at the data pad. "*Internships*?" he said, surprised. "You want us to tell them we got internships?"

"The school the two of you were attending will be closed for several months, until they repair the damage sustained during the initial Dusahn invasion," Michael explained. "It seems only logical that you might seek out a useful way to spend your time until your school reopens."

"That'll probably work for Cuddy's parents," Birk said, "but mine are going to find it pretty hard to believe."

"Just tell them that Cuddy got you the job."

"Are these *paid* internships?" Cuddy wondered. "Because *my* parents are going to want to know why I gave up my part-time job."

"Room and board, and a small monthly stipend," Michael replied. "But I'm afraid you will have to give up your current residence."

"What about all our stuff?" Birk wondered.

"We will send someone to retrieve your belongings, and to notify your landlord that you will be vacating the premises."

"We still have three months left on the lease," Cuddy said. "They're going to charge us for it."

"The Dusahn have declared all such contracts null and void, to make it easier for Corinair's economy to recover from the interruption."

"How nice of them," Birk commented.

"What if our parents try to contact us at this *Kinloch Tech*?" Birk asked, looking back at the data pad.

"The company is owned by someone who supports our cause. He arranged your cover for us. If anyone calls looking for you, they will take a message, which will end up on your personal, secure comm-units."

"Won't someone at Kinloch wonder why they never see us around the office?" Birk asked, finding the whole thing too easy.

"Kinloch Tech is a large company, with several hundred employees, many of whom work in the field and rarely come to the main office," Michael assured him. "No suspicions will be raised."

"Great," Birk said. "My dad will be pleased I'm doing something constructive with my free time. He won't *believe* it," he added, looking at Cuddy, "but he'll be happy."

"How soon can we call them?" Cuddy asked.

"Immediately," Michael replied. "However, I would like to ask you a question first."

"Sure," Cuddy said.

"Do you think you can make the same algorithm work between a surface-based comm-unit and a ship in space?"

Cuddy thought for a moment. "I guess."

"It would depend on *where* the ship was," Birk added. "In orbit over Corinair, no problem. Ships in orbit use the comm-nets all the time."

"What about ships elsewhere in the Darvano system?" Michael asked.

Birk scratched his head, thinking. "Direct link, or general broadcast?"

"General broadcast, I'm afraid."

"*That's* going to be a bit harder," Birk warned.

* * *

"They look like a bunch of teenagers," Cameron declared as she and Nathan headed up the ramp to the Aurora's command deck. "What the hell were you thinking?"

"I was thinking it would be nice to get two more gunships than we had planned, not to mention crews to fly them," Nathan defended.

"Seriously?" Cameron cast a look of disbelief in Nathan's direction as they reached the top of the ramp.

Nathan stopped. "Okay, I wasn't thinking that, really. I was just going on instinct."

"That's what I thought," Cameron said, continuing on. "Same, old Nathan," she added, shaking her head.

"Isn't that what you wanted?" Nathan asked, taking a couple of quick steps to catch up with her. "To be sure that I'm still me?"

"I was hoping for evidence that was a little less risky, to be honest."

"Well, that wouldn't be me, then would it," Nathan quipped as they turned the corner and headed for the bridge.

"What are they, about twelve?" Cameron retorted.

"Captain on the bridge!" the guard at the entrance announced as they passed.

"Status?" Cameron asked her tactical officer, pausing just inside the entrance for his response.

"Threat board is clear, long-range patrols have searched the inbound paths and found nothing," Lieutenant Commander Vidmar reported. "All returning gunships are secure on our decks, Bulldog One is safely aboard the Glendanon, and the Morsiko-Tavi has rejoined the fleet."

"Very well," Cameron replied. "Recall all patrols. Comms, notify all ships that we'll be relocating the fleet as soon as those patrols are back on board."

"Aye, sir," the comms officer acknowledged.

"Lieutenant Commander Kono, leave four recon drones behind, spread wide," Cameron continued. "Set them to meet up with us twelve hours after we jump, each one via an alternate path."

"Yes, sir," the lieutenant commander replied smartly.

"Alert me when the fleet is ready to jump,"

Cameron ended, turning to head aft toward her ready room.

"Aye, sir," the tactical officer replied.

"Recon drones?" Nathan asked, following Cameron.

"To see if anyone is tailing us."

"Why four of them?"

Cameron entered her ready room and moved to hang up her jacket on the hook behind the hatch. "I like to spread them out, hide them. If our tail tries to take them out, at least one of them should make it out to warn us."

"Are you saying we have a tail?" Nathan wondered as he moved around to sit behind the captain's desk.

Cameron finished hanging up her jacket, closing the hatch and turning around, just as he was about to sit. Her eyebrows immediately went up.

"Oh, sorry," Nathan said sheepishly. "Old habit," he added, stepping back out from behind her desk and taking a seat on the couch along the forward bulkhead.

"Not yet," Cameron admitted, moving around in front of Nathan to take her seat behind her desk. "But if we pick one up, we're sure as hell going to know about it."

"Good thinking." Nathan leaned back, his body finally relaxing for the first time in days. "God, it feels good to sit in something comfortable again." He ran his hand across the cushions. "This isn't the same couch, is it?"

"Actually, it is," Cameron said. "I had it reupholstered."

"Why didn't you just get a new one?" Nathan wondered.

"I found out it was from Captain Roberts' home

office," Cameron explained. "He brought it aboard when he first took command. I offered to return it to his family, but his wife thought it would be nice if it stayed aboard...like a piece of him was still with the ship."

"I didn't realize you were so sentimental," Nathan teased.

"It's not sentiment, it's respect," Cameron insisted. "And you still haven't answered the question."

"What was the question?"

"What were you *thinking*, trusting a bunch of kids like that, let *alone* a bunch of kids you don't even know."

Nathan smiled. He had forgotten how much he enjoyed getting Cameron worked up about something. "Oh, *that* question."

"*Oh, that question,*" she mocked. "Did you even stop to consider *why* they offered to join you? Didn't it raise *any* suspicions at the time?"

"At the time, no. *After* the fact, I *did* give it some thought, however," Nathan defended. "I know it sounds a bit conceited, but I think Ensign Walsh offered to help because it was *me*. Nathan Scott, the boy-captain who saved Earth and the core from the Jung. He saw his hero, who he thought was long dead, and felt compelled to follow him." Nathan looked at Cameron. "Pretty stupid, huh."

"Actually, you're probably right," Cameron agreed somewhat reluctantly.

"That's why they woke me up, right?" Nathan joked.

"That's not the only reason Jessica and Telles sought you out after all these years," Cameron insisted.

"You don't need to go there, Cam," Nathan

assured her. "I've had a *lot* of time to think about it... trust me."

"And what did you conclude?"

Nathan looked at her skeptically. "Are you trying to psychoanalyze me?"

"Not intentionally," Cameron replied. "But there is a reason I'm asking."

"What's that?"

"You first," Cameron insisted.

Nathan sighed in contemplation. "It wasn't just one reason," he began. "Yes, they felt they needed me to lead the rebellion, probably more because of my reputation than my leadership abilities."

"Don't sell yourself short."

"I'm not done," Nathan insisted. "But they probably sought me out because they realized that if they didn't try to revive my consciousness now, they might not have gotten another chance." Nathan looked at Cameron. "They sought me out to *save* me." Nathan sighed again. "And now it's up to *me* to save *them*. To save *everyone*."

Both Nathan and Cameron were silent for what seemed an eternity. Finally, after yet another sigh, Nathan spoke again. "Fate has called upon me, yet again."

After another silent pause, Cameron spoke, as well. "Are you up to the task, Nathan?"

"Honestly?"

"Yes, honestly."

Nathan smiled. "I have no idea. Then again, I had no idea the last time fate called upon me."

"Actually, if I remember correctly, you most decidedly did *not* feel up to the task back then," Cameron pointed out.

"The thing is, I don't think I have a choice," Nathan told her.

"You always have a choice, Nathan."

"No, I don't," Nathan argued. "I mean, yes, I could say 'screw this, I'm out of here.' I could take the Seiiki and jump to the other side of the galaxy, where I could live out my life and be long dead by the time the Dusahn, or whoever else wanted to rule the galaxy, caught up with me. But because of who *I* am, I cannot make *that* choice. I can only make one choice."

Cameron thought for a moment. "For evil to triumph, good men must do nothing," she finally said.

Nathan smiled. "Actually, the quote is: 'The only thing necessary for the triumph of evil is for good men to do nothing.'"

"Just checking your memory," Cameron said, the slightest of smiles teasing at the corner of her mouth.

"It's one of my favorites," Nathan admitted. "Timeless. Absolutely timeless. So, you see, I really have no choice. Just like I had no choice when Captain Roberts died, and just like I had no choice that day in orbit over Nor-Patri."

"Because, deep down, you're a good man."

Nathan looked surprised. "Is that a compliment? From Cameron Taylor?" Nathan threw up his hands. "Now I've heard everything."

"I'm being serious, Nathan," Cameron said. "Deadly serious."

"Sorry."

"I've been doing some thinking, as well."

"Is it my turn to psychoanalyze you now?" Nathan joked.

Cameron ignored his quip. "I've been thinking

about why *I* made the decision to give up everything, steal my own ship, and come here to join you."

"Temporary insanity?"

"Nathan..."

"Sorry, I'm tired. It's been a long week," Nathan apologized.

"I once asked Telles why he followed you, of all people. You act on instinct, without thinking things through, and you get by on luck...often *unbelievable* luck at that. Hardly the type of person who someone as logical and intelligent as Lucius Telles should follow."

"And what did he say?" Nathan wondered.

"That it was *because* of those qualities that he followed you," Cameron explained. "You see, anyone can *learn* how to make decisions, how to lead people into harm's way. But few are *born* with that skill. Fewer still are able to listen to others, and learn from their mistakes."

"And few have my incredible luck," Nathan joked.

"Very few," Cameron mused, sighing. "I came when you called because, despite the fact that I question nearly every decision you make, I *know* you will always do what you think is best for *everyone*, with *no* concern for your own well-being. You see, it's your ability to put your own doubts aside and make incredibly difficult decisions...decisions that affect billions, if not trillions, of lives, that makes *you* a great leader. Honestly, Nathan, I don't know if I could deal with that much responsibility."

Nathan was quiet, feeling the weight of her statement. "Is this supposed to make me feel better?" he asked. "Because it's not working."

Cameron looked up, taking a deep breath. "I can't believe I'm about to say this."

Nathan looked puzzled again. "Say what?"

Cameron looked him in the eyes. "I think you should take command of the Aurora."

Nathan's jaw dropped. "Cam... I can't..."

"You have to," she insisted.

"Cam, the Aurora is *your* ship," Nathan exclaimed. "Hell, she's been your ship for way longer than she was mine. I can't take her away from you. You can't ask me to do that."

"I have to," Cameron replied. "It's the only way this rebellion can succeed."

"I can lead from the Seiiki," Nathan argued.

"No, you can't." Cameron shifted uneasily in her seat. "God, I can't believe I'm saying this, either. *Na-Tan* can't lead from the bridge of the Seiiki. He *must* be on the bridge of the Aurora."

Nathan grinned from ear to ear. "Did you just call me *Na-Tan*?"

"Trust me, I nearly gagged," Cameron replied.

"Cam, it wouldn't be right..."

"Nathan, you did *amazing* things with this ship," Cameron explained.

"And so can you," Nathan insisted.

"Perhaps, but in most cases, I'd simply be mimicking you," she admitted. "I can't think on my feet as well as you can. I can't make snap decisions like you. Sure, if it's clearly outlined in procedures, I can, but..."

"Now *you're* selling yourself short, Cam..."

"Perhaps, but that's not the point. If I thought I could do better, I would have taken the fight to the Dusahn on my own, without hooking up with you, Jess, and Telles." Cameron's expression turned deadly serious. "The Pentaurus sector *needs* Nathan

65

Scott. They *need* Na-Tan. The entire galaxy needs Na-Tan."

"Then the entire galaxy is in more trouble than we thought."

"Do you always have to make jokes, Nathan?" Cameron said, becoming irritated.

"Sorry, it's the fatigue."

"I'm offering you my *ship*, Nathan. You have to take her. You have to use her to defeat the Dusahn... *and* Galiardi, *and* the Jung."

Nathan suddenly became quiet. Until now, he had assumed that he had only one enemy...the Dusahn. But he knew that she was right. The Dusahn were only part of the problem. In fact, Galiardi and the Jung were also only part of the problem.

After nearly a minute of silence, Cameron became impatient. "Well?"

Nathan looked at her, sighing as the full weight of his fate landed squarely on his shoulders. "On one condition," he finally said. "You have to be my XO."

* * *

Despite the rapid technological advances over the last hundred years, prisons on Earth were still relatively unchanged. Security systems had changed, tracking chips were used, and surveillance gear was everywhere, but the idea of punishing those guilty of crimes by confining them to small spaces and stripping them of their rights and freedoms was still the norm.

"What have you done to her?" Krispin asked as he stared at the woman he loved on the view screen.

"She is sedated, like all the other inmates," the old man told him.

"Why?"

"It makes them more...manageable."

"Is that what they call it?" Krispin wondered. "How difficult could she be to manage? She weighs barely forty-five kilograms."

"Tell that to the guard she put in the hospital the first week she was here."

Krispin looked back at the view screen. "Did anyone ask why she did that?"

"I do not know," the old man replied.

"I want to talk to her," Krispin insisted.

"I cannot promise she will recognize you."

"I want to talk to her," he repeated.

"I'll see what I can do."

Krispin turned to look at the old man. "Are you my handler?"

"Handler?" the old man asked, unfamiliar with the term.

"The man I will be reporting to. The man from whom I will receive instructions."

"I suppose so."

"What's your name?"

The old man thought for a moment. "You can call me Mister Dakota."

"Very well, Mister Dakota. If you want me to do your bidding, I need to talk to Sara. But first, someone needs to give her something to bring her out of her drug-induced stupor, understood?"

"You are in no position to make demands, Sergeant," Mister Dakota reminded him.

"Do you really think these restraints will stop me from bashing in your skull before the guards can press their remote to immobilize me?"

"Are you threatening me, Sergeant?"

"Just asking a question." Krispin followed his statement with a gaze possessed only by those who had killed with their bare hands and had felt no remorse.

"What makes you think I don't have a similar remote in my pocket?" Mister Dakota asked without emotion.

"Trust must be earned," Krispin told him. "This is your chance to do so."

"It may take some time," Mister Dakota warned.

"Time is all I have," the sergeant replied, turning back to the view screen.

* * *

Aiden looked around the dormitory he and his crew had been escorted to after they had been cleared by medical. "Could be worse," he commented. "When do we eat?" he asked the guard.

"The mess hall has been notified," the guard replied. "Food should be arriving shortly."

"Lots of it, I hope," Charnelle said, plopping down on one of the chairs at the table in the middle of the room.

"The head is over there, and the entertainment system has access to the ship's vid library," the guard explained.

"How long are we going to be locked up in here?" Kenji wondered.

"Until Lieutenant Commander Shinoda clears you," the guard answered. "That's all I know." He looked at Aiden. "Will there be anything else, sir?"

"A change of clothes would be nice," Aiden said.

"I'll see what I can do," the guard promised. He turned to leave, then paused, turning back. "Rumor has it that you people saved Captain Scott. If that is the case, then I'd like to thank you, on behalf of the crew of the Aurora."

"Don't mention it," Aiden replied.

"I just thought you should know."

"Thanks."

Once the guard had left, Kenji spoke up. "Are you happy now?" he asked Aiden. "Is this what you imagined when you volunteered us all?"

"What did you expect them to do?" Aiden wondered. "Trust us implicitly from the start?"

"He's right, Kenji," Charnelle said. "They're just following security protocols. Anyone offering to assist Alliance forces must be treated with suspicion until they can be proven to be trustworthy."

"We *are* Alliance forces," Kenji pointed out.

"But *they* are not," Sari countered. "Not anymore."

"Come on, Kenji," Aiden said. "They're treating us just fine. Besides, you heard the guard. Once we're cleared by the lieutenant commander, we'll be free to move about the ship. We'll probably be assigned quarters and everything."

"And then what?" Kenji wondered. "Fly missions against these 'Dusahn'? Are you even sure this is our fight?"

"I'm sure Captain Scott will explain it all to us, sooner or later," Charnelle defended. "We just have to be patient."

"Why didn't you say something before?" Aiden asked Kenji. "You've had three days."

"We had a Ghatazhak breathing down our necks the whole time," Kenji reminded him. "He would have heard."

"What makes you think they're not listening to us right now?" Sari pointed out.

"To be honest, I don't really care anymore!" Kenji exclaimed. "This was a stupid idea, coming here. Really stupid."

"That's an understatement," Chief Benetti agreed from her bunk.

"I'm sure if you tell them you don't want to be a part of all this, that they'll be happy to put you off on some inhabited world somewhere," Charnelle said.

"A thousand light years from home," Kenji exclaimed. "Lovely. I'm sure that's just what everyone here wants...to be stranded on some world they didn't even know existed three days ago."

"They're not going to leave you stranded," Aiden insisted. "They'll find a way to get you home, if that's really what you all want."

"I'm fine right here," Ledge insisted.

"Me, too," Ali agreed. "After all, we're on the *Aurora,* and we're going to be serving under *Nathan Scott!* No one is going to believe this back home."

"If we ever *make* it back home," Kenji reminded them. "There is a war on out here, remember?"

"And there's probably going to be a war back home, as well," Aiden replied.

"Which is precisely why we should be *there,* instead of *here.* We all took an oath, remember?"

"That oath was to protect members of the Alliance," Aiden told him. "Both there *and* here. Isn't that what we're doing?"

"That oath also said we'd follow the orders of our appointed leaders," Kenji replied. "What about that part?"

"We're just choosing a different leader," Aiden explained. "It's as simple as that."

"That's just it, Aiden, it *isn't* that simple."

"It is," Aiden insisted, raising his voice. "If you let it be." He looked at his long-time friend and second in command. "Now, I need to know if you're going to fight alongside the rest of us...for *these* people."

Kenji looked angry. "If you're going to fight, I'll be right there beside you, Aiden. You know that. But don't expect me to be too enthusiastic about all this, at least not yet."

"Fair enough," Aiden replied. "Thanks." He turned to face his crew, spread out all over the dormitory. "The same goes for all of you. If you don't want to be a part of this, then speak up now."

"You already know how Ali and I feel," Ledge said.

"What about you, Dags?" Aiden asked his sensor operator.

"We've come this far together," Sergeant Dagata replied. "We might as well see it through."

"You people have no idea what you're getting into," Chief Benetti insisted, laughing at them. "But, I can't very well leave you all hanging."

"Thanks, Ash," Aiden said.

"Don't thank me yet," the engineer warned. "I'm still considering killing you in your sleep...sir."

"Good to know," Aiden replied, "I think."

* * *

For as long as he could remember, Krispin Bornet had only wanted to be a soldier. The death of his parents, during the Jung invasion of Earth eight years ago, had only strengthened that desire. The moment the Aurora had driven the Jung from their world, Krispin had lied about his age and volunteered for the new Alliance Marines who were being trained by the Ghatazhak.

For five years, Krispin had volunteered for every training program he could get into. He had worked his way up to the rank of master sergeant, through determination and hard work. He had even been offered a chance to attend the academy, which would have made him an officer. That was the one thing he had declined. His place was on the front lines, with the men. That had always been where he wanted to be. Killing the enemy, in the most efficient manner possible, was his specialty. While many would find that talent horrific, Master Sergeant Bornet took great pride in it. To him, it wasn't about the killing, it was about being *willing* to kill to defend those who could not defend themselves. His job was to stand on the wall, with a target on his chest.

Then he met Sara Jassa. She had shown him a whole new world. A world full of love and laughter. A world full of hope and dreams. A world full of possibilities. For the first time since he had lost his parents, Krispin had begun to see a future that did not include military service. It was something he had never contemplated, as it had always seemed impossible. People like him didn't find love. People like him died in battle, defending their world.

Sara had made him believe otherwise.

Their year together had been the best year of his life. He had even considered accepting the offer to attend the academy, so he could become an officer, marry Sara, and start a family. Then it all fell apart.

For weeks, Krispin had hated her. She had lied to him. She had played him. She was the enemy. But as the weeks turned into months, his hatred faded, eventually replaced by the truth, which was that he still loved her. Krispin had replayed every minute they had spent together, looking for anything that seemed suspicious, but the truth was, there was nothing. She had never asked him about his work, about the Alliance Marines, about their weapons... *nothing*. If she had been a Jung spy, she was a lousy one. At the very least, she had not been playing *him* for information, since she had never tried to get any.

She had never pressed in the slightest when he had avoided talking about his job.

After months of analysis, Krispin convinced himself that, despite her being a Jung spy, their love had been real. She had not lied to him about that. The only lie she had told was a lie of omission and, for that, he had forgiven her long ago.

But now, Krispin stood in front of the door, unsure of what he was feeling. On the other side was the woman he loved, and who loved him. But she was also the reason his life had gone completely awry. What was he to say to her? What would she say to him?

The door buzzed and swung open. He stepped through, pausing as the door automatically closed and locked behind him. She sat there, a couple meters away from him, staring at the table in front of her, undoubtedly expecting another in a long string of interrogators.

Krispin's heart raced, his breath quickened. He felt as if his legs would buckle at any moment. It took all his will to take a step forward. He grabbed hold of the back of the chair in front of him, steadying himself as he moved closer. He pulled the chair out and carefully sat down across the table from her. After swallowing hard, he finally managed to speak. A single, weak utterance... "Sara?"

She raised her head slowly, more out of habit than desire, as if making minimal effort to identify today's inquisitor. Her eyes were cold, devoid of the deep emotions that he expected to see. She looked at him, her eyes narrowing slightly. Her face crinkled, a faint look of disbelief coming over her. The look intensified as recognition hit her. "Kris?" Her mouth opened, her eyes widened slightly, and her bottom lip began to quiver almost imperceptibly. "Is it you?"

"Yes." Kris whispered.

"Oh, God, Kris," she said, barely able to contain her tears. "I'm so sorry. I'm so sorry. I didn't mean for any of this to happen. You weren't my target, I swear it."

"I know."

She looked at him, unable to believe that he would forgive her so easily. That's when she lost control and started to weep openly, her head hung down in shame.

Kris reached out, taking her hands in his. "It's going to be alright, Sara. I'm going to get you out of here."

A small laugh punctuated her sobs, and for a brief moment, a smile pierced through her grief-stricken expression. "You can't," she finally said. "You'll only make things worse. You must forget about me."

"I can't, Sara," Kris insisted. "I love you."

Again, she smiled through the tears. "Sweet Kris," she sobbed. "I cannot live with the guilt of what I've done to you."

"I'm not kidding, Sara. They want me to do something. They say they'll let us both go free if I do. We can be together."

Now she looked confused. "What? What is it they want you to do?"

"I cannot tell you."

"Kris, you can't..."

"Do you love me?" Kris asked her.

"Kris..."

"Do you love me?"

Sara fought to control her emotions, finally

answering, "Of course I love you." She looked down again, adding, "That's why I have to let you go."

"No one is letting anyone go," Kris insisted. "You have to trust me, Sara. You have to believe in me. I need that. I need to know that you'll come with me when I'm done. It's the only way." Kris could see the doubt in her eyes. "You say you love me, but do you trust me?" When she didn't respond, he repeated the question. "Do you trust me, Sara?"

"Yes," she finally answered softly. "You're the only person I *do* trust."

Krispin smiled, his heart filling with love for the first time in more than a year. He rose slightly, leaned across the table, and kissed her on the forehead. "I will be back for you," he promised as he rose to his feet. "We will be together again, I swear it." Krispin stared at her for a moment, waiting for a weak smile from her to carry with him during his upcoming mission.

"When?" she asked meekly.

"I do not know," he admitted, "but I *will* be back."

Krispin turned back toward the door, taking two steps and pausing. "Door!" he barked. A moment later, the door buzzed and swung open, and he stepped through into the next room.

The door closed and locked behind him. Krispin turned to look at Mister Dakota. "I'll do it," he told him. He turned and looked at the old man straight in the eyes with that same, cold stare, adding, "But if you fail to deliver as promised, I will kill you, *and* Galiardi, and no forces, great or small, will stop me."

* * *

It had taken every credit in his possession to convince the guard at the gate to allow him in, and considerable begging of the receptionist to allow him to sit and wait in the grand lobby of House Mahtize in the hopes of getting the briefest of audiences with the lord of the manner. But Tensen Dalott had always had a way with people. His strong, confident manner and unbreakable will had swayed many to support him, despite their various objections.

The hard-nosed receptionist had been a particularly difficult case and had taken him more than an hour to win over. Yet, he had been sitting in the lobby for more than five hours now, during which time he had not eaten, drunk, nor visited the facilities, despite her numerous offers to do so. His mission was vital, and he had this one chance to try to speak with the only man on Takara who might help him.

When he heard the rumble of thrusters from outside, Tensen knew Lord Mahtize had finally returned. Since the Dusahn had taken over, only nobles were allowed to operate private shuttles, and even then, only under Dusahn control.

Another hour passed, during which many staffers bid the receptionist farewell until the next workday. Soon, she would be telling him that Lord Mahtize would be unable to see him, and she would suggest he leave his contact information and await the lord's call another day.

Tensen hated being right at times.

"Mister Dalott," the receptionist called from her desk. "I'm afraid that Lord Mahtize will be busy the rest of the day. If you'd like to leave your contact information, I can see that he..."

Tensen rose from his seat, holding his hand up to interrupt her. "I know you are only doing your job, but the matter I wish to discuss with your employer is of the utmost importance, and I am sure that if he was aware of the subject matter, he would heartily agree."

"No offense, Mister Dalott, but everyone who wishes to speak with Lord Mahtize says as much. It is my *job* to filter them out."

"I understand this, I truly do," Tensen assured her.

"Perhaps if you were to tell me what you wished to speak with him about..."

"Would that I could. I'm afraid you're just going to have to trust me when I tell you that *your lord* will thank you for allowing me to speak with him."

"Anything," she continued, "anything at all."

Tensen sighed, thinking for a moment. If he told her the true nature of his visit, she might lead him to an anteroom and notify the Dusahn to pick him up. But if he told her nothing, his chance would be lost. Tensen normally prided himself on his ability to read people's character, but too much was riding on this very moment.

Then it came to him. "Tell your lord that 'Yassey' wishes to speak with him."

"Yassey?" she asked skeptically.

"Yassey."

"Very well," she replied. After tapping a button on her communications console, she spoke. "Please inform Lord Mahtize that a gentleman named 'Yassey' wishes to speak with him." She looked at Tensen again. "You're sure it's 'Yassey'?"

"Quite sure."

"Yes, Yassey," she assured the person on the other end of her comm-link. "Understood." The receptionist looked at Tensen. "The message is being passed to Lord Mahtize, but I cannot promise that it will change anything."

"I understand," Tensen replied. "Thank you."

Before Tensen could return to his seat, the receptionist's communications console beeped.

"Yes... Understood." She ended the communication and looked up at Tensen. "Mister Dalott, if you'll enter the elevator, it will take you to the top floor, where someone will escort you to speak to Lord Mahtize."

"Thank you," Tensen said, graciously. The elevator doors opened on the far side of the lobby, and Tensen quickly moved to board. Moments later, the doors opened again, revealing a stern-looking gentleman.

"If you'll follow me, Mister Dalott," the gentleman instructed, turning to lead Tensen down the corridor.

Tensen followed the gentleman, his eyes forward, not making eye contact with anyone as they made their way down the corridor. A minute later, after passing through yet two more weapons detection portholes, he was led to a rather nondescript door. The stern-looking gentleman stepped to one side, making room for Tensen to enter.

Tensen opened the door and stepped inside, allowing it to close behind him. The office of Lord Mahtize was just as he expected: massive, lavishly appointed, and utterly useless except to impress all who entered. But Tensen was not easily impressed, especially by Takaran nobility... Not for years now.

"You seem to have me at a disadvantage, Mister Dalott," Lord Mahtize began, stepping out from behind his desk to greet Tensen. "You used my childhood nickname...one that few would know. Yet, I am unfamiliar with the name 'Tensen Dalott'. Is the name even of Takaran origin?"

"It is not."

"From where do you hail, Mister Dalott?" Lord Mahtize asked as he approached.

"I was born and raised on Takara, and have only recently returned after a long absence," Tensen explained.

Lord Mahtize shook Tensen's hand politely, studying the stranger's face. "There is something familiar about you...something in the eyes."

"Is this room secure?" Tensen wondered.

Lord Mahtize smiled, turning toward his wet bar. "You are in a lord's office, Mister Dalott, if that is indeed your name. If you belong among men such as myself, then you already know the answer to your question. Might I interest you in a drink?"

"Thank you, no."

"Then shall we get to the nature of your visit? I was told you have something of great importance to discuss with me," Lord Mahtize said as he poured himself a drink. "What might that be?"

"I have a difficult task to perform," Tensen explained. "One that requires assistance, which only you can provide."

Lord Mahtize sipped his drink, closely examining Tensen's calm demeanor. "I am speaking to you only because you knew my childhood nickname, which means that you and I have similar associates. However, my curiosity is limited, as is my patience." Lord Mahtize took another sip. "What is this task you speak of?"

"I wish to steal the Teyentah."

Lord Mahtize did not react, instead continuing to sip his beverage. "Theft of a Takaran warship, even one not yet completed, is a serious crime, Mister Dalott. The logical thing for me to do would be to signal security and have you turned over to the Dusahn. But of course, you *know* this...which makes me somewhat curious as to why you think that I would provide the assistance you seek. After all, I don't even know you."

"As Tensen Dalott, no. But perhaps you remember an old, childhood friend...one who grew up to become the leader of his own noble house. One who commanded the last capital ship of Takara. One who was the only nobleman to support the true leader of Takara, Casimir Ta'Akar, who was assassinated by those whose nobility was in name only. One who stands before you now, asking if you are still the same man he knew and respected all those decades ago."

Lord Mahtize's mouth fell agape as he examined Tensen's face more closely. "Suvan? Is it you?"

"It is I, Yassey," Tensen replied. "Suvan Navarro."

CHAPTER THREE

Nathan leaned back on his bunk aboard the Seiiki, watching the Ghatazhak battle-cam recordings from the engagement on Kohara four days ago. He wanted desperately to find something to justify his original concerns, but despite viewing more than thirty different battle recordings, he had yet to do so.

What he did see, however, was precision, expertise, and uncompromising discipline. But that was not what struck him the most. It was the composure each of them had while under fire. Alliance Marines were trying to kill them, yet they continued to fire so precisely that only a handful of their attackers suffered serious injury. Based on what he had seen thus far, Nathan was unsure if any Alliance Marines had died at all. Shots to the hands, legs, shoulders, even to the weapons they held, but no actual kill shots. If, in fact, any of them *had* died, it was more likely by accident.

Even more impressive was that the Alliance Marines were quite well trained themselves. Their shots, although not as precise as those of the Ghatazhak, were well placed. The Alliance Marines were by no means equal to the Ghatazhak, but they were not a force to be taken lightly. Had they not had rapid reinforcement by marines stationed aboard the Jar-Benakh, General Telles and his men would have easily overpowered them.

The hardest part had been those recordings that captured the deaths of Ghatazhak soldiers. Nathan had sent men into harm's way before, but rarely did he witness their demise. With each man who fell, Nathan's anger grew, as did his determination.

Someone pounded on his cabin door, breaking his concentration. "What?" he bellowed, stopping the video.

The hatch swung open, revealing an angry Jessica. "What the hell, Nathan!" she exclaimed as she entered, closing the hatch behind her.

"Come right on in," Nathan said, not bothering to get up.

"What do you think you're doing?"

"Watching videos. How about you?"

"I'm talking about Telles," she continued. "What the fuck!" she exclaimed. "It's *Telles!*"

"Yes, I know."

"Then what were you thinking?"

"Well, I was thinking, as the leader of the Karuzari, it was my responsibility to question his decision."

"What? You think you know better than he does?"

"You need to take it down a notch, Jess," Nathan warned, sitting up on the edge of his bunk. "I just wanted to make sure we were on the same page, that's all."

"Of all the people to question…"

"What happened to all that Ghatazhak training you've been taking?" Nathan wondered. "Isn't it supposed to give you more self-control?"

"Fuck you."

"I guess not."

Jessica stewed for a moment. "If you were anyone else, I'd have knocked your ass out by now. You know that, right?" she added.

"I do," Nathan replied. "And if it makes you feel any better, I reviewed the battle recordings from the Ghatazhak, and I believe I owe the general an apology. When he authorized the use of deadly force, I assumed he meant shoot to kill."

"To the Ghatazhak, authorization to use deadly force isn't an order to kill, Nathan. It's *permission* to kill if necessary, and *only* if necessary," Jessica explained. "If Telles had wanted them to kill those marines, he would have given the order 'terminate all targets.' And if he had done that, not a single marine would have survived."

"I can see that, *now*," he told her. "Honestly, though, Jess, I was only trying to understand *why* he made that decision, and to be sure of what *my* role is in all of this. I'm actually surprised the general took offense."

"The Ghatazhak are people just like us," Jessica said, taking a seat at the desk. "Sure, they come off a bit scary..."

"Like they're figuring out how to kill everyone around them?"

"Yeah, something like that. Actually, exactly like that. It's ingrained in us as part of our training."

"In you, as well?"

"Yes." Jessica grinned. "I identified six ways to kill you as soon as I entered...not including just using my bare hands, of course."

"Not sure I needed to know that."

Jessica thought for a moment. "You know, you should take some of their basic combat training."

"A nice idea," Nathan agreed, "but I don't know that I'll have the time."

"Why?"

"Apparently, I'm taking command of the Aurora."

A surprised look came across Jessica's face. "What?"

"Cam's idea, actually."

"Cameron gave you her ship?"

"Yeah, I was surprised, as well," Nathan admitted. "But she made a convincing argument."

"What is she going to do?"

"She's going to be my executive officer again."

"What about Kaplan?"

"She's going to serve as the XO on the Mystic," Nathan replied. "I was hoping you would be my tactical officer again."

"I'm a Ghatazhak, now," Jessica replied.

"Exactly," Nathan said. "One who just identified six ways to kill a friendly the moment she entered the compartment. If that's not a good trait for a tactical officer, I don't know what is."

"What about what's his name?" Jessica asked.

"Vidmar? He's a pilot, as well, so he's going to take command of one of the gunships, at least until we can get some crews trained. After that, he'll be your second."

Jessica sat back, dumbfounded. "I've got to ask Telles," she warned.

"Of course."

"Damn." After a moment, she asked, "What about your ship? What about the Seiiki?"

"She's getting a few improvements," Nathan said, smiling. "More weapons, better shields—eventually she might even get a stealth jump drive, assuming Abby can make a scaled-up version."

"Who's going to command her?"

"Josh and Loki will continue flying her," Nathan explained. "And as needed, I'll take her on missions, myself."

"And Vlad?"

"Vlad will be wherever we need him most, as usual," Nathan told her.

Jessica smiled. "It's going to be just like old times, then."

"God, I hope not," Nathan exclaimed with a wry smile.

* * *

Lord Mahtize looked as if he'd seen a ghost. "I thought the Avendahl was destroyed."

"She was," Suvan confirmed. "I was not aboard her when she was attacked."

"My, God, Suvan... What of your family?"

"My wife is well. We were together, on vacation in the Isa system, when the cluster was invaded. As for my children, I do not know. They are both grown with families on Corinair. I can only hope they are not in Dusahn custody. I have heard troubling rumors..."

"They were only rounding up the families of jump-capable ships who had failed to surrender to the Dusahn," Lord Mahtize explained.

"I also heard they were arresting all active and retired military personnel."

"Active, yes, at least on Takara. They are all being held in the Belanca prison for the time being. The Dusahn have promised their eventual release. As to arresting former military, to my knowledge they have only questioned them and released them. Again, I speak of Takara. My knowledge of Corinair, or any world outside of this system, for that matter, is extremely limited. The Dusahn control all communications and transportation."

Suvan looked down, worry obvious on his face. "I can only hope they went into hiding, somehow."

"Did anyone other than your crew know that you were not aboard when your ship fell?" Lord Mahtize wondered.

"Only my senior staff," Suvan replied.

"Then, surely, the Dusahn believe you to be dead."

"That is my hope," Suvan agreed. He looked at his old friend. "Can you help me, Yassey?"

Lord Mahtize suddenly became even more uncomfortable. "Steal the Teyentah? Are you insane?"

"She is nearly complete, is she not? At the very least, she is space-worthy."

"Yes, but the Dusahn control her now. They control the entire shipyard. Hell, they control everything, Suvan. You know that. Such a thing is impossible. You would be killed before you got anywhere near that ship."

"I must do this, Yassey," Suvan insisted. "It is the only way. With the Teyentah, I have a chance... we *all* do."

"You have always been an idealist, Suvan," Lord Mahtize said, shaking his head. "It was nearly your undoing seven years ago, and it will be your undoing now, if you attempt this foolishness."

"Then you will help me," Suvan stated confidently.

"Have you not been listening?" Lord Mahtize said, throwing his hands up.

"All I need are some credits," Suvan continued, ignoring his friend's protestations. "A few thousand should suffice."

"To do what?" Lord Mahtize exclaimed.

"To put a roof over my head and food in my belly, for starters," Suvan replied. "It took every credit I had on me to buy a new identity, and make my way to Takara."

"They will find you, Suvan. They have ident scanners everywhere...and facial recognition. Sooner or later, you *will* be arrested."

"My entire house was wiped from the records by the Council of Nobles when I stood in support of Casimir. In the records of Takara, house Navarro never existed."

"There is no such thing as complete deletion, Suvan, you know that."

"Perhaps, but the Dusahn have more pressing matters to deal with. They must tame an entire sector of space if they are to keep that which they have stolen. That is why I must strike now, *before* the Teyentah is completed. Once she becomes operational, my opportunity will be lost forever. Yassey, I beg of you. If you have any love for our world, you will help me do this."

"I protect what I love by tolerating the current regime," Lord Mahtize argued. "Just as I tolerated those who preceded them. Just as you did, Suvan. I make that sacrifice for all the people who depend on my house for their survival. Do you think I *like* the Dusahn? They have killed hundreds of thousands... they destroyed Ybara. They destroyed Burgess..."

"In the Sherma system?" Suvan said, realizing the implications.

"Of course, in the Sherma system..."

"Did anyone survive?"

"A few, perhaps, but it is only a rumor. That is not the point..."

"Yassey, the Ghatazhak were living on Burgess," Suvan told him.

"What?"

"That must be why the Dusahn went so far out of their way to destroy it. They knew the Ghatazhak were the only ones who could stop them." Suvan shook his head in despair, plopping down in a chair. "This makes it even more imperative that I take control of the Teyentah."

"Suvan, even if you could steal her, how are you

going to operate her all by yourself? You would need at least a hundred men to run that ship."

"Twelve would be enough to get her away," Suvan corrected. "I was part of the design team, remember? She may need a crew of hundreds, but twelve is enough to fly her."

Lord Mahtize sat down across from his friend. "Even if you could get aboard, the controls will be locked out."

"To all problems there are solutions," Suvan insisted.

"You will not live long enough to find them," Lord Mahtize insisted.

Suvan Navarro, captain of the ill-fated Avendahl, once proud leader of House Navarro, looked at his sole remaining friend on Takara. "If I die trying to save our world, I will die a happy man. I do not judge you for your desire to protect what you have, Yassey. On the contrary, I understand it. But *I* have nothing left *except* my pride."

"You have your wife and your children," Yassey reminded him.

"None of whom I could look in the eyes again, if I did not at least *try* to stop the Dusahn."

Lord Mahtize sighed as he leaned back in his chair. "Credits are not a problem, but you will need more than just credits, Suvan."

"Then you *will* help me?"

"This one time, but that is all. And after this, you must never return."

"You have my word, Yassey."

"I always hated that nickname," Lord Mahtize muttered as he pulled out a card from his suit pocket. "Show this card at the Hotel Entorio. The one in Siskeena, not the one in Willette. They will give you a room. You may stay there as long as you wish."

"I cannot afford a hotel, Yassey," Suvan reminded him.

"I have an account there," Lord Mahtize explained. "It is linked to one of my shell corporations, a thousand times removed from House Mahtize. I use it for my...diversions. You may pull credits from the account without raising suspicion."

"Thank you, Yassey."

"Once you are settled, go to the trades house in Siskeena and ask for Aronis Burklund. Tell him Mikal Yaramin sent you, and that you are looking for work."

"But I am not," Suvan objected.

"Not even as an assembly technician," Lord Mahtize said with a smile, "at the shipyard where the Teyentah is being built?"

Suvan Navarro smiled. He had taken a huge gamble coming to Takara, and an even bigger one coming to House Mahtize. But it had been worth it. "Thank you, Yassey."

"One more thing," Lord Mahtize insisted. "Stop calling me Yassey."

"What shall I call you, then?" Suvan wondered. "Mikal, perhaps?" he added with a grin.

* * *

"Got a minute?" Nathan asked from the doorway of General Telles's temporary office in the Aurora's lower decks.

"Of course," the general replied, setting his data pad down on the desk in front of him.

Nathan entered the compartment, taking a seat across from the general. "I watched some of those battle-cam recordings as you suggested."

"And what did you discover?" the general asked.

"That I should trust you, and your men, without reservation," Nathan admitted. "And that I owe you an apology."

"That will not be necessary," General Telles assured him. "You were right to question my decision, even if only to learn from it. Trust without occasional confirmation is blind, and of little value. Truths must be continually tested to ensure we have not lost touch with reality, since reality itself changes without warning, and sometimes quite dramatically."

"Nevertheless, I do apologize," Nathan said.

"Apology accepted," the general replied. "But again, no insult was perceived."

"Let's just say, *you* were not the one feeling insulted," Nathan explained.

General Telles nodded his understanding. "Ah, yes. She still has a long way to go, I'm afraid."

"Part of her charm," Nathan added with a smile. "Actually, she suggested I take some of your Ghatazhak training. At the very least, to help me understand your operating methods and procedures."

"If you are to utilize the Ghatazhak in the most efficient manner, it would seem a wise investment. However, I do not expect you to have the time."

"Cam told you?"

"Yes. Captain Taylor came by less than an hour ago," the general confirmed.

"Then it wasn't your idea?"

"No, but I was going to suggest it, as it does make sense."

Nathan sighed. "I suppose you're right. I'm not sure how I feel about it, though."

"How you *feel* about it is irrelevant," the general said. "You either take command, or you do not."

"Most humans are not wired that way."

General Telles considered the strange euphemism for a moment. "Perhaps, but I believe that you *are*."

Nathan looked at the general. "Do you ever think about chucking everything and leaving?"

"What do you mean?"

"I mean just quitting all this, packing your bags, and leaving it all behind. Find a wife, a decent job, have some kids, and live out your life on some unknown world out in the middle of nowhere, and just let the rest of the galaxy go to shit as it sees fit."

"No, I do not." The general thought for a moment. "I suppose *I* am not *wired* that way." After a moment, he spoke again. "Have you?"

"What do you think I spent the last five years trying to do?" Nathan wondered.

"You were not aware of your true identity at the time," the general pointed out.

"No, but I knew I was supposed to be more than what I was," Nathan admitted.

"Interesting."

"I mean, I didn't know Connor Tuplo wasn't my true identity, but I always felt like I was destined for something greater. I felt like things had happened in the past that had already set me on that path, but I just couldn't remember them. I knew that when I did, my direction would change accordingly."

"And yet, you did not seek out that direction."

"I tried, but my memories were too fragmented. I still have pieces missing. It's like I remember how something began, and how it ended, but not necessarily what came in between."

"That seems like it would present some difficulties," the general said, concerned.

"Most of the broken memories are inconsequential.

Personal stuff, mostly. I seem to remember most of the events during my previous command with complete clarity, unfortunately."

"Unfortunately?" the general queried.

"Some of them I'd just as soon forget."

"Then your hesitations about taking command have nothing to do with your belief in your abilities, or your mental condition?"

"No, they have to do with the fact that Cameron is giving up her ship," Nathan explained. "One she has now been in command of far longer than I ever was."

"It *is* a considerable sacrifice," the general agreed, "yet, it is one she *chose* to make of her own accord."

"Which makes it even more difficult for me," Nathan said.

"Perhaps you should honor her sacrifice by showing her she made the right choice."

Nathan looked at the general and smiled. "Is that your way of telling me to get off my ass and take the bull by the horns?"

General Telles's eyes widened. "I really do need to study up on Terran euphemisms a bit more."

"Just ask Jessica," Nathan suggested as he rose to his feet. "I'm sure she knows a million of them."

"Indeed," the general agreed.

* * *

"Are you sure you want to do this, Nathan?" Jessica asked as they walked up the ramp to the Aurora's command deck.

"Actually, this is the only thing I *am* sure about right now," Nathan said.

"What if they don't take the news well?"

"I'm willing to take that chance, Jess. These people have risked their lives for me, and if they stay, they're going to be doing so again, and again.

They have a right to know." Nathan stopped short of the entrance to the command briefing room, turning to look at Jessica. "In fact, *everyone* has a right to know; the people in that room, the crew of the Aurora, and everyone else aboard all these ships flying alongside us. If they are going to pledge their loyalty to me, they deserve to know *who* and *what* I really am."

"You risk losing a lot of followers by doing so, Nathan. That's all I'm saying."

"I know that," Nathan agreed. "But I'd rather go into battle with a handful of loyal comrades, than an army of people following a myth." Nathan turned and headed into the command briefing room.

"Jesus," Jessica muttered, rolling her eyes as she turned to follow him.

Nathan headed directly to the head of the table.

Aiden Walsh was the first to spot him, and instantly rose to his feet. "Captain on deck!" he barked, causing the rest of his group to stand at attention, as well.

"Please, as you were," Nathan insisted, holding up his hands. "After all, I'm not technically a captain. At least, not in your military," he added as he took his seat. "I've asked you all here because I assumed you had some questions, and I think you *deserve* answers to those questions."

"No one will tell us what's going on," Aiden said. "They won't even tell us where we are."

"*I* don't even know where we are," Nathan replied, smiling.

"Lieutenant Commander Shinoda and his people have been grilling us for hours," Kenji complained.

"They're just doing their jobs," Nathan insisted.

"I've got a question, sir," Charnelle said, raising her hand.

Nathan looked at her. "I'm sorry…"

"Ensign Tegg, sir. Charnelle Tegg."

"Yes, Ensign. What is your question?" Nathan asked.

"Beg your pardon, sir, but how the hell are you still alive?"

Nathan took a deep breath, letting it out slowly as he contemplated how to answer her. "I'm not."

Nathan's response was met with eight blank stares.

"I am Nathan Scott, son of Dayton and Marlene, born on Earth in the year 3447. However, the body in which I currently reside is *not* my original one. It is a clone."

"You're shitting me!" Chief Benetti exclaimed. When everyone looked at her, she added, "What? You're not thinking the same thing?"

"I have no recollection of my death on Nor-Patri," Nathan explained. "Moments before my death, my consciousness, my memories, everything that makes *me* Nathan Scott, was uploaded onto a portable storage device provided by two rogue Nifelmian specialists."

"The clone race," Aiden realized. "I've heard of them."

"I always thought that was just a rumor," Sari stated.

"Me, too," Charnelle agreed.

"The Nifelmians keep to themselves, don't they?" Sergeant Dagata wondered.

"That's what I heard, as well," Ali agreed.

"But you were in a Jung prison, weren't you?" Kenji challenged. "How were you able to…"

"The how is unimportant," Nathan interrupted. "And, possibly even classified," he added, looking at Jessica.

"Then where have you been the last seven years?" Kenji wondered.

"In hiding, obviously," Aiden said to Kenji. He turned to Nathan and asked, "But why come out now? Aren't you afraid the Jung will find out and come after you?"

"That could spark another war," Kenji added.

"That's probably going to happen with or without me," Nathan commented. "As to your other question, I couldn't just stand by and watch the Dusahn take over the Pentaurus cluster, and God knows how many more systems."

"Lieutenant Commander Shinoda kept referring to the Dusahn, as well," Aiden said. "We thought the Jung had invaded the Pentaurus cluster. At least, that's what they're saying back home."

"We believe the Dusahn to be a rogue Jung caste, banished from the Jung Empire centuries ago. How and why they turned up in the PC, and how they managed to get their hands on jump drive technology, has yet to be determined," Nathan explained.

"And you guys intend to stop them?" Aiden surmised, holding back a look of excitement.

"Precisely," Nathan replied.

"How?" Kenji wondered. "As far as we can tell, you've only got one ship... The Aurora."

"How many ships are we up against?" Aiden asked.

"We?" Kenji added, casting a disapproving glance at his captain.

"Yes, we," Aiden insisted, ignoring his copilot.

Nathan looked at Jessica.

Jessica resisted for a moment, not sure if she should be sharing the intelligence with them just yet. "Currently we have confirmed the presence of thirty-six ships in the Pentaurus cluster," she finally said. "Thirty-three of them are armed, and twenty-one of those thirty-three are classified as warships."

"And you're going after them with *one* ship?" Kenji exclaimed in disbelief. "No disrespect, sir, but that's insane!"

"We don't plan on running headlong into a fight with their fleet," Nathan assured him. "In fact, we have yet to devise any type of plan short of harassing them, in order to prevent their spread to other systems. That's why we needed the gunships. Larger ships have limited jump range. In order to protect our fleet, we must remain outside that range. With the gunships, we can execute hit-and-run strikes, forcing them to protect their infrastructure assets, thereby keeping their forces contained."

"But that will only work for so long, right?" Charnelle surmised.

"Correct," Nathan agreed. "Eventually, we will have to strike more devastating blows, before they can build up their forces."

"Why the fleet of cargo ships?" Kenji wondered. "Why not just create an operating base somewhere?"

"Creating a surface-operating base would be costly and time-consuming," Nathan explained. "And utilizing an existing world that could offer such support would put that world at risk. The Dusahn have already destroyed two entire worlds, neither of which posed any threat. One because their representatives failed to show the proper respect, and the other because the Ghatazhak were based there. Any world safe to operate from would likely be too far away to be strategically viable. A mobile operating base is the only sensible alternative, at the moment."

"But, *nine* gunships, against *twenty-one* warships?" Kenji didn't like the odds one bit.

"Yeah," Chief Benetti agreed. "And what if they have more ships that you don't know about?"

"That's entirely possible," Nathan admitted.

Specialist Leger raised his hand meekly from the far end of the conference table. "Excuse me, sir?"

"Yes?" Nathan said.

"Why?" Specialist Leger asked.

"Why what?" Nathan replied.

"Why are you doing this?"

"Yeah," Chief Benetti agreed. "You were in hiding, weren't you? You were safe and sound, right?"

"What kind of a question is that?" Aiden remarked, annoyed.

"No, it's a fair question," Nathan insisted. "And I have an answer." He looked at the young specialist as he answered his question. "Because it *needs* to be done."

"But why?"

"Come on, Ledge," Aiden begged.

"Because if we don't, the Dusahn will spread to the next sector, and then the next, and so on. Because more people will die. And even more, still, if we end up fighting them later, instead of now."

"But why you?" Leger asked.

Nathan sighed. "I could say, 'Because a handful of people once risked their lives to save me. And then they risked their lives again to bring me back to life.' And I could say, 'Because they *asked* me to lead them.' But that would only be a small part of it. The truth is, I would have taken the fight to the

97

Dusahn without them asking. Because it is the right thing to do."

"Why are you telling us all this?" Kenji wondered.

"Because you have the right to decide for yourselves whether or not you want to join us," Nathan explained. "I know that Ensign Walsh here volunteered you all on the spur of the moment, and under considerable duress. In doing so, he was overstepping his authority as your captain. While I would welcome you all, I want each of you to make that decision on your own, and not have someone make it for you. I will be asking you all to risk your lives, possibly on a daily basis. That is not something I take lightly, and neither should any of you."

Aiden looked at the others at the table, then back at Nathan. "Then, I take it the lieutenant commander has cleared us?"

"That decision now rests with me," Nathan informed them. "If you choose to join us, you will be breaking your oath to the Alliance, just as the crew of the Aurora has done, and just as Captains Roselle and Nash have done."

"What about you?" Aiden wondered.

"To my knowledge, Terran law does not recognize clones, so technically, my allegiance ended with the death of my original body."

"Then just transfer us all into clones of ourselves, and kill *our* original bodies," Aiden suggested, half joking. "Problem solved."

"Not as easy as you might think," Nathan assured him.

"What happens to us if we decide not to join you?" Kenji asked.

"Anyone who does not wish to pledge their loyalty to the Karuzari, and join us in our fight against the

Dusahn, will be transported back to their homeworld as soon as is practicable," Nathan promised.

"Oh, that will be loads of fun," Chief Benetti said. "The interrogations, the dishonorable discharges... Hell, we might even face charges." She looked at Aiden. "Thanks a lot, Aiden."

"Don't listen to her; nobody likes her much." Aiden joked. "I'm in."

"Why am I not surprised," Chief Benetti grumbled.

"So is she," Aiden added, immediately leaning away from Chief Benetti to avoid the angry punch that immediately followed.

"Me, too," Specialist Leger added.

"I'm in, as well," Ali joined in.

"What the hell," Sergeant Dagata agreed. "After all, we've come all this way."

Aiden looked at Kenji. "Just think of all the stories you'll have to tell your children someday."

"If I survive," Kenji replied.

"Count me in, sir," Charnelle said.

"Me, as well," Sari added.

Aiden kept staring at Kenji.

Kenji sighed in resignation. "Well, I can't very well let you all go it alone. Without me, you'll probably do something stupid and get everyone killed on the first mission."

"You mean, like bouncing a gunship off a planet?" Nathan commented.

"Yeah, like that," Kenji chuckled.

Nathan smiled. "Welcome to the team. You should probably remove those Alliance patches from your jumpsuits, though. After all, in the eyes of the Alliance, you're deserters, and in the eyes of the Dusahn, we're all terrorists."

"You really know how to sell it, don't you, sir?" Kenji commented.

Nathan's smile only grew wider.

* * *

"You wanted to see me, sir?" Commander Kaplan said as she entered the captain's ready room on board the Aurora.

"Yes, Commander," Cameron replied. "Please, take a seat." Cameron paused a moment, waiting for the commander to sit before continuing. "How are things going on the Mystic?"

"Slow, but we are making progress. Changing over from a cruise-ship configuration to a residential and support ship is proving to be more difficult than we originally anticipated. Now that the Glendanon has finished building us our own fabricator, things are starting to move a little faster. In another week, we'll get our second fabricator."

"What are you fabricating?" Cameron wondered.

"Mostly structural and compartment stuff. We've been breaking down the luxury suites, and turning them into family suites. We've also been reconfiguring the spa areas to become part of medical. Once finished, we'll have a nice little hospital going. That will take the role of health care for the fleet off the Aurora."

"What about creating defenses?" Cameron asked.

"Once we get the second fabricator, we'll make two more on our own. Then we'll start cranking out point-defense turrets. One of the specialists from Burgess, who was working for the Ghatazhak, provided us with a nice, compact, little design. Each turret is self-powered and wirelessly controlled. We can literally slap them on the outside of the hull wherever we see fit. I've got him working on a field-of-fire plan as we speak."

"How long until you have basic defenses operational?"

"A few weeks, at least. It only takes a couple days to build one. My best guess is that it will take at least twenty of them to give us a sixty-percent intercept rate."

"Sixty percent?" Cameron looked concerned.

"I know, but it's a start. We should be able to get that up to at least ninety in a couple months."

"Maybe if you dedicated *all* of your fabricators to the production of point defense turrets..."

"We thought about that, Captain," the commander said. "Problem is, the Mystic is more important than you might think. We snagged her just in time. The people were not happy all cooped up in cargo pods aboard the Glendanon. We still have a long way to go yet, but just the knowledge that we're working toward something is making a big difference in morale across the fleet. And the extra elbow room isn't hurting, either."

"Sounds like you've really got your hands full over there," Cameron said.

"Yeah, I know I haven't been around much, and you've had to pick up my slack. I apologize for that, sir. I'll try to delegate a bit more of my responsibilities to my department heads on the Mystic, so I can spend more time aboard the Aurora."

"About that... I've decided to make some changes around here," Cameron said.

"Changes?"

"I've decided that it would be best if you were transferred to the Mystic as her full-time executive officer."

"Captain, I can do both jobs, really," the commander insisted. "I just need a little more time to adjust, that's all."

"This isn't about you, Lara," Cameron explained. "It's about what best serves our mission. You said it yourself, the Mystic is far more important than we realize. What you're doing for that ship, and for all of our people, is far more important to our mission. And you are the perfect person for the job. You're quick to solve problems, you adapt to change in the blink of an eye, and you've never met a rule you couldn't find a way around when needed. That's exactly what the Mystic needs right now."

"Of course, sir," Lara replied.

"You do like your role on the Mystic, don't you?"

"Actually, I do. I really do. It's probably the most challenging thing I've ever done. And I've got some great people over there...for civilians, anyway. But I can't help feeling like I've let you down, Cameron."

"Not at all, Lara. I'm quite proud of what you're accomplishing over there. In fact, I'm going to recommend to Captain Scott and General Telles that, in the Aurora's absence, *you* should take tactical command of the fleet."

"I'm honored, sir," Commander Kaplan replied. "I won't let you down."

"I know you won't."

"Is that what you wanted to talk to me about?" the commander asked.

"Yes, that's it," Cameron assured her, a bit of melancholy in her voice.

"Then I guess I'd better pack up my things and move over to the Mystic," the commander said, rising from her seat.

"I'm going to miss you around here, Lara,"

Cameron said as she also rose. "You're probably the best XO I've ever had."

"Thanks, Cam. I'm going to miss you, as well." Commander Kaplan turned to exit, then paused, looking back at Cameron. "By the way, who's going to be your new XO? *Please* tell me it's not going to be Vidmar."

"No, it's not going to be Vidmar. In fact, he's no longer going to be the Aurora's CTO."

"*Really*?" Lara looked quite pleased. "Who's replacing him?"

"Lieutenant Commander Nash."

"*Jessica*?" Lara looked surprised. "I thought she was a lieutenant."

"She *was*. But I can't very well demote Vidmar, and I can't have someone of lesser rank as his supervisor."

"I'm so loving this," Lara exclaimed with a smile. "I wish I could be here to see the look on his face when you tell him."

"I already did," Cameron told her. "You would have enjoyed it."

Lara laughed. "So, who *is* going to be the Aurora's next XO?"

"I am."

"What?"

"I'm turning command of the Aurora over to Captain Scott."

"*What*?" Lara's jaw dropped. "Jesus, Cam, I know he's *Nathan Scott,* and all, but this is *your* ship. Are you sure you want to just hand it over?"

"Do I *want* to? No. But for this rebellion to work, it must be led by Nathan Scott, and he *must* lead it from the bridge of the Aurora."

"Then let him stand on the bridge and impress people while you run the ship," Lara suggested.

"I plan to," Cameron agreed, "but as XO, just like you did with me."

Lara sighed. "I sure as hell did *not* see this coming."

"Actually, I did," Cameron admitted. "The moment I saw his face in that message, I knew I'd be handing my ship over to him to command."

Lara thought for a moment. "Do you really trust him *that* much, Cam?"

Cameron thought for a moment, then smiled. "Actually, I do... I *really* do."

* * *

It had taken only a few minutes for Nathan to pack up his personal belongings from his cabin aboard the Seiiki. Surprisingly, in the five years he had lived aboard her, he had collected very little. Some clothing, shoes, a few sidearms, and a collection of vid-plays and music files that all fit on a single data chip. Along with a few personal mementos, he possessed little of importance. The Seiiki, herself, had been the only possession that meant anything to him, and although she would still belong to him, she would never be the same ship again. She was about to become a tactical combat ship, capable of flying a variety of missions for the Karuzari.

He sat for a moment, looking at the blank walls of his cabin. Despite the fact that he would be back aboard her for any number of missions in the near future, this cabin would no longer be his. In fact, none of the cabins would belong to the individual members of her crew from this point forward. The ship would be based on the Aurora. Her cabins would be gutted to hold reactors for various weapons and shielding systems yet to be installed. The Seiiki would no longer be a *home* to anyone. She was about to become a ship of war.

The side of him that was Nathan saw the advantages the Seiiki brought the rebellion. She was fast, could jump forever, and could carry at least fifty Ghatazhak in her cargo hold. Once armed, she would be quite useful indeed. But the Connor side of him saw the ship as his home…the only thing he'd ever had any control over in his wayward life. The Seiiki represented a dream he had once held. A dream of growing his business into a multi-ship operation, perhaps in some distant system that had yet to be introduced to the wonders of the jump drive. Had he taken the Ghatazhak's fuel, supplies, and repairs, and run as he had originally intended, he would already be well on his way to finally achieving that dream. Not just for him, but for his crew, as well.

Nathan sighed. *His crew.*

He rose to his feet and went to the desk, pressing the intercom button. "Josh?"

"*Yeah, Cap'n.*"

"Have everyone assemble in the galley. I need to talk to the entire crew."

"*Straight away, Skipper,*" Josh replied.

Nathan reached down and picked up the flat holo-chip on his desk that he had missed during packing. He held it in his hand, tapping its surface with his finger to activate it. A three-dimensional image of him and his crew standing in front of the Seiiki's cargo ramp, just before departing on one of any number of runs they had made together, appeared before him. He could almost hear the banter between them. Marcus ridiculing Dalen and Josh. Josh calling Marcus an old man. Neli trying to maintain peace between them all, and Connor, standing in the middle of them, a smirk hiding behind his scruffy beard and tangled mess of hair. It had been a good life, but it was time to move on. He was no longer the same person. He was no longer Connor Tuplo, but he also was no longer Nathan Scott...not entirely. He hoped that his experiences as Connor made him a *better* Nathan. Only time would tell.

Nathan deactivated the holo-chip and placed it in his pocket, then picked up his bag and headed out the door and forward.

Moments later, he found himself following Dalen and Marcus down the port corridor and into the galley, where Neli, Josh, and Loki were already waiting.

"What's going on, Cap'n?" Josh wondered as Nathan followed the others into the galley. "What's with the bag? You going somewhere?"

"Actually, we all are," Nathan said.

"A vacation?" Josh suggested, only half joking.

"I wish," Nathan replied. "We're all moving on board the Aurora. You're all getting cabins down on E deck."

"Together?" Josh wondered, looking fearful.

"No, not together. It will be pretty much the same as it is here. Marcus and Neli in one cabin, Dalen in another, and Josh in the third cabin, with Loki bunking with Josh as needed."

"Hot damn!" Josh exclaimed. "No more of Neli's cooking!"

"Hot damn, no more cleaning up after Josh," Neli followed.

"Does this mean I get to be with my family?" Loki asked.

"In between missions, yes. But you will be

expected to report for duty on a regular basis, even when the Seiiki isn't flying."

"What for?" Josh wondered.

"Training, maintenance, mission planning, that kind of stuff," Nathan explained.

"Why can't we just stay where we are?" Neli wondered.

"We need the cabin space to accommodate the reactors for the plasma torpedo cannons, and for the upgraded shielding," Nathan continued. "The Seiiki is being turned into a tactical combat ship, capable of multiple mission profiles."

"But we're still going to be her crew, right?" Dalen asked.

"That's right," Nathan replied. "You'll still be her chief engineer, Dalen, with a little help from Commander Kamenetskiy and the Aurora's engineering department. Marcus will be the deck chief, and Neli will be support."

"Who's running the gun turrets?" Marcus asked.

"You, Neli, and Dalen, depending on the mission," Nathan told him. "Josh will be the pilot, and Loki will be the copilot, navigator, and weapons officer."

"What will you be doing?" Josh asked.

"If I'm part of the mission, then whatever the mission calls for, I guess."

"We're going to be flying missions without you?" Josh wondered.

"Probably."

Marcus's curiosity was suddenly aroused. "Wait a minute... Where are *you* going to be bunked, Cap'n?"

Despite his best efforts to keep it hidden, a smile crept onto the corner of Nathan's mouth. "I'm taking command of the Aurora."

"You're shittin' me!" Josh exclaimed.

"It's about fuckin' time," Marcus added.

"Uh, how does Captain Taylor feel about this?" Loki wondered.

"Actually, it was her idea," Nathan replied.

"No shit?" Josh asked.

"I hope this doesn't mean we're going to have to wear them dopey, gray uniforms again," Marcus grumbled.

Nathan smiled. "I'm pretty sure you can keep wearing your jumpsuits, Marcus." Nathan looked at his crew. "You should all probably get packed up and moved as soon as possible. Engineering teams are going to start gutting your cabins first thing tomorrow morning."

"Not without us aboard, they're not," Marcus warned.

"That is the plan, Marcus. In fact, I'm counting on you all to make sure they don't screw up our ship permanently. Someday, we're going to want to change her back again. So, make sure they don't do anything we can't undo later."

"You got it Cap'n," Marcus promised.

"Real food, real beds, real showers, and real women!" Josh exclaimed, hopping down from the galley counter. "I'll be moved and trolling the Aurora's mess hall within the hour!"

"Don't forget to pick up comm-sets from the Aurora's quartermaster," Nathan reminded them.

"Uh, Cap'n?" Dalen said. "Are we going to get assigned a rank, or something?"

"To be honest, I hadn't really thought about it, Dalen. Do you need one?"

"I don't know. But how am I going to know who to take orders from, and who to salute, and all that?"

"I'll talk to Captain Taylor about it as soon as

I officially take command. In the meantime, don't bother saluting anyone. Just say 'good day', all right?"

"You got it, Cap'n," Dalen answered, before turning to exit.

His ship might never be the same, but he still had his crew. And to the part of him who was Connor Tuplo, they would always be his *real* family.

* * *

Nathan stood just inside the door of the empty captain's cabin. It was exactly how he remembered it. Except, of course, it was clean; he had never been the tidiest person.

He walked into the center of the main living area, slowly looking around. Memories came flooding back to him. Memories of what had been his refuge; the place where he came to escape the pressures of command, if only for a brief period.

In retrospect, he had done little in this cabin other than sleep, and the occasional 'night before' meetings that had become a ritual for Nathan, Vladimir, Cameron, and Jessica before battles. Those had actually been some of the best times aboard ship. Just the four of them hanging out, doing nothing important.

The door buzzer sounded, and Nathan turned to open it.

"Welcome back, Captain," Vladimir said with a smile. "Have you finished unpacking?" he added as he moved into the cabin.

"To be honest, I don't have much to unpack," Nathan admitted, holding up his duffel bag.

"I'm surprised Cameron gave you her cabin," Vladimir said as he plopped down on the couch.

"She insisted on moving to the XO's cabin,"

Nathan explained. "I tried to talk her out of it, but she kept going on about continuity and appearances... I finally just gave in."

"She never did like this cabin much," Vladimir pointed out. "She always felt like your presence was still in it, like a ghost, or something."

"Really?"

"*Da*. Silly, yes?"

"It's weird," Nathan commented, strolling about the main living space. "To the part of me that is Connor, this place seems completely unfamiliar. But to the part of me that is Nathan, it feels like I've only been gone a few weeks."

"It was only a few weeks that I was sitting right here, watching that message you sent," Vladimir said. "Oh, and I suggest you do not speak of the 'Connor' side of you around anyone but me. It might make people worry."

"And you aren't?"

"Not in the least," Vladimir said confidently.

Nathan looked at him, one eyebrow raised.

"Okay, maybe a little," Vladimir admitted, "but only because you keep talking about the 'Connor' side of you. Josh was right, we should start calling you 'Conathan'."

"Funny," Nathan remarked dryly as he headed into the bedroom to put away his duffel. "Referring to my 'Connor' and 'Nathan' sides is simply my way of dealing with it. Honestly, sometimes I have a hard time telling which memories are from which life."

"Then do not even try," Vladimir suggested.

Nathan paused mid-stride, leaning back to look through the door at Vladimir. "Come again?"

"Seriously. Just pretend you *were* Nathan during the last five years, and that you were *pretending* to be Connor. Like you were hiding out, living under an alias, so the Jung would not discover you were alive."

Nathan stood in the doorway, dumbfounded, staring at his friend.

"What?"

"That's not a bad idea, really." Nathan scratched his head in dismay. "I'm actually kind of embarrassed I didn't think of that myself."

"What can I say?" Vladimir boasted. "I am a genius."

Nathan looked at him cockeyed.

"Okay, I got the idea from Jessica. When they woke your first body and discovered you had no memory, they were going to tell you who you really were, but decided against it."

"Why?" Nathan wondered, still standing in the bedroom doorway.

"Jessica thought it would be easier for you to give up everything you knew, *if* you didn't know about it."

"But I *did* know about it," Nathan argued. "I knew about my *fake* life."

"One where you had no living relatives. No one you would seek out. No one to reconnect with."

"That's crazy," Nathan commented. "Then again, it *was* Jessica's idea, so..."

"Actually, Jessica's reasoning was it would be *easier* to pretend *not* to be Nathan, if you did not know you really *were* Nathan."

"You mean, if I truly *believed* I was Connor Tuplo."

"Isn't that what I said?"

"*That* sounds more like Jessica," Nathan agreed.

"So, just pretend like you *knew* you were really Nathan the whole time, and you are a very good actor."

"In essence, lie to myself."

"Exactly."

"Isn't that kind of crazy in itself?" Nathan wondered.

"Humans lie to themselves all the time."

"That's true," Nathan agreed. He turned and headed back inside the bedroom, opening the closet door. When he did so, his eyes widened, and his mouth fell agape.

Vladimir looked around the room. "Is there anything to eat in here?" When Nathan did not respond, he called again. "Nathan! Do you have any food?" Finally, he got up and headed toward the bedroom. "Did you hear me? Or did the Connor side of you not realize I was calling you?" he teased as he entered the bedroom. He paused mid-stride, spotting Nathan sitting on the edge of the bed, staring at the open closet. "What's wrong?" he asked. Nathan didn't respond, but just kept staring at the open closet. Vladimir moved further inside, looking into the closet, as well. Inside was a full set of men's uniforms, complete with captain's stripes and insignias. Attached to the side of them was a note. Vladimir removed the note and read it aloud. "*You are right where you are supposed to be. Welcome back.*" Vladimir looked at Nathan. "It's signed by Cam."

Nathan looked at Vladimir. "I'm really back, aren't I," he said.

"Yes, my friend. And it's about time."

Nathan looked at the uniforms, then back at Vladimir. "Do you think I'm ready?"

"Hopefully, more so than the first time you took command of this ship," he joked. "Now, let's get something to eat. I'm starving."

* * *

Terig started his day as usual, reviewing the communications logs from the previous day, crosschecking them against the backup logs. Lord Mahtize was adamant about maintaining proper records and backups of all communications, as well as encrypting all files. 'Data is a commodity like any other,' he would often remind his staff. And Terig's primary job was to protect that data, in every way possible.

It wasn't exactly an exciting or challenging job by any stretch of the imagination, but it paid well enough, and he had been lucky to land the position over others. He was fresh out of technical school when he first applied, and had only gotten an interview because of a friend who was on the security staff of House Mahtize. A shared interest in polymorphic circuitry with the woman who had interviewed him had been the clincher, a fact he often reminded his wife of whenever she teased him about his obscure obsession.

Terig had never met Lord Mahtize, nor any of the lord's extended family. Like all the other nobles of Takara, the Mahtize family had taken the longevity serum for decades under the rule of Caius Ta'Akar, allowing them to build a considerable family line. Like every other lord of Takara, Mahtize had dozens of children, and more than a hundred grandchildren and great-grandchildren. He even had a staff whose primary responsibility was keeping track of all of his offspring's birthdays, graduations, and other significant life events, ensuring their lord did not forget to attend with an appropriate present in hand. It was an odd type of family structure, one that only existed among the wealthiest citizens of Takara.

The assassination of Caius, however, had brought

an end to the massive noble families. The nobles had dumped millions into feeble attempts to resurrect the lost formula for the longevity serum, many of which were still in progress. But the dream had all but faded in recent years. Many thought it for the best, believing life-spans lasting centuries were entirely unnatural and had a negative influence on society as a whole. Terig didn't think it as bad as some, but agreed that living forever took much of the value out of life itself. Even without the longevity serum, the average life-span on Takara was well over one hundred and twenty years, enabling families to rival those of the nobles in size, if not in wealth and position.

As he scanned the communications logs, Terig contemplated what it must be like to have so many children that you needed someone to keep track of them for you. What little he saw of the Mahtize household seemed utter chaos in his eyes. Luckily, he had married a woman who only wanted a small family.

The comms log was full of the usual stuff. Business calls by staffers, messages from dozens of people wishing to speak to Lord Mahtize about urgent matters of every sort, and a dozen or so calls made by Lord Mahtize himself. The log was lighter than usual, as Mahtize had been out of the office for most of the day. The lord usually had at least half a dozen meetings with various individuals during a normal business day, but his presence had been required at the Council of Nobles that morning, so the number of personal meetings that had been recorded was only one, a Mister Tensen Dalott.

Terig did not recall the name on any of the previous comms logs, which was unusual. Most meetings with Lord Mahtize required multiple calls to arrange. After further checking, Terig learned that Mister Dalott had shown up that morning, and had somehow convinced those who are supposed to filter out such surprise visits into allowing him to sit and wait in hopes of an audience with the leader of House Mahtize. That really was quite unusual. In fact, Terig could not remember anyone being permitted to speak with his employer without countless prior negotiations.

The fact that this man had done so intrigued Terig to no end.

But it was none of his concern. His job was to back up and encrypt all communication files, and to maintain the infrastructure which supported that function. The content of those files was none of his business.

Yet...

His mind suddenly recalled his brief discussion with Jessica Nash aboard the Mystic Empress, just before he and his wife had boarded the escape pods with the rest of the departing passengers. She had given him a list of things to watch for: movement of Dusahn forces, attacks on other worlds, drastic changes in the political and economics of Takara...in essence, anything that might be of importance to the Karuzari. But most importantly, she had told him to keep an eye out for anything out of the ordinary.

This was, definitely, out of the ordinary.

Terig suddenly felt ill. It had been twelve days since that conversation. Twelve days since he had volunteered to serve as a spy for the Karuzari. This was the first time he had been faced with the decision to actually *do* something. Until now, he had committed no crimes, except one of omission by not reporting his conversation with the rebels to the Dusahn. But *this*...

The ill feeling in his stomach was getting worse. There was a line before him. A line that, if crossed, there would be no turning back from. His wife would be furious with him. She might even leave him. But something inside told him it was the *right* thing to do. He was not a warrior, he wasn't even a brave man by anyone's standards. He had never actually been in a fight. But *this* was something that he *could* do. This was a way he could *resist* the Dusahn. It was a small way...probably one that would amount to nothing. But even if no one ever knew what he had done, *he* would know. Terig Espan would always know that he had done what he could to protect his world.

Terig pulled the data chip from his belt buckle; the one Jessica had given him. It was made of a polymer that would not show up on the security scanners used all over Takara. He leaned forward, as if reaching to adjust his view screen, in order to hide his insertion of the data chip from the camera behind him. Once inserted, he entered a command string to begin the backup process, as usual. Only this time, he added a few extra commands, causing a shadow copy to be sent to the data port containing his special data chip. The last sequence in the command string caused the shadow copy process to be stricken from the logs, so no one would know what he had done. The only way someone could tell he had copied the file would be if they were watching his monitor feed at this very moment. Given that he was usually the first person to arrive in his department, the chances of that were slim.

Still, Terig felt as if he was going to vomit. After

the file was copied, he again adjusted his view screen with one hand, while he removed the data chip with the other, slipping it back into the slot on his belt buckle under the table, where the camera could not see.

Then, just like that, the sick feeling in the pit of his stomach began to fade. Unfortunately, it did not go away completely, and Terig expected it would be with him at least until he got home at the end of the day, if not for days afterward.

But he had done something. He had committed an act of espionage. And while it made him nauseated and light-headed, it also gave him a feeling of exhilaration.

He only hoped he could keep the secret from his wife. She had ways of knowing things that he simply did not understand.

* * *

"Captain on deck!" the security officer at the entrance to the command briefing room barked as Cameron entered the compartment.

"As you were," she instructed, before anyone could rise to their feet. She moved to her usual spot at the head of the table, but did not sit. The chair to her left, the one usually occupied by her executive officer, Commander Kaplan, was conspicuously empty. Cameron looked at the faces of her senior staff, gathered around the table, expecting their usual morning briefing. For a moment, she wondered how many of them already knew what she was about to say, about how their lives were about to change. But she could not dwell on such things. She could not dwell on the fact that she was about to give up her command...her *ship*, without being required to do so. She had once trusted Nathan completely, and

Ryk Brown

it was a trust that had not only been duly earned, but had also come as a complete surprise to her. She hoped he was still the same man, the one whom she had trusted so many years ago. Unfortunately, only time would tell. But the people of the Pentaurus sector did not have the time to spare, and of this, she was quite certain. Just as she had been forced to eight years ago, Cameron Taylor was about to take a leap of faith.

She took a deep breath and began. "Before this briefing starts, I have an announcement to make. First, however, I'd like to say a few words to all of you. Each of you chose to break every rule in the book, and to violate the very oath you swore to uphold. Some of you even left loved ones behind to do so. And you did this simply because *I* told you it was the right thing to do. For that confidence in me, I shall be eternally grateful. And I want you to know that I do not take your confidence in me lightly. Because of that, the decision I made was probably the most difficult of my entire career, if not my life. I only hope you will have as much faith in my decision as I do."

Cameron took a deep breath before continuing. "Effective immediately, I am turning over command of the Aurora to Nathan Scott." Cameron looked at her senior staff, scanning their faces, expecting looks of surprise and confusion, but saw none.

"We already know," Commander Verbeek confessed.

It was *Cameron* who had the look of surprise. She looked at Vladimir, sitting at the other end of the conference table, smiling.

"Don't look at me," Vladimir insisted.

"It was Josh Hayes," Commander Verbeek

118

corrected. "He was telling everyone in the mess hall last night."

"I see," Cameron said, annoyed.

"Where are Kaplan and Vidmar?" Lieutenant Commander Shinoda wondered.

"Commander Kaplan is taking over as the Mystic's full-time executive officer," Cameron explained. "Lieutenant Commander Vidmar is bringing our new chief tactical officer, Lieutenant Commander Jessica Nash, up to speed on the Aurora's weapons systems."

"Who's XO then?" the lieutenant commander wondered.

"What, Josh didn't tell you?" Cameron quipped.

"Actually, I didn't even hear you were passing command to Scott," Lieutenant Commander Shinoda admitted. "I've been going over recon data all night." The lieutenant commander could see the surprise in her face. "Nothing surprises me, Captain. You know that."

"Right."

"So, who's XO, then?" Commander Verbeek asked.

"I am," Cameron replied.

"Now, *that* surprised me!" Lieutenant Commander Shinoda exclaimed. "Alright, it didn't really."

Cameron looked a bit flustered, having expected a more dramatic moment.

"Captain, we understand why you're handing over command, and we all agree with you on this," Commander Verbeek explained. "No insult intended, sir, but Nathan Scott *is* the right person for the job, at the moment."

"Very well, then," Cameron began. "Gentlemen, I give you your new commanding officer, Captain Nathan Scott."

Nathan entered the command briefing room, in

uniform, sporting his captain's insignias, trying desperately to hide his uneasiness.

"Captain on deck!" the security guard at the door barked again.

Everyone in attendance rose to their feet and began clapping.

Nathan looked at their welcoming faces, each a vote of confidence in him, and all his fears suddenly faded away.

CHAPTER FOUR

"You asked to speak with me?" Michael announced as he entered the underground lab where Birk and Cuddy had been working for the last week. "Is something wrong?"

"On the contrary," Birk replied. "I think I've solved the problem."

"*We've* solved the problem," Cuddy corrected him.

Michael looked at them both, surprised. "You only started on this yesterday, and you said it would be more difficult *because* we needed it to be general broadcast, rather than point-to-point."

"I know, but after we broke the problem down to basics, we realized what was needed wasn't a general broadcast from the ground, but, rather, from space." Birk moved to the airborne drawing space along the far wall, swiping his hand in the air to erase the sketches already hovering before him. "Update version number, and save all with same name," he instructed the computer as he swept the floating drawings away with his hands. "New drawing," he instructed as he started sketching in the air.

Michael looked at Cuddy.

"Watch, this is good," Cuddy urged, smiling.

"Communications between all surface-based units is accomplished at three different levels," Birk began. "If the link is between comm-units in the same geographical region—say, within the same city—the signal is routed via local comm-towers, using the relays closest to each comm-unit. If both comm-units are on the surface, but in different geographical regions, like different cities, then the comm-relay routes the signal to the sat-net in orbit, which then sends it either directly to the comm-tower relay nearest the other comm-unit, or if that unit is out of range, to the next satellite in the network, and so on, until it reaches a satellite that can reach the surface relay closest to the other comm-unit."

"Unless the comm-unit is not within range of a surface-based comm-relay," Michael added.

"Precisely," Birk agreed. "And if the other comm-unit is *not* on the surface, but rather in *space*, then the signal is routed outward. If the other comm-unit is in a *ship*, the signal is sent via point-to-point link. If the other comm-unit is on another planet in the Darvano system, the signal is carried by a jump comm-drone. Same thing if the other comm-unit is located *outside* of the system, which of course takes longer."

"I already know all this," Michael assured him. "How does this relate to our problem?"

"The answer is in the routing algorithm," Birk continued. "If the satellite knows the other comm-unit is in space nearby, but doesn't know exactly *where* in space the other comm-unit *is*, it can't initiate a point-to-point link, because it doesn't have any coordinates."

"At which point the system returns an 'unable to connect' signal back to the initiating comm-unit," Michael said.

"It *used* to be that way," Birk explained, "but that changed a few years ago. *Now,* the system first initiates a general broadcast, hoping the intended receiving comm-unit will pick up the broadcast and return its location data, so the point-to-point link can be made, and the connection can be completed. *Instead* of 'unable to connect', you get 'connection delayed, searching for target comm-unit'. The system keeps the link initiation request active for several hours, rebroadcasting the link request every few minutes, before automatically canceling the request."

"And how does that help us?" Michael wondered.

Birk gestured to Cuddy. "It was Cuddy's idea, really."

Michael looked at Cuddy for an answer.

"We embed the message in the link request," Cuddy explained.

"And the Dusahn won't notice this?"

"There are literally thousands of link requests being sent out into space every minute," Cuddy assured Michael. "Who is going to notice one more, even if it *does* have a bit more data in the link string than usual?"

"And the extra data would be encrypted anyway," Birk added.

"But if they *did* notice it, they'd trace it back to the initiating comm-unit, which would be ours," Michael surmised, pointing out the flaw in their plan.

"Unless we use the same trick we came up with to cover our secure comms," Birk told him.

Michael's eyes lit up. "That just might work."

"Of course, it will work!" Birk declared.

"*If* the intended recipient *knows* to be on the lookout for the link requests with extra data tagged to them," Cuddy admitted.

"Aren't the Karuzari monitoring all comms traffic in the Darvano system?" Birk asked.

"We would assume so," Michael agreed.

"Then, sooner or later, they'll catch on to what we're doing," Birk insisted. "And once we have two-way communication, we can devise something more elaborate...one that is even more secure."

Michael smiled. "How soon can you be ready to send a message?"

"About an hour," Birk suggested, looking to Cuddy.

"Two at the most," Cuddy added, always choosing to be more conservative than his cohort.

"Outstanding," Michael congratulated. "The two of you may have just given us the one tool that will help get this rebellion started."

* * *

"I would suggest we cross-train every pilot aboard to fly every *ship* aboard," Commander Verbeek told Nathan and Cameron as they walked through the flight operations support deck toward the ramp. "Not just the active ones, either," he continued. "I'm talking about every *pilot*, period. Officers currently not serving as pilots included."

"How long will that take?" Nathan wondered.

"It's not much of a jump between Eagles and Reapers," the commander stated. "So, all my pilots can be cross-trained in a matter of weeks, depending on our operational load. People who aren't actively flying will likely take a bit longer."

"By that logic, we're going to have to train everyone how to fly the Seiiki, as well," Nathan said.

"And the Ranni shuttles," Cameron added.

"How soon are we expecting the first two?" Commander Verbeek wondered.

"In a few days," Cameron replied.

"How are we going to pick them up?" Nathan wondered. "The Seiiki is already in overhaul."

"And we can't spare any shuttles," Cameron added. "They're too busy running personnel and cargo between ships."

"Maybe we can send one of the boxcars with a couple extra pilots?"

"I'd rather send something with weapons," Nathan told them.

"Why?" Cameron asked.

"Because I'm going along with them," Nathan replied.

"Why?" Cameron repeated.

"Because I want to work on convincing those Gunyoki racers to join us," Nathan explained. "Besides, I *am* a pilot."

"Maybe we'd better start by teaching *you* how to fly a Reaper, Captain," Commander Verbeek suggested.

"Let's teach Jessica, as well," Nathan suggested.

"I wasn't aware the lieutenant commander was a pilot," Commander Verbeek said.

"Neither was I," Cameron agreed.

Nathan paused at the base of the ramp, turning back toward Cameron and Commander Verbeek. "She's not, but she should be. And get Josh and Loki in the sims, as well. I want flexibility as to who flies what on the way back."

"I'll see to it, sir," Commander Verbeek promised.

"Thank you, Commander," Nathan said, turning to continue up the ramp.

Cameron followed Nathan toward the command deck as Commander Verbeek continued on his own toward the main hangar bay. "It might take more than a few days for Jessica to learn how to fly a Reaper," she warned Nathan.

"I suspect Jessica can do anything she wants, once she puts her mind to it," Nathan insisted. "Besides, we'll just stick to the basics for now, and teach her how to use the auto-flight systems...nothing fancy."

"I'm not sure that will..."

"It'll have to be," Nathan insisted, cutting her off. "Don't worry, Cam. Jess will be my last choice as a primary pilot, for now."

"Of course."

Nathan sighed. "I have to admit; this day has been exhausting. Is it always this way?" he asked as they reached the top of the ramp and headed forward.

"I didn't mean to overwhelm you on your first day back, Nathan," Cameron apologized. "I just figured you'd want to get up to speed as quickly as possible."

"You're right, of course."

"Glad to hear it," Cameron said. "Because I left you a collection of files to study. There have been a lot of changes to the Aurora over the last seven years, and her crew has been taught a lot of maneuvers and procedures that you're not aware of."

"So, I've got a lot of homework, then," Nathan surmised.

"Tons."

Nathan looked at her. "You're really making me earn this, aren't you?"

Cameron smiled back as they entered the Aurora's bridge.

"Captain on the bridge!" the guard at the entrance barked.

"Status?" Nathan asked Lieutenant Commander Vidmar and Jessica, both of whom were at the tactical station at the moment.

"No contacts to report," the lieutenant commander replied. "Long-range threat board is clear."

"Very well," Nathan replied. "Mind taking the conn for a while, Captain?" he asked Cameron. "It seems I have some studying to do."

"Actually, I was planning on taking some time

to move into the XO's quarters," Cameron told him. "Have fun, sir," she added, turning to exit.

Nathan sighed. "It seems *you* have the conn, Lieutenant Commander Nash."

"Aye, Captain," Jessica replied with a smile.

* * *

Miri entered the president's office, moving immediately to his desk and activating the sound-suppression field. Every conversation in her father's office was automatically recorded, but there were some things that were left off the record.

President Scott noticed her activation of the field, and set his data pad down to give her his full attention. "What is it?"

"I finally managed to speak with Captain Hunt," she told him. "Covertly, of course."

"I'm not familiar with the name," her father admitted.

"He served with both Cameron Taylor and Nathan. He resigned and took a job as captain of a cargo jump ship, one of many contracted by the Alliance to deliver cargo to our strategic supply depots."

President Scott leaned back in his desk chair. "The ones that Galiardi insisted we establish, in case of an invasion," he recalled.

"So that our forces could continue to fight," Miri finished for him.

"And?"

"He has agreed to help us."

"Just like that?"

"Just like that. He has no family ties, and neither does any of his crew."

"None of them?" the president wondered in disbelief. "Not on the entire crew?"

"Cargo jump ships only have a crew of eight

127

to twelve, and it's pretty common for them to be composed of single men and women, as they are gone for weeks at a time. They also run without escorts, in order to keep a low profile. All of which lends itself to people without families working as their crews."

"And when the ship comes up missing?" the president wondered.

"Actually, Captain Hunt had an interesting idea. It will take a little longer to implement, but it might make it possible to get multiple loads to Nathan without discovery."

"I'm listening," the president told her, smiling.

"He proposes that they rendezvous with a Karuzari cargo ship within the Sol sector, transfer their cargo, and then return to port as if they had actually delivered their cargo to its intended destination. As you know, those supply depots are unmanned. So, Captain Hunt believes he could get four, maybe five, loads transferred before anyone catches on. Possibly even more. However, it would require changing several of Captain Hunt's crew members for ones he can trust. It would also require coordination with several other jump-capable cargo ships, ones provided by the Karuzari."

"Or one *big* one that hung around until it was fully loaded," President Scott suggested.

"That would work, as well, I suppose."

President Scott thought for a moment. "Captain Hunt does realize he would be violating multiple interstellar cargo regulations, not to mention violating his contract with the Alliance. If he gets caught, he and his crew would be imprisoned for some time."

"He is aware of that, yes," Miri promised.

"How did you convince him to help?" President Scott wondered.

"I'm afraid I was forced to tell him everything," she admitted. "That Nathan is alive, and that Cameron Taylor took the Aurora to help him liberate the Pentaurus cluster."

Her father suddenly looked concerned. "Are you sure that was a good idea?"

"Captain Hunt knows people," Miri said. "People just like him...people who would be willing to help Nathan, as well. It may even be possible to get a second ship involved."

"Then he believed you."

"Not originally," Miri admitted. "I showed him the vid-message."

"I see. What type of cargo are we talking about?" the president wondered.

"Mostly consumables," Miri admitted. "Food, water, medical supplies, clothing, some energy rifles, and sidearms. But no real ordnance, as that is tracked much more carefully, and is usually only moved by Alliance crews."

"Well, every little bit *will* help, I suppose," the president said with a sigh. "And you're sure this can't be traced back to this office?"

"If anything, it will appear as if Captain Hunt and his crew were selling the stuff on the black market," Miri assured him.

President Scott rose from his chair and walked over to the large picture window behind him, staring out at the city of Winnipeg. "I never thought I'd be smuggling supplies to my own son," he sighed. "I'm the President of Earth and the leader of the Alliance Council, and I have to run cargo behind the backs of the military leaders who are supposed to answer to us, to men more honorable than those same men who are refusing to support them. How is that even possible?"

"It's the times we live in," Miri told him.

"These times need to end," the president said, "and soon."

"I couldn't agree with you more," Miri told him. "Then I have your approval?"

"As President of Earth, I cannot tell you to ask others to break the law, Miri," the president replied, purposefully nodding his head in non-verbal approval.

"The sound-suppression field is on, Pop," Miri reminded him.

"I know," President Scott replied, smiling. "This way, I can say, 'I did not tell anyone to execute such a plan,' and not be lying."

A smirk came across Miri's face. "That's a pretty fine line you're walking, Mister President."

"Like you said, these are the times we are living in."

* * *

Marcus stood in the newly opened starboard side of the Seiiki, where the cabins that he, Neli, and Dalen had lived in for the last five years had once been. It had taken Vladimir's technicians only a single day to gut the starboard side to make room for the additional reactors and shield generators about to be installed.

"Feeling a bit sentimental?" Neli asked him.

"Don't be silly," Marcus insisted. "It was just a bunch of metal, composites, and shit. Once this overhaul is finished, this is going to be one lean, mean little ship."

"Maybe, but it won't be home anymore."

"It's a spaceship, Neli," Marcus reminded her with a look of disapproval. "Normal people don't live on them."

Neli laughed. "No one is ever going to accuse us of being *normal*."

Marcus dismissed her with a wave as Josh, Loki, and Dalen entered the now wide-open compartment.

"Holy shit!" Josh exclaimed. "That didn't take long."

"We have to reroute all this cabling to the inboard side," Marcus told them, "so the mag-fields on the reactors won't mess with them."

"Can't we just add extra shielding?" Dalen asked. "Moving them's going to be a pain."

"We're going to be adding a lot of additional weight, what with six more reactors and four more shield generators," Loki explained. "That's not going to leave us a lot of useful load with fuel propellant tanks. Every little bit of weight we save counts."

"And that extra shielding would only make it worse," Marcus added.

"Then just make the engines more powerful," Dalen suggested.

"How the hell did you ever get your engineer's ticket?" Marcus wondered.

"I'm not an engineer," Dalen reminded him, "I'm a mechanic. Big difference."

"Apparently."

"Can we just get this over with?" Josh begged.

"Good idea," Marcus agreed. "You head up there, into the crawl space, and start disconnecting the main trunks, so we can pull them out and reroute them."

"Up there?" Josh wondered, looking at the

cramped, dark crawl space above the outboard starboard bulkhead. "Why me?"

"Cuz you're the smallest of us," Marcus replied. "You'll fit better."

Josh rolled his eyes in disgust. "This sucks."

"*Hayes! Sheehan!*" A voice beckoned from the Seiiki's cargo deck, below and aft of them.

"Up here!" Loki replied.

"*CAG wants you both in the simulator bay!*"

"Now?" Marcus bellowed.

"*Yesterday!*"

"Yes!" Josh exclaimed triumphantly.

Marcus looked at Josh. "You set this up, didn't you?"

"Not me," Josh assured him. "But I sure wish I'd thought of it," he added, patting Marcus on the shoulder as he headed aft. "See ya later, old man. Good luck with all this."

Loki shrugged at Marcus, turning to follow Josh.

"Damn," Marcus grumbled.

"I'll climb up and disconnect the trunks," Dalen offered, moving toward the ladder.

"It never ceases to amaze me how Josh always manages to get out of work he doesn't want to do," Neli commented.

"Besides flyin', it's his only other talent," Marcus told her. "He's been skipping out on work since he was in diapers."

* * *

"Good morning, Abby," Cameron greeted as she met Abby at the bottom of the ramp on G deck.

"Good morning, Cameron. You didn't come all the way down here just to meet me, did you?"

"I was just completing a department inspection, and I heard you had boarded."

"Down here in the bowels of the Aurora?"

"I had forgotten how much more exercise an XO gets aboard this ship. I hate to admit that I may have gotten a bit lazy as captain. I'm sure Doctor Chen will be happy to see me lose a kilogram, or two."

"I had forgotten how big the Aurora really is," Abby agreed.

"I spoke with Commander Kaplan earlier," Cameron said as she walked along with Abby. "She promises to get a research lab put together for you aboard the Mystic in the near future."

"I don't mind working here," Abby assured her. "It's only a five-minute shuttle ride from the Mystic. That's better than my commute was on Earth."

"Yes, but there will be times when the Aurora will be away, and we don't want to interrupt your research any more than necessary," Cameron explained. "And we certainly can't take you with us."

"Why not?"

"We'd likely be going into harm's way," Cameron reminded her.

"I've been aboard this ship when she's gone into battle before, Cameron."

"I know. It was Nathan's orders," Cameron explained. "Something about a promise he made to your husband."

"Ah, yes."

"How is he settling in, by the way?"

"Better than expected," Abby stated with a pleased lilt in her voice. "Lieutenant Commander Shinoda has him analyzing the economic systems of the Pentaurus cluster, and the effects the Dusahn occupation is having on it." Abby touched Cameron's arm for emphasis. "Thank you for that. The challenge is helping to take his mind off the forced relocation."

"You're quite welcome."

"The only problem now, is that he's constantly babbling on about economics, which I know nothing about."

"How about the children?"

"Between the rec center, the pool, and the micro-gravity gymnasium, they're keeping quite busy. And there are more than a few kids their ages aboard the Mystic to hang out with. Getting over the language barrier will be a challenge, but they've been through that before. Kirsten has already befriended Jessica's goddaughter, Ania. Did you know that Jessica's mom took it upon herself to start a school for all the children?"

"No, I did not."

"It's only a couple hours a day, over the Mystic's network. But she tutors anyone who needs extra help in person. She's quite an amazing woman. Nothing stops her."

"Well, she did have to raise Jessica."

"From the way she tells it, Jessica pretty much raised herself."

"Why am I not surprised," Cameron said. "Just down this corridor."

"How is Nathan doing?" Abby wondered.

"He seems to be doing well enough," Cameron replied. "He's settling back into the role of captain. He's got a lot of catching up to do. The Aurora has gone through a lot of changes since he was in command. But he seems to soak up information at an amazing rate, now. Something to do with the changes the Nifelmians made to the structure of his brain."

"Yes, I heard about that. You know, I could tell

there was something different about him when I first saw him again on Earth. A calmness...a confidence."

"He's always been confident," Cameron insisted. "Perhaps *too* confident, if you ask me. As I remember it, bordering on arrogance at times."

"That's what's different, I suppose. The *arrogance* isn't there. At least, not like it was."

"They say that arrogance is often a mask for a *lack* of confidence," Cameron commented.

"Then maybe his confidence is *real* this time," Abby suggested.

"Perhaps," Cameron agreed. "If I'd been through everything he has, and survived, I suppose I'd be confident, as well."

"Or a complete basket case," Abby joked.

Cameron wasn't laughing. Luckily, they had reached Abby's destination. "This is it," she said, pausing at the door. "The Aurora R&D lab."

"I guess I'd better get to work," Abby said.

"And I'd best be off to run the ship," Cameron said. "Good luck."

"To you, as well, Captain." Abby turned and punched in her security code, causing the hatch to slide open. Beyond the hatch was a cavernous room, with offices and shops along all sides, and a large doorway into an elevator pad which led all the way to the top of the Aurora, passing through each hangar deck along the way. There were four technicians to one side, working with Deliza on the mini-jump sub they had used to escape from Earth five days ago.

"Abby!" Deliza called out, heading toward her.

"Good morning," Abby greeted as she approached.

"Welcome to the Aurora's R&D bay," she said, waving her arms around as if showing her the space.

"It's actually the port spacecraft maintenance bay. We sort of took it over."

"What are you working on?" Abby wondered.

"We're just doing a deep engineering scan of the jump sub," Deliza explained. "Nathan wants to build a few more of them."

"Why?"

"In order to move operatives on and off Dusahn-held worlds at will," Deliza explained. "I can't wait to see your research on the stealth emitters. I'm dying to help solve the overheating problem."

"Actually, I think I may have already solved that problem," Abby admitted.

"Really?" Deliza exclaimed, barely able to control her excitement. "When?"

"A few days before we left Earth, actually."

"Why didn't you say anything on the ride back?" Deliza wondered.

"I haven't had a chance to give it a proper test," Abby admitted. "I've only run simulations."

"And?"

"So far, the new formulation looks correct. But we need a live test on an actual emitter, which we don't have."

Deliza grabbed Abby by the hand, leading her toward a large shop door on the starboard side. "But we have these," she told her, pointing into the next bay.

As they approached the shop, Abby could see several small machines. "Are those fabricators?"

"Four of them," Deliza proclaimed proudly. "The Aurora's fabrication shop busted their asses making them, too. They installed the last one just a few hours ago. And the next compartment over is full of just about every core material you could imagine. We can pretty much fabricate anything we want, now." Deliza turned to look at Abby. "Please tell me you brought the specs with you."

Abby reached into her pocket and pulled out the data chip she had been carrying since they left Earth five days ago, and held it up for Deliza to see.

"Outstanding!" Deliza exclaimed.

"Let's get started," Abby declared with a smile.

* * *

"You wanted to see me?" Jessica asked as she entered the captain's ready room.

Nathan was busy reading, flipping through screens on his data pad every other second, so he held up his hand to signal her to give him a moment.

Jessica took advantage of the opportunity and plopped down on the couch. "Ah, I missed this couch." When Nathan still didn't respond, she rose and moved over beside him, looking over his shoulder at his data pad as he quickly flipped through the last few screens. "You can't possibly be reading that fast."

Nathan flipped to the last screen in the file, then put the data pad down and grinned. "Pretty slick, huh?"

"Do you actually remember any of it?"

"Every word," Nathan chuckled. "And I was going slowly." Nathan leaned back in his chair. "I don't know what Michi did to my brain, but I like it."

"It's kinda creepy, rearranging things like that."

"According to her, it's more like adding extra pathways, so that electrical impulses move more directly to their targets. She used the analogy of city streets. Ones that are laid out in standard grids are easier and faster to navigate than ones that look like a bowl of spaghetti, meandering all over the place."

"Are you saying my brain is like a bowl of spaghetti?" Jessica challenged.

"Her analogy, not mine," Nathan defended, his hands up.

"What did you need to talk to me about?"

"I just wanted to know how you're settling in at tactical."

"Fine," Jessica assured him. "It's kind of boring, to be honest."

"For a tactical officer, boring is good," Nathan told her. "How is Vidmar taking it?"

"He doesn't seem to mind," Jessica replied. "Actually, he's been quite helpful. He's been teaching me all the standard attack patterns the Alliance has developed over the years, as well as the ones Cameron has devised. Did you know the Aurora's main torpedo cannons are able to cant laterally, and focus all four cannons on a single point anywhere between one and one hundred kilometers?"

"I did," Nathan assured her. "I didn't, but I read that yesterday, when I was reviewing all the weapons systems. You can focus them in pairs, as well, or spread them out a few degrees, so they'll hit different quadrants of a distant target, depending on how far out that target is. Same with the broadside cannons aft. All in all, this ship is now remarkably well armed."

"I'm actually kind of itching to get her into a scrape to see what she can do," Jessica admitted.

"Let's not jump into anything too early," Nathan warned.

"I'm just saying."

"How are our new recruits doing?" Nathan asked.

"For now, they're keeping busy repairing their own ships, with a little help from Vlad's technicians and our fabricators. Three Eight Three has a lot of hull damage to her underside from Walsh trying to skip his gunship off the surface like a flat rock across a pond. You don't really think he *meant* to do that, do you?"

"Doubtful," Nathan admitted.

"Then we may have found someone with your same uncanny luck," she added. "Anyway, they're basically pulling the damaged hull panels—which is most of them—and feeding them back into the fabricators to make new ones. It's faster than trying to repair them."

"That's good thinking."

"Vlad's idea."

"How about Lieutenant Commander Shinoda?" Nathan wondered. "What's your read on him?"

"Good guy; likable, easy to work with, knows his stuff. He's also really good at pulling meaningful intel out of data most people would have overlooked. I can see why Cam thinks so highly of him."

"That's good to hear," Nathan said. "How's Telles doing?"

"Telles is always fine," Jessica said. "That's what makes him Telles. He's got the Ghatazhak helping assemble point-defense turrets to install on all the ships, starting with the Glendanon and the Mystic, which are our two biggest, unarmed assets, at the moment. The Manamu and the Innison will be next."

"Good," Nathan said. "The Aurora can't really leave the fleet until it can at least defend itself."

"That's why we got the gunships, isn't it?" Jessica reminded him. "So we can conduct hit-and-run strikes to harass the Dusahn, without using the Aurora to do so."

"Yes, but it's going to take some time to get all the

gunships back in operational order. Most of them took damage. Besides, we still need to train crews to operate them."

"Well, we've got four good pilots already, and one fully-trained crew on Three Eight Three," Jessica pointed out. "Stick Josh and Loki in two more, and that makes six. Then just fill the gun turrets with Ghatazhak, and you're ready to go."

"Just like that?"

"Yup."

"There's more to operating gunships than just flying and shooting, Jess," Nathan warned.

"Yeah, but not for what we want to do right *now*," she argued. "All that other stuff can come later, can't it? All we need to do *now* is jump in, shoot some shit up, and jump out...hopefully all before the Dusahn can even spin up to fire back."

"I don't know," Nathan said.

"The first missions are all about testing their response, anyway, not about showing them how much damage we can do. Besides, if we jump in like a bunch of amateurs—which is exactly what we'll look like at first—it might make the Dusahn overconfident, making it easier to strike a *real* blow later on, once we get them better prepared."

Nathan tipped his head. "You may have a point."

"Damn right I do," she boasted. "Make them think we're a bunch of wannabes with guns and ships... ones who are too afraid to stand and fight when the Dusahn start shooting back. Then, after a dozen, or so, lame-ass attacks, we jump in with the Aurora and pound the shit out of one of their ships, catching them off guard."

"That's not a bad idea," Nathan agreed. "However, we'll only get to do that once, so maybe we should figure out how to take out more than just *one* of their warships when we do."

"Yeah, I've been thinking about that," Jessica said, a gleam in her eye. "What if we take a few flatbed cargo haulers, remove their cargo pods, and stack a couple rows of mark one plasma torpedo cannons on them. Set them up like our broadside cannons. Just bolt them to the deck, along with a few reactors to power them. Then they can just jump in alongside a target and blast away, launching about a dozen plasma torpedoes at once from close range, and then jump out again. Have two or three of them jump in alongside the same target in a row, and that sucker's got no more shields to protect them. Then the gunships, or the Aurora, can easily finish them off."

"Out on the open deck like that, they wouldn't even need heat exchangers," Nathan realized. "They won't be able to aim, though."

"They don't need to," Jessica insisted. "They're not trying to target any particular point. They're just trying to take down a shield segment or two, so the ships that *can* target critical systems can then make the kills. Even a single gunship can take a warship out of action, if the right shield segment is down."

"We're going to need more intel in order to know *which* shield segments to target," Nathan pointed out.

"That's why we need to engage them with the gunships," Jessica said, "to learn their weaknesses."

Nathan smiled. "I knew there was a reason I wanted you as my tactical officer. You're devious."

"I'll take that as a compliment," Jessica said, smiling and plopping back down on the couch.

* * *

"I still say the Falcon flies better," Josh insisted as he weaved the Reaper through narrow canyons. He rolled the ship to the right, bringing it sharply around the bend, then found himself headed directly toward a vertical face only half a kilometer in front of them. "Whoa!" he exclaimed as he pulled back on the flight control stick, and pushed the throttles to full power. The engines screamed at him in response, and the ship went vertical, barely clearing the rock face in the process. "Falcon climbs better, too," Josh added.

"*The Falcon is a fine ship, but it doesn't have the mission versatility of the Reaper,*" Commander Verbeek said in Josh's helmet comms.

"But it's funner than hell to fly," Josh commented.

"*I've never had the pleasure,*" the commander replied. "*By the way, your passengers are probably splattered against the aft bulkhead by now.*"

"Oops," Josh laughed as he leveled the ship off. "I guess I forgot about them."

"*I don't find that at all funny, Mister Hayes.*"

"Not even a little?"

"*You have a remarkable gift for flight, but I believe it lends itself better toward fighting ships than personnel carriers.*"

Josh pushed the Reaper's nose back down and backed off on the power, diving into the canyons. "Come on, Commander, I was just trying to see what she could do. I *can* fly her gently, you know. Besides, wouldn't the inertial dampeners protect the passengers during a max-G climb?"

"*Assuming they were working, yes,*" the commander agreed.

Josh slipped the Reaper back down into the canyons and continued gleefully snaking his way through them. "Well, I didn't have any indicators that said they weren't, so, going vertical seemed like a good choice to me."

"*You also could have dropped your forward speed and gone vertical in a deck-level attitude,*" the commander pointed out.

"But I didn't *need* to at the time," Josh argued. "*That's* my point."

"*You also didn't need to go vertical in a deck-vertical attitude,*" Commander Verbeek countered. "*If your status indicators had been faulty, and your inertial dampeners would have been out, your passengers would be dead.* That *is* my *point.*"

"But I would have felt that the inertial dampeners had failed as I started the maneuver, and would have changed to a deck-level climb-out," Josh insisted.

"*The Reaper's modular design means the cockpit's inertial dampeners are separate from those in the passenger bay,*" Commander Verbeek explained. He said nothing further beyond that, instead letting the knowledge have its full impact on the young pilot he was attempting to train.

"Oh," Josh replied. "Good point. I'll have to remember that."

"*Agreed.*"

Josh pulled his nose up and added a bit of power, climbing out of the canyons into clear air. "How about you put me back in that canyon, just before the turn, and let me try it again, deck-level?" Josh suggested.

"*Maybe next session,*" the commander replied. "*You're approaching max VR time for the day.*"

"Oh, come on," Josh begged. "I could do this all day!"

The images, sounds, and sensations Josh was

feeling suddenly faded away as the VR helmet disengaged Josh's senses. All he could see was the inside of his VR helmet visor, and the sensation of sitting in the VR training bay returned, instead of the cockpit of a Reaper.

"We don't want to fry your brain, Mister Hayes," Commander Verbeek reminded him as he lifted the VR helmet off of Josh's head. "Four hours yesterday, and four today, is already pushing the limits."

Josh looked around as the helmet cleared his head, spotting Nathan, Jessica, and Loki standing to his right, smiling. "What? I suppose you all did better?"

"I cleared the ridge with a deck-level attitude," Loki bragged, "and I successfully inserted my passengers into their LZ."

"Same here," Nathan added.

Josh looked at Jessica.

"Don't look at me," Jessica replied. "I slammed into the side of the canyon and killed everyone, including myself."

"Remind me not to ride with *you*," Nathan teased.

"Yeah, but you all *wanted* to try going vertical, didn't you?" Josh insisted. "Deck-level is easy, but if there had been stingers on your asses, you'd all be as dead as her," he added, pointing at Jessica.

"Hey, unlike you three, I never *claimed* to be a pilot."

"*Piloting* is only a small part of being an aviator," Commander Verbeek stated as he put Josh's VR helmet back in its cradle. "Knowing what your ship can and cannot do is another, as are how the environment in which you are operating affects your ship's performance. All of you are well aware of this, except for Jessica, who of course has the excuse of
144

never having gone through formal flight training. But the mission itself has an *enormous* impact on your decision-making process. This is what separates pilots from aviators. Anyone can push buttons and get the ship from point A to point B. I could teach an ape to do that."

"Gee, thanks," Jessica said.

Commander Verbeek ignored her. "And any well-trained pilot can yank, bank, and blast their way out of trouble. But true aviators manage to avoid getting their ships into situations that require such radical actions. Unfortunately, that is something that is very difficult to teach. You either have the mindset, or you do not."

"So, what's the verdict with us?" Jessica wondered.

"*You* should limit your piloting to non-combat situations, where only button pushing is required," the commander told her, trying to be as polite as possible. "Captain Scott and Mister Sheehan both seem to have a natural aviator mindset, and should do well under any circumstances."

"What about me?" Josh wondered.

Commander Verbeek sighed. "Mister Hayes, you have an unfortunate condition, one that is very difficult to overcome."

"What's that?" Josh asked, looking concerned.

"You are simply *too* good at flying. Your natural instincts are so good that they override the good aviator side of you. You never have any doubts that you can pull off a maneuver, no matter how difficult it may be. That refusal to consider the possibility of failure is likely to get you into trouble."

"Trust me, it already has," Loki remarked.

"But I always find a way out," Josh insisted.

"But at what price?" the commander asked. "Again,

145

to the aviator, it is about the mission, not about the flying. You would be wise to remind yourself of that every time you strap yourself into a flight seat."

Josh said nothing, but did not look happy with the commander's assessment.

"That will be all for today," the commander insisted. "We'll pick up again tomorrow morning, at zero nine thirty."

"When are we going to learn how to fly a Ranni shuttle?" Nathan asked.

"We're still working on the program," the commander answered, "so it will be a few more days."

"We're supposed to pick them up the day after tomorrow," Jessica said.

"Don't worry," Loki insisted. "Ranni shuttles are fully automated and *really* easy to fly. They were designed that way, so that pretty much anyone could fly them."

"Are you sure?" Nathan wondered.

"Trust me, if you can fly a Reaper, you can fly a Ranni with your eyes closed," Loki promised.

"Good," Nathan said. "Come on, Hotshot," he told Josh, "Let's go get some chow."

"Seriously, I was just seeing what a Reaper could do, honest!" Josh defended as he rose to follow the others out the door.

* * *

Captain Hunt sat at his usual table overlooking the sprawling Sydney spaceport complex. For years now, it had been his custom to enjoy a meal at this restaurant whenever his ship was in orbit around Earth. He had spent nearly six months living in the area after he had ended up stranded there once the Intrepid had gone down, taking out a large section of Sydney in the process.

Perhaps it was the connections he had made with the people and the area during his brief residency. Or perhaps, it had been the guilt he had felt that the ship he had once served on had caused so much death and destruction to the very people it was built to protect. Whatever the reason, he seemed compelled to visit this very spot as often as his flight schedule allowed, in order to witness its continued rise from the ashes.

Of course, after eight years, most of the scars on the great city were healed. There were sections still under construction, and there were, of course, numerous monuments and parks dedicated to the memory of those who had perished on that dreadful day. In fact, unless one knew where to look, one would be hard-pressed to tell the city of Sydney had ever suffered a catastrophic incident.

Today, however, the captain's visit served a dual purpose, one he was most excited about. The last six years of his life had been the most mundane of his existence. Once he had resigned his commission in the Earth Defense Force, he had spent several years working his way up from helmsman to captain, in the burgeoning interstellar shipping community. For the last two years, he had commanded an Alliance-built, but privately-crewed, cargo ship, of the same design as those used to resupply Alliance warships all over the Sol sector. It had been a rather routine assignment; endless cycles of taking on cargo, spending a few days jumping to destinations on the fringes of Alliance space, off-loading, and then jumping their way back. The entire process was one he could have done in his sleep. In fact, he was surprised the entire thing had yet to be completely automated, since so many other tasks once trusted only to humans had recently become.

But, while it had none of the glory and prestige associated with the command of a warship, it also had none of the risks. Or at least, that's what Captain Hunt kept telling himself. The truth of the matter was, he never would have been given command of an Alliance warship. Not only had he served under Nathan Scott and Cameron Taylor, but he had also served as helmsman on two ships that had both been destroyed. Not that the destruction of either vessel had been his fault, but combined, it was enough of an excuse for the leader who replaced Travon Dumar to prevent him from furthering his career in the Alliance.

He was surprised he had been allowed to command a cargo ship contracted by the Alliance. He was certain his current position was the result of a clerical error.

Or was it destiny?

The more he thought about it over the last few days, ever since that call from Miranda Scott, the more he had come to believe it truly *was* fate that had put him in command of the Perryton. And so, he had decided to run with that belief, which was the true reason he had been sitting in this restaurant, picking at his food for the last hour.

"Well, if it isn't the sector's worst helmsman," a voice accused.

Captain Hunt recognized the voice and looked up, smiling. "Denny," he greeted, shaking the man's hand. "Still skin and bones, I see."

"Still short and cocky, I see," Denny countered. "How long has it been?" he wondered as he took his seat. "Six years?"

"Seven, I believe."

"How have you been?" Denny asked as he picked up the menu.

"Busy, bored, but employed."

"Last I heard, you were piloting cargo ships for Walton Cargo."

"I'm captain now," Captain Hunt bragged.

"Someone gave Chris Hunt a captain's chair?" Denny laughed. "Do they know how many ships you've crashed?"

"Zero," Chris reminded his old comrade. "There's a difference between crashing and being shot down."

"Not to the ship, there isn't," Denny teased. "What are you running?"

"An Alliance cargo jump ship," Chris said. "One of those long, modular, ugly bastards."

"The *Alliance* gave you a ship? Whose ass did you have to kiss?"

"I think it was an accident, to be honest. But a lucky one."

"Is the pay decent?"

"Good enough, for a single captain."

"You never married?"

"Not yet."

"Me, either. Too busy, I suppose."

"What have you been up to?" Chris wondered.

"I became a general contractor here in Sydney," Denny explained.

"You must be doing well, then."

"I was. It was like printing money in the beginning. But now, work is getting a bit more scarce. We're hoping things will pick up once people start moving back into the city, but..."

"Yeah. The jump drive is both a blessing and a

curse, I suppose." Chris admitted. "Everyone wants to go someplace else; someplace fresh."

"If we can just get people on other worlds to believe the grass is greener here on Earth," Denny said, "particularly here in Sydney..."

"Well, luckily, cargo shipping is always in demand," Chris said. "Have you ever considered getting back in the navigator's chair?"

"Is that why you called me?" Denny wondered. "To offer me a job?"

"Sort of," Chris admitted. "Actually, I'm trying to round up as many of the old gang as possible."

"What 'old gang' are you referring to?" Denny wondered.

Captain Hunt looked around, trying not to raise suspicion as he pulled a small device from his pocket and activated it. A second later, the sounds of the restaurant disappeared, and they were in complete silence.

Denny looked suspiciously at Chris. "A sound-suppression field? Seriously? What's up, Chris? What 'gang' are you referring to?"

"Those who served under Nathan Scott," he said, a smile creeping onto his face.

"Scott? Why?"

His smile became broader. "Because he's still alive, and he needs us."

* * *

"For Christ's sake, kid!" Marcus bellowed. "Are you ever going to do any real work around here?"

"Sorry, old man," Josh apologized, although only halfheartedly. "But my skills are in demand elsewhere," he joked, walking backwards away from the Seiiki's cargo ramp.

"Skills, my ass," Marcus grumbled. "Pushing

buttons and moving a little joystick around. I never should have let him play all those vid-games when he was growing up."

"Then why did you?" Neli wondered.

"It was the only way to shut him up."

"I heard that!" Josh yelled back at him, picking up his pace to catch up with Nathan and the others as they headed for the nearest Reaper.

"I still don't understand why one of the Aurora's pilots can't fly us," Jessica said.

"They're all flying patrol sorties or recon missions," Nathan explained. "We're lucky we're getting a Reaper at all."

"This is going to be a blast," Josh exclaimed as he caught up to them.

"I thought you said Reapers don't fly as well as Falcons?" Loki reminded him.

"I lied," Josh giggled. "They're a fucking blast to fly, once you turn off all that automation crap."

"Do us a favor, Josh, and leave that automation crap *on* during the trip over," Nathan suggested. "You can yank and bank all you want on the way back, when we're not aboard."

"Alright, but you're taking all the fun out of it."

Josh and Loki quickened their pace, leading Nathan and Jessica to the waiting Reaper. They moved under the overhead wing, from aft forward, meeting with the ground chief to review the ship's condition and sign her out before boarding.

Reaper Eight's systems were already on and humming quietly as they climbed up into her passenger bay, just behind the port forward engine nacelle. Unlike the old Corinairan shuttles, the Alliance ships used engine nacelles with articulating thrust nozzles, much like those on the Seiiki's

151

main engines. The similarity had made their flight-handling characteristics quite easy for Josh to become accustomed to in a minimal amount of sim time.

Once all of them were inside, the ground chief activated the passenger pod hatch from outside, and stepped away.

Josh slid into the pilot's seat, with Loki slipping into the copilot's seat to his right. "Damn, they've already got her spun up and preflighted for us." He looked at Loki. "Talk about service."

"Kind of makes me uneasy," Loki said. "I'm used to doing my own preflights."

"These guys are pros, Lok," Josh insisted. "Relax."

"I never relax when you're at the controls," Loki insisted. "It's too dangerous."

For some reason, the comment tickled Josh to no end as he strapped himself in. "You guys settled in back there?" he called over his comm-set as he placed it on his head.

"*We're ready whenever you are,*" Nathan replied.

"Lok, if you'll do the honors," Josh suggested.

"Aurora Flight, Reaper Eight, ready to cycle out."

"*Reaper Eight, Aurora Flight. Cleared to auto-cycle to starboard side, transfer airlock two.*"

"Auto-cycle to starboard side, transfer airlock two, for Reaper Eight," Loki acknowledged.

Josh fired a half-assed salute back to the ground chief outside his port window, then reached out and activated the auto-taxi system. The Reaper began to roll slowly forward, steering itself onto the pulsing, yellow line which led to the transfer airlock that would take them to the starboard forward flight deck. "We're rolling," he announced over his comm-set.

"How long is the flight?" Jessica asked as she strapped herself into the empty passenger module currently installed in Reaper Eight's midsection.

"There, about four hours," Nathan answered. "Back, about twelve."

"Do we have to take the long way home?" Jessica wondered.

"You, of all people, know the answer to that," Nathan insisted. "We can't chance that someone might follow our jump trail back to the fleet."

"Yeah, I know."

"Besides, I brought movies." Nathan smiled. "From Earth. Seven years' worth that neither of us has seen."

"Did you bring popcorn, as well?" Jessica replied sarcastically.

"No, but I did bring plenty of snacks."

"I thought we were rationing food."

"Rank has its privileges," Nathan said. "Besides, I didn't bring that much. Which reminds me, I have a shopping list the galley chief gave Cam."

"We're going food shopping on Rakuen?" Jessica objected.

"Deliza gave me the number of a lady to contact who can procure everything and deliver it to us. All we have to do is load it. She also gave me authorization to bill it to the Ranni accounts on Rakuen."

"Good, because I *loathe* shopping."

"You're not normal, are you?" Nathan teased.

"You're just now figuring that out?" Jessica rebutted. "I thought the Nifelmians gave you a super-brain."

———

"This never gets old," Josh declared, staring out the forward windows of the Reaper as they rolled out onto the starboard forward flight deck. In front of them, directly across the flight deck, parked along the starboard side, were two of the Cobra gunships they had brought back from Kohara days before.

The Reaper rolled out to clear the transfer airlock, then turned to port to face the open forward end of the starboard flight deck. They could see the bow of the Aurora, its gentle, light-gray curves sweeping downward both forward and starboard from the leading edge of the massive corridor that made up the flight deck.

The ship followed the pulsing, yellow line, coming to a stop at its predetermined transition point.

"Aurora Flight, Reaper Eight," Loki called over comms. "Ready at starboard launch point one."

"*Reaper Eight, Aurora Flight. Cleared for auto-departure from starboard launch point one. Jump point at one zero kilometers.*"

"Reaper Eight copies. Departure sequence received and loaded into auto-flight," Loki reported. "Let's go," he told Josh.

"Oh, boy, I get to push a button," Josh exclaimed with mock enthusiasm. He reached out and pushed the auto-flight button, and the artificial gravity in their area of the flight deck immediately reduced to a fraction of the ship's normal gravity. The auto-flight system took over and fired a tiny burst of translation thrust, pushing the Reaper half a meter off the deck. Another thrust pushed them forward, with several more firing to maintain their rate of ascent and forward translation, so the Reaper passed cleanly out of the forward end of the starboard flight deck before turning to its assigned departure heading. Once on its departure course, the main engines began to power up, and the Reaper accelerated smoothly away, leaving the Aurora and the rest of the Karuzari fleet behind them.

"Thirty seconds to jump point," Loki announced a minute later. "Auto-jump sequencer is loaded and ready, multi-jump series to Rakuen, with a few passes by various class As to hide our flight path."

A few seconds later, the windows turned opaque, and the Reaper's auto-jump sequencer executed the first of a long series of jumps that would take them to the water world of Rakuen.

"Why the hell did we spend three days in the sims if all we were going to do was push buttons and sit on our asses?" Josh wondered.

"In case the buttons don't work," Loki reminded him.

* * *

"Na-Tan, Nathan, I don't care who he really is as long as he gets the job done," Lieutenant Teison insisted as he monitored Falcon One's flight dynamics display.

"I'm just wondering which identity has the most influence on people," Ensign Lassen argued from the back cabin. "The legend of Na-Tan is a powerful one, especially among the more spiritually inclined of the PC. But that of Nathan Scott is more *real.*"

"And it has the advantage of appealing to both groups," Sergeant Nama added.

"Riko's right," Ensign Lassen agreed. "The truly spiritual will see him as the Na-Tan of legend, while the non-spiritual will see him as the man who sacrificed everything, including his own life, to protect billions."

"But that right belongs to both identities, does it not?" the lieutenant suggested.

"That's my point," Sergeant Nama insisted.

155

"So, you're saying that people will see him however they want to see him?"

"Precisely," the lieutenant agreed. "And that's fine with me. It's like the God argument. The power is in the confidence and ability that the belief instills in the individual. That's all that matters. Who is right, or wrong, is irrelevant."

"How can it be irrelevant?" Ensign Lassen argued.

"Because who is right doesn't matter."

"It does to the individual."

"Which is what *faith* is all about," the lieutenant pointed out. "Faith in something that has been proven through science isn't faith; it's fact, at which point it loses all meaning and power."

"What?" Sergeant Nama exclaimed from the sensor station behind the Falcon's copilot seat.

"If I believe something...a God, or some unseen force, or something, and that faith gives me strength and hope where I might otherwise have none, and then science comes along and proves my faith wrong, and I lose all strength and hope, how is that a good thing?"

"It's a good thing because you now have the truth," Ensign Lassen insisted.

"Sure, but it's a truth that destroyed my happiness," the lieutenant explained. "That's why people choose to believe in something even when everything around them points to that belief being false. They'd rather keep the strength and hope their faith provides them. I'm saying that isn't necessarily a bad thing."

"Nobody said it was!" the ensign exclaimed.

"How the hell did we get into this?" Lieutenant Teison wondered.

"I have no idea!" the ensign admitted.

"Guys!" Sergeant Nama tried interrupting.

"I think we were talking about Seena Mayhew, weren't we?"

"Guys!"

"What?" the lieutenant wondered.

"I've got a new contact!" the sergeant explained. "A jump flash, two thousand clicks, bearing two five seven, thirty up relative."

"What is it?" Ensign Lassen asked as he moved forward past the sergeant and climbed back into the copilot's seat.

"The flash was too small to be a ship," the sergeant said.

"One of our recon drones checking in?"

"Right size," the sergeant admitted.

"We're still running cold, right?" the lieutenant asked.

"Affirmative," Ensign Lassen replied. "Zero emissions, minimal heat signature. And the light is too dim for anyone to see us, even if they were sitting on top of us."

"Anything else?" the lieutenant wondered.

"Negative," Sergeant Nama replied. "Just one tiny jump flash. It was in the expected return quadrant, though." The sergeant looked forward at his lieutenant. "Should I ping it?"

"How quick can we jump if it turns out to be a bogey?" Lieutenant Teison asked his copilot.

"We've got plenty of jump juice still left in the energy banks, Lieutenant. So, as fast as you can push the button."

Lieutenant Teison sighed, looking at the time display. "The time is wrong. If it's a recon drone, it's early. Any idea what its trajectory was?"

"Best guess, it'll pass about five clicks to

starboard, slightly below. But that's only a guess," the sergeant admitted.

Lieutenant Teison moved his finger to the escape jump button on his flight control stick, and took a deep breath. "Ping it, Riko."

"Going active...now," the sergeant announced. "Contact! It just lit up. It's a recon drone."

Lieutenant Teison felt a wave of relief wash over him. They had been sitting at the recon drone rendezvous point between the Darvano and Takara systems for hours, running cold to avoid detection by any Dusahn patrols who might pass nearby. It was a risky job, but it was far less risky than jumping into those systems, and collecting data in person. The Dusahn had gotten far too adept at detecting their position based on their jump flash when jumping into a system. But every time a recon drone returned to their position, they had to go through the same few seconds of torment. "Why the hell is it so early?" the lieutenant demanded. "The fucking thing nearly gave me a heart attack."

"It must've picked up something important," Ensign Lassen commented.

"Keep your eyes glued to the threat display," the lieutenant instructed his copilot. "Just in case one of those damned cube fighters followed it out."

"You got it, Lieutenant."

"I'm receiving data from the recon drone," Sergeant Nama announced. After a few moments, he looked up. "It's carrying a message from someone on the surface."

"Who?" the lieutenant wondered.

"Someone who calls himself, 'Willard the mutineer'," the sergeant said, a confused look on his face.

"What does the message say?" the lieutenant asked.

"I don't know. It's encrypted."

Lieutenant Teison adjusted himself in his seat, preparing to get to work. "Plot a stealth course back to the fleet," he instructed Ensign Lassen.

"What about the other recon drones?" the ensign asked.

"They'll move to the secondary rendezvous point, well outside the PC, when they discover we're not here," the lieutenant reminded him. "I have a feeling this message is important."

CHAPTER FIVE

Terig sat at his dining table, staring at the data chip sitting in front of him. His wife had left for a day of shopping over an hour ago, yet, he still had not worked up the nerve to listen to the audio recording he had smuggled out of House Mahtize. Part of him felt like doing so would be the final line of deceit, after which there would be no turning back. But he knew once he had erased the record of copying the file, he had committed an act of treason against his employer, and, quite possibly, against the Dusahn.

But there was still that one problem: his conscience.

Terig kept seeing the image of Nathan Scott in his mind, standing there in the middle of the Mystic's main promenade, calling for people to rise up against the invaders. The man who had been willing to sacrifice his own life to save others. The man who had liberated the entire Pentaurus cluster from the reign of Caius Ta'Akar. The man who had given them the ability to travel between the stars in the blink of an eye.

Nathan Scott had changed everything, for everyone. And he was not a superman. He was just a man, one not much older than Terig. Yet, with only minimal training and experience, he had accomplished great things. Was not such a man worthy of being followed?

Terig took a deep breath, inserted the chip into his data pad, and started the audio playback. After listening for a few minutes, he wondered why he was getting so worried. This appeared to be just another man seeking to gain Lord Mahtize as a customer, or as a means to make contacts with other men of power and influence. Such men came calling frequently. The fact that few of them got this far, made little difference at this point...

Navarro? The name sounded familiar. *Suvan Navarro?* Based on his reaction, the name certainly seemed familiar to Lord Mahtize, as well. His employer was in shock. In fact, Terig had never heard him sound so flabbergasted. Lord Mahtize was acting like he'd seen a ghost.

The more he listened to the tape, the more his mouth dropped open and his eyes widened. This man, this *Suvan Navarro,* was obviously someone the Dusahn would be interested in, and that fact alone meant the Karuzari would be interested in him, as well.

The Avendahl.

Terig suddenly recognized the name. *The captain of the Avendahl. The leader of the exiled House of Navarro, one of the oldest houses of Takara.* The Navarro family had been one of the original settlers, coming over on the first colonization ship from Earth a thousand years ago. House Navarro also had the distinction of being the only noble house to ever be wiped from the records of Takara. In the eyes of his people, the Navarro family never existed.

But he did exist... *The Teyentah? He wants to steal the Teyentah?*

Terig had to back the recording up and listen to that part again, in case he had misheard it.

Oh, my God.

Terig stopped the playback, his mind racing. This was *definitely* something the Karuzari would be interested in. He continued listening to the

161

recording, being careful to commit everything he heard to memory.

By the time he reached the end, he felt weak. His pulse was racing, and he was sweating.

I am not cut out for this kind of work, he thought.

Jessica's instructions ran through his mind; the address on Haven, the molo farm out in the middle of nowhere. He quickly logged onto the net to place an order for molo twine. It was commonly used in candles that kept bugs away during humid nights on Takara, and would not raise suspicion. After several minutes of searching, he found the seller he was looking for. Taggart Farms.

Terig quickly encrypted the file, using the algorithm Jessica had made him memorize before he left the Mystic, then attached the file to the order as a special shipping instruction.

Terig's finger hovered over the 'purchase' button on his data pad screen for what seemed an eternity. *This* really *was* the point of no return. Of that, there could be no doubt. For he was sending intelligence that aided the enemy of the Dusahn. The punishment for that was undoubtedly death...to him, and likely his wife, as well.

He only hoped she would understand.

* * *

"You wanted to see me?" Cameron asked Lieutenant Commander Shinoda as she entered the Aurora's intelligence center.

"Yeah. Does the name 'Willard the mutineer' ring a bell?"

"Actually, it does. Michael Willard, the Corinairan who mutinied and took over the Yamaro. If it wasn't for him, the Aurora wouldn't be around, and Earth would still be ruled by the Jung. But, I've never heard him referred to in that way. Why do you ask?"

"Falcon One just returned with a message that was intercepted by one of our recon drones. Apparently, it was from your Mister Willard."

"What does the message say?"

"We don't know yet," the lieutenant commander said. "It's encrypted, and we don't know the key."

"Can you break it?" Cameron wondered.

"Probably, but it could take some time."

"Then why did you call me down here now?"

"There's a key-clue included in the header," Lieutenant Commander Shinoda explained. "'Why I mutinied.'"

"Why I mutinied?" Cameron looked at the lieutenant commander.

"That's what it says."

Cameron's mind raced. "He mutinied because he didn't want to die."

"Were you about to take them out?"

"I wasn't even there for that part," Cameron said. "I was unconscious, in medical, gravely wounded." Cameron continued to struggle to remember the details from the battle, as told to her later by Jessica during her recovery. "The Yamaro was losing the battle. They ducked behind Corinair, trying to get away from us." Her eyes suddenly lit up. "The Corinairans fired nukes at them, from the surface! They were sitting ducks. Willard mutinied and immediately offered their unconditional surrender. Nathan had to contact the Corinairans and get them to abort the strike."

"So, what do we put in as the encryption key?"

"He mutinied to avoid the nukes," Cameron told him. "Try 'nukes'."

The lieutenant commander entered the word, but it was not accepted. "That's not it."

Cameron thought for a moment. "Willard speaks more Angla than English," she said to herself. "More proper. Uses way too many words."

"But the key can't be that long," the lieutenant commander said.

"Nukes isn't enough," she decided. "Try, 'to avoid the nukes'."

The lieutenant commander entered the phrase. "Nope."

"'To escape the nukes'?"

"Nope," the lieutenant commander replied.

"'To avoid the missiles'?"

"Nope."

"Damn, I know that's the reason," Cameron cursed, "we just have to figure out how he would phrase it."

"Would he use the term 'nukes' or 'nuclear'?" the lieutenant commander wondered.

"Probably 'nuclear', but 'to avoid the nuclear missiles' is too long, isn't it?"

"Maybe just 'nuclear missiles'," the lieutenant commander suggested, entering the phrase as he spoke. "Nope, that wasn't it, either."

"Would 'inbound nuclear missiles' fit in the key variable?" Cameron asked.

"It would," the lieutenant commander replied, entering the words into the computer. "That did it!" he announced as the message began to decrypt.

Cameron leaned over, reading the message. "Willard and many of the ex-Corinari have formed an underground resistance on Corinair, but they need support. They have devised a method for secure surface-to-space communication, and a decryption algorithm." Cameron laughed. "They're using one of the old Terran algorithms...the ones used by the original FTL scout ships. That's definitely Michael Willard. No one else on Corinair would even know about that old algorithm." She looked at Lieutenant Commander Shinoda. "I'll prepare a reply. Have Falcon One deliver it via recon drone, according to the time table in this message."

"They just got back," the lieutenant commander pleaded.

"Tough," Cameron responded plainly, tapping her comm-set. "CAG, XO. I need Falcon One ready to launch as soon as she is recycled and her crew is ready to go."

"*XO, CAG, aye.*"

"Those guys have been gone for twelve hours, Cam," Lieutenant Commander Shinoda reminded her.

"They can take a nap while they're waiting for a reply," Cameron insisted as she typed out the return message. "We've got an intel source from boots on the ground, and I intend to get everything we can out of it."

"Can't we just send a recon drone from here?" the lieutenant commander suggested.

"Once a comm-routine is established, yes," Cameron agreed. "But this is the first contact we've had from Corinair since we arrived. I want to make sure we don't lose this opportunity."

"I understand, but those guys have been flying back-to-back missions for days now, with very little downtime."

"I'll give them a few days off *after* we establish regular contact with the Corinari," Cameron promised as she finished typing the message. "There. Encrypt that using algorithm one five seven tango bravo."

"Tango bravo?" Lieutenant Commander Shinoda laughed. "The tango bravo series hasn't been used in decades."

"It's *never* been used in this part of space," Cameron pointed out. "Use it."

Lieutenant Commander Shinoda shook his head. "As you wish, Captain."

"Damn, I wish Nathan and Jessica were here right now," she exclaimed. "They'd love this. *Especially* Jess."

* * *

"Jump complete," Loki announced from the Reaper's copilot seat. "Welcome to the Rogen system," he added as he entered instructions into the navigation computer. "I'll set us up for the polar approach."

"How long are we going to be on Rakuen?" Josh asked over his comm-set.

"Only as long as it takes to pick up the shuttles," Nathan replied from the passenger module.

"Uh, you do realize we have to do a full checkout of those shuttles *before* we take delivery, right?" Loki asked.

"How long will that take?" Nathan wondered, coming forward into the cramped cockpit.

"A full day, I'd say," Loki warned. "Besides a very thorough inspection, we need to do a couple shakedown flights and a few short jumps, before we take them on a multi-jump series back to the fleet."

"Doesn't the builder do all that before delivery?" Josh wondered.

"Yeah, but they don't *fly* them," Loki explained. "They just put them through diagnostics."

"That's not good enough?" Josh said.

"Not for me, it isn't," Loki insisted.

"Oh, come on..."

"No, he's right," Nathan agreed. "If something goes wrong on the way back, we're going to be a long way from help."

"We'll be a three-element flight," Josh pointed out.

"With no docking capabilities and no pressure suits," Loki countered. "We *need* a thorough checkout."

"Agreed," Nathan seconded. "Besides, it will give me more time to talk with Ito Yokimah again."

"Why?" Josh wondered.

"He owns the biggest, most successful Gunyoki racing team on Rakuen," Nathan explained.

"And he's an arrogant asshole," Jessica called from behind.

"An arrogant asshole who might be the key to getting the Gunyoki to help us fight the Dusahn," Nathan continued.

"Racers?" Josh exclaimed. "You want to get *race* pilots to help us?"

"Gunyoki ships *are* highly maneuverable and, if given full power, their weapons could be quite formidable," Loki told Josh.

"And, they know how to fly them," Nathan added, "*really* well, I might add."

"In simulated combat, yeah," Josh smirked. "They'd probably shit themselves in a real firefight."

"I agree with Josh," Jessica said.

"I don't think so," Loki argued. "The Gunyoki are fearless, and very well trained, with amazing reflexes and instinct, honed by years of experience."

"Bullshit," Josh commented.

"They maneuver at speeds well above what we normally would," Loki insisted. "And in very tight confines."

"Please, I could fly circles around those guys," Josh bragged, "and *without* all that training and so-called *experience*."

"*Unidentified, armed ship at two five seven by one one five, inbound for Rakuen, this is Rakuen Control. State your intentions,*" the controller called over comms.

"Patch me in," Nathan ordered. As soon as Loki signaled him, he replied. "Rakuen Control, this is Reaper Eight. We are here on business for Ranni Enterprises. We are requesting permission to land *at* the Ranni shuttle plant."

"*Reaper Eight, Rakuen Control. You are an armed vessel of unfamiliar design. You are being tracked by our defense batteries. To whom am I speaking?*"

"He's right, they're painting us," Loki told Nathan.

"Rakuen Control, Reaper Eight. This is Captain Nathan Scott, of the Earth ship Aurora."

There was a moment of silence.

"That made him choke on his sushi," Josh chuckled.

"I don't get it," Jessica said, peeking in from behind Nathan. "We didn't get questioned last time, and the Seiiki was armed."

"We filed with Rakuen prior to arrival," Nathan told her. "And they'd seen the Seiiki before. We didn't have a chance to file this time."

"*Reaper Eight, Rakuen Control,*" the controller finally replied. "*You are cleared direct to the Ranni plant. Do not deviate from your course, and do not charge your weapons or shields, or you will be fired upon. Do you understand?*"

"Rakuen Control, Reaper Eight, understood," Nathan replied. "Make sure all weapons and shields are completely offline," Nathan reminded Loki.

"I shut them down just before we jumped in," Loki assured him.

"Good. Take us down," Nathan instructed.

"You got it," Josh replied.

"Uh, Captain?" Loki said. "Two contacts just departed the Gunyoki race platform. They're on an intercept heading and will be on us in thirty seconds."

"Then let's look as non-threatening as possible," Nathan suggested.

"I thought they were just racers?" Josh said. "With their weapons systems dialed down to minimal power."

"Racers or not, the Gunyoki are the Rogen system's primary defense force," Loki reminded him.

"Which means someone on Rakuen doesn't trust us," Nathan remarked.

"That might not be the case, sir," Loki said. "I've heard of them doing this before, when an unexpected, unidentified ship arrives in the system. Sometimes, the Gunyoki just do it for practice. If they really meant to threaten us, I doubt Rakuen Control would have hailed us first. They would have let the Gunyoki pilots do it, for effect."

"Are you sure about that?" Josh wondered, spotting the approaching two-ship element to their port side.

"Uh..."

Two Gunyoki racers, each painted in differing color schemes, but with the same general patterns, streaked across their bow at high speed.

"They're circling around to get behind us," Loki warned.

Josh immediately reached for his flight control stick to take evasive action.

"No!" Nathan warned. "Hold your course and speed."

Josh looked back at Nathan.

"They're in firing position," Loki warned.

"Captain?" Josh asked. "Are *you* sure?"

"Yes," Nathan assured him. "If they were going to shoot us down, they would've already done so. Flying across our bow was only putting themselves in our line of fire, which would be *really* poor intercept policy. Loki's right, they're just taking advantage of the opportunity for a little intercept practice."

"So, they're practicing a poor intercept?" Josh wondered. "And you want these idiots to fly for us?"

"I never said we wouldn't have to teach them a thing or two," Nathan said. "Just get us down, Josh."

"You're in charge," Josh agreed, glancing at two red blips on the threat display.

Nathan moved back into the passenger compartment with Jessica.

"You think Yokimah had a hand in this?" Jessica asked.

"He's trying to show us two things," Nathan told her. "That he has power of the Gunyoki, and that the Gunyoki aren't afraid to take on any aggressor."

"And yet, you look pleased about that," Jessica commented, noticing the satisfied smirk on Nathan's face.

"That's exactly what I hoped he would do."

* * *

"We are at the test position, Captain," Lieutenant Dinev reported from the Aurora's helm.

"Very well," Cameron replied. "Launch the test drone," she instructed.

"Launching drone," Lieutenant Commander Kono replied from the sensor station.

"Captain, it was not necessary to test this on an actual drone," Abby insisted.

"I know," Cameron replied. "But the new emitter design *did* pass all the computer simulations, correct?"

"Yes, that is correct," Abby replied.

"And, testing it on a drone *would* be the next step, wouldn't it?"

"Drone is away, Captain," the lieutenant commander announced.

"Yes, I suppose it would," Abby agreed. "But, there is still a chance of failure...one that could cost you the drone."

"But that chance is minimal, you said so yourself," Vladimir added, standing beside the tactical station. "And this drone is one of our older models, and was scheduled to be taken out of service and scrapped for parts, so it will not affect us from an operational standpoint."

Cameron looked at Abby. "The commander is right."

"Thirty seconds to safe test jump range," Lieutenant Commander Kono reported.

Abby sighed. "It's just that, there are steps one follows in such cases, designed to ensure safety. Skipping steps in this fashion is highly irregular..."

"We're willing to take the risk, Doctor," Cameron reminded her. "*Time* is far more important to us than one old comm-drone."

"It will work," Vladimir insisted. "I checked the simulation results myself."

Abby looked at Vladimir, an annoyed expression on her face.

"I am chief engineer, you know."

"Ten seconds," Lieutenant Commander Kono reported.

Abby turned to face her console in preparation for the test jump.

"Raise forward shields," Cameron ordered.

"Raising shields," Lieutenant Commander Vidmar acknowledged.

"It will work," Vladimir insisted.

"No sense in taking chances."

"Test drone has reached safe range, Captain."

"You may begin the test when ready, Doctor Sorenson," Cameron ordered.

"Yes, sir," Abby replied. She checked the telemetry from the drone, ensuring all its systems were operating properly. "Are you ready, Lieutenant Commander Kono?" she asked.

"Primary sensor array is locked onto the target, and the deep-space array is locked on the destination point," the lieutenant commander acknowledged.

"Maximum magnification on the drone," Cameron ordered. A moment later, the view screen changed its focus, and the drone came into view, despite the fact that it was ten kilometers ahead of them.

Abby took a deep breath. "Initiating stealth jump test."

Cameron kept her eyes glued on the view screen as the drone simply disappeared, without any flash of light. "It worked?"

"Of course, it worked," Vladimir said.

"I wouldn't get too excited just yet," Deliza told them.

"She's correct," Abby added. "So far, it has performed exactly the same as the emitters on your stealth recon drones."

"But with different formulation," Vladimir added. "One that should be able to handle greater power loads required to jump larger vessels."

"We won't know if the new formulation will be able to do that until we get the data back from the test drone," Abby explained.

"Contact at the destination point," Lieutenant Commander Kono reported. "The test drone. It's coming about."

A split second later, the drone appeared, again without any jump flash, on the main view screen.

"Receiving telemetry from the test drone," Abby reported, her eyes glued to her console.

Vladimir moved to stand next to Deliza, who was already looking over Abby's shoulder at the data streaming in.

"It worked," Deliza exclaimed.

"I told you," Vladimir insisted.

Abby did not say anything, only kept studying the data.

Cameron took notice. "Doctor?"

"Emitter temps are well below maximum safe levels, power draw is normal, field strength shows even across the entire field perimeter, and the frequency variations between emitters are well below tolerances. One moment while I extrapolate the current live data into the computer simulation program, and apply it to a maximum range jump on a larger vessel."

"See, it worked," Vladimir repeated.

Cameron waited patiently for Abby herself to make the decision, knowing full well that Commander Kamenetskiy, despite his good intentions, had a habit of being overly optimistic at times.

Vladimir and Deliza continued watching over

Abby's shoulder as she ran the simulations based on the live test data she had just obtained. Finally, she made the call. "I believe the test was a success, Captain."

"Excellent!" Cameron exclaimed. "How big of a ship do you think we can safely jump using the new emitters?"

"I'd have to do some more analysis," Abby replied.

"Best guess, Doctor."

Abby sighed in resignation. "A gunship, maybe. But I'd be very hesitant to try it without further testing."

Cameron sighed, thinking.

"We don't have anything as big as a gunship to test it on," Vladimir stated.

"Could we test it on Josh's gunship? The one we were planning on scrapping for parts?" Cameron wondered.

"It would be better to do it on an intact hull," Abby warned. "The irregularities in the damaged gunship's hull could cause problems establishing a complete jump field."

"What about the Seiiki?" Cameron suggested.

"What?" Vladimir said, his eyes wide.

"It's already opened up for upgrades, right?" Cameron said. "And you're going to upgrade her shields, so you'll be running new power conduits throughout the ship."

"And the shield emitters *are* co-located with the jump field emitters," Vladimir realized. "Nathan will not be happy."

"Trust works both ways," Cameron stated. "Besides, I'd rather lose the Seiiki than a gunship."

"I'm not sure Marcus will agree with you," Vladimir warned.

"I don't need him to," Cameron said sternly. "How quickly can you make it happen?"

Vladimir scratched his head. "Assuming Marcus doesn't kill me? A week? Maybe four days, *if* we pull the teams working on the gunships to help us."

"Make it happen," Cameron decided.

"Are you sure?" Vladimir wondered.

"Nathan will be back before we run the test. He can countermand my decision then, if he so chooses. Worst-case scenario is that we have to change the emitters back to the original ones. Either way, the Seiiki will be back in action on pretty much the same schedule."

Vladimir tipped his head in agreement. "A very good point," he conceded. "I'll get started," Vladimir promised as he turned to exit.

Abby looked skeptically at Cameron.

"Like I said, time is of the essence," Cameron reiterated.

"If you're going to jump directly to upscaled live tests, I'd like to first conduct a few more test jumps with the drone," Abby suggested, "since we're already out here."

"Of course," Cameron agreed.

* * *

"I was surprised when I got word that you had returned to the Rogen system, Captain," Mister Yokimah said as he led Nathan and Jessica to his office. "After all, it has only been two weeks."

"About that, yes," Nathan replied. "I haven't bothered to do the conversions."

"So, am I to understand that you are still in command of the Aurora? I find that rather surprising."

"Actually, I have only recently taken command of her again, after a long absence."

"I see," Mister Yokimah said, swinging the double doors to his office wide open for all to enter. "Welcome to my refuge," he added proudly, his arms wide.

Both Nathan and Jessica's eyes opened in amazement as they entered the massive office.

"My God," Nathan exclaimed. The office was long and rectangular, with high arched ceilings. Along either wall were massive windows, also arched. In between the windows were bookcases, each of them neatly organized and similarly clad in the same bindings and covers. Placed strategically about the office were numerous games, obviously meant as distractions from the occupant's work. At the far end was an equally massive desk, backed by even more arched windows that opened out to the planet-wide oceans of Rakuen.

The entire office felt as if someone had stuffed a library and a game room into an old-Earth cathedral. Nathan found the decor odd, and out of place, on a world that echoed Asian influences in most of its architecture. Here, there was none of that influence.

"Are these books real?" Jessica wondered.

"In the sense that you can open them and read them, yes," Mister Yokimah replied. "However, they are all reprints made from digital versions. I had all the greatest works of humanity, from as far back as I had access, printed and bound for this collection."

"Why?" Jessica asked.

"The collapse of civilization on Earth after the bio-digital plague was primarily due to the fact that printed books no longer existed. Knowledge and history were lost for nearly a millennium. Imagine if a library such as this had been maintained back then. Where would Earth civilization be now? How much more advanced would we all be? How much further out into the galaxy, or perhaps even the universe, would we have traveled? All but for the lack of printed books," he finished, gesturing toward his towering stacks of literature.

"How many books do you have here?" Nathan asked.

"Just over thirty-eight thousand, in this room alone," Mister Yokimah bragged. "And this room only contains works of fiction. Science, religion, history, philosophy...those are all contained in other rooms...rooms two or three times this size. So far, we have reproduced over two hundred thousand books. Unfortunately, we are running out of material to print."

"You mean paper?"

"No, I speak of content," Mister Yokimah corrected. "The original expeditions that escaped the plague and settled this system carried a limited amount of digital content in their data banks. However, I have been able to obtain additional content from other worlds, both in this sector and neighboring sectors, thanks to the jump drive that you bestowed upon us all."

Nathan looked around. "Amazing." He spotted a small practice putting green in one corner. "You play golf?" he asked with surprise. "I didn't know they *had* golf out here."

"Sadly, I have yet to play a real round of golf," Mister Yokimah admitted as he picked up a remote from a side table and pointed it at the wall. "There are no golf courses in this sector, or in any of the neighboring sectors, that I am aware of. *This* is the best I can do."

A portion of the wall slid open, revealing a small side room. It was curved, forming a dome much like the main view screen that wrapped around the Aurora's bridge. The walls were stark white, and the room was poorly lit until Mister Yokimah entered, and the projections came alive.

"Wow," Nathan exclaimed, following their host inside the room. Before them was a golf course, one that appeared as real as he could remember. He could hear the breeze rustling through the distant trees; he could feel it on his face. The sound of birds in the distance. Even people playing neighboring holes.

"What do you think?"

"It looks quite real," Nathan admitted.

"Have you played, Captain?"

"Not for years," Nathan confessed. "Ice hockey was always my game. I did play a little golf in college, however, just for fun. Although, I was never very good."

"I have been trying to teach myself the game using this simulator I had custom built," Mister Yokimah explained. "I feel that I have gotten pretty good with my irons and with my driver, but my short game needs some work. Especially my putting. I feel that on a real course, where the greens are not flat, I would have difficulties."

"Maybe someday you will be able to play for real," Nathan encouraged.

"Perhaps we can play a round together?" Mister Yokimah said hopefully. "Perhaps even on Earth?"

"It may be some time before I am free to visit Earth," Nathan admitted. "In their eyes, I am still deceased."

Mister Yokimah looked confused. "Then how is it you are in command of the Aurora? Isn't she an Earth ship?"

"She was," Nathan replied. "It's complicated."

"Of this, I have no doubt."

"Why don't you just build a course?" Jessica suggested. "I mean, if you can print a few hundred thousand books, surely you can build a golf course."

"Alas, Rakuen *is* a water world," Mister Yokimah explained. "Land is a very expensive commodity."

"What about Neramese?"

"The conditions on Neramese would not be conducive to growing and maintaining a real course. The best I can hope to do is to someday build a floating mini-course on Rakuen. I believe they call such courses a 'pitch and putt'?"

"Surely, there are worlds nearby where you could build a course?" Nathan wondered.

"Building in another system would be prohibitively expensive at this time," Mister Yokimah said, "even for someone with my wealth. I could *afford* to do so, but there would be no return on the investment, and I cannot justify the expense. Not if I intend to continue operating my Gunyoki racing teams."

"You have more than *one* team?" Jessica asked.

Mister Yokimah turned off the golf simulation, leading them back into the main office. "I have eight teams," he bragged. "A total of twelve Gunyoki racers, including the backup ships. I'm afraid *that* is where my true passion lies. Until such time as others in the Rogen sector share my interest in golf, playing on a real, tournament-level course shall have to remain a dream."

Nathan and Jessica continued to follow their host down the length of his office toward his desk at the far end. "I'm surprised you can get any work done at all in here," Nathan commented. "I'd be too distracted with all these games."

"There is actually very little for me to do at this point in my career," Mister Yokimah admitted. "My companies pretty much run themselves. I have one or two meetings each day, and I visit one of my factories at least once per week, but otherwise, my time is mostly my own. This is more my sanctuary than my work space. I spend much of my time either reading or playing one of these games that I have collected."

"A tough life," Jessica commented.

"I have no complaints," Mister Yokimah admitted, "other than a lack of golf courses, that is." Mister Yokimah reached his desk, moving around it to take his seat. "But you did not come to Rakuen to play games, did you, Captain Scott?"

"Actually, I came to pick up a few shuttles from the Ranni plant."

"Really?" Mister Yokimah took his seat. "Why would the Aurora need Ranni shuttles?"

"They are very useful little ships," Nathan insisted.

"So much so that Deliza Ta'Akar instructed her plant to start producing them for the Karuzari," Mister Yokimah stated, a pleased expression on his face. "Knowledge is a very powerful tool," he added, noticing the surprised look on the faces of his guests.

"Or a dangerous one," Jessica warned, "depending on who has it, and how it is used."

Mister Yokimah either did not notice the veiled threat, or chose to ignore it. "I simply *like* to be aware of what is going on...on *my* world. Nothing sinister about it, I can assure you."

"I'm sure Lieutenant Commander Nash did not mean to imply otherwise," Nathan assured him.

Jessica's expression remained unchanged.

"Of course," Mister Yokimah agreed. "So, tell me,

Captain, why *do* I have the pleasure of your company this day?"

"I was hoping that you'd given further thought to the potential threat the Dusahn pose to your world." Nathan told him.

"I can't say that I have, to be honest," Mister Yokimah replied. "Until a few days ago, that is."

"What happened a few days ago?" Jessica wondered.

"I was contacted by a Takaran businessman by the name of Jorkar Seeley. It seems he is interested in becoming the sole distributor of Yokimah water purification systems in the Pentaurus cluster. He apparently has the full support of the Dusahn in this venture."

"Really," Nathan stated with a suspicious tone.

"It seems that, rather than spread their area of control further out into space, the Dusahn are interested in establishing trade with other worlds for the things they need."

"I thought you said the Takarans have their own water purification systems," Jessica reminded him.

"According to Mister Seeley, the primary manufacturing plant in the Takaran system was destroyed during the invasion," Mister Yokimah stated. "Seems it was too close to one of their surface-to-orbit plasma cannons."

Nathan looked at Jessica for confirmation, but got no response. "And this Mister Seeley, he sought you out?" Nathan asked. "How did he get here?"

"In a Ranni shuttle, actually. There are hundreds of them in use by the Takarans. Of course, now they have all been fitted with Dusahn transponders and remote override capabilities."

"And you are sure this man is who he claims to be?" Jessica asked.

"I have no way to verify his identity, I'm afraid," Mister Yokimah admitted. "However, I see little risk in doing business with him, as long as the terms he proposes are satisfactory."

"Then you haven't done any actual business with him yet," Nathan surmised.

"Not as of yet, no," Mister Yokimah confirmed. "We have a meeting later this evening, over dinner. Perhaps you'd like to join us, Captain? Both of you. You can meet him yourself, if you'd like. Who knows, he may even be a good source of intelligence for your little rebellion."

Nathan looked at Jessica, who nodded discretely. "I think we'd like that."

"You'll have to find something else to wear, I'm afraid. The restaurant is rather upscale. I don't think your uniforms would be appropriate. Shall I send a car for you?"

"That would be appreciated," Nathan agreed.

"What hotel are you staying in?" Mister Yokimah wondered.

"We have yet to arrange accommodations," Nathan admitted. "To be honest, we weren't sure how long we were going to be on Rakuen."

"Please, allow me. I will have my assistant arrange accommodations for you. My treat, of course," Mister Yokimah insisted. "How many in your party?"

"Four, thank you," Nathan replied.

"It is my pleasure, Captain. Now, if you'll excuse me, I do have *some* business to attend to this afternoon. I will have someone take you to your hotel."

"Thank you," Nathan repeated. "I look forward to our engagement later."

"Until then, Captain, Lieutenant Commander," Mister Yokimah said, standing and bowing politely as Nathan and Jessica departed.

"Where the hell are we going to get dinner attire?" Jessica asked under her breath as they made their way back across the massive office.

"I'm sure there are plenty of places to buy clothing here," Nathan insisted.

"How are we going to pay for it?"

"I have the company credit chip, remember?" Nathan said, tapping his shirt pocket.

* * *

"What the hell?" Josh exclaimed as he stood looking at the Ranni shuttles. "I thought you had a hand in the design of these things?"

"I did," Loki replied. "What's wrong?"

"They look like armadillos."

"Arma-what?"

"Armadillos. An Earth creature. Kind of like the dasypia on Haven."

"Never heard of them."

"Well, they're ugly, just like these shuttles," Josh insisted. "Didn't anyone consider that when they were designing these things?"

"Actually, the shape is one of the reasons they are so fuel efficient," Loki explained. "They are based on the shape of the esani beetle."

"Great, an ugly bug," Josh complained as he walked up to the first ship. "Jesus, Loki. Harvesters are better-looking than these things. What were you thinking?"

"We were thinking that customers cared more about efficiency and operational costs than looks."

"*Bean counters* think about efficiency and operational costs," Josh commented. "The people who own them, and fly them, or ride in them want them to *look* cool." Josh looked at the shuttle again. "*This* is *not* cool."

"I rather like them," Loki insisted as he opened the hatch on the nearest shuttle.

"Big surprise there," Josh muttered, following Loki inside. "Jeez, you didn't even make them cool-looking on the *inside*."

"What are you talking about? They are quite comfortable."

Josh shook his head. "You just don't get it, do you?"

"I guess I don't."

"You guys have invented the Clarkson Evolution of jump shuttles."

"What is a Clarkson Evolution?" Loki wondered, certain that he would not care once he found out.

"The first electric car on Earth, *after* they recovered from the bio-digital plague. They were ugly as hell, but they were very efficient, and very economical to operate."

"But they were unsuccessful because they didn't look *cool*?" Loki surmised, moving forward into the cockpit.

"Actually, they sold millions of them," Josh said. "Made the Clarkson company the biggest maker of vehicles in the NAU for decades to come."

"Then there may be a method to our madness, after all," Loki stated as he sat down in the pilot's seat.

Josh said nothing as he climbed into the copilot's seat.

"It never ceases to amaze me how much trivial

knowledge you seem to have about Earth," Loki commented as he began turning on systems.

"I've had a *lot* of downtime the last seven years, remember?" Josh looked the shuttle's main console over, getting familiar with the layout. "This looks pretty basic."

"It is, actually. Very intuitive, and very easy to operate. You need almost *no* flight training to fly it."

"What are you trying to do? Put us out of our jobs?"

"Hardly," Loki insisted. "Deliza's market research shows there is no way anyone can build commercial, passenger transport ships fast enough to meet the growing demand to move both people and goods between systems. The Ranni shuttle is designed to meet that demand. They are inexpensive and quick to build, and easy for the layman to operate. It also allows individuals, or small companies, to run their own shuttle services, making jump transport more affordable for those who cannot afford their own personal shuttles."

"Like space taxis," Josh surmised.

"Something like that, yes."

"These things come in cargo versions?" Josh wondered.

"There is only the one version, but the interior is easily reconfigurable, and the top of the fuselage can be detached to allow easy loading and unloading of cargo that is too large to fit through the main boarding hatch. There is also an escape tunnel from the back of the main cabin that leads to an aft hatch at the bottom of the stern, which can be fitted with a conveyor belt to be used for smaller cargo."

"Single-pilot certified, I assume?"

"Of course," Loki confirmed. "But it is not

recommended unless that single person actually *is* a pilot."

Josh sighed. "So, what are we doing, here?"

"I thought I'd go over the basic layout with you, and then you could start the checkout on the second ship," Loki suggested.

"Are we gonna fly them both at the same time, in formation?"

Loki cast a disapproving glance at Josh. "No. That would be foolish. The initial flights should be done by *two* qualified pilots."

"Just so you know, I'm okay sitting second seat on these flights," Josh told him as his comm-unit beeped. "Seems like a real snooze-fest anyway," he added, taking his comm-unit out of his pocket to answer it. "You got Josh."

"You guys can take your time," Nathan told him over the comm-unit. *"We're probably not going to depart until sometime tomorrow."*

"Why? What's up?" Josh asked.

"Yokimah invited us to dinner."

"What about us?" Josh wondered.

"You guys will have to fend for yourselves," Nathan told him. *"The hotel has room service, and the bill is on Yokimah Industries, so enjoy yourselves."*

"Outstanding!" Josh declared gleefully.

"But don't go crazy," Nathan added.

Josh rolled his eyes in disappointment. "Wait, what hotel?"

"The Gorsica, on the south side of the center plaza," Nathan explained.

"I know where it is," Loki announced.

"Where are you guys now?" Josh wondered.

"Shopping," Nathan replied. *"It seems we don't have the proper attire."*

186

"We'll finish the primary checkout, and maybe even get the first flight in before we head to the hotel, Captain," Loki promised.

"Sounds good. Keep a low profile, and don't let Josh get into trouble."

"I'm hurt," Josh insisted.

"Yes, sir," Loki acknowledged.

"I'm having dollag steaks, palyama, and a few of those tall ales they serve here," Josh decided, putting his comm-unit back in his pocket.

"You're on a planet that is ninety percent water, and you're ordering dollag steaks?" Loki wondered. "Do you know how expensive that will be?"

"You heard the captain," Josh said. "Yokimah's paying for it."

"He also said not to go crazy," Loki reminded him.

"It's not like I'm ordering two steaks," Josh argued.

"Most people order seafood when on Rakuen," Loki told him.

"Most *stupid* people."

Loki rolled his eyes as he continued his checkout.

* * *

Cameron stepped through the hatch, returning to the intelligence department for the second time today. "Don't tell me you got an answer already?"

"They must have had a reply already written," Lieutenant Commander Shinoda commented, handing the data pad to Cameron.

Cameron read the message. "Well, it's definitely Michael Willard," she decided as she read. "He answered every test question correctly, *and* he used the proper encryption algorithm."

"What does he say?"

"All the ex-Corinari have gone into hiding to avoid

arrest," Cameron told him. "Many of them have formed an underground resistance, but they have been unable to take any action as of yet. They say they could convince most of the Corinari to come out of hiding and join their cause, *if* Nathan was to show his face on Corinair."

"Why would he want to do that?"

"It seems that most of the Corinari are not convinced Nathan is still alive."

"Can you blame them?" Lieutenant Commander Shinoda agreed. "Even *I* saw him buried."

Cameron looked at the lieutenant commander. "I guess Nathan is going to have to go back down to Corinair. General Telles is *not* going to like this."

* * *

Suvan Navarro walked down the corridor leading from the shuttle docks to the number two assembly bay of the Takaran shipyards. It had taken him five days to finally land a position on one of the hull-painting crews. Five days of sitting around the trades house, waiting for an opening. Even then, an opening had only come due to an accident in which a member of the paint crew, to which he was now assigned, had lost his life.

Although Suvan did not wish ill will on any of his fellow Takarans, he knew the time would come when he might have to take one or more of their lives in order to accomplish his goals. If killing a few innocent Takarans was the price of liberation for the entire Pentaurus cluster, then it was a price Suvan was willing to pay, and ten times over, if need be.

Stealing the Teyentah was going to be hard enough. Finding people to help him was going to be even more difficult. The men building this ship were all gainfully employed, in trades the Dusahn desperately needed. Their futures were secured, as were those of their families. Convincing such men to risk everything on so risky a plan would not be easy, and would take a great deal of time.

Unfortunately, *time* was something that was in short supply. Once the Teyentah was completed, she would be assigned a Dusahn crew and put into service, at which point her theft would be impossible. If he was going to make off with a three-kilometer-long warship, he would have to do it soon.

He followed the line of workers, turning the final corner. Before him was the Teyentah, floating motionless in her assembly bay, separated from him only by massive windows lining the bay-side deck on which he now stood.

The Teyentah was a beautiful ship, despite being all function over form. She followed the modular design that had become so popular toward the end of Caius's reign. The concept allowed sections to be removed or added to a ship's core structure, making it easy to reconfigure to meet its new mission by either adding, removing, or reorganizing her modules as needed.

The Teyentah had been configured as a battleship. She was smaller than the Avendahl had been, by a considerable margin, and she had nowhere near the firepower Suvan's former ship had possessed. But she had three flight decks: two for fighters and one for heavier ships, all of which were already partially loaded with spacecraft. In addition, she had four gun pods, each carrying two, independently-powered, double-barreled mark three plasma cannons, as well as multiple point-defense turrets. All in all, she had ten mark three turrets, four missile launchers, forty point-defense turrets, and four forward-facing mark five plasma torpedo cannons. She also had the ability to launch any number of automated, self-guided weapons from her flight decks, such as jump KKVs. Combined with the upgraded Dusahn shielding, she would likely be a match for a ship twice her size.

Yet, the Dusahn did not seem to be in a hurry to finish the work that Casimir Ta'Akar had begun more than seven years ago, just before he was assassinated and his house dissolved. It seemed an odd decision, but Suvan was not one to question such a gift, for this delay was the one thing he had going for him in this crazy scheme of his.

And so, Suvan Navarro would bide his time, painting the exterior of the ship he planned to someday steal, all the while keeping his eyes and ears peeled, looking for any opportunities that might come his way. At this point, he had no plan. For plans were born from intelligence, of which he had almost none. So, his first order of business was to gather as much intel as he possibly could.

But for now, he would paint.

CHAPTER SIX

Nathan stood at the hotel bar, nursing his cocktail and tugging every now and again at the tall collar that wrapped completely around his neck. The stiff, white collar reminded him of the priests on Jerenbaugh. He had always hated taking runs to that world, as it was almost impossible not to get tripped up by any number of rules imposed by their theocratic government. Josh, himself, had been arrested there, for nothing more than saying hello to, who he perceived to be, an attractive, single woman. She *had* been attractive, just not single, as evidenced by the parallax earring hanging from her left earlobe. Of course, Josh had no idea of the significance of that particular piece of jewelry; a fact that had nearly gotten him executed, and had cost the Seiiki the entire profit from her haul.

Nathan smiled, remembering the look on Josh's face when Connor had come to pick him up after paying off the young woman's husband to convince him to drop the charges. He looked like a scared kid who finally spotted his long-lost parent. It was the first time Connor had ever seen Josh take a tongue-lashing from Marcus without defending himself. Even Neli had given him a piece of her mind, which was something Josh *never* tolerated...not from Neli.

"Are you going to buy me a drink, or what?"

Nathan turned to look at Jessica, his mouth dropping to the floor. "Wow."

"Good reaction," she said, taking his drink from his hand and tossing it down her throat.

"You clean up nicely...especially for a soldier-girl."

"Two more," Jessica told the bartender, signaling to him.

Nathan couldn't stop staring. "Can you even breathe in that thing? It looks like it's painted onto you."

"It's surprisingly comfortable, actually."

Nathan looked her up and down again. "I can't believe you're eight years older than when I first met you."

"And you started off so well," Jessica said, shaking her head as she picked up her drink.

"No, I mean, you look like you're nineteen…twenty tops. You're actually making me feel embarrassed. I mean, you can bounce a credit chip off your abs." Nathan picked up his drink and tossed it back in a single gulp. "I need to start doing some crunches, or something."

"Aww, I think that little layer of baby fat around your belly is kind of cute," Jessica teased, pinching the side of his belly. "That suit does *not* look comfortable."

"That's because it isn't," Nathan agreed, tugging at his collar again. "Are all the men on this planet long-necked, or something? I feel like this collar is digging into my jaw."

Jessica reached up and touched the back of his collar, causing it to soften along the top edge. "Didn't you bother reading the instructions?"

"I don't intend to wash it," Nathan replied. "What did you do?" he wondered, finally able to relax.

"They're smart clothes, Nathan," she explained. "How do you think I got into this thing?"

"What are you talking about?"

"It felt about three sizes too big when I put it on.

Then I pressed a spot up here, and it just formed to my body in all the right places, all by itself."

"So, this is a 'smart jacket'?"

"You'd know that if you'd read the instructions."

"Who the hell reads instructions on clothing?" Nathan wondered. "Shall we?" he asked, offering her his arm.

Jessica took his arm, and the two of them walked out of the bar and into the hotel lobby, where they found their driver waiting for them.

"Captain Scott?" the man asked, a twinge of local accent in his speech.

"Yes," Nathan replied.

"Your car is waiting, sir," the driver said, turning to lead them out.

Nathan and Jessica followed the driver out and climbed into one of a dozen, or so, limousines sitting in front of the hotel entrance.

"Nice," Jessica commented as the driver closed the door. "I haven't been in a limo in at least a decade."

"What was the occasion?" Nathan wondered.

"Prom, I think."

"A decade?"

"I said *at least* a decade," Jessica defended. "And if I remember correctly, I didn't look half as good as I do now."

"Of that, I am certain," Nathan replied as the driver climbed into the front seat.

The limo rose up from the ground and began gliding away from the hotel on a cushion of anti-gravity. Nathan looked out the window as they pulled out of the hotel property. The streets of the city were lit in pale hues of blue and green, with other colors mixed in to compliment the city decor and architecture. The limo pulled out onto the main

193

road, which ran along the water's edge and wrapped around the perimeter of this section of the massive floating city. All three of Rakuen's moons were out, providing a dazzling mixture of blues and reds, causing lavender sparkles in the crests of the waves in the distance.

Nathan could imagine how the view must have captured the hearts of the first settlers to colonize Rakuen. It was a truly beautiful world, blessed with an abundance of water that was home to a multitude of plant and aquatic life, most of which were not only edible, but quite delicious.

As Connor Tuplo, Nathan had visited this world a few times before, but he had never been able to afford to partake in its offerings. The landing and facilities fees imposed on foreign ships were steep, and Connor had always been forced to underbid his competition in order to win such runs. Most of his trips to Rakuen had barely paid for their return, as nothing was ever hauled *from* Rakuen in a foreign ship, not since they first received jump drive technology a few years ago, thanks to Ranni Enterprises.

"What are you going to say to him?" Jessica asked.

"I haven't really thought about it," Nathan admitted. "I guess I was planning on letting the conversation take its natural course, and see if I can comfortably steer it toward a discussion on the threat the Dusahn pose to, not only Rakuen, but, the entire quadrant."

"What about this Takaran businessman?" Jessica wondered. "You're not buying that cover, are you?"

"I'm neither buying, nor *not* buying it," Nathan admitted. "I *am*, however, somewhat suspicious."

"Our latest intel suggests the Dusahn are still

quite selective about who they allow to travel in and out of their systems within the Pentaurus sector."

"But that water purification plant *was* destroyed, wasn't it?" Nathan said.

"It was."

"Then he may *not* be a spy."

"Or, he may not *know* he is a spy," Jessica pointed out.

"The Takarans use Corinairan nanites," Nathan reminded her.

"Which can be completely flushed out in only a few weeks' time, and we're now a month into the Dusahn occupation."

"That's cutting it a bit close," Nathan said.

"Doesn't mean it isn't possible," Jessica replied. "Just keep your wits about you, and don't reveal anything about our strengths, or lack thereof."

"If this person *is* a spy, couldn't we use that to our advantage?" Nathan suggested. "Feed him some false intel to take back to the Dusahn. Maybe set a trap to take out a few of their ships while keeping our risk low?"

"False intel ops can be tricky," Jessica warned. "If not done correctly, they can bite you in the ass. Better to just keep things simple for now. Remember, we're here to pick up a couple of shuttles and try to talk Yokimah into convincing the Gunyoki to join us." Jessica looked out the window as the limo transitioned from the thoroughfare to the city streets. "To be honest, I'm not sure Yokimah has as much power and influence as you think he does. At best, I don't think he could do more than give us *his* Gunyoki racers. We'd still need pilots for them."

"He's got more influence than you think," Nathan insisted. "And there are hundreds of Gunyoki racers in the Rogen system. Honestly, though, I'd be happy with just his twelve. Put jump drives in them, and they'd be nearly as deadly as gunships, and definitely more maneuverable."

"Let's hope you're right," Jessica said. "We're pulling up to the restaurant now."

Nathan looked out the front windows just in time to see the crowd of people gathered in front of the restaurant. "What the hell?" He looked at Jessica.

"Don't look at me," she told him. "I have no idea what's going on."

"Driver," Nathan called, tapping on the window dividing the driver's compartment from theirs.

"Yes, sir," the driver replied as the window lowered.

"What's with all the people? Is this some kind of grand opening, or something?"

"No, sir, the Porta Constantona is one of the oldest establishments in the city."

"Then why the crowds?" Jessica wondered.

"They are here to see you, sir," the driver said, surprised they did not know. "They are here to see Na-Tan," he added, smiling.

"Great," Jessica said sarcastically.

"You guys wanted to use me as a recruitment tool," Nathan reminded her. "I guess this is where it starts."

"Yokimah is up to something," Jessica told him. "I can feel it."

"People like him are *always* up to something," Nathan assured her as the limousine pulled to a stop and settled slowly back onto its gear.

Bright lights on a dozen different vid-cams snapped on as the driver got out and rushed back to open the door for Jessica. He graciously extended his hand, bowing slightly, so as not to block the view of any of the vid-cams. Jessica stepped out, smiled at the crowds, and did her best to look sexy rather than menacing. She stepped to one side to make room for Nathan, who followed her out of the limousine.

The crowd erupted in cheers for the legend they had all thought long dead. People randomly shouted *Na-Tan* as he offered his arm to Jessica and escorted her into the restaurant, politely waving at the crowd as they passed by.

"I'm glad I dressed up for this," Jessica said. "It would've been awfully embarrassing if we had shown up in those drab, gray uniforms of ours."

"Yeah, I think I'm going to need to adopt a different image in the future," Nathan told her as they entered the restaurant. The buzz of the crowd quickly diminished as the doors closed behind them, and they were immediately enveloped in the restaurant's sound-controlled environment.

"Captain Scott, welcome!" the maître d' gushed, stepping forward to offer his hand. "And the infamous, and stunning, Lieutenant Commander Nash," he added, lightly kissing the back of her hand. "We are honored by your presence. Please...if you'll follow me, Mister Yokimah is expecting you."

"We didn't get this kind of reception last time," Jessica said under her breath as they followed the maître d' into the main dining room.

"They probably didn't believe us last time," Nathan replied.

The main dining room was eerily silent, with the only sounds being those of the staff moving about, ducking in and out of the sound-suppression fields surrounding each table. As they moved through the room, every pair of eyes eventually fell upon them.

People spoke silently to one another as they watched Nathan and Jessica, and a few even raised their glasses in salute to the famous duo.

Nathan felt that familiar, unpleasant feeling once again. The same feeling that had plagued him throughout his life. It was the feeling of every eye being upon him, which had caused him to enlist and seek a position that would take him into deep space, where he could take refuge in obscurity. Unfortunately, that had not gone as planned.

The maître d' led them to a private dining enclave that was slightly elevated and surrounded by shimmering windows, through which one could not view the interior from the main dining room. The maître d' led them inside, then stepped aside, handing them off to the private maître d' who stood watch over Ito Yokimah's party. He led them to their seats, taking care to ensure they were comfortable and had fresh beverages to quench their thirst before stepping back.

"Welcome, Captain, Lieutenant Commander," Mister Yokimah greeted. "I trust your ride in was pleasant?"

"Quite so, thank you," Nathan replied.

"I believe you already know my wife, Jana. And this is Jorkar Seeley, of Takara."

"A pleasure, Mister Seeley," Nathan greeted.

"The pleasure, or should I say, *honor*, is all mine, I assure you," Mister Seeley replied. "Your name is quite well known among my people."

"This is Lieutenant Commander Jessica Nash," Nathan said, introducing her to the Takaran businessman.

Mister Seeley's eyes lit up. "Mister Yokimah, you didn't tell me..." He looked at Jessica. "*The* Jessica

Nash? The one who fired the shot that ended the reign of Caius Ta'Akar?"

Jessica nodded, smiling perhaps a bit too much. She felt Nathan's elbow gently poking her side. "It *was* a hell of a shot."

"That would be the understatement of the century," Mister Seeley said. "That shot changed Takara forever."

"Not all would say for the better, I understand," Nathan said.

"True, there are many who benefited greatly from the reign of Caius. I assure you, however, that I was not one of them. In fact, my fortunes did not turn until well after that shot was fired."

"Which house is it you serve?" Jessica asked.

"Straight to business," Mister Seeley remarked. "I like you."

Jessica just smiled politely.

"I currently serve House Jolenza," Mister Seeley announced proudly.

"Currently?" Nathan wondered. "I was under the impression that one's loyalty to their house was for life."

"In the old days, yes. However, even before the fall of Caius, changing ones house affiliation was not uncommon, albeit somewhat difficult."

"Which house did you serve before House Jolenza?" Jessica asked.

"I proudly served House Navarro, until it fell from grace in Takaran society and was disbanded."

"Some would say *looted*," Nathan remarked as he sipped his glass of wine.

"And I would agree with them," Mister Seeley replied. "Suvan Navarro was a man of principal, one of the few who deserved his title. I ended up with

House Jolenza when they were bequeathed a portion of House Navarro's lands."

Nathan did not look pleased.

"It was a tumultuous time," Mister Seeley added, noticing the captain's expression. "The assassination of Prince Casimir was most distasteful, in the eyes of the commoners. But, as you are well aware, the nobles of Takara have always been more concerned with maintaining their own wealth and position than anything else."

"Exactly the type of behavior that destroys civilizations," Nathan commented.

"An interesting observation," Mister Seeley agreed.

"Mister Yokimah tells me you seek to bring his water purification systems to Takara?" Nathan asked, changing the subject.

"Indeed. As you know, the factory that produced such equipment on Takara was destroyed during the initial occupation by the Dusahn. My lord is hoping to bring Mister Yokimah's products to Takaran markets *before* House Ansonte can rebuild their factory."

"I'm surprised the Dusahn are allowing you to travel outside the system, unsupervised," Jessica commented. "It is my understanding that they do not allow such freedoms."

"In the beginning, no, but they have begun to ease such restrictions as of late...in the interests of maintaining the economies of the Pentaurus cluster. I assure you, however, they are keeping close tabs on my travels. My ship is fitted with a logging device. Upon my return, the Dusahn will know everywhere I have been, and precisely how long I was there. If I go anywhere other than where I had planned, without good explanation, there will be a high price to pay."

"Then the nobles of Takara are *cooperating* with the Dusahn?" Nathan asked.

"I understand your inference, Captain," Mister Seeley said. "But they have little choice, really. We all saw what happened to Ybara. And two houses have already been seized since the Dusahn arrived."

"What happened to their leaders?" Jessica asked.

"No one really knows," Mister Seeley replied. "We suspect they are still alive, however. The Dusahn seem to consider public executions a method of deterrence."

"So we've noticed," Nathan commented.

"Mister Yokimah tells me you have taken command of the Aurora once again," Mister Seeley said, obviously steering the conversation in a direction he preferred. "Is that *really* true?"

"It is," Nathan replied. "Why do you ask?"

"We were under the impression the Alliance had abandoned the Pentaurus cluster because they have their own threats with which to contend."

"It is true the Alliance is otherwise occupied, at the moment," Nathan admitted. "However, the *Aurora* is not. She is *here*, and under *my* command."

"The Aurora is in the Rakuen system?" Mister Seeley asked, his eyes wide.

"Her exact location is, as you might expect, classified," Jessica stated, taking note of Mister Seeley's interest.

"Let's just say that she is *nearby* and leave it at that," Nathan suggested.

"Of course," Mister Seeley agreed. "I did not mean to pry, Captain."

"Captain Scott means to drive the Dusahn out of

201

the Pentaurus sector," Mister Yokimah told Mister Seeley.

"Would that he could," Mister Seeley said. "The Dusahn are fairly well established already. It will take more than the *Aurora* to drive them away, I'm afraid." He looked at Nathan and Jessica.

"The Aurora has dealt with forces greater than those of the Dusahn," Nathan stated confidently. "I am confident we will find a way to contain them and, eventually, remove them from all the systems they have illegally invaded."

"Legality is a matter of interpretation, is it not?" Mister Yokimah said. "It always depends on whose laws are to be used."

"The taking of anything by force, and against the will of the civilization from which it is taken, is wrong by any reasonable measure," Nathan asserted. "*Might* does *not* make right."

"There are those who would argue that point," Mister Seeley responded.

"Like the Dusahn, for example," Jessica said in an almost seething tone.

"And the Jung, and our own nobles of Takara," Mister Seeley added. "I am not disagreeing with your ethics, Captain. I am merely pointing out that every society has its own point of view, in such matters. I am told you are a student of history, Captain. If so, then surely you must agree with me."

"I agree that many civilizations throughout human history have believed in their right to take what they need by force, if necessary," Nathan replied. "I do *not* agree that it is *right, or* that such beliefs should be *respected.*"

"Ah, but you expect *your* beliefs to be respected, simply because a *greater* number of people believe as *you* do," Mister Seeley countered. "Do you not see the hypocrisy in that?"

"I see no hypocrisy in protecting the weak from those who might prey upon them," Nathan told Mister Seeley. "Lines must be drawn somewhere, or chaos will consume us all."

"But do not the lines become less critical the further out into space we are able to travel?" Mister Seeley asked. "Does not the very jump drive you introduced to this quadrant of space make those lines less necessary than before?"

"If anything, it makes them more necessary, Mister Seeley," Nathan argued. "For threats that were once out of range, are no longer so." Nathan turned to address his host. "Which brings us back to the purpose of my visit, Mister Yokimah. I was hoping you might have given some more thought to the threat the Dusahn pose to the Rogen sector, and to Rakuen."

"The Dusahn have no interest in Rakuen," Mister Seeley insisted.

"How would you know this?" Jessica wondered.

"Well, for one thing, they didn't even know where Rakuen *was* when I filed for an interstellar travel permit."

"Well, they certainly do now, don't they?" Jessica said in an accusatory tone.

"I expect the Dusahn know where *every* human-inhabited world is located within this quadrant of space," Nathan added in an attempt to soften her accusation. "They could not have pulled off such a quick, overwhelmingly successful invasion of *multiple* systems without excellent, prior intelligence."

"Which is precisely why I do not see the Dusahn

as a threat to the Rogen system," Mister Yokimah said.

"The only reason the Dusahn have not invaded your system is because they have yet to get around to it," Nathan warned. "What your system has to offer them is not worth risking the loss of either Takar or Darvano. But once they have secured those systems and have added a few more ships to their fleet, they will come. It could take months, or even years. But they *will* come. It is what they do."

"How is it you know so much about the Dusahn, Captain?" Mister Seeley wondered.

"The Dusahn are just a rogue caste of the Jung, Mister Seeley. And believe me when I tell you, I *know* the Jung."

"And I *know* the Rakuen people, and especially the Gunyoki who protect them."

Nathan leaned back in his chair a moment. "How long has it been since your Gunyoki have seen actual combat?"

"I assure you, Captain, our Gunyoki are *quite* well trained," Mister Yokimah boasted.

"Training and facing *real* battle are two entirely different things," Nathan assured him.

"The Gunyoki risk death every time they fly," Mister Yokimah asserted. "They face *live* fire, as well."

"Live *low-power* fire," Nathan corrected. "I've read the history of your races, Mister Yokimah. No Gunyoki has ever died as a result of weapons fire during a race, only of pilot error, sometimes occurring as a result of weapons fire. There is a *big* difference."

"I would disagree," Mister Yokimah replied.

"You would be displaying your ignorance," Jessica said, interrupting them. Mister Yokimah looked irritated. "The Ghatazhak train relentlessly, from the time they enter puberty until the day they retire from service. Their training is like nothing you can imagine. Yet, every one of them will tell you that until you have been battle-tested, *multiple times*, you cannot know for sure how you will perform."

"Have *you* seen such battle?" Mister Yokimah asked, as if challenging her.

"I have," Jessica replied, with a cold, hard stare. "I have killed more men than I can remember, and I have nearly died on several occasions."

"Actually, you did die once," Nathan reminded her. "Technically."

"And you, Captain?" Mister Yokimah asked. "We have all heard the tales of the brave Captain Scott, and how he has faced overwhelming odds and still come out victorious. But have *you* taken lives, face-to-face, like Miss Nash?"

"Does it matter?" Nathan wondered.

"I believe it does," Mister Yokimah stated. "After all, you're the one who is suggesting that our Gunyoki would be unable to stop a Dusahn invasion of Rakuen, simply because they have never faced *real* combat."

"Your Gunyoki couldn't even stop me," Nathan replied.

"What?" Mister Yokimah was shocked.

"What?" So was Jessica.

"Something happens to you in combat," Nathan explained. "The first time, you're just scared out of your mind, and if you are well trained, that training kicks in and saves your ass. But the next time, and the time after that, and the time after that... Well, that's when the changes take place. That's when you develop instinct. That's when you develop insight. That's when you develop the ability to see all possible outcomes in the blink of an eye and make near instantaneous decisions... Decisions that *win* battles. That's why the Jung were so difficult to stop. *They* are battle-hardened, just like the lieutenant commander and myself. And so are the Dusahn."

Mister Yokimah smiled in a manner that Nathan had not yet seen. "You seriously believe you could beat the Gunyoki?"

Jessica suddenly wished she could gag Nathan.

"I do," Nathan responded confidently.

"Perhaps you'd like to back up your rather outlandish claims with action, my dear captain?" Mister Yokimah suggested. "Perhaps even make a wager on the outcome?"

"That's just silly," Jessica declared, trying to derail things before they went too far. "We're trying to fight a rebellion here, not fly races for your entertainment."

"Perhaps if I sweeten the pot?" Mister Yokimah suggested.

"What do you have in mind?" Nathan asked, still looking completely confident.

Oh, God, Jessica thought.

"If you lose, ownership of the Ranni shuttle plant is transferred over to me."

"And if I don't lose?" Nathan asked.

"My Gunyoki racers are yours," Mister Yokimah promised, "to do with as you wish."

"I'm pretty sure the Ranni shuttle plant is worth far more than your twelve Gunyoki racers," Nathan argued.

"You underestimate the profitability of my racing teams," Mister Yokimah told him. "Besides, if a Dusahn invasion *is* inevitable, as you say, the Ranni shuttle plant will no longer be of strategic value to you."

"What am I going to do with twelve Gunyoki racers, without pilots to fly them?" Nathan wondered.

"I cannot bet the lives of the pilots," Mister Yokimah told him. "However, I can *loan* a few of them to you, to train your people."

"Mechanics, too," Nathan insisted.

"Mechanics, as well, *assuming* you win. However, you must promise to keep them out of harm's way."

Jessica saw the look of determination in Nathan's eyes, and it worried her. "Captain..."

"It's a bet," Nathan replied without hesitation. "We can work out the details later, I assume?"

"Of course," Mister Yokimah agreed. "Ah, the main course has arrived," he said as the waitstaff appeared, carrying large trays of Rakuen delicacies.

Jessica leaned closer to Nathan, speaking in low tones, so no one else could hear. "When Cam finds out, she's gonna kill you."

* * *

"No fucking way," Marcus declared with a wave of his hand.

"Marcus," Vladimir said as he followed him up the Seiiki's cargo ramp, trying to reason with him.

"There's no way you're using this ship as a test bed."

"I think it sounds cool," Dalen said from the top of the cargo ramp.

"Nobody asked you, dumbass," Marcus snapped as he passed Dalen on his way forward.

"You have no problem flying the Seiiki into danger, but you refuse to install experimental emitters?" Vladimir questioned, hoping to make Marcus realize the hypocrisy of his position.

"This is different," Marcus insisted.

"How?"

Marcus stopped dead in his tracks, and turned to face Vladimir who was still following him. "We have no *control* over *this*. If those emitters fail...if even *one* of them fails, some part of the ship ain't making the jump...*possibly* a part one of *us* is *in*!"

"That's a good point," Dalen agreed, in support of Marcus.

"That will not happen," Vladimir promised.

"You don't know that. That's why they're called *experimental*."

"If even a single emitter shows sign of malfunction, the entire system will refuse to accept the jump energy," Vladimir assured him. "The same way the safety protocols work on your current emitter array."

"He's got a point," Dalen told Marcus.

"That's how they're *supposed* to work," Marcus countered. "They ain't never been tried."

"He's got a point, too," Dalen told Vladimir.

"Now you are just splitting hairs," Vladimir exclaimed. "It does not matter. Captain Taylor has already given the order to install the test emitters."

"She ain't *my* captain," Marcus argued. "And she ain't in charge of *this* ship. This is Nathan's ship, not hers. And when he's away, it's my job to look after her."

"Oh, he's got a *really* good point there," Dalen agreed. "A couple of them, in fact."

"Actually, Nathan appointed me as his second in command of the Seiiki," Vladimir reminded him.

"That's also a good point," Dalen told Marcus.

"Shut up," Marcus told Dalen. "That was before he took command of the Aurora again," Marcus told

Vladimir. "Besides, you're not even *on* this crew, anymore!"

"That's a good point," Dalen told Vladimir.

"Shut up," Vladimir scolded. "Marcus, be reasonable. The Seiiki *needs* stealth jump capabilities. Probably more so than any other ship, at the moment."

"He's got another good point there," Dalen told Marcus.

"SHUT UP!" both Marcus and Vladimir shouted in unison.

"Sorry," Dalen apologized, his hands up.

"Besides," Vladimir continued, "Cameron agreed *not* to conduct the first test jump until Nathan returns and signs off on it. All we would be doing is installing the emitters *now*, to save time."

"And if he says no, which I'm sure he will, we're going to have to swap all the emitters back," Marcus declared. "Sounds like a dumbass plan to me."

"Me, too," Dalen agreed. Marcus scowled at him. "I know...shut up."

"There's no way I'm taking down a *functioning* jump drive. Not while there's a risk we'll get caught on deck, unable to jump away, if the Aurora comes under fire."

"Now you're just being silly," Vladimir accused.

"What I'm *doing* is *protecting* our silly asses."

Vladimir sighed in resignation. "What if we *add* the stealth emitters instead of replacing them, leaving the original system intact? As a secondary array?"

"You'd still have to tap the stealth emitters into the same power conduits," Marcus insisted. "There ain't room to run another whole network of conduits, or weight allowance neither."

"Fine," Vladimir agreed.

"And we can only tap them in one at a time, so the existing system is never down for more than an hour at a time."

"That will add *thirty hours* to the process," Vladimir argued. "*Two* at a time…*simultaneously.*"

Marcus scowled at Vladimir. "Agreed," he finally conceded, although somewhat begrudgingly.

"*Spaseebah!*" Vladimir exclaimed with relief.

"Sweet!" Dalen exclaimed. "We're gonna have big guns, *and* be stealthy!"

Marcus and Vladimir both scowled at Dalen.

"I know…shut up!" Dalen exclaimed, turning to get back to work.

Marcus looked back at Vladimir. "You break my ship, I break your face," he warned, poking his finger at Vladimir's chest.

Vladimir laughed at Marcus's threat as he turned and walked back down the ramp, muttering something in Russian.

"What did you say?" Marcus yelled after him. He turned to look at Neli, who had been standing in the corner of the Seiiki's cargo bay the entire time. "What did he say?"

"I don't know," she replied, smiling, "I don't speak Russian."

"Then why are you smiling?"

"Because I'm picturing you trying to kick his ass," she replied as she turned and headed up the ladder to the main level.

* * *

The ride back to the hotel was a quiet one, as was the walk through the lobby, the ride in the elevator, and the walk to their rooms.

"Good night," Nathan said as he turned the doorknob to his room and pushed the door open.

"Not so fast," Jessica remarked, following him into his room. As soon as the door closed behind them, and she knew they were in private, she laid into him. "What the hell were you thinking?"

Nathan started to open his mouth, but was unable to get out a single utterance.

"A Gunyoki race?" she continued. "When was the last time you were even in a cockpit?"

"I've been flying the Seiiki for..."

"I mean a *real* cockpit, Nathan! Like a fighter! Let me guess...*flight school*?"

"Well..."

"Exactly. You let that pompous ass Yokimah *trick* you into risking your life."

"We need those fighters, Jess..." Nathan said as he removed his dress jacket and hung it in the closet.

"Oh, and let's not forget about that bet. The Ranni shuttle plant? It's not even yours to bet, Nathan!"

"Did it ever occur to you that I might *actually* know what I'm doing?" Nathan asked her.

"He baited you, hooked you, and reeled you in..."

"Actually, *I* baited *him*," Nathan corrected.

"What?" Jessica couldn't believe what she was hearing.

"I thought the Ghatazhak were supposed to be calm and collected," Nathan commented. "Oh, yes, 'there is still much work to be done,'" he said, mimicking General Telles.

"What the hell are you talking about?"

"If you'd calm down for a moment, I'll explain it to you."

Nathan's calm demeanor only frustrated her more.

Nathan noticed Jessica looked like she was about to explode. "Take a breath, and listen," he said calmly. "Please...... I can make it an order, if you'd like."

"Don't push it," she snapped.

"Have a seat," Nathan suggested.

Jessica stared at him for a moment, then sat as he had suggested.

"I started the entire premise by saying the Gunyoki couldn't even stop me."

"What?"

"Think back," Nathan said.

Jessica thought for a moment, trying her best to recall the evening's events as best she could. "So, you're saying it was your idea all along?" she asked, still skeptical.

"Well, to be honest, I don't think I really had a race in mind when I made that statement," Nathan admitted, "but it quickly became apparent that it *was* the best way to get our hands on some of those fighters."

"But you bet the Ranni shuttle plant," Jessica reminded him. "You've never even *flown* a Gunyoki. You've never even seen the cockpit. There's no way you can outfly one of them."

"I'm a better pilot than you realize," Nathan insisted.

"Oh, come on, Nathan..."

"Thanks for the vote of confidence."

"We *need* those shuttles. Within a couple months, we can have about a dozen of them..."

"We're not going to defeat the Dusahn with Ranni shuttles, Jess," Nathan insisted.

"We're not going to defeat them with twelve Gunyokis, either," Jessica argued.

"But we can get both."

"And how do you propose to accomplish that?"

"By winning," Nathan replied.

"Got a better plan?"

"Those shuttles aren't free, you know. There are material and labor costs involved in creating them. If I win, we get twelve Gunyoki fighters, and a few pilots and maintenance specialists to teach us how to use them. *And*, we still get the shuttles."

"And if you lose, which I'm *pretty sure* is the most likely case scenario here..."

"Then we still get the shuttles, but at a slightly higher price," Nathan explained. "And who knows? Yokimah might even give us a price break out of respect."

"Yeah, right."

"Don't you see? The risk is very small, and the reward is potentially huge for us."

"You're forgetting one thing," Jessica said. "You could die."

"It's a race around a preset course, with automated defense pods firing low-power weapons. I wasn't kidding when I said I read the accident histories from the Gunyoki races. Most of those pilots died because they were too proud to punch out, and tried to recover control of their ships. *I'm* not that stupid."

"Are you sure about that?" Jessica questioned, still not impressed. "I think you should get Josh to fly against them instead."

"No, it has to be me," Nathan insisted.

"Why?"

"For the same reason you and Telles pulled me into this," Nathan explained. "To inspire others to join the rebellion. If I fly against the Gunyoki and *win*, I'll earn the respect of not only the Gunyoki and the Rakuens, but probably of everyone in the sector. These people may have *heard* of me, but they have never really been *affected* by my actions. *This* will change that. I will become *their* legend, as well."

"And if you lose?"

"As long as I don't lose by much of a margin, it will likely have the same effect. They'll respect me for trying, and coming close to beating them." Nathan looked at her, smiling, waiting for her to see the beauty of his reasoning.

Jessica just smirked and said, "I think some of your brain got left behind in the cloning chamber."

The door chimes sounded. Nathan turned toward the door as the automatic, embedded view screen on their side of the door activated, showing Josh and Loki standing on the other side in the corridor. Loki had his usual look of concern, while Josh looked excited about something. "Open," Nathan instructed.

The door swung open, and Josh came bursting into the room. "Oh, my God! You're going to race the Gunyoki! Are you nuts?"

"How did you know?" Nathan wondered.

"It's all over the Rakuen nets!" Josh exclaimed. "Every media outlet is talking about it. The forums, the news, the race nets, everyone! It's going to be *huge*!"

Nathan looked at Loki as if seeking confirmation that Josh wasn't blowing things out of proportion, as usual.

"They're saying it's going to be the biggest race in over a century," Loki confirmed. "Tickets are already selling like crazy."

Nathan looked at Jessica.

Jessica smirked. "Yup, played him right into your little trap, didn't you, slick."

CHAPTER SEVEN

Nathan and Jessica followed the man, in the official Gunyoki Combat Racing Association jacket, through the GCRA headquarters on Rakuen. They had been summoned early in the morning, and the GCRA had sent an airship to the hotel's rooftop landing pad to pick them up.

"What's this all about?" Jessica asked the man they were following.

"I am sorry, but I'm afraid I really do not know," he replied. "I was simply instructed to escort you from the landing pad to the committee chambers."

They continued following him down the long corridor that crossed over the main lobby. The corridor was a clear, enclosed tube, passing between tall, four-story walls of transparent aluminum. At the far end of the corridor was a set of double doors, each adorned with the GCRA logo. Once they reached the end of the corridor, the doors swung open automatically, revealing a large meeting room. In the center of the room was a massive conference table able to seat at least fifty people. Around the perimeter of the room were three more tiers of seating, bringing the capacity of the room into the hundreds. Finally, on the walls hung the Gunyoki banners, similar to the ones that had hung everywhere on the Gunyoki racing platform.

"Welcome, Captain Scott," the man at the far end of the table greeted as he bowed. "I am Master Chiisun, leader of the Gunyoki. I believe you already know Mister Yokimah," he added, gesturing to the man on his right.

"A pleasure, sir," Nathan said, bowing. "Mister

Yokimah. Allow me to introduce my tactical officer, Lieutenant Commander Nash."

"An honor, Lieutenant Commander," Master Chiisun replied, bowing to her, as well.

"An unusual title, 'master'," Jessica commented. "What does it denote a mastery of, if I might ask?"

"I am a master of the Gunyoki Arts, having dedicated my life to the ways of the Gunyoki."

"Then, you're like the master of all of them?"

"No, I am one of sixteen Gunyoki masters. In my current position, I oversee all GCRA operations and events. That is why I have asked you here today. We have much to discuss."

"Of course," Nathan agreed.

"Please, be seated," Master Chiisun instructed, taking a seat himself. "This morning, we were informed of the challenge that has been made by you, and accepted by Mister Yokimah."

"It wasn't really a challenge," Nathan said. "It was more like a statement of opinion."

"Perhaps, but an invitation was made by Mister Yokimah for you to prove your statements through action, specifically to engage in a combat race with a Gunyoki."

"Captain Scott's statement was that the Gunyoki could not even stop *him*," Mister Yokimah stated. "This infers that Captain Scott was challenging *all* of the Gunyoki, not an individual pilot or ship."

Master Chiisun looked at Nathan. "Is Mister Yokimah's understanding of your meaning correct, Captain Scott?"

"It is," Nathan admitted. "However, I meant no disrespect, Master Chiisun. I was trying to make Mister Yokimah understand that the Gunyoki are no match for the Dusahn, whom I believe will eventually invade the Rogen system, just as they have invaded the systems of the Pentaurus cluster."

"Your intent is to get the Gunyoki to help you fight your battles," Mister Yokimah stated.

"My *intent* is to secure allies in my fight against the Dusahn," Nathan explained, "so that *all* the human-inhabited worlds of this quadrant can be free of the Dusahn, and any other threat which may come their way."

"The Gunyoki do not fight the wars of others," Master Chiisun stated plainly. "The Gunyoki exist only to protect Rakuen. They were formed during the Water Wars of our forefathers, and have remained a viable deterrent for many would-be aggressors for centuries. I would be inclined to agree with Mister Yokimah's assertion that the Gunyoki are capable of defending Rakuen, *should* the Dusahn make the mistake of attacking our world."

"With all due respect, Master Chiisun, I believe you are overestimating the capability of your defenses," Nathan warned. "*That* is the reason I made the statement, and *that* is the reason I chose to accept Mister Yokimah's wager."

"Which brings us to this meeting," Master Chiisun stated. "The Gunyoki Council cannot sanction a dogfight between an outsider and a Gunyoki, unless you choose to attack Rakuen, of course."

"I would most certainly prefer *not* to," Nathan assured him.

"There is another way for you to settle your wager, however," Master Chiisun continued. "While the Gunyoki Council frowns on the idea of turning over twelve Gunyoki warships to someone *not* of Rakuen, those warships *are* the legal property of Mister Yokimah, and we have no authority to stop him from turning them over to you, in the unlikely event that you should win them. However, we *do* control all Gunyoki operations within the Rakuen system. The only way we can see for you to fulfill the obligations of your wager is as an entrant in the upcoming Gunyoki races."

"You want me to fly a Gunyoki?" Nathan questioned. "Uh, I was thinking that I would fly one of our ships...perhaps one of our fighters."

"Was not your assertion that the Gunyoki lack the skills one can only attain in actual combat?" Mister Yokimah reminded him.

"Yes, but..."

"If this is the case, then *you*, as someone who has *been* in actual combat on *numerous* occasions, should have an edge, even in a ship with which you have little experience."

"But I have *no* experience in a Gunyoki," Nathan replied. "I only saw them for the first time a couple weeks ago."

"The point Captain Scott was trying to make was that superior weaponry and spacecraft are ineffective when operated by warriors without combat experience," Jessica explained, "and that someone *with* such experience could *beat* the Gunyoki with lesser weapons."

"If that is the case, then giving the captain a weapon of equal capability should improve his odds," Mister Yokimah argued.

"Not if he's never flown one," Jessica countered.

"Perhaps, if Captain Scott was given some instruction, and some experience?" Master Chiisun suggested.

Both Nathan and Jessica looked at Master Chiisun. "What?"

"Not all of the Gunyoki racers are corporate teams such as Mister Yokimah's," Master Chiisun explained. "Many are independents who are either privately funded or have managed to gather some sponsorships. All they need to compete is a Gunyoki ship that meets the requirements, the entry fee, and the ability to successfully complete a qualifying run."

"I have no such ship," Nathan replied.

"I would be more than happy to loan one to you, Captain," Mister Yokimah offered. "I'll even provide you with a maintenance chief to show your people how to maintain it."

"I know nothing of the Gunyoki racers," Nathan pointed out.

"I can provide you with an instructor, as well," Mister Yokimah added.

"No doubt some second-rate, washed-up..." Jessica stopped when she felt Nathan's elbow in her side.

"I assure you, Lieutenant Commander, that I will provide the best instruction available," Mister Yokimah promised. "After all, I wouldn't want it said that Captain Scott did not lose fairly, and of his own accord."

Jessica glared at Mister Yokimah, taking offense to the arrogant smirk that accompanied his last statement.

"If this is not acceptable to you, Captain, the Gunyoki Council is willing to disapprove the challenge, thus saving your honor," Master Chiisun offered.

Nathan looked at Mister Yokimah. "I thank you for the offer, Master Chiisun, but that will not be necessary, especially considering Mister Yokimah's gracious offer. I would be honored to compete in the Gunyoki races."

"You still have to qualify, first," Mister Yokimah reminded Nathan. "That, in itself, will be quite an accomplishment."

"Are you sure about this?" Master Chiisun asked Nathan. "The Gunyoki train for years before entering the races. You will have only days."

"A challenge, to be sure," Nathan admitted graciously, "but one I am willing to face."

"You are aware the Gunyoki face, and fire, live weapons?" Master Chiisun asked.

"I am."

"Very well, the challenge is approved," Master Chiisun stated. "Mister Yokimah, you will make available a Gunyoki racer, in good operational condition, and a chief mechanic to tutor Captain Scott's team in its maintenance. Furthermore, you will provide him with a flight instructor of the highest caliber. All of these things must be made available to Captain Scott as quickly as possible."

"I will see to it personally," Mister Yokimah said with a smile.

Master Chiisun turned to look at Nathan. "You are either a very brave man or a fool, Captain. Either way, I will be quite interested to learn which."

"Me, too," Nathan said under his breath to Jessica.

* * *

As expected, Suvan's first day on the job had consisted of orientations and safety seminars, as well as a general review of the operational plan to paint the Teyentah's hull with her final primer coat. During all of this, Suvan had quickly concluded that the paint boss, Tor Asken, took himself entirely too seriously. However, Suvan knew he was lucky to have gotten this far. Had he arrived on Takara even a week later, he might have missed this phase, and would not have gotten hired. Applying primer to the outside of the ship did not require any special talent, as everything that wasn't covered got painted the same.

But now, Suvan faced a new challenge as he wandered through the crawler bay looking for the hatch that led to his assigned unit, crawler four four two. Unfortunately, they were rarely in any logical order, as the digital displays above each hatch simply showed the identification number of the crawler that was attached to it on the other side.

Suvan had spent hours studying the crawler operations manual the night before, as he was expected to already be fully qualified to operate the tiny vessel. While the flight mechanics were basically the same as any spacecraft, its control inputs were quite different. Crawlers, when flown, were controlled entirely with the operator's feet, not a flight control stick and throttle. Although the models in use on the Teyentah were fully automated, and could get anywhere on the ship's surface with simply the push of a button, experienced operators rarely used automation on the job. Suvan needed to do the same, so as not to raise suspicion. He had already received a few double-takes from passersby who thought they recognized him. One man even asked his name, sure that he had seen his face somewhere before. The gruff facial hair and more common hairstyle Suvan had been cultivating since the Dusahn first invaded was helping to disguise his identity, but it was not enough. Only seven years had passed since the exile of House Navarro and the subsequent expungement from the rolls of nobility, so there were still people who remembered the Navarro name, as well as Suvan's face, many of them former citizens of the Navarro lands.

Four four two. Suvan stopped and turned toward the hatch, pressing the control panel. The hatch slid open, revealing a cramped airlock only a meter square, and two meters tall. Suvan stepped inside and pressed the button on the interior control panel, causing the inner hatch to close behind him. A moment later, the outer hatch opened, revealing the backside of crawler four four two, a meter away.

Suvan leaned forward and pressed the control pad on the crawler's hatch. There was a small hiss of pressurized air, after which the small hatch swung upward, coming to rest against the ceiling of the stubby little tunnel, connecting the airlock to the back of the crawler.

Suvan stepped into the tunnel, feeling the artificial gravity disappear as he left the airlock. There were cameras everywhere, and Suvan needed to look like he knew what he was doing. As he had rehearsed the night before, Suvan grabbed the rail suspended over his head on the inside of the hatch, pulled his feet up to form his body into a ball, then swung forward, inserting his feet through the tiny hatch and down into the bottom of the crawler. Once his feet were inside, he hooked his toes into the control pads and pulled himself slightly downward by bending his knees as much as the confines of the crawler's interior allowed. Bending at the waist and neck, he passed his head and body through the hatch, thankfully not hitting his head on the upper edge of the hatch, a sure sign of an inexperienced crawler operator.

Once inside, Suvan immediately activated the hatch, causing it to close behind him, sealing with another hiss of pressurized air. Once closed, the hatch formed the crawler's seat and backrest, allowing Suvan to properly secure himself to the unit. He quickly scanned the console, checking various buttons and switches according to the prestart checklist he had memorized the night before. Satisfied that the previous operator had shut the crawler down correctly, he turned on the master power switch and began the short startup routine.

Two minutes later, the crawler was ready to go. "C-Op, Crawler Four Four Two, ready to punch," he called over the comms as he tightened his restraints. While he waited for clearance, Suvan twisted his feet left and right, pulling the toes of the pedals up and down, finally raising and lowering the pedals themselves, all in a test of the crawler's flight controls.

"*Four Four Two, C-Op, negative,*" the controller replied. "*Incoming units. We'll move you to your work sector with booms. Sorry.*"

"Four Four Two, understood," Suvan replied, a wave of relief washing over him. Crawler row was tightly packed, and was probably the most dense area in the shipyard. It was the last place Suvan wanted to conduct his first crawler flight.

"*Four Four Two, you're number three,*" the controller informed him.

"Four Four Two is number three for the arm," Suvan replied, trying to sound like the calm, experienced crawler operator he was pretending to be.

What Suvan really found amusing was that he was far more nervous now than he had been going into battle for the first time. He wasn't sure if it was due to having only the thin, single-walled shell protecting him from the vacuum of space, or that his limited propellant supply meant that inefficient flying could leave him unable to get back to crawler row, thus requiring an arm to retrieve him, or worse yet, a rescue tug. Most likely, it was the fact that any of these would reveal him to be an impostor, which would surely stir Dusahn interest and eventually lead to his death.

Suvan took the extra time to look out the windows surrounding his head. On either side, crawlers were being plucked from their docked positions by large, spidery arms connected to tracked base trucks. Above him, and at least half a kilometer away, was the Teyentah herself, her dark gray base coat glistening from hundreds of lighting panels lining the assembly superstructure surrounding her.

Eventually, one of the arms came his way. At first, the grappler at the end of the arm looked as if it were coming toward his face, and would crash through this canopy and kill him, but at the last second, the arm lowered slightly and grabbed hold of the grappling point on the front of his crawler, in between his arm sleeves, causing a slight jolt.

"Four Four Two, good connect," Suvan reported as he pressed the docking release button to detach from crawler row. Another jolt as the docking clamps released their hold on his crawler's backside, and Suvan moved quickly away from the safety of crawler row, riding on one of the many limbs of the giant, mechanical spider that shifted crawlers, materials, and other items from place to place about the massive assembly bay.

The view outside was surreal, as more than

a dozen arms carried crawlers to and from the Teyentah, passing by one another in a seemingly choreographed, mechanical space-dance. At times, Suvan feared he would collide with crawlers being carried in the opposite direction, but they never came within a few meters of him. Just close enough to exchange a wave to the passing operator.

"Four Four Two," the controller called. *"Confirm paint load."*

"Four Four Two is carrying one thousand kilograms of P two seven," Suvan replied, noting his gauges.

"One K, P two seven, copy."

"C-Op, Four Four Two. Is there a problem?"

"Negative, Four Four Two. The last paint loader forgot to log your load. We had you down as two hundred kilograms, but your data link shows one K. We just wanted to be sure you were seeing the same, before we assigned you to a work sector."

"Understood."

"You'll be at two eight seven five to start," the controller told him. *"Probably move laterally from aft forward."*

"Sounds good," Suvan replied, mimicking the lingo he heard from the other, more experienced, crawler operators.

Suvan watched as the arm moved him under the Teyentah and up her starboard side, closing on her hull as he approached his assigned work sector. As he neared the hull, he activated his utility arms, causing all four of them to extend fully, with only a partial bend in their elbow joints. Seconds later, the magnetic pads on the ends of his utility arms made contact. "Four Four Two has mag lock at section two eight seven five," Suvan reported. "Ready to work."

"Copy that, Four Four Two. Releasing."

Suvan felt a small bump as the arm released its grip on his front, and slid down and away from him. He charged his painting system and then extended the applicator arm until it was only a few centimeters from the hull of the ship. Once he verified that the applicator arm was parallel to the hull surface, he used the utility arm to energize the area of the hull he was about to paint, and started the applicator pumps. The metal-infused paint, attracted by the magnetized area of the hull, flowed out of the applicator arm and adhered to the hull surface like magic, in a smooth, even coating.

Suvan had been lucky. An arm had taken him to his work sector, and the area he was working on was pretty much flat, with very few protrusions that would require either manual maneuvering of his crawler or a hand application operation. He needed to impress his foreman with his skill and professionalism. New hires always started outside, painting the ship. If they were good, they moved on to exterior assembly tasks. If they were very good, they sometimes got moved inside.

That was where Suvan needed to be... *Inside* the Teyentah.

* * *

"I still think you should have insisted on flying a Super Eagle," Jessica said as they entered Nathan's room.

"Insist on flying a ship I've never flown, to avoid flying a ship I've never flown?" Nathan wondered. "Yeah, that makes sense."

"You flew Eagles back at the academy. Isn't a Super Eagle just an Eagle with a jump drive and plasma cannons?"

"The only thing about the Super Eagle that's the same as an Eagle is its airframe," Nathan corrected. "Trust me, it wouldn't have been that much of an advantage."

"But a whole fucking race?" Jessica exclaimed as the door chimes sounded. She turned around and saw the image of Josh and Loki on the door view screen, and opened the door. "How many actual heats is that?"

"Seven or eight, I think."

"What's going on?" Josh asked as he and Loki entered the room.

"Nathan is going to compete in a Gunyoki race," Jessica exclaimed.

"Yeah, we already knew that," Josh replied.

"No, I mean the *whole* race," Jessica explained. "All eight rounds."

"What?"

"There are only six rounds maximum in the upcoming race," Loki corrected.

"I thought there were at least eight," Nathan said.

"The next race is a mid-month race," Loki explained. "Not as many entrants."

"What's a mid-month race?" Jessica wondered.

"Just like it sounds," Loki said. "In the middle of the month. The big races are at the top of the month. The ones in the middle of the month have about half as many entrants, so there aren't as many rounds." He looked at Nathan. "Am I to understand that you're going to be an entrant?"

"Yup," Nathan replied.

"What are you going to fly?"

"A Gunyoki."

"You don't have one," Loki reminded him.

"Yokimah is loaning me one," Nathan told him.

"And before anyone says, 'You don't know how to fly it,' they're sending along someone to teach me, and someone to teach us how to maintain it."

"Us?" Loki wondered.

"You should've asked them to let *me* fly it," Josh insisted.

"That would sort of defeat the purpose," Nathan told him.

"Can I fly second seat?" Josh begged.

"Actually, I was thinking that Loki would fly second seat."

"What?" Josh couldn't believe it.

"No offense, Josh. You're a great pilot, but Loki's much better with systems than you are."

"You've got a point there," Josh admitted.

"Captain, Gunyokis are not easy ships to fly," Loki began. "They are complex and have gimbaled engine nacelles that are used for both thrust vectoring and aiming the main cannons. They are a balance of power distribution and timing, harkening back to the days when reactors were not as popular, and the crew had to choose which systems would get power at any given moment."

"Yeah, I know," Nathan assured him, "I read up on it on the way back," he added, holding up a Rakuen data pad. "Yokimah gave me some homework. We don't get the ship until late tomorrow."

"Captain, we only have six and half days until the race."

"Then I have a lot of work to do, don't I?" Nathan replied.

"We should find a simulator," Josh suggested. "We can help you train…"

"No, I need you two to take the Ranni shuttles back to the Aurora."

"Captain..." Josh began to protest, before Nathan cut him off.

"I need you to tell Cameron and General Telles what's going on, and tell her to relocate the fleet to a position in the Rogen sector from which she can move between the fleet and here in a single jump."

"You want the Aurora here?" Loki wondered.

"Yes," Nathan replied. "I have a feeling there's more going on than we realize, and I'd feel a lot better if the Aurora was nearby, instead of several days away."

"But we can *help* you train," Josh insisted.

"After you update Cam and pass on my orders, take a Reaper and return as quickly as possible. And bring Vlad, Deliza, Marcus, Dalen, and Neli back with you. We need a crew for the races."

"And bring Telles and a squad of Ghatazhak," Jessica added. "We need security, and no one is better at tactics than Telles. He could be a big help with race tactics."

"Good thinking," Nathan agreed. He turned back to Josh and Loki. "You guys got all that?"

"Yes, sir," Loki replied.

"Max throttle, gentlemen," Nathan urged.

"You got it, Cap'n," Josh replied, turning to exit.

Loki just stood there, staring at Nathan.

"What?" Nathan wondered.

"Jesus, Captain. I can't believe you're going to try to race the Gunyoki."

"Yeah, neither can I," Nathan admitted as Loki turned to follow Josh out the door.

"Neither can I," Jessica said, flopping down on the couch. "I'm ordering lunch," she told Nathan. "You start studying."

* * *

Makani Koku sat patiently in the sitting room of Ito Yokimah's vacation home on the Isle of Jikura, just south of Rakuen's equator. It had been nearly a decade since he had spoken to his former employer, and it had come as a considerable surprise when his presence had been requested a few hours ago.

Normally, Makani would have ignored such a request. When he retired, he had completely disconnected himself from Rakuen society and media. These days, he rarely even connected to the net. His days were spent sleeping in, playing chonka with his friends in the park, and fishing for seoli in the evening surf. It was island life at its finest, and he had earned it.

Unfortunately, Ito Yokimah was the *reason* Makani could *afford* the island lifestyle. Although he had rightfully earned every credit to his name, he never would have had the opportunity to do so, had Mister Yokimah not given him a hand up when he had been at his lowest. Ito Yokimah had seen honor, where Makani had once believed there was none left. He had shown Makani that honor was not just in what a man did, but was also in what he *had done*. More importantly, he had taught Makani that even the most honorable men made mistakes, and that the truly great men learned from their mistakes and continued on. Were it not for Ito Yokimah, Makani would not likely be alive today, enjoying his retirement years, and reveling in the children and grandchildren that would carry on the Koku name.

Of course, Makani did not live in a home like the one in which he currently waited. Such homes were reserved for the wealthiest of Rakuen, like Ito Yokimah. They were not the homes of men of true honor and sacrifice, but rather of men who were willing to do what was necessary to achieve their goals. The honor code of the Gunyoki placed little value on fame, fortune, and power. Their code had been about tradition, dedication, and sacrifice. Gunyoki pledged their lives to the protection of Rakuen. Every moment of every day was spent in the service of that promise. Even now, after not having sat in a Gunyoki fighter for over two decades, Makani would gladly return if his world was threatened.

He only hoped that such a threat was not the reason for this visit with his former employer.

"Mak," Mister Yokimah greeted enthusiastically as he entered the room. "How have you been, old friend?" Ito reached out, embracing his former employee and trusted advisor. "You look quite well, for such an old man," he teased.

"I am in good health," Makani replied. "You look quite well yourself, Mister Yokimah."

"Mister Yokimah? Please, we have too much history together, you and I, for such proper forms of address." Mister Yokimah moved toward the wet bar. "May I offer you a drink, Mak?"

"No thank you, Ito."

Ito smiled. "That's better. So, tell me, how have you been? How is retirement treating you? Do you miss the excitement of the races?"

"I am enjoying the peace of island life," Makani replied. "And no, I do not miss the excitement of the races. Such addictions are the purview of young men, not old masters."

"Quite right, of course," Ito agreed, pouring his drink and taking a seat. "I trust you have been following the nets?"

"Normally, no," Makani told him. "However, I did

check them on the way over. I thought I might find a clue as to why you requested my presence."

"Then you have heard of this brash, young man's ridiculous assertions, I take it."

"I have," Makani confirmed, "although I would not be as quick to take them so lightly."

"No one is taking them lightly, Makani," Ito promised. "Of this, you can be certain. But remember, there are over five hundred Gunyoki on Rakuen…"

"Most of whom are an embarrassment to the code," Makani added, interrupting Ito. "And, more importantly, would be of little use in the defense of Rakuen."

"Still the same, old, traditional hardliner, huh Mak?" Ito laughed. "Of course, that is what I always liked about you… And so did the media, I might add." Ito sipped his beverage. "So, what do you think of all this? Should Captain Scott be allowed to race?"

"The races have been open to all for more than a decade now," Makani reminded Ito. "I believe you were one of the biggest proponents of that change."

"It was necessary, Makani, you know that. Interest was fading. The Gunyoki would have closed for good, and Rakuen would have lost her deterrent. The Nerameseans would have again come for our water, not to mention all the other rabble in the sector. You *know* that."

"So, for the good of Rakuen, we diluted the Gunyoki's effectiveness."

"We increased the number of Gunyoki fighters from thirty to over five hundred," Ito reminded him. "Was that not proof enough for you?"

"Quantity is a poor substitute for quality," Makani stated.

"Please, spare me your Gunyoki proverbs," Ito

chided. "Times are different, now. The jump drive has made the galaxy a much smaller place. Distance no longer serves as the protective buffer it once was, old friend."

"You may have been able to buy your way into the Gunyoki, Ito, but you cannot buy your way into the Rakuen Leadership Council. You must still be elected, or at least, that's how it was the last time I checked."

"Don't be so certain," Ito told him as he took another sip of his drink.

Despite the life debt Makani owed Ito Yokimah, he was quickly tiring of the man. "Perhaps you should get to the point of my visit?" he suggested.

"Excellent idea," Ito agreed. "Makani, I need you to teach Nathan Scott how to fly a Gunyoki fighter."

"You wish me to train your challenger how to defeat you?" Makani was confused. "Why would you want this?"

"There is no way that arrogant, young man is going to beat five racers and win the event," Ito insisted with a dismissive wave of his hand.

"From what I've read about him on the way over, he will beat the first few," Makani warned. "He already has more training and experience than most of the independents. Perhaps if, as I had suggested, you had kept the training requirements of the Gunyoki when you opened up the races to all, Captain Scott's odds would be more to your liking." Makani smiled, having enjoyed his last statement.

"Captain Scott *will* lose," Ito insisted. "But when he does, I want no one to be able to accuse me of not giving him a fair chance of success. *That* is why I want *you* to teach him. *You* were one of the *best*... not only as a pilot, but as an *instructor*, as well. If

Makani Koku trains Nathan Scott, no one will be able to say he did not get a fair chance. *No one* can say the race was rigged."

"An odd choice of words," Makani commented. "But I do see your point. Unfortunately, it makes little difference. I am retired, and I intend to stay as such."

"Makani, please," Ito begged. "It must be you."

"There are plenty of decent instructors out there," Makani argued.

"But none with your impressive credentials and reputation."

"And none that are so beholden to you," Makani replied.

"The fact that your own wealth is the result of my employment of you, back when no one else would hire you, should not be an issue, Makani," Ito insisted. "You repaid that favor tenfold, by not only winning many races for Team Yokimah, but for training other pilots who went on to make our team one of the top ten in the sport."

"*That* was always the difference between us, Ito," Makani pointed out. "To *you*, the Gunyoki races are a sport. To *me,* they are training exercises, meant to maintain the Gunyoki's ability to defend our world. Where I see lives, *you* have always seen *credits*, Ito."

"And yet, you continued to work for me for all those years," Ito reminded the old Gunyoki master. "Was it *really* just for lives?"

"The answer to that question only matters to myself," Makani replied.

"If the safety of Rakuen is what you hold dearest, then you *must* train Nathan Scott."

Makani looked suspiciously at his former employer. "I do not see the connection."

"If you do as I ask, I will push for the training requirements that you hold so dear."

"You said they would strangle the Gunyoki races."

"That was then, long before the jump drive. Our economy is booming, and more people can afford to attend the races. We are holding them twice-monthly now."

"Enforcing my training standards would slow down the enrollment," Makani reminded him.

"We would phase in the requirement over time," Ito explained. "Besides, we can afford it. The Gunyoki races are now the number one form of entertainment on all of Rakuen. And with the jump drive, we have people attending from all over the sector. Improving the quality of the pilots will only enhance the product that we offer, making it more exciting. Don't you see, Mak, you can finally get what you wanted. The *rebirth* of the Gunyoki, in all their former glory. And all you have to do to make it happen is teach one man how to fly a Gunyoki fighter."

"And if he surprises you, and wins the event?" Makani wondered.

"That's not going to happen," Ito insisted.

"But if it does?"

"I am not asking you to teach him how to *win*, Makani. I am only asking you to teach him how to *fly*."

Makani Koku, the last of the true Gunyoki, and the only Gunyoki master who refused to sell out for the profit and power the races offered, was being given a chance to resurrect all that the Gunyoki had lost, and all that he had once held dear.

How can I turn my back on such an opportunity?

* * *

"Loki wasn't kidding about the engine nacelles,"

235

Nathan said to Jessica as he sat on the sofa in his hotel room, studying the Gunyoki operations manual. "About eighty percent of its in-flight maneuvering is accomplished using them. Its attitude thrusters are generally used for docking. It's a wild system." When Nathan got no response from Jessica, he turned to look at her, sitting at the desk on the other side of the room. "What are you reading?"

"Everything I can find on the net about the history of the Gunyoki and their races," she replied. "Did you know the races weren't even a big thing until about forty years ago?"

"I did not," Nathan admitted as he continued to study.

"They were just regular military exercises, conducted once per month, so the Gunyoki could keep their skills up and maintain a level of deterrent that kept the Nerameseans from raiding their water," Jessica explained. "They nearly had to give it up due to some accident in which eight Gunyoki died." Jessica turned to look at Nathan. "Did you know they're not even a military organization?"

"I did not."

"They were originally just a bunch of wealthy men who funded the construction of their own fighters to defend their world during the Water Wars with Neramese. Their ships were handed down from father to son over the centuries, continuing to participate in the monthly training exercises until the accident. That's when the Rakuen government stopped funding the Gunyoki."

Nathan realized that she wasn't going to stop, and put down his data pad. Truth was, he needed a break, anyway, and her diversion was at least along the same lines. "How did they become such a big thing, then?"

"Get this," Jessica began enthusiastically. "Ito Yokimah proposed turning the training exercises into racing events, using attendance and viewing revenue to fund the ongoing Gunyoki operations *without* using government funds. But, apparently, the Gunyoki objected to the idea of turning their training into a spectacle, primarily because the proposal required lifting the training requirements to become a Gunyoki."

"Why did they decide to lift the training requirements?" Nathan wondered.

"To be successful, they needed more entrants. So, instead of requiring years of extensive training, they changed it to simply being able to pass a flight test, which was something that anyone with enough aptitude for spaceflight could learn to do using a simulator."

"So, all they had to do was fly a simulator, and then they could race?" Nathan questioned.

"No, you can *learn* on the simulator, but you still have to pass a flight test in the real thing before you can race," Jessica explained. "Yokimah even started a loan program that enabled newly certified Gunyoki race pilots to purchase their own Gunyoki racer."

"So, any fool with a Gunyoki rating gets an armed fighter? That's insane," Nathan exclaimed.

"Not really. Yokimah thought of that, as well," Jessica continued. "The power levels of your weapons systems are controlled by the Gunyoki Council. During races, your weapons only have the power necessary for that level of the race. As you advance, so do the power levels of your weapons."

"Then, if they had to *really* defend Rakuen, their weapons would have full power," Nathan surmised.

"Precisely."

"I have to give it to Yokimah," Nathan said. "It was a pretty good plan."

"It's how he became so rich and powerful," Jessica added.

"I thought his money came from manufacturing water purification systems," Nathan said.

"It does now, but back then, he was just a junior executive at a banking firm. Somehow, he managed to get the funding he needed to make his idea work and to start his own racing team. His team has won more Gunyoki championships than all the other teams combined."

Nathan shook his head in disbelief. "Something doesn't track here," he said. "Why would he bet *all* his ships?"

"Because he's sure you're going to lose?" Jessica said with a grin.

"Thanks," Nathan replied, noting her sarcasm. "Although you could be right, I don't think that's it. Yokimah doesn't strike me as the type to take such risks."

"You saw the size of his office," Jessica said. "I'm sure he can afford to buy new racers."

"You're probably right," Nathan admitted, "but I still think there's more to it. Ito Yokimah is not the type of man who *likes* to lose, especially in such a public fashion, even if he *can* afford it."

"Well, he gets a full third of the profits generated by the races, so he stands to make a bundle, *regardless* of whether he wins or loses," Jessica explained. "I'd call that pretty good motivation. Hell, he'll probably make enough to buy a hundred racers."

Nathan sighed. "You don't risk *that* much, just for profit," Nathan insisted. "Not men like Ito Yokimah," he added, returning to the sofa and picking up his data pad. As he sat, the view screen on the wall came to life, displaying the image of one of the hotel staff.

"*You have an incoming call,*" the voice announced.

"Accept call," Nathan instructed, facing the view screen. "Hello."

"*My apologies for the intrusion, Captain Scott,*" the hotel staff member on the view screen said. "*You have numerous messages, but in particular, one from Miss Hia Donti, from the Rakuen National News Service. I have examined her credentials and find them to be authentic.*"

"Did she leave contact information?"

"*Indeed, she did, sir.*"

"Why notify me of *this* message, and none of the others?" Nathan wondered.

"*This was the first one from a well-known, well-respected agency,*" the staff member explained. "*I thought you might be interested. I can connect you, if you wish.*"

"One moment please," Nathan told the staff member. "Mute call." Nathan turned to Jessica. "What do you think?"

"I think the less attention you draw to yourself, the better," Jessica replied.

"I thought the purpose of getting me involved in the rebellion was to use my reputation to legitimize it and help with recruitment. This could be our chance to do exactly that."

"It could also be our chance to attract the attention of people we'd rather not notice us," Jessica argued.

"I'm pretty sure we're passed that point already," he told her. "Continue call," he instructed, turning

239

back toward the view screen. "Please send the contact information to my room terminal, along with all the other messages, if you will. I'll contact Miss Donti myself."

"*As you wish, sir.*"

The image on the view screen disappeared, and the contact information, transferred to the room terminal, displayed for a few moments to confirm that the data was now available to him.

"Miss Donti probably slipped her a few credits to push her message to you," Jessica warned.

"Probably," Nathan agreed. "That doesn't mean she's not legit, though. It just means she's determined."

Jessica sighed in resignation. "Well, if you're going to do the interview, we'd better review what you're going to say, first."

"I'd rather just wing it," Nathan insisted.

"Bad plan, Nathan. Very bad plan."

* * *

"*XO, Sensors,*" the intercom on the captain's ready room announced.

"XO, go ahead," Cameron replied.

"*Two contacts just jumped in. Ranni shuttles.*"

"What about the Reaper?" Cameron asked.

"*Just the two contacts, sir.*"

"*XO, Comms,*" another voice interrupted. "*Flash traffic...*"

It was too late. Cameron was already out of her seat and headed for the hatch.

"XO on the bridge!" the guard at the door announced as Cameron stepped through the hatch onto the Aurora's bridge.

"What's the traffic?" Cameron inquired from the comms officer as she passed the comms station, and came to stand next to Lieutenant Commander Vidmar at the tactical station.

"Mister Sheehan, sir," the comms officer replied. "He and Josh are piloting the shuttles. He is requesting that you meet him in the hangar deck."

"Did he say anything else?"

"Negative, sir. But he did use the flash traffic hail, and he sounded urgent."

"Any other contacts?" she asked.

"Negative, sir," Lieutenant Commander Vidmar replied. "Threat board is clear, and long-range patrols have no contacts."

"How long until they land?" Cameron asked.

"They're on final now," the lieutenant commander replied.

"You've got the conn, Lieutenant Commander," Cameron ordered as she turned and headed for the exit. "I'll be on the main hangar deck."

"Aye, sir," the lieutenant commander acknowledged as he exchanged glances with Lieutenant Commander Kono at the sensor station. "This does not bode well," he said to himself as Cameron left the bridge.

Cameron moved quickly aft, turning left then right, and then down the main ramp to the flight deck below. It took all of a minute and a half for her to get from the bridge to the main hangar deck at no more than a brisk walk. She didn't like the urgency of the situation; nor did she like not knowing what was going on. But there was a reason Loki had not broadcast an update over comms, and there was also a reason he requested to speak to her as soon as possible.

Cameron entered the flight deck, heading immediately aft, across the cavernous hangar, toward the smaller transfer airlocks at the far end.

By the time she got halfway across the massive deck, the first Ranni shuttle was rolling through the airlock doors.

The small, odd-looking, rounded shuttle cleared the airlock door and turned to the right, rolling forward to provide room for the other Ranni shuttle waiting to cycle through the airlock, as well. Before it could come to a stop, the shuttle's hatch split laterally across its middle and opened up like a clamshell. As the shuttle rolled to a stop and its systems cycled down, Loki came quickly down the air stair, jumping the last half meter to the deck, obviously in a hurry.

"Captain," he called to Cameron as he walked toward her.

"What's going on, Loki?" Cameron asked. "Where are Nathan and Jessica?"

"They're still on Rakuen, Captain," Loki replied.

"Why?" Cameron asked, pretty sure she wasn't going to like the answer.

"You're not going to believe this, but Nathan's going to fly in a Gunyoki race."

"Again, I have to ask...why?"

"He made a bet with... I can explain it all in detail later, but first, I have to pass Nathan's orders on to you."

Cameron was beginning to get nervous. "And they are?"

"He wants you to move the fleet to the Rogen sector, immediately, so the Aurora can go to Rakuen."

"Did you tell her?" Josh yelled from the boarding hatch of his shuttle as it came to a stop behind Loki's shuttle.

"Of course, I told her!" Loki replied, somewhat annoyed.

"Did you tell her what he bet?" Josh asked.

"I was getting to that..."

"Maybe we should go someplace else to talk about this," Cameron suggested.

"Can we get something to eat first?" Josh begged. "We didn't have a chance to pick up any snacks before we took off."

"But you've got to get the fleet moving first, Captain," Loki insisted.

"It's not like I can snap my fingers and get them all to jump to the same place," Cameron reminded him. "But I will get the process started," she assured him. "Meet me in the command briefing room in fifteen minutes."

"You might want to have General Telles and Deliza there, as well," Loki suggested.

"And Vlad," Josh added.

"General Telles is on the Glendanon right now," Cameron told them. "Better make it thirty minutes."

"Yes, sir," Loki replied.

Cameron tapped her comm-set as she headed back forward, walking alongside Josh and Loki. "Helm, XO. Plot a fleet jump course for the Rogen sector and feed it to all ships. We're jumping as soon as the fleet is ready."

"*Helm, aye.*"

* * *

"*Good afternoon, Rakuen. I'm Hia Donti. Joining us today from a remote location on Rakuen is Captain Nathan Scott, otherwise known as the savior 'Na-Tan' from the Legend of Origins. As many of you may know, Captain Scott led the rebellion against the Takaran Empire, defeating the forces of Caius Ta'Akar, and liberating all the worlds of the Pentaurus cluster. He then returned to the Sol sector and drove their enemy,*"

*known as the Jung, from not only Earth, but from all
the original core worlds of humanity. Those worlds
now enjoy a tenuous peace, made possible only by
Captain Scott's sacrifices. Captain Scott, welcome to
Rakuen."*

"Thank you, Miss Donti," Nathan replied politely
toward the view screen in his hotel room.

*"The question on everyone's mind is obvious. Why
have you chosen to enter the Gunyoki races?"*

Nathan took a deep breath, pretending to
contemplate the answer, despite the fact that he had
already rehearsed it with Jessica several times over.
"There are two reasons, actually. The first is simple:
we need the Gunyoki ships to fight the Dusahn."

"In the Pentaurus cluster?"

"Correct," Nathan confirmed.

*"We, on Rakuen, were under the impression that
the Pentaurus cluster was part of the Sol-Pentaurus
Alliance. Shouldn't the Alliance be providing forces
against the Jung?"*

"Technically, yes," Nathan explained. "However,
since the assassination of Casimir Ta'Akar, the
rightful heir to House Ta'Akar, and the true leader
of Takara, the relationship between the Sol and
Pentaurus sectors has suffered to the point of only a
formality. In addition, the Sol sector believes that it
faces a renewed threat from the Jung Empire."

*"The empire to which your surrender secured a
peace?"*

"Yes. Unfortunately, the Jung Empire is still
quite strong, and has considerably more ships than
the Alliance."

*"But they don't have jump drive technology yet, do
they?"*

"To our knowledge, they do not. And that is

providing the edge the Alliance needs to maintain control, for the time being. Unfortunately, this means the people of *this* quadrant are left to deal with the Dusahn threat on our own."

"*You use the term 'our',*" Miss Donti pointed out. "*Do you consider yourself a citizen of this quadrant, and not of Earth?*"

"I have been living in this quadrant, under an alias, for the last five years. So, yes, I do consider this area of the galaxy my home. And I am willing to fight for it, as well. Which brings me to my second reason for entering the race."

"*Which is?*"

"To demonstrate to those on Rakuen who believe the Gunyoki can protect them from the Dusahn, that they are sadly mistaken."

Hia Donti looked skeptical. "*Captain Scott, the Gunyoki have protected Rakuen for over three hundred years, during which time we have enjoyed a level of peace that is unprecedented in this quadrant.*"

"I understand that," Nathan assured her.

"*Do you realize the Gunyoki accomplished this with fewer than fifty ships, and that they now number over five hundred?*"

"I do."

"*Then how can you possibly think they are incapable of protecting Rakuen from the Dusahn who, I should add, are more than three hundred light years away and, by our understanding, have neither the ability, nor the desire to attack the Rogen system.*"

"Because I know the Jung," Nathan replied.

"*But the Jung are nearly thirteen hundred light years away from the Rogen sector.*"

"The *Dusahn* are merely a rogue caste of the Jung Empire, exiled centuries ago to wander space in search of an empire of their own. The only thing that kept them from being a threat to anyone was the limitations of linear FTL systems. Now, with jump drives, they are a threat that you cannot imagine."

"Captain, many Rakuens believe the best way to protect ourselves from the Dusahn is to pose no threat to them. In fact, many believe the Dusahn would be just as willing to accept us as allies, since their own forces are limited."

"For the moment," Nathan pointed out. "What happens when their forces have doubled, or tripled?"

"That could take decades," Miss Donti said.

"The Takaran and Corinairan industrial bases are capable of doubling the Dusahn forces in as little as five years," Nathan insisted. "And when they do, they will expand their empire as they see fit."

"But would not an alliance with the Dusahn protect us from that expansion?" Miss Donti suggested.

"It would not," Nathan replied.

"How can you be sure?"

"I cannot," Nathan admitted. "But I *am* sure of several things. The Dusahn have no respect for human life. They have no respect for the rights of others. They wiped out an entire civilization simply because the representatives of that civilization failed to show the Dusahn leader the proper respect. I have personally witnessed the Dusahn wipe out all life on Burgess, simply because a small force, one that had never made an aggressive move toward the Dusahn, had the *potential* to be a threat. They did not attack that military force exclusively, even though they could have easily done so. They glassed the entire planet. Only a couple thousand escaped, and they are now under the protection of myself and the Karuzari. So, you see, Miss Donti, the Dusahn, just like the Jung from which they came, cannot be trusted."

"If that is the case, then what would you have us do, Captain Scott?"

Jessica smiled from off camera. Hia Donti had set Nathan up perfectly, and without even being asked.

"Ally yourselves with the Karuzari," Nathan said. "Help us drive the Dusahn *out* of the Pentaurus sector, and *out* of this quadrant of the galaxy."

"That's an awfully big request," Miss Donti said. *"Especially from a people who have enjoyed peace for so long."*

"Indeed, it is," Nathan agreed. After taking a breath, he continued. "I was once a student of Earth history," he explained. "One of my favorite quotes, from long before the bio-digital plague nearly wiped out humanity and sent us fleeing to the stars, was this: 'The only thing necessary for the triumph of evil is for good men to do nothing.' You see, Miss Donti, it is easy to say that peace is the answer. It is easy to believe in the goodness of humanity. But the truth is, humanity is an ugly beast, ready to pounce on the unsuspecting and the weak. Peace, like that which Rakuen has been lucky enough to enjoy for all these years, requires effort. It requires those *good men* to stand ready to respond when humanity shows its dark side. Your Gunyoki were once those good men, and likely still are. But if they fail to respond to such an obvious threat, your peace will be lost, and it is always more difficult, and more costly in lives, to take that peace back again. *That* is why I am here, and *that* is why I have challenged the Gunyoki. My intent is not to mock them, but to inspire them to do exactly what they were designed to do...to rise up and meet the danger that looms on their horizon."

247

Miss Donti was silent for a moment. Unfortunately, like the seasoned journalist she was, she changed direction, catching Nathan off guard. *"Captain Scott, everyone once believed you were dead. In fact, many witnessed your burial on Earth, which, I might add, was an open-casket ceremony. Can you explain how that is possible?"*

"Quite easily," Nathan replied, without missing a step.

No, Jessica thought. She even started shaking her head from off camera.

"My body died on the Jung homeworld, but only after my consciousness, memories, and everything that makes me Nathan Scott, was copied into a holding device to be transferred later into a clone of my original body."

Seasoned journalist or not, Hia Donti appeared stunned. *"Are you saying you're a clone?"*

"My body is, yes."

Oh......my......God, Jessica thought.

* * *

"He did what?" Deliza exclaimed, nearly jumping out of her seat.

"I'm sure he had good reason," Yanni insisted, trying to calm his wife down.

"Why is everyone so worried?" Vladimir wondered.

"I don't understand," Abby said. "What's made at this plant?"

"Jump shuttles," Yanni told Abby. "It's probably Ranni Enterprise's biggest revenue stream."

"It's our *only* revenue stream, now that the Dusahn have taken over the Pentaurus sector," Deliza reminded him. "If we lose that plant, how are we going to continue to fund the Karuzari?"

"He will win," Vladimir insisted.

"We have plenty of credits in reserve," Yanni reminded her.

"That's not going to go as far as you might think," Deliza warned. "A few months, at the most."

"I believe the captain's logic is sound," General Telles commented.

"You think betting our only revenue stream is a sound one," Deliza said in disbelief. "Where are we going to get shuttles if we lose the plant?"

"While your shuttles are a very efficient design, they will not win this war for us," General Telles stated. "Besides, they are not free. You still have to pay for them."

"I'm telling you, he will win," Vladimir repeated.

"I'm not following you," Cameron admitted.

"If Captain Scott loses, we can still purchase whatever shuttles we need. But even if he loses, as long as he does well, he will likely win the respect of many on Rakuen. While it may not sway public opinion enough to choose to openly support us, it will likely bring us quite a few volunteers, quite possibly even a few Gunyoki, as well. And if he *wins*, then at the very least, we will get twelve warships that, once fitted with jump drives, will be quite formidable against the Dusahn."

"Are twelve Gunyoki worth risking our only revenue stream?" Abby wondered.

"Is no one listening to me?" Vladimir wondered. "Nathan *will* win."

"Deliza's assessment of her ability to fund this rebellion is correct," the general admitted. "However, if we have not beaten the Dusahn by then, it is quite probable that we'll no longer be alive, and thus the lack of funds will be of little concern."

"Why do you all have such little faith in him?"

Vladimir demanded to know. "Nathan would not have made such a challenge if he did not believe he could win!"

Everyone became quiet, staring at Vladimir, since it wasn't like him to yell in the middle of a meeting.

"How can you be so sure?" Cameron asked Vladimir directly.

"I have played poker with Nathan, *many* times. He never bets more than he can afford to lose. And the more he bets, the more likely he is to have a *very* good hand. Nathan *must* have a card up his sleeve to bet this much."

"I would have to agree with Commander Kamenetskiy's assessment," General Telles announced. "It is in line with Nathan's character, *and* his tactical style."

Cameron looked at Loki. "You know more about these races than any of us. What does Nathan have to do to win?"

"Basically, he has to win a minimum of four matches to get into the final round," Loki explained.

"What happens in the final round?" Deliza wondered.

"First, the number two and three ships battle it out. The victor then faces the number one ship to determine the winner of the event."

"What do you mean by 'battle it out?'" Cameron asked.

"The first two rounds are a race course laced with targets you have to take out while trying to beat the other guy to the finish line," Loki explained. "In the third and fourth rounds, those targets start shooting back, which means you have to use your shields to avoid taking damage that costs you both time and points. But in the final rounds, you are flying the course, trying to take out automated defenses that are firing at you, *and* you have to fight with the ship you are competing against. At the end of the course, the two ships are vectored away from each other, and then back to meet head on in the dogfighting arena, where they 'battle it out.'"

"Is it dangerous?" Abby wondered.

"Very," Loki replied.

"I heard the Gunyoki used low-power weapons," Deliza said.

"Compared to the ones used in actual combat, yes," Loki confirmed. "But there is still plenty of risk. Someone is injured in nearly every event, and a Gunyoki pilot dies at least once every season."

"That's the whole point of it," Josh added. "They're trying to simulate actual combat, including the threat of death. It's exciting as all hell."

"Not my idea of entertainment," Abby commented.

Cameron sighed. "I'd feel more comfortable if Josh was doing the flying."

"Thanks," Josh said, "I think."

"You know what I mean," Cameron insisted.

"That's why I said thanks... I think."

"It's not like he's going to be completely on his own," Loki pointed out. "It takes two to operate a Gunyoki fighter; a pilot *and* a weapons operator. You are also allowed a controller and a tactician, both of whom are in communication with the flight crew throughout the race. Captain Scott asked me to be his weapons operator, and Josh to be his controller."

"Who did he want as his tactician?" Cameron wondered.

"General Telles," Loki replied. "I brought all the data about the Gunyoki races, including ship specs, course layouts, targets and defenses, and the details of every race flown over the last twenty years. I also brought several books on Gunyoki combat tactics. I figured we're all going to need them."

"Us all?" Cameron asked.

"He also needs support crew. Technicians, computer programmers and engineers, mechanics... Our fighter will take damage during the race. Someone has to be able to fix it before the next heat, or we will be disqualified."

"I'll pack my things," Vladimir announced.

"He wants Marcus, Dalen, and Neli to come, as well," Josh said.

"They're still working on the Seiiki," Cameron said. "They're installing stealth emitters on her."

"Whose bright idea was *that*?" Josh wondered.

"Mine," Cameron stated.

Josh just shut up.

"How long before they're finished?" General Telles asked.

"Three days," Vladimir replied, "*if* we get more of my people to help them."

"It will take us five days to get the fleet moved all the way to the Rogen sector, and then to Rakuen ourselves," Cameron explained. "As soon as they finish with the Seiiki, we'll have them take her to Rakuen ahead of us."

"That's going to be cutting it close," Loki warned.

"Can't be helped," Cameron stated. "I don't like the idea of the Seiiki sitting on deck, half-finished."

"I *guarantee* you that Marcus doesn't like it," Vladimir added.

* * *

"*My body died on the Jung homeworld, but only after my consciousness, memories, and everything that makes me Nathan Scott, was copied into a holding device, to be transferred later into a clone of my original body."*

"Are you saying you're a clone?"

"My body is, yes."

Lord Dusahn pressed the remote, pausing the playback as a sinister smile came across his face. "This just came in?"

"From one of our informants on Rakuen," General Hesson replied. "It was broadcast just a few hours ago."

"And when is this race to take place?"

"In seven Rakuen days, my lord. Approximately five point seven Takaran days."

"Barely enough time to get one of our ships to the Rogen sector," Lord Dusahn surmised.

"Can we afford to take such a risk, my lord?" General Hesson wondered. "The Gunyoki *are* formidable fighters, and the Rakuens have more than five hundred of them."

"Can we afford *not* to take the risk?" Lord Dusahn said. "If Nathan Scott will be racing in the Rogen system, then surely the Aurora will be nearby. To rid ourselves of both, or better yet, to capture them... We would then stand unopposed, free to take over the entire quadrant."

"While I see the logic of your plan, and I *do* feel its temptation, I am obligated to remind you that our forces are hard-pressed to maintain control over the worlds we have *already* seized. I *also* feel obligated to point out the *danger* of making an enemy of the Rakuen, *especially* before we are able to add to our forces."

Lord Dusahn thought for a moment. "Transfer twenty heavy fighters from my ship to the Jar-Morenzo, then dispatch her and four gunships to the

Rogen sector. Position them within striking distance of Rakuen."

"The Jar-Morenzo is slower and will barely have enough time to make it to Rakuen," General Hesson warned.

"You are the one who is worried about risking our forces in the Rogen sector," Lord Dusahn reminded the general. "Would you prefer that I send one of our newer ships? The ones better able to defend the Pentaurus cluster?"

"The Jar-Morenzo may not have the firepower to defeat the Rakuen, my lord."

"They do not need to *defeat* the Rakuen," Lord Dusahn told him. "They merely need to defeat the Aurora and kill, *or capture*, Nathan Scott."

CHAPTER EIGHT

"Marcus!" Vladimir called from the bottom of the Seiiki's cargo ramp. He was holding a duffel bag and pulling a cart full of various tools and technical equipment.

"*He's under the port side,*" Neli replied from inside the cargo bay.

Vladimir dropped his duffel and parked his cart, bending over to look underneath the Seiiki as he moved around to her port side. "Marcus!" he shouted again, spotting a pair of stout legs hanging down from an opening between the port engine nacelle and the main body of the ship. "Marcus!" he called again as he moved closer.

"*What?*" Marcus replied, his voice muffled by the compartment around him.

"I need to tell you something."

Marcus lowered himself down, obviously annoyed. "If you're coming to tell me that I have to finish upgrading the Seiiki on my own, I already know."

"You do?"

"Josh was by ten minutes ago," Dalen said as he climbed down from the topside of the ship.

"You are not angry at me?"

"At you? No," Marcus said. "You're not the one who decided to do something as stupid as challenging the Gunyoki to a race. Now, *Nathan? Him*, I'm angry at."

"I have assigned four more engineers to help you. They are young and somewhat inexperienced, but they learn quickly," Vladimir promised. "Just try not to scare them."

"No promises," Marcus grumbled as he worked.

"Marcus..." Vladimir scolded.

Marcus squatted down low, turning to look under the fuselage at Vladimir. "What the hell are you still doing here?" he barked. "Go and keep Nathan from killing himself, already!"

"I'll see you in three days!" Vladimir said as he turned to depart.

"No, you won't," Dalen declared. "Cuz we'll be all *stealthy* and shit."

Marcus stood back up, inserting his upper body back into the underside of the ship. *"Most likely, we'll be in pieces...about six or seven of them, I'd guess."*

Vladimir scurried out from under the Seiiki, grabbing his duffel and tool cart again, and headed quickly toward the Reaper waiting fifteen meters away.

"Finally!" Deliza declared as Vladimir approached. "What took you so long?"

"I had to gather a few things," Vladimir replied. "Put all this in the aft bay," he instructed one of the deck crew.

"Yes, sir."

"Everyone's aboard," Deliza told him. "We were just waiting for you," she added, leading him to the side hatch just aft of the forward port engine nacelle.

Vladimir waited for Deliza to climb up into the Reaper and then climbed in himself. *"Bozhe moi,"* he declared as he looked inside. The interior was nearly full. Deliza and Yanni were sitting opposite the door. Next to them was General Telles, along with four Ghatazhak soldiers, all of them dressed in civilian attire, but looking just as deadly and serious, as usual.

"Button up back there!" Loki yelled from the cockpit.

Vladimir pressed the button to close the hatch,

then turned to sit down. "You're coming with us?" he asked, spotting Abby in the seat next to his.

"Since you'll be dealing with new technology, I thought you could use a physicist," Abby said, her voice dripping with sarcasm.

"Oh, wonderful," Vladimir replied in similar tone.

* * *

Nathan and Jessica stood in front of the Gunyoki Museum. The building was dark, like every other building at the waterfront. "It's closed."

"No kidding," Jessica replied. "Everything's closed. The driver must've thought we were crazy to come down here this early."

Nathan turned to look out across the vast ocean on the other side of the street. The Rakuen sun had just started to rise from the watery horizon, sending shimmering reds and oranges across the cresting waves. "This is where the message said to meet him."

"Are you sure it wasn't a prank?" Jessica wondered. "The old fart could be sitting at home, laughing."

"If he's still at home, he's probably sleeping like everyone else," Nathan surmised.

"That's what *we* should be doing," Jessica agreed, peering through the windows into the dark lobby. "Wait, someone is coming."

Nathan turned to look in the window as a young man came to the front doors from deep within the darkened lobby of the museum.

"Captain Scott?" the young man asked as the doors opened.

"There's no way you're the guy we're supposed to meet, right?"

"No, I am not, but I will take you to him."

"He's *here* already?" Jessica asked, surprised.

"For some time now. If you will please follow me."

"Well, someone's an early riser," Jessica said as she and Nathan entered the museum, following the young man.

They crossed the dimly lit lobby, entering the main pavilion on the other side. The pavilion itself was massive and contained many different fighter spacecrafts, each of them hanging from cables attached to the ceiling, poised at differing angles of display as if they were in flight and maneuvering. A maze of winding walkways rose from the floor of the pavilion from various points, each of them rising up and snaking around and between the various ships, providing views from every imaginable angle.

They continued deeper into the pavilion, toward floor displays of various uniforms, flight suits, helmets, and other gear associated with the Gunyoki. At the center of the displays was a collection of simulation booths, and standing in front of them was an old man with long, gray whiskers, bound neatly into a point at about the middle of his chest. The old man's hair was tied back in similar fashion, and he wore the blue and yellow jacket of a Gunyoki warrior, adorned with numerous patches that spoke of his countless victories.

The young man leading them came to a stop, bowing respectfully to the old man in the center of the pavilion. The old man bowed back, although in a far less pronounced fashion, as if accepting the payment of respect from the much younger man.

The young man turned to face Nathan and Jessica, standing beside the old man. "Captain Scott, I present Gunyoki master, Makani Koku."

"Holy crap," Jessica mumbled, only half to herself.

"Holy crap?" the old Gunyoki master asked.

"She means to say, 'It is an honor to make your acquaintance,' Mister Koku."

"The correct term, is *Master* Koku."

"My apologies, Master Koku," Nathan replied. "May I introduce my chief tactical officer, Lieutenant Commander Jessica Nash."

"A pleasure," Master Koku said, bowing his head in respect. "It is rare to see one so lovely in such a dangerous profession. You are surely an amazing, young woman to hold such a position."

"Uh, thanks." Jessica looked at Nathan. "Do you know who he is?"

"Uh, yeah...he just introduced himself."

"This guy...I mean, Master Koku, has racked up more simulated kills, and won more races, than any Gunyoki in the history of Rakuen. He was a Gunyoki for *forty years.*"

"I am still Gunyoki," Master Koku corrected. "Gunyoki cannot cease being Gunyoki, any more than a tocan can cease being a tocan."

"What's a tocan?" Jessica wondered.

Master Koku gave her an odd look.

"A dog, right?" Nathan said, recognizing the Rakuen term.

Again, Master Koko looked puzzled.

"It doesn't matter," Nathan insisted. "I don't mean to sound ungrateful, Master Koku, but how was I lucky enough to get *you* as my instructor?"

"When the impossible must be accomplished, one naturally enlists the help of someone who is known for accomplishing the impossible," Master Koku stated.

"Mister Yokimah?"

"He is a difficult man to refuse," Master Koku admitted.

"Tell me about it," Nathan remarked. He looked around the pavilion, gazing at the ships all around him. "This place is amazing," Nathan exclaimed. "Are these *all* Gunyoki fighters?"

"Every model since the beginning of the Water Wars between Rakuen and Neramese," Master Koku explained. "The Gunyoki were once the protectors of Rakuen. Men who worked normal jobs, went home to normal families, lived normal lives. But when their peaceful world was threatened, they used their own money to build their ships, and they spent every spare moment training themselves to fly them. The Gunyoki have kept Rakuen safe for generations, and all they have ever asked for in return was simple respect."

"And here I thought they were just a bunch of race pilots," Jessica said under her breath.

"The *races* are a relatively recent development," Master Koku stated.

"Oh, you heard that?" Jessica was suddenly embarrassed.

"I am old, not deaf."

"Right."

"Are all the people in your service so brash and outspoken?" Master Koku wondered.

"The lieutenant commander is a special case," Nathan assured him. "She takes some getting used to, but she's worth it."

"Gee, thanks," Jessica said. "You know, I didn't want to drag my ass down here at zero dark thirty. Maybe I'll just go over there and take a nap while you teach my CO how to fly one of these things, so he doesn't kill himself next weekend."

Master Koku smiled. "I like her."

"Why *did* you have us come down here so early?"

Nathan asked, hoping to steer the conversation away from Jessica's insubordinate attitude and her sleep-deprived lack of respect for everyone, and everything, on Rakuen.

"To test your level of commitment," Master Koku replied.

"Seriously?" Jessica asked, her face somewhat contorted in disbelief.

"Actually, I wanted to conclude our business here before the museum opened and the crowds became a distraction," Master Koku explained. "The commitment thing was my subtle attempt at humor."

"Very subtle," Jessica smirked.

"You brought us down here before sunrise to look at old Gunyoki fighters?" Nathan wondered. "Couldn't we have just looked at pictures?"

"Indeed, we could have. But I was more interested in these." Master Koku turned to the side, gesturing toward the collection of simulator booths behind him, at the center of the pavilion.

"Simulators?" Nathan said.

"Precisely."

Nathan walked over and peeked into one of the booths. "But these are just toys," he commented, "games, like the ones we saw at the racing platform. Surely you have something more advanced than this?"

"Prove to me that you can fly a toy, and *then* I will take you to a *real* simulator," Master Koku stated in a calm, yet firm, tone.

"Couldn't we just skip straight to the advanced sims?" Jessica suggested. "It's not like we have time to waste."

"Nor do I," Master Koku agreed. "And if training your CO is a waste of *my* time, I'd prefer to find out now, while I still have time to return home and go seoli fishing."

"Seoli fishing," Jessica laughed. "If you weren't a living legend..."

Master Koku looked confused for a moment, then turned back to Nathan. "Please, Captain, indulge an old man, if only for a moment."

Nathan took a deep breath, letting it out in a long sigh. "Of course, Master Koku. I put myself in your hands," he added with a bow.

* * *

"The ship is at condition one, Captain," Lieutenant Commander Vidmar announced. "The last recon Reaper has reported in, and the first jump destination is still clear."

"Alert all ships," Cameron ordered from the command chair at the center of the Aurora's bridge. "Start the clock for jump one."

"Starting the clock for jump one, aye," the comms officer replied.

"Jump clock is running," the navigator reported.

"Who has rear guard?" Cameron wondered.

"The Morsiko-Tavi," the lieutenant commander replied. "She's got a pair of mark one plasma cannon turrets strapped to her deck, so she can provide cover fire, if needed."

"Thankfully, the need is unlikely," Cameron stated. Although she hadn't voiced as much to anyone, she was happy to move the fleet. They had been in the same area for more than a week, which made her nervous. They were in the middle of nowhere, and well away from any known shipping lanes. She knew the odds of them being found were astronomical, but there was still something about staying in the same hiding place for long periods of time that made her uncomfortable.

"Thirty seconds to jump one," the navigator warned.

The first jump was the Aurora's. When moving the fleet, it was her job to jump to their destination first, and send a jump comm-drone back to the fleet, signaling that it was safe for them to jump, as well. It was overkill, since recon Reapers had been jumping in and out of the first jump destination for the last hour and had detected no threats. But for the safety of a dozen unarmed vessels, and the thousands of lives at stake, she had chosen the more cautious approach. It would take twice as long to reach their final destination, within the Aurora's single-jump range to Rakuen, but it could not be avoided. The last thing they needed this early in the game was for the fleet to be forced to disperse in numerous directions, and attempt to rejoin later. Most of the ships in the Karuzari fleet still depended on one another to survive, and some of them would not last more than a few days on their own. It was a precarious condition for them to be in, and they were working to improve upon it, but there was still much to do.

"Five seconds," the navigator warned. "Three...... two......one......jumping."

On the Aurora's main view screen, the familiar wave of pale blue light spilled out across her forward hull, immediately covering her, and then building to a flash of blue-white light that was greatly subdued by the view screen's filters. A second after the wave of light began spilling out of their emitters, the view screen was back to normal; the visible stars having shifted an almost imperceptible amount.

"Jump complete," the navigator reported.

"Scanning the area," Lieutenant Commander Kono added from the sensor station.

Cameron sat patiently, waiting for word from her sensor officer. If there was a warship in the area, they would either attack immediately, or wait for them to feel comfortable enough to let their guard down. They might even wait to see if any other ships were following the Aurora. But the lieutenant commander was scanning with active, high-powered sensor arrays, using every detection method possible. If there was a ship out there, she'd find it, but they'd also be announcing their position to that ship, as well.

It was a chance Cameron had to take.

"No contacts," Lieutenant Commander Kono reported. "Beginning long-range scans."

"Prepare the all-clear drone," Cameron ordered.

"All-clear comm-drone loaded and ready for launch," the comms officer acknowledged.

Cameron watched the jump clock display on the center console directly in front of her, between the navigator and the helmsman, as another minute passed. Their fleet-movement protocol called for a five-minute delay between the Aurora's arrival at a jump destination and the launching of the all-clear jump comm-drone. It was just enough time for them to determine that there were no immediate threats in the area. If the fleet did not receive the all-clear signal within ten minutes, they were to jump to an alternate location and wait for a predetermined length of time before executing a series of emergency evasion jumps. Again, it was overkill under the current conditions, but necessary.

The minutes ticked by, finally reaching the five-minute mark.

"Still no contacts, Captain," Lieutenant Commander Kono reported.

"Launch the all clear," Cameron ordered.

"All-clear drone away," the comms officer confirmed.

"Move us out of the arrival zone, Lieutenant," she added.

"Aye, sir," Lieutenant Dinev replied from the helm.

Two minutes later, Cameron switched the view on the Aurora's spherical screen to the aft-facing cameras and was rewarded with multiple jump flashes as the fleet jumped in behind them.

"The fleet has jumped," Lieutenant Commander Kono reported.

"The Morsiko-Tavi has reported in," Lieutenant Commander Vidmar added from the tactical station. "Jump one is complete."

"Six hours to the next jump," the navigator reported.

Cameron sighed. Every ship in their ragtag fleet had different jump ranges and recharge times. The smaller ships, such as the flat-bed pod haulers like the Morsiko-Tavi, could perform endless back-to-back jumps with only a few minutes between them. Larger ships, like the Mystic Empress, the Innison, and the Glendanon, had to wait to recharge their jump drives between each jump. Although the Aurora was fitted with two completely independent jump drives and could perform two max-range jumps in succession, no one else in the fleet could. Furthermore, they had to limit the range of each jump, so every ship still had enough jump energy left to make a series of short emergency evasion jumps. The result was that the fleet moved like a turtle.

Alas, it could not be helped, and as much as Cameron wanted to move the Aurora to the Rakuen system within the day, her primary responsibility was the protection of the fleet which had just jumped in behind her. It was this responsibility that greatly limited the Aurora's ability to take the fight to the Dusahn, which was precisely why Nathan was taking such a gamble to secure a handful of Gunyoki fighters.

* * *

"This is a joke," Nathan insisted as he stared at the simple display and control inputs. "There are no docking thrusters, no translation thrusters, not even weapons controls."

"This is a *flight* simulator," Master Koku replied in his usual calm demeanor. "I am using it to introduce you to the complexities of piloting a Gunyoki fighter."

Nathan shrugged slightly, resigning himself to his instructor's methods. "You *do* know that I am both trained and experienced in space flight, right?"

"Terran fighters, large warships, and small cargo vessels," Master Koku stated. "None of this training will translate well to piloting a Gunyoki fighter. If anything, these experiences will make it more difficult for you."

"How?"

"The primary propulsion and maneuvering thrust points on a Gunyoki fighter are located on either side at the stern of the ship, well aft of its center of gravity. This causes rapid attitude changes in yaw, roll, and pitch, with only the slightest application of thrust. Too much thrust, and the motion of the ship can easily become uncontrollable."

"Gunyoki fighters are equipped with auto-recovery, aren't they?"

"Indeed, they are," Master Koku confirmed. "However, it uses considerable propellant to correct your attitude. Use this system too many times, and you will have insufficient propellant to complete your mission."

"My *mission*?"

"The race, or 'heat', as it is called."

"Why do I get the impression that you don't care much for the Gunyoki races," Nathan wondered as he ran through the simplistic demonstration of the simulator's basic flight control inputs.

"For what the races have done to foster support of the Gunyoki, and to increase the number of ships and pilots, I am grateful, and am proud of the small part I have played in its success."

"But?"

"But what?" Master Koku wondered.

"You don't *like* the races."

"You should worry less about my likes and dislikes, and more on the challenges you face."

"What challenges?" Nathan chuckled. "I'm sitting in a children's game at a museum. A couple hours from now, this place will probably be swarming with kids on a school field trip, arguing over who gets to play with this thing next."

"Field trip?"

"Never mind," Nathan replied. "How do you start this thing?"

Master Koku leaned in from the side of the simulator booth and pressed the start button. The screen in front of Nathan switched from the flight control introduction display, to a view of space. A moment later, a green square appeared in the middle of the screen and was moving slowly toward him.

"You are currently on a heading to pass through that first training gate," Master Koku explained. "No thrust is currently being applied."

Nathan stared at the green, square gate floating in the middle of the screen. "The gate is drifting to port," he observed.

"Indeed, it is. As your course tracks further away from safe passage through the gate, it will change color. First yellow, then to orange, then to red. When it is flashing red, you have only seconds to correct your trajectory in order to pass through it. If the gate disappears completely, it means you are no longer able to navigate through the gate. At that point, an alternate gate should appear."

"And the purpose of all this is?"

"To give you a simple way to become accustomed to the difficulties of maneuvering a Gunyoki fighter."

Nathan took a deep breath. "I've studied the flight manuals. I can do this." He placed his left hand on the flight control stick at the left side of his seat, and his right hand on the throttle at the opposite side.

"Note your thrust level display," Master Koku urged, noticing that Nathan had his hand on the throttle.

"I know. I'm at five percent thrust right now." Nathan instinctively pushed his flight control stick to the left, attempting to steer toward the drifting gate. Instead, the ship rolled to port, but its course remained unchanged. "Oops," he said, reversing his control input to stop the roll. He then increased the thrust level to his starboard engine, hoping to yaw to port, so he could then increase thrust evenly to both engines to propel the ship toward a new course line that would take him through the center of the gate.

"You are thinking like the pilot of a cargo ship," Master Koku warned.

"How so?"

"You are attempting to find the perfect course through the center of the gate."

"And there is something wrong with that?" Nathan asked.

"Nothing at all," Master Koku agreed, "*if* you are flying a cargo ship. The gate is ten times the width of your ship. Any path through the gate is as good as another. *This* is your first lesson."

The gate turned yellow. Nathan increased the power to his right engine, bringing his nose further left, then evened the thrust levers and increased power equally to both engines. The gate turned orange for a few seconds as it drifted further to port. A few seconds later, it began drifting back towards the center of the screen, turning yellow and then green. Nathan increased power to the left engine as he reduced power to the right, bringing his nose back left, before again adding power equally to both engines. As the gate grew closer, he realized he might not clear the right side of the gate and immediately pushed his flight control stick ever so slightly to the right, releasing the pressure a split second later, causing his ship to roll to starboard. A bit of opposite control input stopped his roll, and he slipped through the gate, causing it to disappear from the screen.

"Nicely done," Master Koku congratulated. "For a cargo ship pilot."

Nathan glanced at Master Koku, noticing his implacable expression as two more gates appeared on the screen, moving toward him more quickly than before.

It was going to be a long day.

* * *

Nathan lay on the bed in his hotel room. It was only noon, and he was already exhausted. With his eyes closed, he could see orange and red training gates speeding past him on all sides. He had spent three hours in that children's simulator, and another two hours in a more advanced one in the museum's maintenance shop.

Although his ability to control his flight path had improved over those five hours, he continually felt like he was barely on the edge of control, convinced that most of the gates he had managed to successfully navigate had been more by accident than by skill. If either simulator were the slightest bit accurate, he didn't stand a chance of even qualifying, let alone participating in the actual event.

Nathan lay there, forcing himself to drift away, knowing that in a few short hours, he and Jessica would be face-to-face with the Gunyoki fighter spacecraft that Mister Yokimah had loaned him.

His eyes suddenly popped open, awakened by the door chimes. "Damn," he cursed, sitting up. "Doesn't she ever sleep?"

Nathan rose and headed for the door where the embedded view screen displayed a group of familiar faces.

"Are you insane?" Deliza asked, charging in as soon as Nathan opened the door.

"I'm sorry, it's all I had to wager," Nathan apologized.

"I'm over that," Deliza insisted as she pushed past him, Yanni following close behind. "I'm talking about entering the race. Do you even realize how risky it is? Do you know how many credits we spent cloning, and recloning you?"

"I'm touched," Nathan said as he began greeting the others.

"We brought them here as quickly as we could, Captain," Loki assured him as he walked by.

"Nathan!" Vladimir exclaimed. "The Gunyoki design is amazing! I have been studying it since we left the Aurora!"

"*We* have been studying it," Abby corrected, following Vladimir past Nathan and into the room.

"*Da, da, da.* When do we get to see one?"

"Later today," Nathan replied. "General," he nodded as General Telles entered.

"Captain," the general replied. "I have taken the liberty of posting my men at key positions on this floor as a security measure."

"Do you really think that's necessary? This hotel is pretty exclusive," Nathan assured him.

"They let us in, didn't they?" Josh joked as he passed.

Nathan leaned through the door, peering into the hallway. "Where are Marcus, Dalen, and Neli?"

"They'll be here in two days," Vladimir explained. "They're finishing some extra upgrades."

"What *extra* upgrades?" Nathan asked, closing the door.

"Cameron ordered them to install the new experimental stealth emitters on the Seiiki, in order to test them on something larger than a recon drone," Abby explained. "I tried to talk her out of it."

"On *my* ship?"

"She is only trying to expedite matters in much

271

the same way you did with the original jump drive," Vladimir told him.

"In Captain Taylor's defense, she did not intend to actually *test* the emitters on the Seiiki *without* first getting your approval," General Telles added.

"But if they don't work..."

"Relax," Vlad said, cutting Nathan off. "Marcus insisted we install the new emitters as a secondary array, feeding off the same power grid, so that the original emitters would *still* be operational."

"Thank God."

"Have you started your training yet?" Josh wondered.

"Yes," Nathan replied, sitting on the edge of his bed. "Early this morning. *Very* early."

"Who is your instructor?" Deliza asked.

"An old Gunyoki master named Koku," Nathan replied. "Real pleasant fellow. Loves to speak in circles."

"Koku?" Loki exclaimed, stunned. "*Makani* Koku."

"That's the guy."

"Are you kidding me?" Loki said excitedly.

"Why?" Josh wondered. "Who's Makani Koku?"

"Possibly one of the greatest Gunyoki masters of the last century!" Loki exclaimed. "Possibly of all time!"

"Yeah, well, he's old enough to have been around a century ago, that's for sure," Nathan commented.

"Captain, you don't know how lucky you are," Loki explained. "If anyone can teach you to fly a Gunyoki racer in less than a week, it's Master Koku."

"Huh," Nathan said, surprised. "I figured Yokimah sent me some old, washed-up racer pilot, just to make sure I'd lose. I guess I misjudged him."

"Who, Yokimah, or Master Koku?" Josh wondered.

"It is possible Mister Yokimah was simply making certain that everything appeared fair," General Telles stated. "Despite Mister Sheehan's high regard for this Master Koku, there may be other reasons Mister Yokimah selected him. Ones that are not yet apparent. Ones that may be detrimental to our goals."

"This is Makani Koku we're talking about," Loki insisted. "He actually *opposed* the whole race idea decades ago. He doesn't even *like* Ito Yokimah."

"Yet, he worked for him for many years as both a pilot and an instructor," General Telles pointed out.

"How did you know that?" Nathan wondered.

"I have been reading the history of the Gunyoki, and the races," the general explained.

"He didn't have a choice," Loki said. "I read all about the guy while I was attending flight school here. He only worked for Yokimah to keep the level of training as close to the original Gunyoki edicts as possible. Unfortunately, he failed. All Yokimah was interested in was the profit, not the defense of Rakuen. He believed increasing the number of ships and pilots was a faster way to build Rakuen's deterrent levels. Master Koku retired two decades ago because the Gunyoki training edicts had all but been abandoned, and the racing commission was letting anyone who could buy a ship and become proficient enough to pass the flight test, enter the race and become an official protector of Rakuen."

"What's this?" Vlad asked, pointing to the metal case on the floor.

"It's a Gunyoki flight simulator," Nathan explained. "I'm supposed to be able to plug it into the view screen on the wall. It's got a basic flight control stick and throttle to go with it. Master Koku gave it to me to practice on my own, before my first real flight tomorrow."

"Have you tried it?" Josh said, excited.

"Actually, I was taking a nap."

"Maybe we could adapt it to work with the VR sim rig?" Vladimir suggested.

"You brought one?" Nathan asked in surprise.

"*Konyeshna*," Vladimir replied.

"Everything on Rakuen uses the same operating system and base code," Yanni said. "We had to learn it to make the interface between our shuttles and the Rakuen computers work. It shouldn't be too difficult to adapt the code in the simulator to work on the VR sim gear."

"How long?" Nathan asked Yanni.

"I should be able to have it ready by tomorrow, at the latest," Yanni assured him.

"Great," Nathan agreed. "Where are you guys staying?"

"Here," Vladimir replied. "Our Reaper is parked on the rooftop pad."

"Isn't this place expensive?"

"You bet it is," Deliza agreed. "You should see the deposit I had to put on the company account."

* * *

It had taken some doing, but Nathan convinced the managers of the Gunyoki racing platform to allow them to use the Reaper as their support ship, and to park it in the auxiliary bay next to bay seventy-five, where the Gunyoki fighter Mister Yokimah had loaned him was housed. The fact that their ship was armed had been the biggest sticking point. Only the promise that neither their weapons systems, nor their shields would be powered up while in the vicinity of the race platform had won them permission.

Their bays were located on the underside of the outermost ring of the platform, where all entrants who had yet to qualify for the upcoming event were placed. The Reaper flew in under the platform, coming up under the opening to transfer airlock seventy-five, and translating upward through the open hatch.

Once inside, the bay doors slid in under them, forming the floor of the bay. The Reaper dropped its gear, after which the artificial gravity in the bay slowly increased, pulling them gently down to the deck.

After a few minutes, the transfer airlock was pressurized, and the inner doors opened.

"Rolling forward," Josh announced, guiding the Reaper through the inner doors which were now opening before them. As their nose rolled across the threshold, their Gunyoki fighter came into view.

"There it is," Loki announced. "Starboard side."

"I'll put us in the opposite corner," Josh said as he steered the Reaper to port. He looked out the starboard side at the Gunyoki fighter. "Why doesn't it have a number on it?"

"He has to qualify, first," Loki replied.

The Reaper pulled into the corner and then rotated its gear, so it could pivot around to face its nose back the way it had come. Finally, the hatch opened, and Nathan jumped out, followed by Jessica and the others.

Nathan let out a long whistle as he approached the Gunyoki fighter on the other side of bay seventy-five. "These things are even more impressive up close. They sure didn't have any of *these* in the museum."

"I should say not." A man came around from the

opposite side of the Gunyoki fighter and headed toward them. "Captain Scott, I presume?"

"Correct," Nathan replied, offering his hand.

"Quoruson Insimi," the man replied, reluctantly shaking Nathan's hand.

"This is my team," Nathan began, preparing to introduce them each, one at a time.

"No offense, but my time is limited, and the only one I *really* need to meet is your chief engineer," Mister Insimi said, interrupting Nathan.

"That would be me," Vladimir said, stepping forward. "Vladimir Kamenetskiy, at your service."

"You have worked on Gunyoki fighters before?"

"*Nyet.*"

Mister Insimi looked at Nathan.

"That means no."

"Of course." Mister Insimi sighed in disappointment. "Then this may take more time than I'd hoped."

"No disrespect, Mister Insimi," Abby began, "but while the design of the Gunyoki is unique, the technology behind it is not terribly advanced."

Mister Insimi was at a loss for words.

"I'm curious," Abby continued, "why don't you use static-state fusion generators instead of variable-state? You'd get far more power with half the weight volume costs, *and* you won't be forced to constantly adjust the power distribution between the primary systems."

"Balancing the power is *part* of flying a Gunyoki fighter," Mister Insimi insisted.

"But aren't the Gunyoki supposed to serve as a deterrent to potential aggressors?" General Telles pointed out.

"Well, yes..."

"Then would it not make more sense to have as much available power on board as possible?"

"I'm sorry, you are?"

"Lucius Telles," the general replied.

"He's my tactician," Nathan added.

"I see." Mister Insimi turned back toward the group. "My job is to instruct you on the basics of maintaining and repairing a Gunyoki fighter, *not* to debate the strengths and weaknesses of its design."

"Of course," Nathan agreed. He stepped forward, putting his arm around Mister Insimi's shoulder, leading him off to one side. "We appreciate you sharing your expertise with us, Mister Insimi, but you should understand that the people you are about to *instruct* are probably some of the most intelligent, well-educated people you will ever meet."

Mister Insimi looked back over his shoulder at what appeared to be a rather motley group of people. "Are you sure about that?"

"Mister Kamenetskiy is also chief engineer for the Aurora."

"He is?"

"He is. And the blonde lady, Doctor Sorenson, well, she and her father *invented* the jump drive."

"*Really,*" Mister Insimi exclaimed, looking back again.

"And that's *General* Lucius Telles, leader of the Ghatazhak. I'm sure you've heard of them."

"Of course."

"And the petite young woman there is Deliza Ta'Akar, *daughter* of Prince Casimir of Takara, and *founder* of Ranni Enterprises. I'm *quite* certain you've heard of *her.*"

"Oh, absolutely," Mister Insimi gushed. "Everyone on Rakuen knows of Deliza Ta'Akar."

"So, you see, Mister Insimi, you might want to treat these people with a little respect. After all, they are all *way* smarter than either of us...no insult intended."

"Oh, no, I mean, yes, sir."

"In fact, you might even learn a few things," Nathan added. "Things you could apply to the ships *you* normally work on."

Mister Insimi looked at Nathan, suddenly very interested. "You think?"

"I do."

Mister Insimi looked back at the group. "What about the others?" he asked. "Those three guys, the attractive woman, and the four guys standing by your ship?"

"My weapons officer, controller, and my security team."

"I see." Mister Insimi straightened his coat, his attitude obviously changed by his discussion with Nathan. "We're wasting valuable time, Captain. I have so much to show them."

"Thank you, Mister Insimi," Nathan said graciously. "Thank you ever so much."

"Welcome!" Mister Insimi announced, heading back to the group, his arms wide and a smile on his face. "I'm *so* happy to meet you all, and I cannot *wait* to show you this wonderful ship, and share with you *everything* I know about it. My name is Quoruson Insimi, but all of *you* can call me Quory."

Nathan smiled. For the first time since he had arrived on Rakuen a few days ago, he felt like he had the upper hand.

* * *

Nathan studied the control panel in his Gunyoki fighter, checking to ensure that all systems were operating properly while he finished reviewing his checklist. "Prelaunch is complete," he announced over his helmet comms. "All systems are green. We're ready to launch."

"Very well," Master Koku replied from the seat directly behind Nathan. "You may arm the auto-launch system."

"I thought you said I wasn't allowed to use any automation during this stage of my training."

"Only for departures and arrivals," Master Koku explained. "Unfortunately, it is required when operating in the vicinity of the race platform... supposedly, for the safety of the spectators."

"But there are no spectators today."

"Precisely," Master Koku agreed with great annoyance.

"And I don't have to call for clearance?"

"It would be redundant to ask for permission to be controlled by the departure computer," Master Koku said, again sounding annoyed. "Simply select 'nearest available practice area' as your destination, and the system will fly you clear of the platform, headed in the direction of your selected destination."

"How do I know when it's okay for me to take the controls?" Nathan wondered.

"The system will notify you. Auto-flight will disengage, and the auto-pilot will take over, holding your course and speed constant until you disengage it and take manual control."

"How do I know when we're going to launch?" Nathan asked.

"The departure control system will launch you as soon as it is ready. Once you arm the auto-flight system, select a destination, and press the 'ready to depart' button."

"Is it quick, or do we have to wait a few minutes?" Nathan asked as he armed the auto-flight system and pressed the appropriate buttons. The ship immediately rose a half meter off the deck and began moving into the airlock. "That answers that question."

"There are only a few ships practicing today, so the wait time is minimal," Master Koku explained.

"Non-existent would be more accurate." Nathan watched his systems and flight status displays, paying attention to which thrusters were firing in case he ever had to depart the facility manually. When he had been at the EDF Academy on Earth, he had not cared for automated flight systems, and neither had his basic flight instructors. 'If you can't do it manually, you've got no business using automation.' "Does anyone use the auto-pilot during the race?" he wondered.

"No Gunyoki would use automation during a race," Master Koku replied. "So, yes."

"What?"

"Unfortunately, there are few real Gunyoki flying these days. Most of the pilots are brash youngsters, with little respect for the ways of the Gunyoki. To them, 'Gunyoki' is the ship they fly. It has lost its true meaning."

"Yeah, time has a way of changing things," Nathan commented as the ship came to a stop in the transfer airlock, and the inner doors began to close. "When I was a teenager, my grandfather taught me to fly in this old, piston-engine biplane. There was not much in the cockpit. Just a stick, rudder pedals, throttle, and mixture. It only had three gauges: airspeed, altitude, and engine tachometer. It was a great plane to fly. Later, after he passed away, my father hired someone to restore it and upgrade a few things. I'm not sure why. Anyway, he replaced the gas-powered piston engine with a solar-charged electric engine, and replaced the three simple gauges with a fancy digital display, which gave me all kinds of information I had no idea what to do with. It took me longer to learn how to use that digital display and all the automation, than it did to learn to fly the plane in the first place."

"Did it ruin your enjoyment of flying?" Master Koku asked as the outer doors opened below them, and the ship began to descend out of the airlock and into space.

"For a while, yes," Nathan admitted. "And to be honest, I still wish it was that same, old plane that my grandfather taught me to fly, but I adapted. In fact, I flew it a little over a week ago."

"You were back on Earth?"

"For a few days, yes."

"Did anyone know you were there?"

"It was more of a *covert* visit. A long story."

"I suppose it had something to do with the whole 'clone' issue," Master Koku commented.

His observation took Nathan by surprise. "You might say that." He turned to glance over his shoulder at the old man. "Does that bother you? That I'm a clone?"

"If I understood correctly, it is only your body that is a clone. And if your body is a copy of your original body, then you are no less the man you were in your original body."

"Not everyone sees it that way."

"People tend to see what they *wish* to see, long before they see the truth," Master Koku said as the ship cleared the airlock and thrusted forward.

"Should I be ready to take control?" Nathan asked as the ship passed under the massive race platform.

"Departure Control should release flight control to your auto-pilot as soon as we have cleared the outer perimeter, which is one thousand kilometers from the platform."

"A thousand kilometers?" Nathan said. "At this speed, it'll take forever."

"Brace yourself," Master Koku warned.

As the words left the Gunyoki master's lips, the ship's two main engines went to twenty-five percent power, pushing Nathan back in his seat. "Whoa!" he exclaimed, struggling to breathe. "Aren't there any inertial dampeners in this thing?"

"Yes, but they only lessen the forces, they do not remove them completely."

"Why the hell not?" Nathan wondered, still pinned against his seat.

"A Gunyoki must *feel* the forces of flight, in order to perform properly. Without them, he knows not what those forces are doing to his ship."

"Yeah, well, I'm feeling those forces, alright!"

"Nine hundred kilometers from the platform," Master Koku announced. "Prepare to take manual control."

The thrust levels decreased slightly, and Nathan managed to reach out and grab the flight control stick and the throttles. He adjusted himself in his seat, better preparing himself, both physically and mentally, for the task ahead.

"Nine-fifty."

"I'm ready," Nathan assured him.

The warning light on the auto-flight system began to blink, indicating that control was about to be turned over to the onboard auto-pilot system.

"One thousand."

The warning light turned green.

"Auto-pilot has the ship," Nathan announced. "Going to manual," he added, pressing the button on his flight control stick to disengage the auto-pilot.

At first, everything seemed fine. The ship wavered slightly, but Nathan kept on course.

"Try a twenty-degree, level turn to the left," Master Koku suggested.

Nathan did as instructed, angling his starboard engine nacelle, so the thrust nozzle pointed slightly toward the ship's centerline, and increased the thrust level of that engine. The ship began to turn left, as commanded. A quick set of opposite inputs stopped his turn, and he continued flying on the new course.

"Now return to your original heading," Master Koku instructed.

Again, the maneuver was simple enough.

"Nicely done."

It was the first compliment Nathan had heard come out of Master Koku's mouth.

"Now, give me a rolling, descending left turn, coming about ninety degrees and pitching down thirty degrees."

Nathan adjusted his engine deflections and power settings, executing the maneuver as requested. However, he was a little late stopping his roll and had to roll back in the opposite direction to correct for it.

"Remember, both turns and attitude are controlled by both engine deflection *and* thrust levels. As the point of thrust is well aft of the center of gravity, the center of rotation will always feel somewhat off. You will become accustomed to this over time.

Meanwhile, it is important that you restrict your inputs to tiny changes. Gently coax your ship to do your bidding, do not manhandle her. The results are often unpredictable."

"I'll try to remember that," Nathan replied as he continued maneuvering.

"Change course to one five two, by six seven, and accelerate to five-seventy," Master Koku instructed.

"Five-seventy?" Nathan asked. "Isn't it too soon to be flying that fast?"

"That is not even half of her top speed. You cannot win a battle at slow speeds."

Nathan sighed. "You're the boss," he agreed, increasing power as he changed course. "Where are we going?"

"There is a small group of closely packed asteroids nearby," Master Koku explained. "Most of them are small enough that they will not penetrate your shields."

"Most of them?" Nathan wondered as he got the ship on its new course and speed.

"Try to pick a line that requires the least maneuvering," Master Koku told him. "Study the movement of the asteroids. Anticipate where they will be when you reach them. Use their movement to your advantage."

"I'll do my best," Nathan promised.

"Hopefully...better."

"Right." Nathan looked down at his sensor display, noting the movement patterns of the nearest asteroid. His mind flashed back to Haven, and negotiating her dense rings in the Aurora many years ago. "Okay, I've got this," he verbalized.

"What is it you have got?" Master Koku wondered.

"A figure of speech," Nathan explained. "It means: I'm confident that I can do this."

"Then by all means, *have* this."

Nathan's brow furrowed slightly at his instructor's turn of phrase. He set his course for the large asteroid directly in front of him, which was passing right to left. He then grabbed the throttle to decrease power, just to be safe.

"Maintain a constant speed throughout the asteroid field," Master Koku insisted.

"What?"

"Slowing down or speeding up, to avoid a collision, requires no particular talents," Master Koku said. "Do not alter your speed."

"Whatever you say," Nathan agreed, adjusting himself in his seat in preparation. He glanced at his sensor display, tapping the image of the large asteroid directly ahead to call up its course and speed. A quick, mental calculation told him the asteroid's lateral motion was not enough to move it out of his way before impact. However, it was also moving slightly away from him, which bought him a few more seconds. He altered his course slightly to starboard, then rolled his ship onto its port side as he approached, looking up at the surface of the asteroid less than fifty meters away. "Why isn't the gravity well of this guy pulling me toward it?"

"These asteroids are composed of extremely porous rock," Master Koku explained. "Despite their size, their mass is negligible."

"It would have been nice to know that ahead of time," Nathan said. "I would have cut it even closer."

"Perhaps you should have studied the geology of the Rogen system prior to attempting to navigate its contents."

"Right," Nathan replied, rolling his ship back and over on its right side in order to pull around the next approaching asteroid. "Uh-oh," he said as he cleared the second asteroid. A sea of smaller asteroids was coming toward him, all of them spinning wildly and bouncing off of one another. "This is *not* good. A few of them must have collided and broken apart."

"Not an uncommon occurrence in a densely packed group of floating rocks," Master Koku said dryly.

Nathan pulled his ship over hard to port, then pulled his nose up. The maneuver caused his engine nacelles to reposition dramatically, and the ship began to yaw to starboard as it rolled to port. "Uh..."

"You are applying too much thrust," Master Koku warned.

The ship's aft end slid to one side as Nathan tried to correct its motion, but every input he made only worsened his situation. "This is not working," he exclaimed.

"Concentrate," Master Koku insisted. "Clear your mind of fear. See your course. See what your ship, what your engines, must do to find that course."

A group of spinning, rocky debris struck his port shielding, causing it to light up in opaque ambers.

"Oops," Nathan said as he continued struggling to control his ship.

"You are not concentrating."

"This would be a lot easier if you'd let me use my throttles," Nathan insisted.

"And if your throttles were stuck?"

"But they're not," Nathan reminded him, "and I'm not going to get any better if I'm splattered across a rock in space."

Master Koku took control of the Gunyoki fighter,

recovered it from its tumbling spin, and then guided it smoothly through the tight groupings of spinning rocks and dust.

Nathan watched in amazement as the old man piloted the complex and difficult-to-maneuver ship around and between the obstacles dancing about them as if he could do so in his sleep. "You've done this before."

"I have."

Nathan sighed. "Well, I don't think I did that badly for my first time. What do you think?"

"I think you are hopeless," Master Koku replied.

"Not the answer I was hoping for," Nathan said to himself.

* * *

"The design of the Gunyoki fighter is based on two principles. The first is durability. Every system has at least one redundancy; many three," Quory explained to the team as he led them around Nathan's ship. "In addition, all components are considerably overbuilt. This gives the Gunyoki fighter a remarkable ability to sustain damage, yet remain combat effective."

"What's the second design element?" Vladimir wondered.

"The modularity of its construction. Every section is designed to be easily removed and replaced. Likewise, every component *within* each section is designed with such rapid serviceability in mind."

Josh looked around the bay, noting numerous tool cabinets and diagnostic equipment, but no spare parts. "Where are all the spares?"

"I do not believe that Mister Yokimah provided them," Quory admitted.

"Uh, won't we *need* them?" Loki asked.

"Doubtful, as the chances of your captain advancing past the third round are negligible."

"Can we *buy* some spare parts?" Deliza asked.

"It is difficult, as they are in high demand. However, if you have the funds, most can be obtained through the shadow markets."

"Perhaps you can make us a list of what we might need?" Deliza suggested.

"I would be happy to, Miss Ta'Akar," Quory assured her.

"What's so significant about the third round?" Abby wondered.

"It is when the targets start shooting back," Quory replied with a smile. "If, by some miracle, your captain makes it past the third round..." Quory's smile became more pronounced. "You will definitely need those parts."

"Don't you mean, we?" Vladimir said.

"Yes, you."

"No, we, as in, all of us...*including* you?" Vladimir corrected.

"I am not allowed to assist in the servicing of your Gunyoki fighter," Quory insisted. "I am an employee of Yokimah Racing. If I help you maintain your ship, I will most certainly lose my job."

"Then why are you here?" Vladimir wondered.

"I was told to instruct you on the basics of Gunyoki service and repair."

"By whom?" Deliza asked.

"By Mister Yokimah, of course."

"That doesn't make sense."

"Perhaps he is just protecting his property," Abby suggested.

"Doubtful," Quory said. "This ship is nearing the

end of its useful service life. After this event, it will be disassembled and recycled."

Deliza, Abby, and Vladimir all exchanged concerned glances.

"So what?" Josh exclaimed. "Half the parts on the Seiiki are past their useful service life."

Deliza, Abby, and Vladimir all looked at Josh.

"What?" Josh wondered.

"You're not helping," Deliza told him.

* * *

"I swear, that kid is awfully creative when it comes to finding ways to get between a rock and a hard place," Roselle declared, letting go a raucous laugh.

"Just how dangerous *is* this race?" Robert asked Cameron.

"The first two rounds are just two ships racing each other through a course, shooting at targets as they go," Cameron explained. "So, as long as he doesn't fly into any of the race gates, he should be fine. From what I've read, however, it's the third round where things get interesting. That's when the targets start firing back."

"He's got shields, doesn't he?" Robert asked.

"Yes, but Gunyoki fighters are under-powered, and the flight crew has to constantly juggle power distribution between propulsion and maneuvering, weapons, and shields."

"Crew?" Robert wondered.

"Nathan is doing the flying, and Loki will be the weapons officer," Cameron said.

"Doesn't sound that bad," Gil said.

"It gets worse," Cameron warned. "In the final rounds, they use an asteroid field instead of race gates, and the ships have to fight each other, along with the automated weapons emplacements. And if both ships make it through the course, they engage in a dogfight at the end."

"And the weapons are not simulated?" Robert surmised by the concern in Cameron's voice.

"No, they are not. They *are* low-power, but more than enough to cause significant damage if their shields fail."

"Has anyone ever died in these races?" Gil asked.

"At least once or twice per year. Although, usually it's due to pilot error, and not to weapons fire, at least not directly."

Gil shook his head. "Like I said... A rock and a hard place."

"Why is he doing this?" Robert wondered.

"He's trying to show the Rakuens that their Gunyoki are not enough to stop the Dusahn..."

"By beating them in a race?" Gil said, laughing again.

"...*And* to win their respect, and possibly their support," Cameron added. "There's also a bet."

"Oh, this just keeps getting better and better, doesn't it," Gil said.

"What's the bet?" Robert asked, nowhere near as amused as Gil.

"If he wins, we get twelve Gunyoki fighters."

"And if he loses?"

"Yokimah Enterprises takes ownership of the Ranni shuttle plant on Rakuen."

Robert shook his head. "Why are we moving the fleet to the Rogen sector?" he wondered.

"Nathan's orders," Cameron replied. "Both he and Jessica have an uneasy feeling about all of this."

"Did he elaborate?"

"No. I'm assuming it's just a hunch."

"Jess doesn't do hunches," Robert said. "If she suspects something's amiss, she's got good reasons."

"If so, she hasn't shared them with us."

"What's this got to do with us?" Gil asked.

"After we park the fleet within single-jump range of Rakuen, Nathan wants the Aurora to go to Rakuen for the race. General Telles agrees that it's a good idea, but I'm a little uncomfortable leaving the fleet unprotected."

"You can be back within a minute or two," Robert reminded her.

"Think you could take out our entire fleet in less than a minute?" Cameron pointed out.

"More like thirty seconds," Gil surmised.

"Precisely," Cameron agreed.

"So, you want us to protect the fleet in the Aurora's absence?" Robert assumed.

"To be honest, I'm not sure," Cameron said with a sigh. "I just think it would be best if every armed ship we have is in a ready state, especially while this ship is away from the fleet."

"Well, we've got four gunships that are fully operational, and two more that *could* be combat-ready in a few days, but really *should* be kept out of action, if possible," Robert told her.

"The problem is, we don't have crews for them all," Gil added.

"I can provide enough engineers and sensor officers to crew three ships," Cameron offered. "And I can give you a couple of copilots to fly with the two of you. Plus, we have one full crew from Three Eight Three, and the flight crew from Three Eight Two."

"You want to use the kids?" Gil questioned.

"They *are* trained," Cameron reminded him.

"They're straight out of flight school, Cam," Robert

argued. "That's a *long* way from being fully trained and ready for combat."

"They did alright on Kohara."

"They got lucky," Gil insisted.

Cameron leaned back in her chair, sighing. "Right now, I'll *take* lucky."

CHAPTER NINE

"While you are no longer flying like a cargo ship pilot, you are *now* flying like you are in a conventional fighter," Master Koku observed from the backseat of the Gunyoki fighter.

"What's wrong with that?" Nathan wondered as he snaked his ship through the gates on the practice course.

"Nothing, if you are flying such a fighter. The nature of the Gunyoki engine nacelles demands a different approach. You must consider the movements that your nacelles must make, in order to transition from one maneuver to the next. In a conventional fighter, such considerations are not necessary, as they have thrusters scattered about the ship, and pointing in every conceivable angle needed."

"Which makes them much more maneuverable and easier to fly," Nathan commented.

"It may make them easier to fly, but it does not make them more maneuverable. What it *does* make them is overly complex and difficult to maintain. It also makes them easier to disable. Destroy only a few thrusters, and a conventional fighter loses half of its maneuverability, making it an easy target."

"Take out one of a Gunyoki's two engine nacelles, and you get the same result," Nathan argued.

"Ah, but doing so is quite difficult. *That* is the beauty of the Gunyoki design. Simple, rugged, and deadly...once you *master* it."

"I'm trying, believe me," Nathan insisted.

"No, you are trying to force it to do your bidding, instead of allowing it to do what it was *designed* to do." Master Koku placed his hands on the flight controls on either side of him. "May I demonstrate?"

"Please."

"Do not expect much," Master Koku said. "It has been several decades since I have piloted anything other than a wave rider. My controls?"

"Your controls," Nathan replied.

"I have control," Master Koku announced. At first, he simply guided the ship through the next few gates while he refreshed his memory on the feel of the Gunyoki fighter. "The feel of the controls has improved since my day," he commented as he guided the ship through the next gate. "They seemed to have recovered much of the feeling of direct connection that was lost over the years."

Nathan watched as the old pilot skillfully guided the ship through one gate after another, without any wasted motion. Every maneuver flowed smoothly into the next, and the engine nacelles seemed to rotate constantly, pausing as needed to apply thrust in the appropriate direction, their angles relative to the ship's longitudinal axis changing when appropriate, as well. The difference was the lack of hesitation which existed when Nathan was flying. The movement of the engine nacelles never abruptly changed direction as they did with disturbing regularity when Nathan was piloting.

Nathan glanced in his auxiliary view screen, which was currently displaying the camera focused on Master Koku behind him. The old man was calm and relaxed, his expression serene. His steely, gray-blue eyes darted from canopy to console and back again, with amazing speed. His head, upper body, and arms never moved more than necessary, just like the engine nacelles outside. The old Gunyoki master was one with his ship, even after decades of separation. It was truly a marvel to behold.

Finally, Master Koku steered the fighter through the final training gate and brought it into a slow, graceful, one-hundred-and-eighty-degree turn.

"That was amazing," Nathan declared. "Everything was so fluid. Not just the movements of the ship, but of yourself."

"When you are truly connected with your vessel, the ship's movements, and your own, are as one," Master Koku explained.

"But, can you really fly the ship so gracefully in a combat situation?" Nathan wondered. "It seems to me that a more aggressive style would be necessary, in order to survive."

Master Koku smiled. "All young pilots believe such nonsense. Allow me to demonstrate." Master Koku pressed several buttons on his starboard control pad.

Movement on his center display screen, the one that displayed the course layout, caught Nathan's eye. "What's happening?"

"I have selected a more difficult level. The course is reconfiguring itself."

Nathan squinted, studying the layout while it reformed. "It looks like it's getting shorter."

"Not shorter, but more compact," Master Koku corrected. "Brace yourself, Captain Scott."

Nathan barely had enough time to do so, before Master Koku had taken the ship to full power, and the acceleration forced him back into his seat, threatening to crush him. His eyes wide, he watched, in both horror and amazement, as the old man dove full speed through the first gate. The ship rolled over to the left, its nose coming up as he turned toward the next gate. Their rolling motion continued as they passed through the second gate and dove down for the third gate. In fact, it felt like the ship never stopped rolling, pitching, and yawing, sometimes in ways that felt contradictory to their flight path. With every gate that approached, Nathan was sure they would collide with its boundary, but his fears were never realized. Master Koku cut every corner precisely, always clearing the gate by the same single-meter distance, and always taking the most direct, effortless line to the next gate.

"It's about to get interesting," Master Koku stated calmly.

Warning alarms sounded in the cockpit, informing them their ship was being targeted by more than fifty weapons turrets. Nathan's eyes widened as Master Koku armed both their shields and weapons, delicately balancing power amongst the three primary systems, ensuring the right amount of power was always being delivered to the system that needed it most, exactly when required. Stub-missiles launched from their weapons pods on either side; two, three, sometimes four at a time, each of them finding and disabling their targets. Laser turrets on the upper and lower sides of the aft end of the ship danced about, expertly neutralizing weapons turrets as weapons fire, from those very same turrets, streaked past them on all sides. Although Master Koku was careful to ensure that every shield had adequate power just before it might absorb a weapons blast, none ever struck their shields, as the old pilot always managed to shift the fighter just enough to move it out of the path of incoming fire. Finally, as he approached the final gate, the old man cut his engines, allowing him to use the plasma cannons on the front of each engine nacelle to disable the last four weapons turrets that were firing on them.

And throughout the entire flight, the old Gunyoki master maintained his serene demeanor. Never did he appear stressed, and never did it appear as if he was not certain that what he was doing would work the way he expected.

Finally, the fighter leveled out, and Master Koku throttled the engines back down. "Not my best effort," he said with a tinge of disappointment.

"Well, it has been a few decades," Nathan said. "Uh, just out of curiosity, what difficulty level was that course set at?"

"Master; Level Ten."

"Of ten, I assume?"

"Correct," Master Koku confirmed.

"And what level was I at?"

"Novice; Level One."

"Then, I still have a ways to go, yet," Nathan said.

"Correct, again."

* * *

"All due respect, Captain, but that sucks!" Aiden said.

Captain Nash dipped his chin slightly, looking at the young ensign.

"Sorry, sir, but Three Eight Three is fully operational. I know she looks like shit, but that's just on the outside. We've been busting our backs getting her ready for action. If I tell my crew we're moving to another gunship now, I'll have a mutiny on my hands."

"Don't you think you're exaggerating things a bit, Ensign?" Robert suggested.

"Have you *met* my chief engineer, sir?" Aiden

asked. "I call her 'honey badger', behind her back, of course."

Robert's eyes narrowed. "They have honey badgers on Kohara?"

"I was born and raised on Earth, sir," Aiden explained. "We moved to Kohara when I was sixteen."

"I see."

"Sir, the only things we have left to repair, other than the damage to the bottom of our hull, of course, are all minor and wouldn't interfere with our ability to fight," Aiden said, pleading his case.

"We're not *expecting* a fight, Ensign. We just need ships to fly guard over the fleet while the Aurora is one jump away."

"That's all the more reason to let us *stay* on Three Eight Three, Captain."

"So everyone in the fleet can look out the window and say, 'Look at that banged up ship that's protecting us.'"

"More like, 'Hey, that's the ship that skipped off the surface of Kohara and saved Captain Scott's ass!' uh, sir."

A small chuckle came out of Robert's mouth. "Do you have your latest readiness report handy, Ensign?"

"You bet," Aiden replied, handing his data pad to Captain Nash.

Robert looked over the long list of systems still needing attention on the ensign's gunship. "You call this a *few* things?"

"I never said that, sir," Aiden corrected. "I said we were fully operational."

"I suspect you and I have very different ideas of what 'fully operational' means, Ensign." Robert handed the data pad back to Aiden. "Do me a favor, fix that glitch in your targeting sensors next. I don't want to get one of your plasma torpedoes up my ass."

"Does that mean…"

"Congratulations, Ensign. Your ship has been activated," Robert said as he turned to walk away. "Your new call sign is Striker Three."

"Yes, sir!" Aiden replied. "Thank you, sir! And I promise, no plasma torpedoes up your ass!"

Robert shook his head as he walked away, wondering if he had just made a terrible mistake.

* * *

"Looks like you're getting the hang of it, Captain," Loki commented from the back seat of their Gunyoki fighter as Nathan threaded their way smoothly through one gate after the next.

"*I see your weapons officer knows as little about the ways of the Gunyoki as you,*" Master Koku's voice said over their helmet comms.

"Eight training flights in two days, and he still won't let me move past grandma level," Nathan muttered.

"*You are in luck, Captain, as the 'grandma' level has no targets for your weapons officer to engage.*"

"So, we're bumping up to, what, advanced grandma level?" Nathan joked as they passed through the final gate on the training course.

"*Intermediate; Level One,*" Master Koku replied. "*Try not to make me regret doing so.*"

"Someone's never heard of positive reinforcement," Nathan said under his breath.

"*The Gunyoki do not believe in… What was that expression you used?*" he asked, his voice trailing as if he were speaking to someone near him, instead of to Nathan and Loki.

"*Blowing smoke up your ass,*" Josh replied.

"*Ah, yes. The Gunyoki do not believe in blowing smoke in one's ass.*"

"*Close enough,*" Josh decided. "*Remind me what my job is here, again?*"

"*To be quiet and to learn,*" Master Koku advised.

"That's an awfully tall order for Josh," Nathan teased.

"*What happened, Lok?*" Josh wondered. "*You fall asleep back there?*"

Nathan pulled the fighter into a tight turn, coming back around as the training course reconfigured itself into tighter groupings.

"*Unlike the previous level, in which all gates were evenly spaced, the intermediate course has clusters of three to four gates that are close together, with longer distances between each cluster. There are targets for your weapons officer to hit at the first and last gates in each cluster.*"

"I'm ready," Loki assured him.

"I'm turning into the first gate now," Nathan announced.

"*Increase your forward speed by ten percent,*" Master Koku instructed.

"Increasing speed by ten percent," Nathan acknowledged as he applied forward thrust and waited for his speed to build.

"*You will need to roll and turn at a faster rate, due to your increased speed and the tighter spacing of the gates,*" Master Koku warned.

"I know."

"I'm picking up a target," Loki reported. "Top right corner of the first gate. I'm tagging it for lasers."

"*Lasers are generally used for close-in targets,*" Master Koku advised. "*From further out, missiles would be your first choice.*"

"I thought I'd take it one weapons system at a time for now," Loki replied. "Until I get used to the system's responsiveness."

"*As you wish. However, had the targets been live...*"

"I know," Loki replied, cutting him off. "We'd already be taking shield hits and losing points."

"*Or worse.*"

Loki fired the starboard dorsal laser turret, disabling the first target.

"Nicely done," Nathan congratulated as he brought the fighter into a tight turn for the second gate, just as they passed through the first.

Loki studied the gates on the sensor display in the center of his console for a moment. "If you take the next gate low, I can take out the outbound target with one of our ventral turrets now, instead of later."

"Copy that." Nathan pushed the nose of the fighter down, bringing his intended flight path away from the left side of the gate and down toward the bottom right.

Loki waited until the ship passed through the second gate and pitched upward, giving him a clear firing line at the target on the fourth gate, still two gates ahead of their current position. He fired the port ventral laser turret, sending a beam of highly-charged laser energy passing under the edge of the third gate, striking the target on the fourth. "Got it."

"Nice shot," Nathan said as he pulled the ship into a roll and arced over the bottom edge of the next gate, its border passing over their heads by no more than two meters.

"*A good shot, but a lousy tactic,*" Master Koku scolded. "*The maneuver will add two seconds to your time, which the early shot will not replace.*"

301

"*I could've told you that,*" Josh boasted.

"But it would be a good tactic in battle," Nathan argued.

"*There are no gates in battle.*"

Nathan steered the ship through the fourth gate and into the longer stretch between the first and second cluster.

"Two targets on the first gate in the second cluster," Loki reported. "Locking missiles on targets. Missiles away," he added, pressing the missile launch button.

Two stub-missiles darted away from the missile pods on either side of their fuselage, streaking toward the next gate. A few seconds later, two flashes of light appeared on the top and bottom of the next gate.

"Targets disabled," Loki reported confidently.

"*And in proper fashion,*" Master Koku confirmed.

Nathan dove through the first gate of the second cluster, rolling the ship over and entering a climbing left turn, allowing his engine nacelles to continue their sweeping movements without changing direction as they moved from one thrust position to the next.

As they approached the last gate in the cluster, Loki deftly fired their lasers, disabling another target just before they passed through the gate.

"This is easy," Loki bragged in a fashion unlike him.

"*You expected it to be difficult to disable things that do not fire back?*" Master Koku wondered.

"*This guy is killin' me, Lok,*" Josh exclaimed in delight.

Loki looked at the next group of gates, noticing something peculiar. "Uh…"

"*Yeah, I see it,*" Josh replied.

"There are more than four gates there," Loki warned.

"*I thought you said there were only three or four gates in each cluster?*" Josh said to Master Koku.

"*It is possible that I was not entirely forthcoming,*" Master Koku replied.

"Am I seeing things, or are those gates moving?" Nathan wondered.

"*Holy crap,*" Josh exclaimed.

"*Too easy for you now, Mister Sheehan?*" Master Koku inquired.

"*I'm calculating the gates' drift rates and directions for you now, Cap'n.*"

"I can't use missiles," Loki decided. "I'm going manual with the lasers," he added, grabbing the laser controls.

"I can match my drift angle with that of the gate's, if it helps," Nathan offered.

"*If you pass through the gate without disabling the targets on it, you will lose points,*" Master Koku warned.

"I know!" Loki barked, feeling the pressure. "Crap, there are two of them."

"I'm matching the drift," Nathan decided.

Loki took his first shot with the starboard dorsal turret, but missed the target by more than a meter. "Damn it!" he cursed, firing again. "Got it!"

"Gate threshold in five seconds," Nathan warned.

"*Roll her to starboard, Cap'n!*" Josh urged.

"That's going to make the next turn more difficult," Nathan said as he rolled the ship to the right.

Loki fired the port ventral laser turret as the ship rolled over, disabling the second target on the left side of the gate as they passed through. "Got it!"

"*You just lost ten points,*" Master Koku announced.

"But I got it!" Loki insisted.

"*The position transponder is in the nose of your ship,*" Master Koku explained. "*You disabled the second target, but not before the nose of your ship had breached the gate threshold.*"

"*You can make up the lost points by flying faster!*" Josh urged. "*Increase your roll rate, and hold it through the next two gates! And speed the fuck up!*"

"Got it," Nathan replied, trying to remain calm. He kept his thrusters firing as he rolled, increasing their forward speed as he passed the next gate, then held the roll as he eased the ship to starboard, on course for the third gate.

"*Pause your roll for a few seconds as you pass the gate,*" Josh advised. "*Then start it up again at half the previous roll rate as you turn toward the fourth gate.*"

"Are you sure?" Nathan asked.

"*Of course, I'm sure,*" Josh insisted, sounding slightly insulted.

Nathan stopped their roll as he passed through the next gate, starting it again at a slower rate a few seconds later, pulling the ship into a shallow left turn, despite the fact that he was rolling right. "This doesn't feel right."

"The next gate is going to be too close, Josh!" Loki warned.

"*Flip her as you pass through the gate,*" Josh instructed. "*Nose over ass! Then neutralize your nacelles and fire full thrust for three seconds!*"

Nathan had no time to acknowledge the instruction, already pitching the fighter's nose up hard, flipping the ship over as it passed through the gate. Two seconds later, his engine nacelles reached their neutral position, and he jammed his throttles all the way forward, holding the thrust button for three full seconds as instructed, shaving off a tremendous amount of forward speed in the process.

"*Now flat spin left ninety!*" Josh ordered.

Nathan complied, immediately bringing the nose of the ship ninety degrees to the left, so they were essentially flying sideways.

"*Full burn for three!*" Josh barked.

Thrusters fired as Nathan pressed and held the button. The fighter jumped forward, instantly shifting their flight path a few degrees to the right of their original course.

"*That's it!*" Josh announce proudly. "*Another ninety left, and then burn for five to get back up to original entry speed, plus five percent to make up the lost points!*"

Nathan completed the last turn and fired his thrusters as instructed, passing through the fifth gate, which was sliding away from them from left to right.

"Firing!" Loki announced as laser bolts streaked over their head toward the sixth gate.

"*You have regained your lost points,*" Master Koku announced. "*You have even regained the two seconds you lost earlier, thanks to your controller.*"

"Good work, Josh," Nathan congratulated.

"*You should be doing the piloting, young man,*" Master Koku said to Josh.

"*That's what I told them!*"

* * *

"Ensign Tegg, Ensign Wabash," Captain Nash began. "This is your new crew. This is your engineer, Master Sergeant Biller; your sensor operator, Sergeant Kotai; your med-tech and gunner, Specialist Havins; and your systems tech and gunner, Specialist Aris."

Robert turned to the crew. "Ladies and gentlemen, this is your new captain, Ensign Charnelle Tegg, and her first officer, Ensign Sari Wabash. Your new call sign is Striker Four," he added, turning back toward Ensign Tegg. "Any questions?"

"No, sir," Charnelle replied, smartly.

"Then I suggest you get acquainted with your crew and familiarize them with your ship. You have less than two days to get them ready."

Great, Charnelle thought as Captain Nash departed. "How many of you have experience with a Cobra gunship?" she asked her new crew. When no one raised their hand, she asked, "How many of you have even *seen* a Cobra gunship?" When everyone's hand went up, she added, "Other than the one behind me, that is."

Everyone's hand went down.

"Great." Charnelle turned to look at Sari. "This should be fun."

"How about I take Havins and Aris and show them their guns," Sari suggested.

"Good idea," Charnelle agreed. "I'll show the other two their consoles, and review combat protocols with them."

"Looks like another sleepless night," Sari joked as he turned and headed toward their gunship. "Havins! Aris! On me!"

"That leaves you two with me," Charnelle told the others. "Biller, right?" she asked the master sergeant as they followed the others toward the gunship.

"That's right."

"Which engineering department were you attached to on the Aurora?" Charnelle wondered.

"Waste systems," the master sergeant replied.

"Wonderful."

* * *

"Jesus! This is insane!" Loki exclaimed as their fighter twisted and rolled, pitched and yawed.

"These gates are moving *way* faster than the last time!" Nathan exclaimed as he barely managed to avoid colliding with the gate as he passed through it.

"Another gun emplacement!" Loki warned. "Upper left of the gate, two gates from this next one."

"I see it," Nathan replied, glancing at his sensor display.

Something suddenly slammed into them, sending the ship's aft end sliding to starboard.

"What the hell was that?" Nathan exclaimed.

"We're hit!" Loki warned.

"*Moving targets!*" Josh announced over comms. "*Four drones! Closing on you from your seven high! They've got plasma cannons!*"

"Why the hell didn't you warn us?" Loki wondered.

"*I didn't even* know *there were drones, let alone armed ones,*" Josh defended. "*They came out of nowhere!*"

"My ass, they did!" Loki insisted. "Missile launches!"

"*The drones have missiles?*" Josh said in surprise. "*What the hell?*"

"Popping countermeasures!"

"Get ready to drop two missiles, but without engine ignition!" Nathan instructed.

"What? Why?"

"Just do it!" Nathan ordered as he snaked around and through the next gate. "And be ready to remotely detonate them!"

"Whatever you say."

Nathan glanced up at the approaching gate.

"Drop the missiles! Pop two spinners, as well! Now!" he ordered as they passed through the next gate.

Two missiles slid smoothly out of the missile pods, but their engines did not fire. Nathan thrusted up and away from the drifting missiles, just enough to avoid hitting the next gate as he passed through it. As they did, two spinners launched out of their aft, starboard countermeasures pod, and began drifting forward just like the stub-missiles.

"*Fuck!*" Josh cursed. "*Four missiles! Five seconds!*"

"Detonate!" Nathan ordered.

Loki pressed the button and remotely detonated the two drifting stub-missiles, just as they were about to make contact with the gate they had just passed through. The explosions caught the drifting countermeasures, breaking them up and creating a debris field in the area of the gate, into which all four pursuing missiles flew.

Four more detonations behind them.

"*Fuck yeah!*" Josh exclaimed over comms with glee. "*Nicely done, guys! But don't forget about the gun turrets on the last gate!*"

"Trust me, I haven't," Loki assured him.

"Don't forget about those drones, either," Nathan reminded him. "They're still back there."

"I'm telling you, there are no attack drones in the Gunyoki races!" Loki insisted.

"*I am using them to simulate the opponent you would face in the final round,*" Master Koku explained. "*Assuming you get that far, of course.*"

Loki was sure he could *hear* the old Gunyoki master smiling through the comms.

"Incoming fire!" Nathan warned. "From the last gate!"

Their forward shields lit up as bolts of plasma

energy slammed into them. Nathan tried to dodge the incoming fire by jinking about wildly, but it was to no avail.

"*You look like a kalla bug on a hot walkway,*" Master Koku laughed. "*Just fly the ship.*"

"They're shooting at us," Nathan replied.

"*That is why you have shields,*" Master Koku reminded him.

"But we lose points with every hit!"

"*Not exactly,*" Master Koku corrected. "*Every hit reduces your available shield strength, but points are not taken away for the hits; they are subtracted at the end of the race, not during, which gives you time to recharge the shields to avoid losing those points.*"

"You could have told us that before!" Nathan exclaimed.

"*You could have, and should have, read it in the rule book,*" Master Koku replied indignantly. "*There will be time to recharge your shields toward the end of the race.*"

"I'm sorry, Captain," Loki said. "I should have known that."

"Don't worry about it," Nathan insisted. "Just keep those fucking drones off our ass!"

"I'm locking missiles on them," Loki announced. "As soon as you can, do an end-over, so I can launch!"

"After the next gate," Nathan told him. He continued his rolling turn, then cut his thrust and flipped over, passing backward through the gate.

"Launching four!" Loki announced.

Four stub-missiles leapt from their launchers, streaking behind them toward the pursuing drones. As Nathan rolled the ship back over nose first, the missiles spread out and found their targets.

"Hell, yeah!" Loki exclaimed as all four drone contacts disappeared from his sensor screen.

"*Uh, Cap'n, you need to fly faster,*" Josh warned.

"I'm already doing three-twenty, Josh," Nathan replied.

"*I know! You need to fly faster, trust me!*"

"What's up?" Nathan asked as he boosted his thrust.

"*There are four gun turrets on the last two gates! They're going to pound the fuck out of you, and it's going to cost you a bunch of points, because you won't have any time to recharge your shields before you reach the finish gate! Flying fast is the only way I can see to make up for it,*" Josh explained.

"It would've been nice to know that ahead of time, Josh!" Nathan scolded.

"*I know, Cap'n, I'm sorry. I should've studied the course better. I'm not used to being on comms while someone else is doing the flying!*"

"If you can swing wide when you transition between gates thirty-two and thirty-three, I might be able to target at least two of those turrets with missiles," Loki suggested.

"That will cost us time," Nathan said as he rolled the fighter over and pushed the nose down, just in time to make the next gate.

"*Not if you fly faster!*" Josh urged.

"I am flying faster!" Nathan insisted. "Be ready, Loki! I'll cut gate thirty-two danger-close and swing wide."

"*Use the same maneuver I gave you yesterday, Cap'n!*" Josh urged. "*Flip, burn, spin, and burn again!*"

"That's the plan!" Nathan confirmed.

"Oh, my God," Loki exclaimed, glancing up as the

310

edge of gate thirty-two missed their canopy by half a meter.

Nathan pulled hard on his flight control stick, applying full thrust for a full second, grunting as he squeezed the muscles in his abdomen and legs to keep from passing out as the blood tried to leave his head. "Here we go!" he warned as he cut thrust and pushed his nose back down hard. He suddenly felt himself being pushed upward, his restraints digging into his shoulders. A quick twist to the right on his control stick, and his Gunyoki fighter yawed to starboard, just enough to bring his nose around to point at the last gate no more than a kilometer away.

"Locking missiles onto targets!" Loki announced.

That's when Nathan saw it. Flashes of red-orange in the distance as the plasma cannon turrets Loki was targeting opened fire on them.

"Missiles away!" Loki announced.

Nathan didn't wait to be sure the missiles were clear, as plasma bolts were already streaking past them on all sides. He pressed the thrust button on his flight control stick, firing his main engines at full power, pushing him back into his seat hard and nearly knocking the wind out of him. He glanced out the window as he commanded his fighter to yaw back to the left. His engines were burning at full thrust, but he was still sliding directly toward the edge of gate thirty-three.

"We're not going to make it!" Loki exclaimed.

Nathan said nothing. He just kept adjusting his yaw in an attempt to get maximum delta from his engines. He rolled the ship onto its right side, engines still burning at full power.

"Fuck!" Loki exclaimed.

"*You'll make it!*" Josh insisted.

Master Koku said nothing.

Nathan glanced upward. They were headed for a collision.

"Five seconds to missile impact!" Loki announced. "Are you at full power, Captain?" he pleaded.

"I am," Nathan stated calmly.

"Missile impact!" Loki announced. "Two targets down!"

The fighter shook as its engines burned at maximum power. Nathan glanced upward every few seconds, trying to judge whether or not they would collide with the approaching gate.

"We're not going to make it, Captain," Loki warned again.

"*You'll make it!*" Josh repeated.

"No, we won't," Loki insisted. "You've got to abort and miss the gate!"

"No way," Nathan insisted.

"Captain!"

"*Shut up, Loki!*" Josh yelled. "*You'll make it!*"

"We're going to hit!" Loki declared. "Aft, just forward of the countermeasures pods!" Loki braced himself for impact. "FUCK!"

Nathan glanced up as the collision alarm began to sound. The gate's edge now filled his view. Loki was right.

Oh, God.

He removed his finger from the thrust button, cutting his engines.

"What are you doing?" Loki demanded.

Nathan armed his docking thrusters and fired, pushing his nose upward, and sliding past the gate, missing it by only a few centimeters.

"*I FUCKING TOLD YOU!*" Josh screamed over comms.

* * *

Nathan climbed slowly down the ladder from the Gunyoki fighter's cockpit. Every muscle in his body ached, and he felt mentally exhausted.

"That was some sweet flyin', Cap'n," Josh exclaimed as he came walking across the hangar bay. "Some pretty good shootin', too, Lok."

"Thanks," Nathan said as he set his feet on the deck.

"I'm going to go take a nap," Loki said as he stepped down from the ladder.

"Good idea," Nathan said.

"You showed improvement today," Master Koku said as he approached. "However, I would suggest, that in the future, you do not allow yourself to lose mental focus under pressure."

"What are you talking about?" Nathan wondered.

"All that yelling and arguing. It disrupts one's concentration, and causes one to make rash decisions. When one remains serene, even under pressure, one's mind remains clear, and answers come with ease."

"I'll try to remember that," Nathan replied halfheartedly.

"See that you do," Master Koku urged. "You will need it in your next training flight."

"I thought we were done for the day," Nathan said, looking disappointed.

"Although there is still much that I could teach you, there is still one thing you have not yet tried in a Gunyoki fighter."

"What's that?" Nathan asked.

"The one thing the Gunyoki was originally designed to do. I believe your people call it 'dogfighting'."

"But that only comes in the finals, right?"

"Correct."

"*You* said I wouldn't make it to the finals. Have you changed your mind?" Nathan wondered.

"I have not," Master Koku replied. "However, stranger things have happened, and you should be prepared, nonetheless."

Nathan leaned back, nearly falling against the ladder. The thought of enduring a few more grueling hours, fighting the ever changing G-forces as he wrestled his fighter to get it to do his bidding, was disheartening.

Then it occurred to him. "Who am I going to fly against?"

Master Koku smiled, which was unusual for him. "I recommend you get some rest," he said as he walked away. "You will need it."

Nathan turned to look at Master Koku as he walked away. "Who am I flying against?" he asked again. Nathan threw his hands up in frustration as the old man headed toward the large bay doors that separated their hangar from its transfer airlock. The doors began to part slowly, revealing a vintage Gunyoki fighter that had just arrived. Nathan grabbed Quory as he and Vladimir walked past on their way to inspect Nathan's ship after its last training flight. "Whose ship is that?" he asked Quory, pointing to the vintage fighter his instructor was walking toward.

"Why, Master Koku's, of course," Quory answered.

Nathan's head fell back. "You've got to be kidding me."

* * *

Vladimir was shoulders-deep in a Gunyoki shield generator, when he felt a tap on his shoulder. "I'm busy," he grunted. The tap repeated. "I said I'm busy."

"Vladimir."

Vladimir rolled his eyes. "*Bozhe moi.*" It was her again. "What is it, Abigail?"

"We think we solved the problem."

"We?" Vladimir extracted his arms from the shield generator and turned around to see Abby and Deliza, both with data pads in their hands. "*Da, konyeshna.*"

"We *can* convert their reactors to static-state," Abby said, "and with minimal effort."

"Impossible..."

"That's what I thought..."

"The entire structure of the core would have to be reconfigured..."

"Not if the reaction mass is reduced to half its current size," Abby explained.

Vladimir looked at Abby. "I believe I suggested this two days ago, and you told me it would not work."

"Because you didn't suggest adding a second containment field *within* the first. *You* wanted to put a bunch of limiters in there to maintain the static-state, which would have been a nightmare to keep balanced. A containment field that small is self-balancing." Abby handed her data pad to Vladimir, so he could see for himself.

Vladimir studied the designs on Abby's data pad. His brow furrowed at first, then his left eyebrow went up. After several more facial contortions, he said, "This might work. But this is not the work of a physicist."

"My idea, Deliza's engineering," Abby replied.

"You mean, *my* idea, *your* changes, and *her* engineering."

"Really, Commander?"

Vladimir waved his hand dismissively, handing

the data pad back to Abby. "It does not matter. The Gunyoki Council would never approve the changes. We would be disqualified."

"We checked the rules," Deliza said. "The only limit is the introduction of *new* technology and technology that comes from *outside* Rakuen science. This is simply a modification of their existing technology, *and* it uses components already in existence *on* Rakuen. There is no way they can disqualify us."

"If it is so easy, why has no one on Rakuen done this before?"

"Their understanding of physics, especially in the area of power generation and containment fields, is surprisingly limited, considering how advanced they are in other areas," Abby explained.

"We have seen this in other societies, when Ranni Enterprises has ventured beyond the Pentaurus sector," Deliza said. "Civilizations usually have limited resources, forcing them to choose which areas to research and improve upon. Areas that are adequate to the immediate needs are often neglected. The Rakuen fusion reactors use seawater as their reactive material, which is abundant on their world. They also position their reactors on the seafloor, which means *size* is not an issue for them. And they have never cared to be an interstellar civilization. So, you see, it comes as no surprise that they never bothered to fool with static-state reactors."

Vladimir still appeared skeptical. "How will this change help Nathan?"

"It will give him at least thirty percent more power," Abby told him.

"So, he could have full power for *two* of his three primary systems at the same time, instead of just one?" Vladimir rubbed his head. "I am not sure that will be worth the risk."

"How can *more* power be *not* worth it?" Deliza wondered.

"What if we make the modifications and it does not work?" Vladimir pointed out. "We only have a single spare reactor. If something goes wrong with *it*, we will be finished."

"The race lasts an entire Rakuen day," Deliza argued. "And it's highly unlikely his variable-state reactor will fail in the first three rounds, so we'll have plenty of time to convert the spare *back* to a variable-state configuration."

Vladimir sighed. "How long will it take to make the conversion and test it?"

"At least twelve hours, I'm afraid," Deliza said. "Maybe longer."

"There will be no time to test it *in* the ship." Vladimir looked at Deliza. "Is there time to get another spare, just in case?"

"Maybe."

"It's your call, Commander," Abby stated. "You're the chief engineer."

Vladimir was surprised by her statement. "Very well, get started."

"Yes!" both Abby and Deliza exclaimed.

"Doctor, just one question."

Abby turned back to look at Vladimir. "Yes?"

"Why did you listen to *Deliza,* and not to *me*?"

Abby smiled. "Because Deliza is *not* you."

"*Shto*?" Vladimir said as they walked away.

* * *

"All patrols report negative contacts," Lieutenant Commander Vidmar reported from the Aurora's tactical station. "Strikers One through Four are on station."

"Very well," Cameron replied from the command chair. "Mister Bickle?"

"Evasive jump route to Rakuen plotted and ready, sir," the navigator replied.

"Comms, let Commander Kaplan know she now has command of the fleet."

"Aye, sir."

Cameron felt a sense of dread wash over her. The Aurora had been by the Karuzari fleet's side, protecting the ragtag group, for twenty-five days now, and other than that first day over Corinair, they had not fired a single shot in its defense.

"Commander Kaplan confirms she has command of the fleet, Captain," the communications officer confirmed.

"Very well." Cameron took a deep breath. She worried the fleet had become complacent, secure in the knowledge that the odds of the Dusahn locating them were beyond astronomical. "Helm, take us to Rakuen."

"Aye, sir," Lieutenant Dinev replied.

"Starting jump series in three......two......one..."

But so had been the Aurora's super jump into the middle of a battle, in the Pentaurus sector, eight years ago.

* * *

"How are you feeling, Captain?" Master Koku asked over comms. *"Did you get sufficient rest?"*

"I don't think that's going to come until well *after* the race," Nathan admitted.

"Do not worry. Odds are, it will be over quickly."

"Thanks."

"He's just trying to get in your head, Cap'n," Josh insisted.

"There are already two people in there, as it is," Nathan joked.

"If you're trying to inspire confidence, you're failing," Jessica told Nathan over comms.

"Sorry, I'm not feeling terribly inspiring, at the moment."

"What happens next?" she asked Josh, who was sitting next to her in their control room back on the race platform.

"They're approaching the practice area, now," Josh said. "Race protocol states that, as soon as they pass the last gate, they peel away in opposite directions and start the fight with head on passes. So, that's probably what Master Koku is going to have them do now."

"Head on is the most difficult shot," General Telles said.

"It's also the most equal," Josh added. "Neither ship has an advantage, unless one has more available power for their shields than the other."

"It is the most deadly, as well," General Telles added. "It is the only angle at which the Gunyoki can bring all her weapons onto its target at once. It is said that a *true* Gunyoki requires *only* the first shot," General Telles stated.

"Then this could be a very long day," Josh replied.

"In a few moments, we will break in opposite directions," Master Koku instructed over comms. *"Each of us will enter the dogfight area from opposite sides. All Gunyoki dogfights begin with a head on pass."*

"Understood," Nathan replied.

"*According to Telles, they usually end that way, too,*" Josh added.

"They used to," Loki corrected. "Not as often, since the independents started having more success."

"Something tells me Master Koku is a single-shot kind of guy," Nathan muttered.

"*You will break right, I will break left,*" Master Koku instructed. "*In three......two......one......break.*"

Nathan rolled the ship to the right, pulling up on the nose as he fired his main engines to begin his turn. "Give me an intercept angle, Loki."

"Should be on your screen now, Captain," Loki replied.

Nathan glanced at his view screen, noting the green arc. He held his thrust just long enough to bring his ship onto the arc, then rolled back left, and fired his thrusters again to come around to port to begin the fight.

"He's coming around on an intercept heading," Josh reported as Vladimir and Quory entered the control room.

"What are you doing here?" Jessica asked Vladimir.

"We're waiting for a part to be fabricated," Vladimir replied. "How is Nathan doing?"

"They're setting up for the first pass now," General Telles said.

"Any sign of the Seiiki?" Vladimir wondered.

"We got word from the Aurora via comm-drone about an hour ago," Jessica told him. "They were still finishing up with the upgrades and decided to just stay aboard the Aurora until she reached Rakuen. They should be jumping in at any time."

"Good. We have a lot of spare parts that need to be tested before the race tomorrow, and I will be up all night going over every system in Nathan's ship, to be sure it is ready."

"You mean *we* will be up all night," Quory corrected.

"I thought you were afraid of losing your job with Yokimah Racing," Jessica said.

"Miss Ta'Akar has assured me that I will have a position at her shuttle plant, if need be. Assuming, of course, that the captain wins."

"I imagine your job with Yokimah Racing will be secure if he loses, as well," General Telles observed.

"This is true," Quory admitted. "But it will be so much more exciting if he wins, don't you think?"

───────────

"*You're crossing the dogfight perimeter now,*" Josh reported.

"Copy that," Loki replied. "We're clear to engage, Captain."

Nathan tapped his targeting system, selecting the twin plasma torpedo cannons on the front of his engine nacelles. The system immediately locked onto Master Koku's older fighter and began adjusting the nacelle angles inward to account for the target's diminishing range. "Target acquired."

"*If you've got him, he's got you,*" Josh warned.

Nathan pressed his firing button three times in rapid succession, sending twelve plasma torpedoes streaking toward the oncoming fighter. As soon as the last four torpedoes left their tubes, he rolled the ship to the left, into the course of his opponent, and pitched down as he fired his main engines again. As the ship rolled and dove, four plasma torpedoes streaked past them, missing by less than a meter.

"No joy," Loki reported. "He jinked at the last second, just like us."

"*He's breaking left, your right,*" Josh warned. "*He's diving, too!*"

"He's trying to get under us, the same way I'm trying to get under him," Nathan announced. "I'm going to let him."

"*I'd continue diving,*" Josh argued. "*Make him come at you from above, where your countermeasures are more effective.*"

Nathan held his dive a few seconds longer.

"*I thought you were going up,*" Josh wondered.

"Not yet."

———

"This is too easy," General Telles observed. "I suspect that Master Koku is setting a trap."

"He is an old man, you know," Josh said. "And he hasn't really flown that thing in twenty some-odd years. Maybe he's just rusty, or a bit senile."

"He is neither," the general replied. "The Gunyoki training rivals that of the Ghatazhak. That level of training stays with a man for all of his days."

"They're both diving," Jessica noticed, looking at the view screen.

"They're both showing the other their most protected side," Josh explained.

"But one of them must break first," General Telles pointed out.

"So, he's playing *chicken* with Nathan?" Josh wondered.

"I believe so. Remember, Master Koku is also attempting to *teach* Nathan to fight, not necessarily to *win* the fight himself. He may be attempting to test the captain's resolve."

Josh turned back toward the view screen as he

tapped his comm-set. "Cap'n, we think the old man's laying a trap..."

"...*He's playing chicken with you, to see if you'll break first.*"

"Are you suggesting we bail now?" Nathan wondered.

"*No way! If you do, he'll just turn into you and take a kill shot at your belly. He's expecting you to pitch the whole ship up, just like you would in an Eagle. Hold as long as you can, but when you break, keep your topside to him and engage with your dorsal laser cannons.*"

"And how exactly do I do that?" Nathan wondered.

"*Fly your nacelles, not your ship,*" Josh insisted.

"Okay, yeah," Nathan replied, his voice unsure. "That's different, but I think I understand what you're saying. In fact, I believe that's what he's been trying to get me to do for the last few days."

"It would've been nice if he'd just *told* you that to begin with," Loki commented.

"He doesn't work that way, trust me."

Loki's attention was suddenly diverted to the sensor screen in front of him. "What the...?"

"*He's breaking early!*" Josh exclaimed. "*He's transitioning down! Flip now and hold your course!*"

In a split second, Nathan calculated his next step. He pushed his stick in the opposite direction that he wanted his nose to move, knowing that doing so would keep his engine nacelles thrusting in the same direction, while he swung his nose downward to keep his dorsal side pointing toward his opponent. He felt his restraints digging into his shoulders and the blood rushing to his head as the ship pitched over rapidly on the lateral axis that connected the aft end of the fighter to its engine nacelles.

"He's leveled off," Loki warned. "Jesus! He's locking his plasma torpedo cannons on us!"

———

"How the hell did he get his gungines on target so fast?" Josh wondered.

"What the hell's a gungine?" Jessica asked.

"An engine with a big gun on the front," Josh explained. "He's firing! Roll left! Pitch up! Max thrust!"

"That's stupid," Jessica said.

"I don't know. Gungine has a nice ring to it," Vladimir commented.

"Thank you," Josh said as he watched the view screen.

———

The fighter shook violently as the plasma torpedoes slammed into their dorsal shields, causing them to glow a brilliant red-orange for several seconds.

"Dorsal shields are down fifty percent!" Loki warned.

"From a single blow?"

"That was *four* torpedoes at once, Captain," Loki reminded him.

"*I believe Master Koku is attempting to weaken your dorsal shields, thus forcing you to show your weaker, ventral side, so he can finish you off quickly,*" General Telles warned. "*This is a common tactic used when a kill shot is not made in the opening, head-on pass.*"

"Then we don't show him our topside again," Nathan concluded. "At least not until our dorsal shields have recharged."

"If we keep pouring power into weapons *and*

maneuvering, it will take at least five minutes to get our shields back up to full strength," Loki warned.

"How many hits can our ventral side take?" Nathan wondered.

"One hit like that will likely blow the emitters."

"Okay, we want to avoid that," Nathan decided as he brought the fighter into a steep turn and rolled it to the right.

"*Aurora calling Lieutenant Commander Nash, do you copy?*"

Jessica tapped her comm-set. "Aurora, go for Nash."

"*Stand by for XO, sir.*"

"What's going on?" Vladimir asked, noticing Jessica's response.

"The Aurora is here."

"Finally."

"*Nash, XO,*" Cameron called. "*Status?*"

"XO, Nash. We're good here. We're on the Gunyoki race platform. Actual is on a training flight. You should be able to see him in sector four two seven. Two-ship element."

"*We have them on sensors,*" Cameron replied. "*Which one is Actual?*"

"Unfortunately, he's the one getting his ass handed to him."

"*Lovely.*"

Master Koku's fighter slipped smoothly under Nathan with such speed and precision that Nathan barely had time to realize his opponent had done so, let alone change the attitude of his ship to protect his weakened dorsal shields. The ship rocked again as both plasma torpedoes and laser bolts slammed into his port shields.

"Damn it!" Loki exclaimed. "He's moving around so much I can't get anything to lock on him."

"I can fire blind the next time he tries to slip under us," Nathan suggested.

"Anything is better than just getting pummeled by this guy."

"*I thought he was one of your heroes?*" Josh teased.

"He is," Loki admitted. "But right now, I just want to put a stub-missile in his backside!"

"Well, maybe you should," Nathan suggested as he flipped his engine nacelles over, and fired his main engines at full thrust.

"What are you doing?" Loki yelled.

"Putting some distance between us, so you can launch stub-missiles," Nathan explained.

"*Fuck yeah!*" Josh exclaimed over comms.

"I don't have a lock!"

"Just fire a full spread!" Nathan ordered. "Eight per side! Now, now, now!"

"Firing!" Loki replied, his fingers dancing across the launch control pad. "Missiles away!"

Nathan kept his engines burning, but changed the angle on his nacelles in relation to their fuselage, so the ship would descend below their opponent while still keeping their nose facing in the same direction. As he did so, two flashes of light appeared directly in front of them, no more than a kilometer away.

"Two hits!" Loki declared. "He just lost his starboard shield!"

"Fuck, he's closing on us," Nathan realized as the range to his target suddenly started falling off rapidly. "He must've reversed thrust, the same as us." Nathan took his finger off the thrust button, and rotated his engine nacelles back around, so his thrust nozzles were again facing aft, then pressed the button again, throwing them back in their seats.

"Jesus, would you stop doing everything at full power?" Loki complained. "You fly like Josh!"

"*I heard that!*"

"Note to Vlad," Nathan said. "Loki wants more juice for the inertial dampeners." Nathan cut his thrust again as the range to his opponent approached zero. He pitched his nacelles down and opened fire with his plasma torpedo cannons, just as Master Koku's fighter passed under him. Unfortunately, his opponent rolled his ship onto one side, allowing the shots to miss him entirely.

"How the hell does he do that?" Nathan wondered.

"*He's on your six again,*" Josh warned.

"No shit," Loki replied, sounding irritated. The ship rocked again as more energy weapons slammed into their aft shields.

"They just lost their aft shields, sir," Lieutenant Commander Kono reported from the Aurora's sensor station. "And their dorsal and port shields are almost gone, as well."

"This is a training flight, right?" Lieutenant Commander Vidmar asked.

"Not like any training I remember," Cameron admitted.

"Should we put a search and rescue Reaper on standby?" the lieutenant commander asked.

"That might not be a bad idea," Cameron agreed.

"Look at that guy fly," Lieutenant Dinev said in amazement. "Who is he?"

"I don't know," Cameron replied. "But I hope he's on *our* side."

———

Nathan flipped his ship over, rolling to starboard while he tried to bring the plasma cannons on the front of his engine nacelles toward Master Koku's fighter, but it was too late.

"We just lost our ventral shields!" Loki exclaimed.

"*You have to make a run for it!*" Josh urged. "*Stay out of his crosshairs until your shields recharge!*"

Two more plasma cannon torpedoes slammed into them, rocking the ship, and causing them to lose all power.

"We've lost all power!" Loki declared. "Shields, weapons, propulsion…Everything is down."

"*I believe they call that a kill,*" Josh announced.

Nathan took his hands off his controls, content to just drift for a few minutes. "Well, at least we made him earn it. How long did it take him? Five, six minutes? That's not too bad for our first Gunyoki dogfight, right?"

"*Actually, it was a minute thirty,*" Josh corrected. "*And General Telles is pretty sure he was playing with you the whole time.*"

"*By the way, the Aurora is here,*" Jessica added.

"Great. Please tell me they didn't see that," Nathan pleaded.

"*Would you like to land and take a break, Captain?*" Master Koku wondered.

"Why, are you tired?"

"*Not in the slightest,*" Master Koku replied.

"Then let's go again," Nathan insisted.

"Just as soon as we get our power back on," Loki added.

* * *

Jessica walked across the Gunyoki bay, looking about. The hour was late, but everyone was still hard at work. Abby, Deliza, and Vlad were working on upgrades for the ship's reactor. Marcus, Dalen, and Neli were getting the ship ready for tomorrow's races, under the watchful eye of Quory. In the control room, General Telles and Loki were reviewing past Gunyoki races to better understand the strategies and habits of the men who Nathan might be facing.

"Where's Nathan?" Jessica asked Vlad as she approached the workbench where the three of them were working.

"In the lounge, with Josh and Yanni," Vladimir replied, his eyes never leaving the project in his hands.

Jessica continued across the bay, nodding at the Ghatazhak soldier in plain clothing who stood at the entrance from the bay to the race platform. General Telles had positioned a man at both entrances, and changed them out every two hours.

She made her way into the side offices, past the control room, and down the corridor, finally reaching the lounge. She had expected to see Josh and Yanni goofing off, and Nathan napping. But that wasn't what she saw, at all.

In the middle of the room sat Nathan, in a VR training helmet, his hands moving about in the air as if he were flying a Gunyoki fighter. Sitting at a table next to him was Josh, who was talking to Nathan as his controller, and Yanni, who was doing his best to play Loki's role during the simulation.

"What's he doing?" Jessica asked Josh as she entered.

"What does it look like?" Josh quipped.

"Shouldn't he be getting some rest?" Jessica insisted. "The qualifying runs start in three hours."

"Master Koku already signed him off," Josh replied. "He doesn't have to fly in the quals. He's already in."

"Does he know that?"

"Yup," Josh replied. "He just wants to make sure he's ready."

"Well, *is* he?"

"Oh, hell no," Josh exclaimed with a slight giggle. "But he's doing better. Yanni here came up with a sweet little training algorithm that uses simulated drone targets that shoot at you. Nasty little buggers."

"I call the program 'drone dancing'," Yanni said.

Jessica sighed. She had half expected that she, Vlad, and Nathan would hang out together, just as they had always done the night before a battle. It had become a ritual of sorts. She knew Cameron couldn't attend, since she was in charge of the Aurora in Nathan's absence, but the three of them... "Just make sure he gets some rest."

"You got it," Josh assured her.

Jessica turned and headed out. There would be no gathering of friends before the battle this night.

* * *

Master Koku entered the lounge as Josh was removing the VR helmet from Nathan's head. "Is this the device you have been using to train?" he asked as he entered.

"Yes," Nathan replied.

"How does it work?"

"You wear it on your head, and it sends signals to your brain to make you see, feel, hear, and smell. It's as if you were there, in the cockpit of a Gunyoki."

"Does it make you feel the G-forces, as well?"

"Fortunately, it does not."

"A pity," Master Koku said. "I rather like those forces. It makes one feel that he is *connected* with his ship." Master Koku touched the helmet lying on the table. "Seems a poor excuse for reality."

"It is," Nathan agreed. "But it's better than nothing."

"Does it teach you to fly like a *real* Gunyoki?"

"No, it does not."

Master Koku looked at Josh and Yanni. "May I have a moment alone with your captain, gentlemen?"

Josh looked at Nathan, who nodded.

Master Koku feigned interest in the VR helmet as he waited for Josh and Yanni to leave the lounge. "Do you have birds on your world?"

"Yes, thousands of different species," Nathan replied, looking confused.

"We have them, too, although, I think not as many. There is one, a bird of the sea, mostly. The kamohame. It is a large bird, with a wingspan of two meters. Since there is not much land on Rakuen, the kamohame must sometimes make long flights. They are experts at using air currents to glide upon, thus making their journey between islands less difficult." Master Koku closed his eyes as he spoke, looking back in his mind. "As a boy, I used to sit and watch them for hours, gliding effortlessly on the afternoon breeze. They would sail about, looking for prey. To hunt, they would dive, accelerating to incredible speeds before piercing the surface of the water to come back up with their meals moments later." Master Koku opened his eyes and looked at Nathan. "Do you have such birds on your world?"

"Yes, we do."

"And did you ever just sit and watch them?"

"Actually, I have," Nathan admitted. "I always marveled at how they could just hover in one position by simply facing into the wind, making tiny adjustments with their wings. Later, when my grandfather taught me to fly, we spent many hours riding thermal currents, practicing powerless flight. Not as efficient as a bird, but fun, nonetheless."

"This does not surprise me," Master Koku admitted. "I have seen this in your flying."

"Seen what?"

"The efficiency of using everything you have available to you to achieve your goal, but with the least amount of wasted effort. It seems most important to you."

Nathan smiled. "My grandfather used to tease me about how orderly I liked to keep the cockpit of the aircraft we flew in. I liked order."

"And it shows in the way you fly."

"Is that a compliment?" Nathan wondered, smiling.

"I am merely stating fact." Master Koku looked away, toward the view screen on the far wall that was showing the names of the men who had entered tomorrow's event. "The Gunyoki were once like the kamohame; efficient, fearless, dedicated. Now, that is all but lost. You see those names? I recognize only twenty-seven. Twenty-seven *true* Gunyoki, out of hundreds. Yokimah's dream of rebuilding Rakuen's defenses has failed," he admitted, hanging his head.

"Then, you *don't* believe the Gunyoki can defend Rakuen if the Dusahn invade."

"I do not," Master Koku admitted in disgrace.

"Then why don't you say something? Tell all of Rakuen what you think."

"I am but an old, and forgotten, man," Master Koku said.

"You are one of the greatest Gunyoki of all time," Nathan insisted. "Perhaps not everyone would listen to you, but many would. It would at least get people talking about it."

"Much like your entrance into tomorrow's event?" Master Koku wondered.

"You mean *today's* event," Nathan corrected, pointing to the time display on the wall, which indicated that it was three o'clock in the morning.

Master Koku smiled. "Perhaps, if you win, you will change the minds of those who matter," he said, tilting his head at the names on the view screen. He rose from his seat slowly, his old bones fatigued from a full day of flying, something he had not done in decades, but had thoroughly enjoyed, nonetheless. "Your grandfather, did he fly in battle?"

"He did," Nathan replied. "It was before I was born, however. He never really talked about it."

"Men who have seen war, feel no need to discuss it further," Master Koku said as he headed for the exit. As he passed, he patted Nathan on the shoulder. "Your grandfather would be proud of you, young captain."

Nathan sat, thinking, as the old Gunyoki master headed for the exit. "Master Koku?" he called out. Nathan turned to look at the old man. "Do I even have a chance?"

Master Koku smiled. "You would have made a fine Gunyoki, Captain Scott. Now, get some rest. You will need it."

Nathan watched as the old man left the room and disappeared into the corridor. For the first time in a week, he had hope.

* * *

Captain Garo was awakened rudely by the intercom in his quarters. Unlike the newer Dusahn warships, the Jar-Morenzo's accommodations were spartan, at best, even for her commanding officer. Although automation had been installed over the years, to reduce her crew requirements to only a handful, no effort had been made to turn the freed-up space into creature comforts for her remaining crew.

Captain Garo knew his hardships did not go unnoticed by his lord. He also knew that for his successful false-flag operations in the Sol sector, he would be getting command of one of the first new Dusahn warships that would soon be built in their newly acquired Takaran shipyards. He only hoped it would not take as long to build them as it had back in the Esinay system. The Esinayans had been a slow and difficult people to work with; too methodical, too careful. He had never met people so unwilling to take risks in the name of glory. The knowledge that soon they would be able to cut ties with that world delighted him to no end. He only hoped his ship would be given the honor of sterilizing that miserable little world, when the time came.

"What is it?" the captain grunted into the intercom. He rolled out of bed, sitting on the side of his bunk as the man on the intercom spoke.

"*We have arrived at our destination,*" the man said. "*We are now eight light years outside the Rogen system and have made contact with our informant on Rakuen.*"

"And?" the captain wondered, becoming impatient.

"*Captain Scott, and the Aurora, are there.*"

Captain Garo looked at the time display on the

bulkhead above the hatch. "There are still three hours until the races begin. Wake me again in two."

"*Yes, Captain.*"

Captain Garo lay back on his bunk. If he captured Captain Scott and destroyed the Aurora, he would surely get his new ship, perhaps even the very next one built.

CHAPTER TEN

Vladimir entered the control room, a concerned look on his face. "I need to speak with you," he announced.

Jessica and General Telles both looked at him.

"Where is Nathan?" Vladimir asked.

"He's sleeping, finally," Jessica answered. "What's up?"

Vladimir handed her his data pad. "I found this attached to the main power trunk that connects the reactor to the power distribution system."

"What is it?"

"A remote cut-off switch," Vladimir replied ominously. "And it is not in the ship's schematics or specifications. I have checked."

"When was it put there?" General Telles wondered.

"It had to be added *before* we received the ship," Vladimir insisted. "I have been with her *every moment* that she has been in the bay...ever since we first arrived. It could *not* have been installed during that time *without* my knowledge. In *fact*, I do *not believe* we would have discovered this device if we had *not* pulled the reactor in order to install the one we are upgrading." Vladimir shook his head. "If this device were to be activated, all power would be lost, and there would be no way to restore it in flight."

"Maybe Quory installed it?" Jessica suggested.

"It is possible," Vladimir admitted. "He was with the ship, alone, prior to our arrival. But he did not try to stop us from upgrading the reactor. If *he* planted the device..."

"Who else knows about this?" General Telles asked.

"I have told no one," Vladimir promised. "You are the first."

"Did you remove it?" Jessica wondered.

"No. It has tamper sensors. If I remove it, whoever put it there *will know*."

"Can you bypass it *without* disturbing the device?"

"I can install a bypass trunk to go around the device, but it would be best if I kept the original power trunk active, in case the device monitors power flow, as well."

"If you install a bypass trunk, won't there be a drop in the power levels traveling through the original trunk?" General Telles asked.

"Yes," Vladimir confirmed. "Perhaps thirty to forty percent. If we were using the original, variable-state reactor, it would definitely be noticeable. But the static-state reactor we are installing will produce thirty percent *more* power, so it might go unnoticed."

"And you're sure that bypassing it will be enough?" Jessica asked. "The last thing we need is for Nathan to lose power in the middle of a race."

"Yes, it will work," Vladimir assured her. "But that is what bothers me. This is a stupid way to cheat. After such a catastrophic power loss, there is sure to be a detailed inspection by race officials *after* the ship is recovered."

"Perhaps winning the race is *not* the goal of this device," General Telles suggested.

"If they activated it at the right moment, he could smash into an asteroid and be killed," Jessica surmised.

"Or worse," General Telles added.

Vladimir looked confused. "Worse than being dead?"

"Bypass the device, and do everything you can to

ensure that whoever is monitoring it will not learn that you have rendered it ineffective," General Telles instructed. "And you are to tell no one, understood?"

"Not even Nathan?"

"Especially not Nathan," Jessica insisted. "He's got enough to deal with right now."

"If you think that is best," Vladimir agreed.

"Good work, Vlad," Jessica congratulated. "You probably just saved Nathan and Loki's lives."

"*And* this rebellion," General Telles added.

"You think the intent is to capture him?" Jessica asked.

"*Bozhe moi,*" Vladimir gasped.

"Killing him makes him a martyr. Capturing him, so that he can be interrogated and tortured, makes him appear weak and uninspiring. And information gleaned from him would likely lead to our own destruction."

"You think the Dusahn are responsible?" Vladimir wondered.

"Either the Dusahn or Yokimah. Either Yokimah, or someone in his organization, is involved."

"If the Dusahn *are* pulling the strings, then it's through that Takaran businessman, Jorkar Seeley," Jessica insisted.

"A possibility," General Telles agreed. "Unfortunately, we have no way to be sure. We have yet to establish communications with Mister Espan, so we have no way to check on Mister Seeley's background."

"Perhaps I should...*investigate*?" Jessica suggested.

"Immediately," General Telles agreed.

Vladimir got a concerned look on his face as Jessica left the room with both purpose and enthusiasm. "What does she mean by *investigate*?" he asked the general.

"Better that you do not know."

* * *

"The first heat is about to begin," Josh announced.

"Are we recording every camera and sensor feed?" General Telles asked Loki, who was sitting next to Josh at the controller desk.

"Every drone camera, every static camera, and all the cameras mounted on both ships. We're also recording the main sensor feed from Race Control."

"Who is racing first?" Nathan asked.

"Ichi Aza," Master Koku replied.

"Is he good?"

"'Ichi' means 'clan' in old Raku," Loki explained.

"There are three Gunyoki clans," Master Koku elaborated. "Aza, Bonsa, and Konsai, named after the founders of the Gunyoki. The Gunyoki Council uses these names to identify the different race groups to honor the original Gunyoki clans."

"Which clan were you in?" Nathan wondered.

"I am of Ichi Aza."

"What clan am I in?"

"You have been assigned to Ichi Konsai," Master Koku replied. "But it is only a name, now. It has no meaning beyond identifying which group you are competing within during this event."

"Then why do you still consider yourself a member of Ichi Aza?" Nathan wondered.

"There are a handful of us who still race. Every group has at least one true member representing the original ichi. When I raced as a member of the true Ichi Aza, I was obligated to fly in that group. Nika Salenger, Tariq Taira, Tham Kors, Alayna Imai, and

Ryk Brown

several others, are all true members of their ichis, having trained under the masters of those clans."

"So, if you're a member of a *real* ichi, then you have to fly within that group; otherwise, they just assign you to whatever group they feel like."

"Incorrect. The Gunyoki Council chooses the ichi to which an entrant will be assigned."

"Based on what criteria?" Nathan wondered.

"The order of selection is based upon each ichi's standing, based on either the current season, or the standings at the end of last year's season."

"So, first, second, third, first, second, third, and so on?"

"Correct."

"I'm not sure I want to ask which round I was chosen in," Nathan commented.

"A wise decision," Master Koku agreed.

"The first heat is Ichi Aza," Loki reported. "Suli Noma versus Kylen Kunai. Both of them are independents."

"They're approaching the starting gate now," Josh reported.

Nathan leaned forward, his eyes darting between each set of camera views, and then from shot to shot within each set, as he tried to glean as much knowledge as possible. First the view from just over the pilot's left shoulder, which showed him the flight controls and console, as well as the view outside. Then the two chase drones, one of which was high left and slightly aft of the ship, and the other high right and just forward.

"The heat is on," Josh declared.

The first thing Nathan noticed was that both pilots pushed their throttles to full power, just before they passed through the starting gate. "They throttled up before they passed through the gate," Nathan said. "Isn't that cheating?"

"It takes one and a half seconds for a Gunyoki engine to go from zero to full power," Master Koku stated. "The rules dictate that they cannot be at full power until the race transponder in their nose *reaches* the starting gate threshold. They are attempting to gain an edge. However, at this level, it is generally not as effective as they believe."

"Especially if the next gate is greatly displaced," Loki added.

"Good to remember."

They continued to watch as the fighters danced about one another, each trying to get the best line through each gate.

"Remember, it takes more than being the first to cross the finish threshold to win the heat."

"Points; I remember," Nathan assured his instructor.

"Most important is that you do not make contact with the gate."

"That one's kind of obvious, isn't it?" Nathan replied.

"Not even with your shields."

Nathan looked at Master Koku. "You get penalized if your shields touch the gate?"

"No, but making contact with the gate will drain your shields of energy. Depending on how late in the heat the contact takes place, you may not have time to recharge your shields before you reach the finish threshold, and points will be deducted."

"Right," Nathan replied, his attention turning back to the race. "How long are the first heats?"

"Five minutes," Loki replied.

"These guys are pretty good," Nathan said, his

eyes still glued to the array of camera views on the massive view screen in front of them.

"You are easily impressed," Master Koku said.

"You're not helping," Nathan replied, his eyes never leaving the view screen.

"I am not here to help, I am here to teach."

"You're better than these guys," Josh insisted.

"Suli Noma is female," Master Koku pointed out.

"I didn't know there were female Gunyoki pilots," Nathan admitted.

"There were none in the original Gunyoki centuries ago, as our population was not yet at safe levels, and the women's lives were considered too critical to the future of Rakuen to risk them in combat. That changed more than a century ago, although to this day, it is still a male-dominated event. I did not think this would surprise you," Master Koku said. "Do not the women of your world fight alongside the men?"

"Oh, they do," Nathan assured him. "It's just that the further away from Earth we travel, the more common it seems to be that the women do not partake in risky professions. Usually, for the same reasons."

"Noma just took the lead," Josh reported. "She forced Kunai to swing wide on gate eleven, and he almost didn't make gate twelve."

"It is a common tactic," Master Koku explained. "She used his fear of collision against him, sliding in between him and the next gate, and then accelerating momentarily to force him to the outside."

"How many points are taken off for missing a gate?" Nathan wondered.

"Fifty."

Nathan glanced at the old man. "But you only get one hundred points for winning the race."

"And eighty for finishing second," Loki added.

"Precisely why one wishes to avoid missing a gate. Unless your opponent performs as poorly, it is nearly impossible for you to win once you have missed a gate."

"Noma just tagged gate fifteen," Josh said. "Her starboard shield is down to eighty percent."

"There are only five gates left," Master Koku stated. "She will likely finish with ninety percent shield strength."

"How many points is that?" Nathan wondered.

"A single point for each percent," Master Koku explained.

"Kunai just tagged eighteen!" Josh reported. "But he's only down ten percent."

"He must have barely brushed it with his shields," Master Koku observed.

"Through nineteen, burning for the finish gate!" Josh exclaimed. "And......Noma wins it by half a length!" he announced, throwing his hands up. "This shit is so cool!"

"How do we know who won?" Nathan asked.

Josh pointed to the status screen. "Noma took it, by four points."

Nathan sighed. "What's the purpose of the points again?"

"I thought you studied the Gunyoki races?" Loki said.

"I was concentrating more on flight tactics than race rules," Nathan admitted. "I was counting on you guys for that."

"The champion from each ichi advances to the final round. The ichis scoring second and third in overall points face one another to determine who will face the ichi with the highest score at the start of the finals."

"So, it's by the *ichi's* score, and not by the *pilot's*?" Nathan asked.

"That is correct."

"That seems weird."

"The races are deeply rooted in the tradition," Master Koku explained, "even if the training and commitment, once demanded of the Gunyoki, has been all but lost."

"I didn't really think Noma was going to win," Josh said.

"Why, because she's female?" Master Koku wondered.

"No, because Kunai jumped out in front of her from the start. That was one tough move she pulled to get around him." Josh laughed. "I *love* tough chicks."

"Speaking of which, where is Jessica?" Nathan wondered.

"She is on a recon assignment, elsewhere on the platform," General Telles replied.

"When do I fly?" Nathan asked.

"You will be flying in heat six, Ichi Konsai's second heat of round one," Master Koku explained.

"Are they going to have that reactor ready by then?" Nathan asked General Telles.

"They have been working on it all night," he assured him. "Commander Kamenetskiy promises it will be ready."

* * *

"Vlad, mind if I borrow Quory for a minute?" Jessica asked.

Vladimir looked over at her from his position

below the Gunyoki fighter, a curious expression on his face. "*Da?*"

"That means yes," Jessica told Quory, taking him gently by the arm, and leading him away from the others.

"But they might need me to..."

"They'll be okay for a couple minutes," Jessica insisted, refusing to take no for an answer.

"Very well," Quory agreed, realizing that he didn't have a choice. "What can I do for you, Lieutenant Commander?"

"I was wondering about something," Jessica began. "The transfer airlock logs indicate the ship was delivered to the bay two and a half hours *before* we arrived. Is that correct?"

"I believe it was more like three and a half hours," Quory corrected.

"Oh, yes," Jessica agreed, "Rakuen timekeeping is still a little confusing to me."

"Of course."

"The logs also show that a second ship arrived less than an hour before we did, and departed half an hour later."

"Yes, that was the shuttle I was on."

"Why did it take half an hour to unload one guy?" Jessica wondered. "For that matter, why didn't they just use the passenger bay for the main platform?"

"I brought my own tools and diagnostic equipment along with me," Quory explained. "Those black cabinets over there," he added, pointing to the far wall.

"But you were sent to *instruct* us on maintaining and servicing the Gunyoki fighter. Why *your* tools?"

"I don't go anywhere without my tools."

"Even if you don't expect to use them?"

"I felt your team deserved a fair chance, like anyone else," Quory explained. "I did not know if you would have the proper tools. I'm sorry if I offended you. I assure you, I only had good intentions."

"And you did not use those tools on our ship, *before* we arrived?"

"Why would I?" he asked, a confused look on his face.

"I don't know...to check that everything was in order before turning it over to us?" Jessica suggested.

"It was completely inspected by one of our lead mechanics just hours before it was moved to your bay. Further inspection would have been a waste of time."

Jessica looked the Rakuen engineer directly in the eyes as her tone turned ominous. "You are aware of my reputation; my training; the things I have done?"

"Uh, yes," Quory replied, suddenly becoming nervous.

"Did you know that I have been training with the Ghatazhak for the last seven years?"

"I was not aware," he replied, becoming more uncomfortable with each passing moment.

"So, you're telling me that you did not lay a hand on that ship while you were waiting for us to arrive."

"No, I did not. Why do you ask?" Quory's expression suddenly changed. "Did you find something wrong with it?"

"What was the name of the mechanic who performed the inspection prior to moving it here?" she asked.

Quory looked from side to side, and then leaned in closer to Jessica. "Are you going to rough him up?" he wondered.

"I'm just going to ask him a few questions, just like I'm asking you," Jessica assured him.

Quory thought for a moment. "I'm not sure I should say," he admitted, recoiling slightly in case his inquisitor did not care for his response.

"Trust me," Jessica said, reaching up and straightening his collar rather firmly. "You should."

"Uh, Darrien Genn," Quory told her, becoming nervous again. "But you did not learn this from me."

"Learn what?"

"The name of the…" The light came on. "Ah…"

"Where would Mister Genn be right now?"

"Here, on the platform, of course. Yokimah Racing has three entrants in this event."

"Which bay?"

"I am not sure," Quory admitted. "But it will be any of the bays between thirty and thirty-nine. Those all belong to Yokimah Racing."

"Thank you, Quory, you've been most helpful," Jessica said, turning to leave.

"You're not going to hurt him, are you?" Quory asked, his conscience getting the better of him.

"Not if he's as forthcoming as you have been," Jessica replied. She stopped and turned to look over her shoulder at Quory. "You *have* been honest with me, right? Because I'd hate to have to *rough you up*."

"No, that would not be pleasant," Quory agreed, quickly adding, "and completely unnecessary, I assure you."

Jessica just smiled. "Good."

* * *

Nathan's heart raced as he guided his Gunyoki fighter down the start corridor. To his right was his opponent, Valen Takoda, his Gunyoki fighter painted in reds and greens, with a logo of some type of ferocious-looking animal on its side.

Nathan glanced at his flight display as his ship vibrated mildly from the low-power, constant burn of his engines, to bring his ship up to start speed.

"*Okay, Cap'n, this guy's no problem,*" Josh assured him over comms. "*He's a newb, just like you. His first event. He barely passed his quals. He's got nothing. Just fly clean lines, keep your speed up, and you'll smoke him. By the time...*"

"I got it, Josh," Nathan said, cutting him off. "I appreciate the pep talk."

"*Okay, twenty gates, even spacing, nothing too wild,*" Josh reminded him. "*Five to six is a tight turn to port, and fifteen to sixteen is tight to starboard, followed by tight to port to seventeen.*"

"I remember," Nathan assured him. "How are we looking back there, Loki?"

"All systems are good, and our new reactor is putting out thirty-two percent more power than the old one. Race Control should be releasing us from auto-flight in about twenty seconds."

"Outstanding," Nathan replied, trying to sound confident. "Just keep your eyes on my lines and, whatever you do, don't let me tag a gate."

"You got it, Captain."

Nathan glanced forward, spotting the start gate coming at them fast. He moved his right hand down to his throttles and placed his finger on the thrust engage button.

"*Ten seconds to start gate,*" Josh warned.

The auto-flight indicator light shut off, releasing control of the ship to Nathan, so that he could fly the race.

"*Be ready on that throttle,*" Josh added, "*in......
five......four......three......two...THROTTLE!*"

Nathan jammed his throttles all the way forward,
his engines spooling up to full thrust in fewer than
two seconds, pushing him back into his seat as his
ship lunged forward.

"Engines are at full power," Loki reported.
"Acceleration curve is good. Five seconds to the first
turn."

Nathan glanced from the sensor display at the
center of his console to the forward window, spotting
the flashing marker lights of the first gate, still a
kilometer away and closing fast. Another glance
out his window showed him that his opponent had
accelerated right along with him, and they were
running neck and neck. That would give him the
advantage for the first two gates, both of which were
left turns. If he kept his speed up and used his nacelle
angles properly, he could gain a small lead, which he
could use to keep his opponent behind him, going
into the first right turn at gate three.

Nathan rolled his fighter a bit to the left. The
center of the approaching gate was below his flight
path, and the next gate was high and left, so he
wanted to pass through the gate high and left, as
well. Seconds later, the upper left curve of the gate
streaked over their canopy, only a meter away.

"Not sure you want to cut it that close, Captain,"
Loki warned. "Remember, when deployed, our aft
laser cannons sit nearly a meter above the hull."

"Understood," Nathan replied as he pulled his
nose up and held his power at maximum.

"*Thirty seconds to the next gate,*" Josh warned.
"*Fifteen seconds to planned max speed.*"

"Turn rate looks good," Loki reported. "Bogey is half a length back and two meters below."

"Keep your gate entry low, so he has to fall back to avoid tagging it," Josh suggested.

"That's the plan," Nathan replied. "Entry angle check?" he asked Loki.

"A little high," Loki replied, confirming Nathan's suspicions. "One more degree on the gungines."

"Do we really have to call them that?" Nathan wondered.

"Yes," Josh insisted.

"That's it," Loki reported. "Thrust cut-off in five......four......three......two......one......MECO."

Nathan held his engines for two more seconds, then switched them off and pulled his throttles back to idle.

"We're a little fast, Captain," Loki warned.

"Nah, you're fine," Josh insisted.

"Ten seconds. Bogey is swinging wide to avoid falling back," Loki reported.

Perfect, Nathan thought as he glanced up at the approaching gate. A few seconds later, the bottom edge of the gate slid under them at dizzying speed, and Nathan increased his throttles to thirty-two percent, pressing and holding the thrust button as he changed the angles on his engine nacelles to turn a little more, in order to line up with the next gate.

"You're going to need extra thrust..." Loki began. "Never mind, I see you already added the extra two percent."

"Cap'n doesn't fly like an old lady, Lok," Josh teased.

Cameron sat in the command chair at the center of the Aurora's bridge, her eyes, like everyone else's, glued to the feeds on the main view screen provided as a courtesy by Gunyoki Race Control. So far, Nathan appeared to be holding his own, but the race had just started.

"Go to full power as soon as you clear gate three," Josh recommended over the loudspeakers in the overhead.

"We're already faster than planned," Loki warned.

"He's right," Nathan argued. *"Takoda's going to add power and try to overtake us, and it's a diving right turn to the next gate, which favors him."*

"Just don't overdo it," Loki warned. *"Or you'll have to reverse your thrust to slow down for the turn to the following gate."*

"Just give me a number to stop at," Nathan instructed.

"Oh, crap, just a second," Josh pleaded. *"Uh, six seven five...no...yes...six seven five."*

"Six seven zero would be safer," Loki suggested.

"Of course it would, grandma, but Takoda's already at six six eight."

"Gentlemen, which is it?" Nathan asked.

"Six seven five!" Josh insisted. *"You can make the turn and there's no way Takoda can pass you on the inside without tagging the gate."*

Cameron turned her command chair slowly around to face her tactical officer, a worried look on her face. "This does not sound promising."

"At least he's in the lead," Lieutenant Commander Vidmar replied, trying to keep a positive attitude as they listened to the comms chatter.

"That's it," Josh urged from their control room back on the race platform. "Six seven three...six seven four...six seven five! Now, tighten your line and force him to fall back, Cap'n!"

"*Tightening,*" Nathan replied, trying to sound calm.

"Takoda is not going to yield," Master Koku warned.

"He doesn't have a choice," Josh insisted.

"He does not want to be the first Gunyoki pilot to lose to an outsider."

"But his only play is to fall back or tag the gate," Josh replied. "Either that, or... Oh, fuck." Josh quickly turned back to his console. "Cap'n, he's going to try to force you to move."

"He already is," General Telles said, watching the view from the chase cameras as the opponent's fighter moved closer to Nathan's. "And he's accelerating."

———

"He's four meters and closing!" Loki warned.

"At six seven five?" Nathan exclaimed. "Is he crazy?"

"*It's an ego thing!*" Josh explained. "*Master Koku called it!*"

"Three meters!"

"Channel all available power to the starboard shields," Nathan instructed.

"Already on it," Loki assured him. "Shields at one hundred and ten percent." Loki glanced out the window to his right at the opponent's fighter, its cockpit slightly aft of theirs. "Jesus...two meters!"

"*Hold your line!*" Josh urged. "*Gate in five seconds, then a hard climbing left turn!*"

Nathan's eyes danced between his flight displays and the fighter that was about to collide with him, gritting his teeth, determined not to yield.

"Three......two......one..."

As their ship passed through the gate, there was a sudden bright flash to their right, followed a split second later by a second flash and a bone-shaking jolt, which knocked their ship to the left.

"*He tagged the gate! He tagged the gate!*" Josh exclaimed with glee.

"He tagged us!" Nathan exclaimed nowhere near as joyfully as he struggled to maintain control and pull their ship into a climbing left turn.

"Shield power dropped twenty percent," Loki reported, "but we were at one ten, so we should be able to recharge in time."

"What about our systems?" Nathan demanded.

"We're good!" Loki assured him. "A little fluctuation in the starboard shield emitters, but we're good!"

"*Nice job, Cap'n!*" Josh congratulated. "*You fucking showed him!*"

"Where's he at?" Nathan wondered, looking around.

"He's on your six, two lengths back!" Josh reported, sounding as if he was about to burst from excitement. He spun around to look at Master Koku. "Did you see that?"

"I did."

"Just hold your lines tight, and keep your speed up through the rest of the gates, and there's no way he'll get past you in time!" Josh told Nathan over his comm-set.

"*I can do that,*" Nathan assured him.

"*In a stunning display of determination and skill, Nathan Scott has increased his lead over Valen Takoda...*" the commentator announced over the Aurora's loudspeakers.

Cameron looked at Lieutenant Commander Kono at the sensor station. "How's he doing?"

"He's up to two ship lengths now," the lieutenant commander replied. "The other ship is having to channel extra power from his propulsion system to recharge his port shield, which is having a hard time maintaining its integrity. If he falls back any further, the captain has the first race locked up."

"*...The only way Takoda has a chance now would be if the one they call Na-Tan tagged a gate, as well, but there's not much chance of that with only three gates to go in the sixth heat of the day!*"

Cameron smiled.

"Final gate coming up!" Josh announced, barely able to contain himself.

"Where's Takoda?" Nathan asked.

"Low left, now," Loki replied, "but he's managed to close to half a ship length."

"*It's now or never!*" Josh exclaimed. "*Max power, Cap'n!*"

Nathan came out of his turn, the last gate now directly ahead and closing fast. He pushed his throttles to full power, the force of acceleration pushing him back into his seat again. The Gunyokis were incredibly powerful, probably even more so than the Falcon had ever been. And although they were difficult to handle, they were, without a doubt, amazing ships to fly.

"*YES!*" Josh exclaimed at the top of his lungs as the nose of Nathan's Gunyoki fighter pierced the threshold of the final gate, claiming the team's first victory of the day.

Nathan felt a wave of relief wash over him as he backed off on the throttles and waited for Race

Control to activate his auto-flight systems and bring him home.

"Good job, Captain," Loki congratulated from the back seat.

"Thanks, Loki. I couldn't have done it without you," Nathan replied. "Without *all* of you."

* * *

Although she had heard the commentary about Nathan's race and the official announcement of his victory, Jessica had not been able to share in the celebration that had undoubtedly occurred in bay seventy-five afterward. In fact, she wondered if she was going to get back in time for his next race. She had been trying to find a way into Yokimah Racing's Gunyoki suites for over an hour. As it turned out, her credentials showed her to be a member of the competition, which made it even more unlikely for her to gain access. She had even searched for a way to *break* in, but without success.

So, she had been forced to pocket her ID badge and blend in with the throngs of racing fans prowling the corridors outside the Yokimah suites, hoping to get a glimpse of their favorite Gunyoki pilot.

Fortunately for Jessica, she was not interested in pilots, only mechanics. The pilots rarely left the safety of their team suites, for fear of being mobbed by fans. Mechanics and technical support personnel did not have that problem. Early on, Jessica had noticed one of them slipping out for a few minutes to visit with friends attending the event. Not long after, another person stepped out and disappeared into the crowds, returning a few minutes later with an attractive young woman in tow.

With a pattern established, Jessica now had a viable plan. But after forty-five minutes of waiting, she was starting to wonder if anyone else would leave.

By the end of the second hour, she was beginning to contemplate her chances of successfully overpowering the guard at the entrance to the Yokimah suites, and getting inside to obtain the information she needed before security stunned her and dragged her away, unconscious.

Another thirty minutes passed, and the race commentators were already reporting that Nathan Scott and Azel Senza were on their way to the approach lanes for the next heat. Assuming Nathan won, the following race would only be an hour away, and she was no closer to getting answers than she was two and half hours ago.

Just as she was about to give up, a skinny young man in a Yokimah Racing uniform came through the door and into the crowd. Jessica immediately followed him, weaving her way through the shifting mass of spectators, being careful not to lose sight of her target.

She quickly determined that the young man was up to something. He kept looking around, as if checking for a tail, although he was not very adept at it, as he never once looked Jessica's way. If the man *was* a spy, he was a lousy one.

Two minutes later, as the commentators announced the start of Nathan's second heat, the young man slipped into one of the many public vid-com booths located throughout the race complex. Jessica continued to move closer, eventually coming to stand just outside the same booth, as if awaiting her turn.

Less than a minute later, the young man turned and opened the door, startled by Jessica's presence as she forced him back into the booth and closed the door behind her, trapping him inside.

"What are you doing?" the young man demanded. "I don't have any credits, if that's what you want."

"You work for Yokimah Racing?" Jessica began.

"Yes..." The young man realized how attractive his assailant was and then added, "but I'm not a pilot, I'm just a tech."

"What kind of tech?" Jessica wondered, her arm up against the young man's chest, holding him firmly against the vid-com screen behind him.

"You're hurting me."

"What kind of tech?"

"Sensors and comms," the man replied.

"Do you know someone named Darrien Genn?"

"Who are you?" the man demanded to know, trying to get free from her.

Jessica grabbed him forcefully by the chin, pinning his head against the view screen, as well, and pressing her body against his while pushing her knee into his groin just enough to make him worry. "Give me any trouble, and you'll be singing falsetto for the rest of your life," she threatened. "Darrien Genn. Do you know him?"

"Yes," the young man admitted. "He's the lead mechanic for two zero seven."

"The Gunyoki fighter that Ito Yokimah loaned to Nathan Scott?"

"Yes, why do..."

Jessica pushed her knee into him a little more firmly, shutting him up. "Where is he?"

"Darrien?"

"No, Santa Claus, asshole."

"Who?"

"Is Darrien Genn working here today?"

"No, no. He hasn't been in all week," the young man squeaked, fearing additional pressure by Jessica's knee. "He got the week off, since they loaned out his ship. He was supposed to come in yesterday for a staff meeting, but didn't show. Everyone figured he went out of town, or something."

Jessica thought for a moment, her grip weakening slightly. "Do you know where he lives?"

"Well, yes, but..."

Jessica tightened her grip again.

"Okay, okay... He lives in the Obi district."

"What's his address?"

"I don't know, one of the newer tenement buildings. Pison, Pisa... No, Pianeese! Pianeese Towers! On the seventeenth floor! That's all I know! I swear!"

Jessica eased up a bit, looking him in the eyes, their faces only centimeters apart. "Are you being honest with me?" she asked.

"Yes, I promise you."

Jessica moved back a bit more, lowering her knee at the same time. She looked at him crossly. "Why did you come out here to make a call? You guys don't have vid-comms in the Yokimah suites?"

"I wanted to make the call in private," the young man admitted.

"Why? What are you hiding?" When the young man didn't answer, she pushed her knee back into his groin a bit. "Tell me..."

"I was making a bet," he admitted.

"What kind of bet?" Jessica wondered. "On the races? Isn't that illegal?"

"I need the money."

"So, you bet on a Gunyoki race? What are you, stupid?"

"It was a sure thing."

"What was?" Again, the young man didn't want to answer. "Tell me," Jessica instructed crossly.

"One of our ships is experiencing power fluctuations, and they can't figure it out."

"Yokimah's got spares."

"One spare is down, and we loaned the other one to Nathan Scott."

"So, how is that a sure thing?" she wondered.

"If the pilot goes over ninety percent on her reactor, it might blow a bus, and she'd lose one of her primary systems," the young man explained.

"Whose ship are we talking about?"

"Suli Noma," he replied. "They discovered the problem during her first heat."

"But she won that heat."

"It didn't start fluctuating until the heat was over," the young man explained.

"So, you bet against your own team?" Jessica sighed, shaking her head. "You should be ashamed of yourself, young man. What could possibly be so important that you would betray the trust of an asshole like Yokimah?"

The young man looked confused. "I need the money to quit my job and go back to school."

"What for?"

"I want to change careers. I want to be a marine biologist."

"Ocean world...makes sense, I guess," Jessica agreed. "What's your name?"

"Milan."

"Milan what?"

"Milan Jento."

"Listen carefully, Milan Jento. This conversation is going to be our little secret, okay?" she said, straightening his collar and then brushing his bangs from his eyes.

"Our little secret...right," he agreed, relaxing a bit, but still on guard.

"And since I know your name now, if I find out that you *told* anyone about our little rendezvous here in the vid-com booth, I'll hunt you down and *really* introduce my knee to your nuts. Understand?"

Milan nodded.

"Good boy."

"Say, you wouldn't want to meet later, maybe, after the races..."

Jessica touched his lips with her index finger, quieting him. "Don't ruin it, kid." She winked at him, then reached behind her and opened the door, stepping out and closing him back in before she turned and walked away. "I always get the freaks."

* * *

"*Twenty down, twenty gates to go!*" Josh exclaimed over comms. "*You're halfway there! Just keep your lead and keep squeezing him out!*"

"You make it sound so easy," Nathan commented as he bore down against the G-forces of his turn, bringing his fighter's nose around toward the next gate.

"Two stub targets on twenty-one," Loki reported. "Locking missiles on targets."

"*Senza will try to slip under you as you launch missiles,*" Master Koku warned. "*He likes to use the flash of their rocket motors to blind you to his actions. Just before you launch, descend a few meters to block him.*"

"Copy that," Nathan replied.

"Five seconds to launch," Loki warned. "Gate threshold in ten."

Nathan pushed his flight control stick down, causing his engine nacelles to angle downward. A second later, he pressed the thrust button for a full second, causing the ship to transition downward several meters and accelerate slightly.

"Missiles away!" Loki announced as the missiles' rocket motors flashed as they left the pods on either side of the cockpit.

"*Senza's climbing!*" Josh warned. "*He's trying to slip over you!*"

"Damn," Nathan cursed, pulling his flight control stick up and firing his thrusters again. He glanced out the window as his opponent's ship tried, but failed, to slip over the top of them, nearly colliding in the process. "Nice try, buddy."

"*He is more clever than I anticipated,*" Master Koku admitted.

"Targets disabled!" Loki announced. "We are taking points from this guy at every gate!"

"We need more lead on him," Nathan decided as they passed through the next gate. "Otherwise, he's going to try that shit again, and again."

"*You're already at six-twenty, Cap'n, and these gates are more widely spread,*" Josh warned.

"Would you go faster?" Nathan asked.

"*Well, yeah, but I'm crazy. Just ask Loki.*"

"He's not lying. He *is* crazy," Loki happily agreed.

"But he could still pull it off," Nathan said as he inched his throttles forward to accelerate in his turn. "And so can I."

"You're at six-thirty," Josh warned as they watched the sensor display and camera views of the two Gunyoki fighters, battling for position as they dove through the twenty-eighth gate.

"Can he handle that speed?" Neli wondered, watching nervously from the back of the room.

"He can handle it," Vladimir assured her. "*Davai*, Nathan, *davai*," he added, under his breath.

"Six-thirty-five," Josh reported. "He's still matching your speed."

"He's locking missiles on the next gate targets," General Telles announced, noticing the opponent's status displays.

"Those targets are for lasers," Josh exclaimed. "Can he do that?"

"He can," Master Koku confirmed. "He will lose a few points for not using the required weaponry, but he *will* gain points. More importantly, he will deny your captain of them."

"He realizes that he cannot continue at Nathan's speed, so he's trying to make up the difference by stealing points from him," General Telles surmised.

"Correct."

"A sound tactic," the general observed.

"Indeed," Master Koku agreed.

Josh turned back to his console. "Okay, guys, listen up…"

———

"…*the bottom line is, you're going to have to go faster,*" Josh explained to Nathan and Loki.

"He's barely able to make the turns as it is," Lieutenant Commander Vidmar declared as he watched the race feeds on the transparent screens at the front of his console.

Cameron quickly did the math, using a portion of the tactical console that she was standing at with the lieutenant commander. "If he takes the next ten gate targets, all with missiles, he can finish two full ship lengths behind Nathan, and still win," she concluded. She looked at the lieutenant commander. "He needs to go even faster."

"Senza just took out three more targets with missiles," Lieutenant Commander Kono reported from the sensor station. "He missed one, though. Loki just took it out with lasers."

"Every point counts," Cameron muttered, staring at the camera feeds as Nathan rolled his ship through the next gate. "I have to admit, he is flying the *hell* out of that ship."

"*Five gates left!*" Josh announced over comms. "*By our calculations, you still have a ten-point lead!*"

"Loki, is the last gate in missile range?" Nathan asked.

"Uh, yes, but…"

"If I swing wide, right after the next gate, can you get a lock on those targets?" he asked as they approached the thirty-sixth gate.

"Yeah, but…"

"*I know what you're thinking, Cap'n,*" Josh interrupted, "*and I like it, but if you swing wide, I don't know that you'll make gate thirty-seven. If you miss that gate, you're done.*"

"If we deny him those last few targets, we'll have him by the balls," Nathan exclaimed as they slid past gate thirty-six, clearing it by just under two meters.

"*I would not advise this,*" Master Koku warned.

Nathan pondered his idea for a split second, then moved his flight control stick to the right, swinging wide of his line. "Do it, Loki," he ordered.

"Locking stubs on the finish gate targets," Loki replied.

"*Senza's accelerating,*" Josh warned. "*He's trying to slip past you to port!*"

"Missiles away," Loki reported as four missile rocket motors flashed on either side of them, lighting up the cockpit for a brief moment.

Nathan rolled his ship back left, pushing his nose slightly downward as he jammed his throttles all the way forward.

"What the fuck!" Josh exclaimed. *"You're accelerating!"*

"Captain!" Loki yelled in alarm.

"Ready four flashers!" Nathan barked as he struggled against the G-forces induced by his accelerating turn.

"Four flashers, ready!" Loki acknowledged without question.

Nathan slid his fighter in front of the pursuing Gunyoki fighter, dropping slightly below his opponent's flight path. "Drop four! Now, now, now!"

Loki's finger had pressed the button before the first 'now' had left Nathan's lips.

Four, small, cylindrical objects jettisoned from the top, aft end of Nathan's Gunyoki fighter, popping directly up into Azel Senza's line of flight. The four objects ignited, creating brilliant fireballs directly in front of the advancing fighter. Stunned by the sudden appearance of the bright objects, his opponent instinctively dove under the glowing countermeasures in order to avoid colliding with them, and weakening his shields with only three gates left.

It was a mistake.

"He tagged the gate! He tagged the gate!" Josh squealed in delight. "Fuck yeah! That was some serious pilot shit right there!" he exclaimed to everyone in the control room.

"Senza's losing control," General Telles observed coldly.

"He is going to collide with the next gate," Master Koku added.

Two seconds later, Gunyoki Four One Eight slammed into gate thirty-nine and broke apart.

"Oh, shit," Loki exclaimed.

"What?" Nathan asked as he turned toward the final gate.

"Senza just slammed into gate thirty-nine."

"He tagged it?" Nathan asked, excitement in his tone.

"No, he *slammed* into it. He broke apart."

"Oh, my God," Nathan exclaimed, easing his throttles back.

"*It's okay!*" Josh exclaimed over comms. "*They punched out! They're both out! Their beacons are on, and Race Control has launched search and rescue ships!*"

"Are they okay?" Nathan asked as they glided through the final gate, claiming victory of their second heat.

"They hit that gate at seven hundred meters per second, Captain," Loki warned. "The punch-out had to be automated."

"Josh, was the punch-out automated?" Nathan asked as Race Control activated his fighter's auto-flight to bring them back to the race platform.

"*What?*"

"Did they punch out *before,* or *after* they hit the gate?"

"*Stand by one,*" Josh replied.

Nathan had a sinking feeling in the pit of his gut. He was willing to do anything to win this event, but he had not expected this, especially in only the second round. But the Gunyoki races were designed to simulate both the act and the risks of combat, and Nathan's argument had been that the current Gunyoki pilots lacked the edge that combat gave a person. Was this not a demonstration of that edge?

"*Before!*" Josh finally announced. "*They punched out before impact, Cap'n.*"

Nathan felt a wave of relief wash over him, his head falling back against his headrest.

"*Race Control just confirmed that both men are alive,*" Josh added.

"Are they injured?" Loki asked.

"*They're not saying,*" Josh replied. "*They're just reporting that both of their med sensors are sending back strong vital signs, so they* are *alive.*"

Nathan sighed, closing his eyes. He could feel his hands shaking as he placed them on his thighs. For once, he was terribly grateful for auto-flight.

* * *

"Hey! Jess! Where have you been?" Josh exclaimed as Jessica entered the lounge for bay seventy-five. "Did you hear? Nathan won his second heat!"

"I heard," Jessica replied, although with far less enthusiasm than Josh. She turned to General Telles. "Where's Nathan?"

"He's on his way back, now," the general replied. "He should be landing in about five minutes. What have you learned?"

Jessica took the general by the arm, leading him away from the celebration as she spoke. "I'm pretty sure Quory had nothing to do with the device. In fact, I don't even think he knows it's there. Turns out, some guy named Darrien Genn was the last one to work on our bird. He's the chief mechanic for it."

"Were you able to speak with him?"

"He's not here. No one has seen him all week; not since our bird was delivered."

"Then, we are at a dead end?"

"Nope. I got his address. But I'll have to go to Rakuen to find him."

General Telles looked at the clock on the wall. "If this is all part of some conspiracy, whatever is going to happen *will* happen during one of Nathan's races. His next race is just over an hour away. I would prefer that you were here."

"I'll try."

"Perhaps you should take someone along?"

"I'll be less conspicuous on my own."

General Telles nodded begrudging agreement. "Transportation?"

"I was going to take the Reaper."

"Are you comfortable piloting it?"

"What piloting? I push a few buttons. With any luck, Rakuen Control will auto-flight me directly to my destination. All the buildings have landing pads on top."

"Flying a Reaper back to Rakuen is not exactly inconspicuous," the general reminded her.

"If I take one of the public shuttles, it will take twice as long," she pointed out. "Besides, I'm not planning on taking the Reaper into combat, or anything. Just a simple hop down to Rakuen and back. It's really the only way I have a chance of getting back *before* his next race."

"Very well," the general agreed. "Need I remind you of the importance of this?"

"Any and all measures necessary," Jessica assured him. "I know the drill."

* * *

Cameron stared at General Telles's image on her view screen. "You should have told me right away," she finally told him in a stern voice.

"*I was in error,*" the general admitted. "*I shall not make that mistake again.*"

"You should tell Nathan, as well. I know you think he has enough on his plate, but if you expect him to be in command, he has to know everything. He is not a child who needs to be protected, and you and Jessica need to stop doing so."

"*Agreed,*" the general replied.

"So, do you think the Dusahn are involved?"

"*It is the most logical theory. Jessica is in the process of gathering more information. I expect to hear from her within the hour. In the meantime, I believe it is best if we assume that is the case.*"

"I'll put all forces on alert, but not charge shields or weapons, so as not to tip anyone off," Cameron said.

"*A wise precaution,*" General Telles agreed.

"That was some race, wasn't it?"

"*Indeed, it was,*" the general agreed. "*Captain Scott's piloting skills are more impressive than I had anticipated.*"

"Yes," Cameron agreed. "He's always been a very instinctive pilot with a natural aptitude, but I have *never* seen him fly like *that* before. For a moment, I thought Josh was doing the flying."

"*Trust me, he wanted to,*" General Telles assured her. "*I will contact you as soon as we know more.*"

"And you will speak to Nathan?"

"*Directly. Telles out.*"

Cameron picked up her remote and turned off the view screen, ending the call. She leaned back in her seat a moment. By now, Nathan had proven that he was himself again, and more. At first, the 'more' aspect worried her. Now, she was beginning to see it as a significant asset.

* * *

General Telles entered the lounge, finding Nathan sitting in the room by himself. "A moment of contemplation?" the general asked as he approached.

Nathan looked at the general, exhaustion and guilt evident on his face. "Just reviewing things in my head, I guess."

"The race?"

"Yup. What I could have done differently. What I could have done better."

"You were victorious," the general reminded him. "Isn't that all that matters?"

"I nearly got those men killed."

"Those men chose to climb into that cockpit, fully aware of the risks, same as you and Loki. And that pilot made a bad decision. It was his decision that nearly got him killed."

"I ordered the countermeasures launch," Nathan reminded the general. "They could not have anticipated that move."

"If you had been in that pilot's position, and those flashers had suddenly appeared in your path of flight, what would you have done?"

"That doesn't work."

"Humor me."

"I would have plowed right through them."

"And taken the loss of points because of the drain on your shields?" General Telles questioned.

"Pull up, and you make the gate, but your turn

to the next gate is so wide you'd lose more ground to the leader. Dive down, and, well, we saw what happened. Myself, I would've held my course and plowed right through the flashers. The shields can take the impact just fine. Probably no more than a five percent drop, if that. But I can't know for sure that I'd do that."

"You would've," General Telles insisted. "For the same reason you thought of launching those flashers. At the moment, you put yourself in the other pilot's seat and ran those options through your head, just like you explained them to me just now. You determined that two of the three possible reactions by the pilot would assure your victory, and that the third option, the one *you* would have chosen, still kept the odds in your favor, although, less so than the first two possible reactions. Did you consider any other maneuvers?"

"Several," Nathan replied. "Fly faster, take a tighter line to the gate to block him out...but his ship was a bit faster than mine. I could tell. And the turn to the next gate would have favored him, if I had let him get in above me."

"So, you chose the maneuver that offered the highest probability of success. And you did so in a split second, in the heat of simulated battle."

Nathan looked at General Telles. "You and I both know that those races are nothing like real combat. No fighter pilot with actual combat experience would've pulled such a dumb maneuver."

"Isn't that what you are trying to prove to the Rakuens?" the general asked. "That their pilots lack the necessary experience? If so, I believe you just gave them a wonderful example."

Nathan looked at General Telles again. "How do

you do it?" he wondered. "How do you maintain your belief that what you are doing is right?"

"What else am I supposed to believe?"

"Don't you ever question yourself?"

"Of course," the general insisted. "I just don't sit around looking like someone just stole my favorite goba doll."

"Goba doll?"

"A small, stuffed doll popular with Takaran children."

"Did you just make a joke?"

"I was attempting to poke fun at you, to point out the folly of your self-introspection."

Nathan couldn't help but laugh. "So, you were trying to make me feel better?"

"Precisely."

Nathan laughed again. "Finally, we found *something* you suck at."

* * *

Jessica had wasted little time upon landing atop the Pianeese Towers tenement building. However, she had been surprised that, for a technologically advanced world, their security measures were sorely lacking in sophistication. It had taken her all of five minutes to locate the security office, bust her way in, and subdue the two men inside, and then locate the seventeenth floor unit in which Darrien Genn resided. The two security officers had even been kind enough to loan her their restraints to ensure that they could not sound the alarm before she had concluded her business.

As expected, she found a global door pass, as well, which she used to gain unannounced access to Mister Genn's residence. What she had *not* expected, was to find him long dead, lying in a pool of his own, coagulated blood, his neck sliced open in a way that she found familiar and troubling at the same time.

A quick examination of the wound was all she needed, and within a few minutes of entering the man's residence, she was on her way to the roof and to her Reaper's communications gear.

* * *

"What do you mean, you didn't remove it?" Josh exclaimed.

"The device has tamper sensors," General Telles explained to the group assembled in the lounge at Gunyoki bay seventy-five.

Nathan listened, but did not comment.

"I assure you the device has been rendered harmless," Vladimir promised. "And whoever is operating it will be unaware that it has been bypassed."

"When was this thing installed?" Marcus wondered.

"To the best of our knowledge, prior to delivery. Jessica has found the mechanic who we *believe* installed the device," the general explained.

"*Believe*?" Deliza wondered.

"Yeah, didn't Jess beat the truth out of him?" Josh asked.

"He is dead."

"She *killed* him?" Josh exclaimed. "Damn, Jess..."

"He was long dead when she found him," the general added.

"I knew Yokimah was a cheatin' bastard!" Josh declared.

"We do not believe it was Yokimah," General Telles said. "At least, we have no proof that he is involved."

"He wants Nathan to lose," Josh exclaimed. "What more proof do you need?"

"The general's right," Loki insisted. "If we lost all power in the middle of a heat, race officials would be crawling all over our ship as soon as it was recovered. They'd find the device, and Yokimah Racing would lose its accreditation."

"Damn, this is some crazy shit," Dalen exclaimed.

"If it wasn't Yokimah, then who?" Abby wondered.

"The most logical explanation is that the Takaran businessman, Jorkar Seeley, is a Dusahn operative. The mechanic was killed with a Ghatazhak blade, and in a manner consistent with Ghatazhak training."

"Seeley is Ghatazhak?"

"I cannot say. All I *can* say is that Darrien Genn was killed by a Ghatazhak weapon, by someone with Ghatazhak training. It could have been a Ybaran, for all we know."

"Why would a Ybaran work for the Dusahn?" Neli asked. "They glassed their *entire world*."

"The Ybaran can be incredibly duplicitous," General Telles assured her. "We also cannot overlook the possibility that the Dusahn may have resurrected the Ghatazhak programming system used by Caius."

"I thought *your* people were the last of the Ghatazhak," Yanni stated.

"There are bound to be more of us out there; some in hiding, others who simply gave up and blended into civilian life. However, I do find it hard to believe that a *true* Ghatazhak would collaborate with someone like the Dusahn."

"My money is on a Ybaran," Deliza said, disdain in her voice.

"I would agree," General Telles replied.

"So, what happens next?" Josh wondered.

"If the Dusahn *are* involved, their likely goal is to capture or destroy both Nathan *and* the Aurora."

"If they wanted to kill me, they would've installed something else," Nathan insisted, finally speaking up. "Like a bomb."

"A bomb would be too easy to detect," Vladimir insisted. "The beauty of this device is that it appears to be a safety aspect. Like an emergency power interrupter. I almost did not notice that it had a transceiver built into it."

"Then put the device on a fuel line, or on the plasma trunk, or on any of twenty different things that would kill us instantly," Nathan argued. "No, they want to capture me, interrogate me, torture me, and use whatever information they glean from me to find the rest of you and destroy you."

"What about the Aurora?" Loki asked.

"*That*, they'd just as soon destroy once and for all," Nathan concluded.

"The captain is correct," General Telles agreed. "I believe their intention is to activate the device, robbing the captain's fighter of all power, then jump in and capture him."

"When are they going to try?" Josh wondered.

"In the final round, in the asteroid course, when we're at the furthest point from the race platform," Nathan surmised. "That will make it impossible for the Gunyoki to respond fast enough, since they don't have jump drives. That means the Aurora must respond. They'll jump me with gunships, or something just large enough to grab my ship and jump away. As soon as the Aurora jumps to me to intervene, something larger will jump in, like a battleship."

"No offense intended, Cap'n, but how would the Dusahn know if you'd even *reach* the final round?" Marcus asked.

"By planting similar devices on all the ships I face," Nathan concluded.

"Whoa," Josh said in a low tone. "That would take more than just one mechanic."

"Jessica discovered that one of Yokimah's ships was experiencing unexplainable energy fluctuations. That ship eventually lost in the next heat."

"You think Senza's ship was sabotaged, as well?" Loki suggested.

"It is a possibility," the general agreed.

"No way," Josh argued. "You totally outflew that guy, Cap'n."

"If I may?" Quory said, raising his hand for permission to speak.

"Please," General Telles insisted.

"There is no way that Mister Yokimah is *not* involved in this," Quory insisted. "His security is too tight, and he oversees every aspect of these events personally. He has too much invested in the entire Gunyoki Racing Association, *and* in his racing team."

"Then why did he bet all his ships?" Josh argued.

"Because he planned on fixing the race," Nathan explained. "He gets a portion of the ticket sales…"

"A *significant* portion," Quory added.

"…He hands me and the Aurora over to the Dusahn, believing he is securing an alliance and protecting both his world and his profit machine, which he would *lose* if the Gunyoki decided to join our rebellion," Nathan explained.

"I told you he's a sneaky bastard," Josh exclaimed.

"You said he was a *cheating* bastard," Loki corrected.

"Same thing."

"Ito Yokimah never had any intention of losing," Nathan concluded.

"So, what do we do when they attack?" Josh asked.

"The same thing we always do," Nathan replied. "We fly, we fight, and we win."

"Damn right!" Josh exclaimed.

"Uh, has anyone considered telling the Rakuens about all this?" Abby wondered.

"That would be ill-advised," General Telles insisted.

"Assuming Seeley is Dusahn, he'd simply notify the warships lying in wait, and they'd just attack outright, for fear of losing the opportunity to destroy the Aurora," Nathan concluded. "It's safer for Rakuen if we let them believe their plan has worked, so they attack at a place of *our* choosing."

"Which is where?" Josh asked.

"The same place they probably wanted us to. At the furthest point in the asteroid course," Nathan replied.

"Are we going to be able to take them?" Dalen wondered.

"There are at least fifty Gunyoki on this platform at the moment," Quory reminded them. "And another few hundred who would respond from the surface of Rakuen within five minutes."

"None of which will make a difference without jump drives," Nathan argued.

"But we've got the Aurora," Josh bragged.

"The Dusahn will undoubtedly send a battleship, perhaps even two," General Telles insisted. "We may be able to repel the attack, but it is doubtful that we will be able to destroy the Dusahn warship. We simply cannot risk losing the Aurora at this point."

"What about the gunships?" Josh asked.

"They are guarding the fleet," General Telles replied.

"I have some ideas," Nathan announced, glancing at the clock on the wall. "For now, though, we have another race to fly."

"Nathan is right," Vladimir agreed. "Let's get back to work."

Nathan exchanged glances with General Telles as everyone rose and headed out of the room. He strolled over to the general's side, waiting for everyone to leave before he spoke. "You should have told me about the device from the start."

"Your executive officer has already chastised me for that mistake," General Telles assured him. "There is another matter to consider. Should we tell Master Koku about our suspicions?"

Nathan sighed. "Honestly, I'm just not sure. I'm going to have to think about that one."

"Agreed."

Nathan took a deep breath and let it out. "You know, there *is* a way to test your theory."

"I know," the general replied.

Nathan nodded. "We need to speak with Cameron."

* * *

Jessica was out of the Reaper within seconds after it rolled to a stop inside bay seventy-five on the Gunyoki race platform. Despite her best efforts, she had not been able to get back prior to the start of Nathan's third heat.

After sprinting across the empty bay, she reached the control room where Master Koku, Josh, and General Telles were monitoring Nathan's performance. "How's he doing?"

"He is holding a very small lead," the general

replied. "But his opponent is challenging him at every turn."

Jessica's eyes darted toward Master Koku.

General Telles shook his head, confirming that they had not told the old man about the device, or about the suspected plot between Yokimah and the Dusahn.

"Gate fifty-six, coming up," Josh announced. "You're in the homestretch now, Cap'n..."

"*...Watch your line in the next turn, or Salenger will try to slip under you again,*" Josh warned.

"Understood," Nathan said, holding his breath as he bore down against the G-forces. He finished his turn, rolled level, and pushed his throttles forward again, having chosen the utilization of constant changes in speed instead of the smooth, traditional style of the true Gunyoki, of which his opponent was one of the remaining few.

"This would be far less tiring if we had better inertial dampeners," Loki observed.

"That would not be the way of the Gunyoki," Nathan stated, mimicking Master Koku.

"*Surprisingly, your impressions are worse than your flying,*" Master Koku proclaimed dryly.

Nathan smiled. "I think I'm pissing Salenger off with all these speed changes," he commented as they accelerated toward the next gate. "He's almost rear-ended us at least a dozen times now."

"Locking lasers on the next set of targets," Loki announced. "Firing."

"*Oh, yeah!*" Josh exclaimed. "*Ten more points for the good guys!*"

Nathan glanced at the rear camera view as he

rolled his ship over and dove for the next gate, backing his throttles off more than usual.

"Uh, isn't this where you usually punch it?" Loki wondered.

"I don't want too much speed, or I won't make the next turn," Nathan insisted.

"You've made turns like this at a faster rate before, Captain," Loki reminded him.

"We're further off line than I'd like," Nathan replied.

"*He's making his move!*" Josh warned. "*Low to port! Translate down and left! Quickly!*"

Nathan paused a split second before moving his control stick, and failed to rotate his engine nacelles quickly enough to move his ship down and left to block his opponent's attempt to get around him. Nathan jammed his throttles forward as his opponent's fighter slid under him and took the lead.

"*Fuck!*" Josh cursed over comms.

Nathan followed his opponent through the next gate, allowing the distance between the two ships to increase slightly.

"*Keep your throttles at max power!*" Josh yelled. "*You've only got three gates to catch him!*"

"What about points?" Nathan demanded. "Do we have him on points?"

"*If he finishes first, Salenger will have you by ten points,*" General Telles chimed in. "*Your only hope is to pass him before you reach the last gate.*"

Nathan left his throttles at full power, switching back to the fluid, traditional piloting style that Master Koku had taught him. Although he was able to keep up with his opponent over the next two gates, he was unable to gain on him, let alone pass him. As they breached the fifty-ninth gate and entered the final turn, all hope appeared to be lost.

Then there was a small flash in the leader's port engine, and the fighter started drifting off course.

"*He just lost his port engine!*" Josh screamed. "*GUN IT!*"

"All power to the main engines!" Nathan barked.

"What about shields?" Loki warned as he channeled all available power into the engines. "There are still two targets left."

"*If you cross the finish line first, you'll still have enough points to win, even after the penalty for not taking out the targets,*" General Telles assured them.

As Nathan's fighter began to pass on his opponent's port side, several smaller explosions went off within the other ship's malfunctioning engine. "He's coming apart!" Nathan exclaimed. "Transfer power to starboard shields!"

Nika Salenger's port engine exploded, setting off a chain reaction in his port propellant tank, then his port missile bay, working its way across through the entire ship, killing its crew in the process.

Several large pieces of debris slammed into the starboard side of Nathan's fighter, before their shields had adequate energy, sending their ship sliding sideways.

"Shit!" Nathan exclaimed as he struggled to regain control.

"Multiple damage warnings!" Loki announced. "Starboard engine is losing hydraulics! Reactor containment is fluctuating! Missiles and lasers are offline..."

"All I need is maneuvering!" Nathan yelled. "Quickly! We're going to hit the gate!"

Loki quickly channeled all remaining energy

that their damaged reactor could produce into their maneuvering systems. "I'm restarting maneuvering!" he announced. "You should at least have docking thrusters in ten seconds!"

"You're gonna hit the gate in twenty!" Josh warned.

Jessica and General Telles exchanged glances.

"*Docking thrusters coming up!*" Loki announced.

"His docking thrusters may not be enough," Master Koku warned. "Not with so little time before impact."

"Docking thrusters online!" Loki reported.

Nathan twisted his flight control stick, leaning it to the right to put their ship into a fast roll.

"*What the hell are you doing?*" Josh yelled.

Loki said nothing.

Nathan kept his eyes looking out the window, catching a glimpse of the area of the gate they were going to collide with, trying to judge their closure rate and time his roll rate. Tiny squirts from docking thrusters adjusted his roll rate as they drifted toward the last gate, debris from his opponent's obliterated fighter drifting alongside them.

Nathan's eyes widened as they entered their final roll before impact. "Hold on!" he warned as he fired and held his thrusters to slow their roll at the last second. He held his breath, looking up as the ship rolled, their canopy rolling past the gate's edge, missing the structure by less than a meter.

"YOU'RE CLEAR!" Josh exclaimed, jumping out of his seat. "YOU WON!"

Master Koku, as usual, showed no reaction at all.

"I hope your mechanics are good," he warned. "As you will have just over an hour to repair the damage, or you will forfeit the next race."

General Telles and Jessica again exchanged glances as Master Koku silently left the control room.

CHAPTER ELEVEN

Nathan sat at the control room console next to Josh and Loki, while Master Koku, Jessica, and General Telles stood behind them. All eyes were glued to the assortment of camera views and sensor displays as they watched the final heat to determine the champion of Ichi Aza.

"Suli will take the next gate higher than expected, leaving room below for Alayna to slip under her," Master Koku stated. "Do you know why?"

"Because she's stupid?" Josh joked.

"To bait her pursuer," Nathan surmised. "The next gate is high right, and the gate after is in the same direction. If Alayna goes under, she'll be outside on both turns and she'll fall further behind."

"Correct," Master Koku agreed. "It will also expose her to the defenses on gates sixty-three and sixty-four."

"But those are on a different leg," Josh argued. "They're still eight gates away. Are they even active?"

"All gun emplacements become active the moment the race begins," Loki stated.

"Mister Sheehan is correct," Master Koku agreed. "This round is meant to simulate an attack on a heavily defended position."

"Then why are they flying against one another?" Josh asked in a sarcastic tone.

"Because it adds to the excitement," Master Koku replied. "Unfortunately, much of the race is designed for that purpose."

"Yup, she's going high right, just like you said," Josh noticed.

"She's not going for it," Nathan realized as the

second ship held her position directly behind the leader.

"Hell, she's translating up," Josh added.

"She will make her move at the next threshold," Master Koku predicted.

Moments later, the two ships passed through the next race gate, and the second ship translated further upward and began accelerating.

"Where the hell is she getting the extra thrust?" Josh wondered.

"Her weapons officer is taking power from weapons and shields in favor of propulsion," Master Koku explained.

Nathan looked at the sensor readout for Alayna Imai's ship. "She's using a zero-twenty-eighty split." Nathan turned to look at Master Koku. "No power to weapons and only twenty percent to shields?"

"A clever tactic," General Telles commented.

"Alayna is betting that Suli's weapons officer will destroy the targets."

"But *twenty percent*?" Nathan questioned. "A single direct hit, and her shields will be gone."

"A gamble, yes," Master Koku agreed. "But she has taken the lead away from her opponent."

Nathan turned back just as Alayna's ship overtook Suli's, and she returned her power levels to a more balanced distribution, although still favoring propulsion. "Damn. I'm glad we don't have to maintain a three-way balance like that."

"That was a slick move," Josh exclaimed. "I'd like to meet this Alayna chick. She looks hot."

"Alayna is married, with six children, and a husband who is twice your size," Master Koku stated calmly.

Josh's eyebrows jumped. "Thanks for the warning, grandpa."

"How many gates left?" Jessica asked.

"Twenty-five," Loki replied.

"How many gates are in this race?" she wondered.

"Eighty," Loki answered.

"That's a long-ass race."

"The final is twice as long," Master Koku told her.

"And through asteroids," Loki added.

"And the other guy is allowed to shoot at you," Josh chimed in.

Jessica looked concerned. "You're kidding."

"In the final heat, one ship is the aggressor, and the other the defender," Master Koku explained.

"What's the difference?" Jessica wondered.

"The aggressor must deal with both the fixed defenses, and his or her opponent. The defender only has to worry about their opponent, and not the defenses."

"How do they decide who's the aggressor, and who's the defender?" she wondered.

"The ship from the ichi with the greatest accumulation of points is allowed to choose. In nearly all cases, they choose to defend."

"No surprise there," Jessica said.

The door to the control room burst open, and Quory stepped inside. "I have news!" he blurted out with excitement.

Everyone in the room turned to look at Quory.

"Tham Kors has withdrawn from Ichi Konsai's final heat. The damage to his ship cannot be repaired in time. They just announced it throughout the platform. Congratulations, Captain. You are now going to the final round as the Ichi Konsai Shenshomi!"

"Shen-what?" Jessica wondered.

"The warrior of Ichi Konsai," Loki explained.

There was not as much surprise in their faces as Master Koku would have thought. "One has to wonder, however, why they did not use an alternate ship. After all, Tham Kors flies for Yokimah Racing, and two of their pilots are already out of the competition, which makes their ships available as backups."

"They can do that?" Josh wondered. "Just use whatever ship they want?"

"Within the same team, yes," Master Koku replied.

"They can change pilots, too," Loki added.

"In the same team?" Josh asked.

"Not always," Master Koku corrected. "If a pilot is too badly injured to continue, he or she may select an alternate to fly in their place. However, the alternate *must* be of the same ichi."

"Alayna Imai will win this heat," Nathan announced. "Yokimah wants his pilots to face me in the finals, and *she* is on his team."

"She'll also be the first woman in race history to make it to the final heat," Loki added.

"Which only serves to support Yokimah's assertion that the Gunyoki are capable of defending Rakuen," Nathan continued. "He's orchestrated this entire event to serve his purposes."

"You are accusing Ito Yokimah of cheating?" Master Koku asked, surprised.

"People like Yokimah don't consider it cheating," Nathan insisted. "They refer to it as 'doing what is necessary for the greater good', which *usually* means for the good of the one doing it."

"If you do not trust him, why did you accept his challenge?" Master Koku wondered.

Nathan looked at the old man. "If there's one thing that combat has taught me, it's that you rarely get to choose *who* you fight, or *when* you fight them."

"Uh, Nathan's right," Josh interrupted. "Alayna just won."

General Telles looked at the screens, quickly tallying up the scores. "This means you will have your choice of roles in the final heat," he concluded. "Ichi Konsai now has five more points than Ichi Aza."

"Congratulations, Captain," Master Koku offered respectfully. "You have gotten further in the competition than I would ever have imagined. It seems your reputation for being *lucky* is not an exaggeration."

* * *

Makani Koku entered Ito Yokimah's office deep inside the Yokimah Racing Center on the Gunyoki race platform. The call from his former employer was unexpected, and he feared it was related to Captain Scott's suspicions. That fear, as well as the life debt that Makani owed Ito, compelled him to answer the call.

"Makani," Ito greeted as he entered the room from a side door. "I trust all is going well in bay seventy-five?"

"As well as can be expected," Makani replied.

"They will have their ship repaired, and ready for action, in time for the finals, will they not?"

"I cannot say for sure, but I would be surprised if they did not. They are quite a determined and resourceful bunch."

"Excellent," Ito exclaimed. "That's precisely what I'd hoped. A *tremendous* event this has turned out to be, wouldn't you say?"

"It appears to be the usual folly that the public now calls Gunyoki."

"Ticket sales are through the roof!" Ito exclaimed. "Paid viewership, both in viewing arenas and at home, is off the charts, as well. The Gunyoki Combat Racing Association will earn more credits from this *one event*, than they will from the entire season."

"I imagine you, as the one of the founders, stand to receive a substantial percentage of those credits."

"Indeed, I do," Ito bragged. "And it's all because of you, my old friend."

"My role in all of this is marginal, at best," Makani insisted humbly.

"Don't sell yourself short, my friend. There are still many who remember the name Koku. Your reputation, alone, probably accounts for a sizable portion of our sales. Everyone wants to see the legend, who was trained by a legend, fly against their favorite Gunyoki pilots of today. The publicity around your name, and that of Captain Scott's, well, you simply cannot buy that type of publicity. Not for all the credits on Rakuen. And this deal is but a stepping-stone. I have plans for Rakuen that you would not believe..."

"Deal?" Makani wondered.

"Event," Ito corrected. "This *event* will make Ito Yokimah a household name. 'Ito Yokimah', the protector of Rakuen."

Makani looked puzzled. "How exactly are you *protecting* Rakuen?"

"It is a long story," Ito said, dismissing the subject with a wave of his hand. "One you do not have time for, my old friend."

"I do not?"

"Has no one informed you?" Ito grinned. "Alayna

Imai has invoked the right of s*on bukai kawa no.* And *you* are her kawa no."

Suddenly, all of Captain Scott's suspicions no longer seemed unfounded. "I am honored."

"I expected you would be," Ito replied. "You have the opportunity to make Gunyoki history, old friend. Beat Nathan Scott, and *you* will become the greatest Gunyoki since Yuki Muto."

"I will do my best, as always," Makani promised, bowing respectfully. "I will need to return to bay seventy-five, to collect my things, before I report to my ship."

"Take your time, old friend. I promise you, the final heat will not start without the great Makani Koku."

"You honor me, sir," Makani said, bowing again as he stepped backward toward the exit.

Ito Yokimah watched as the old man turned and left. He picked up his glass of wine and took a sip, pleased with himself. Everything was going as he'd hoped.

* * *

Makani nodded at the surprisingly confident-looking guard at the entrance to bay seventy-five. Although he was aware that Captain Scott had brought in his own security detail, the men filling that role seemed a unique bunch, as did their leader, General Telles.

In fact, it had not escaped Makani that everyone in Captain Scott's team seemed unique; an odd assortment of characters. In his experience, humans tended to associate with those of similar ilk. Whereas, Captain Scott's group appeared to cover a broad spectrum of personality types, cultural backgrounds, and accents. If they were all part of the same military organization, it was unlike any that he had ever known.

Despite his best efforts to remain detached, Makani had developed a begrudging respect for the lot of them. Nathan, most of all. In just six short days, he had gone from never having even sat in a Gunyoki, to flying as if he had been doing so all his life. Makani had never seen anything like it. He had trained countless pilots, both true Gunyoki, and those who simply wished to race. Many of them had possessed natural instincts and abilities, but not one of them had ever accomplished so much in so little time. He was beginning to understand the reality behind the legend of Na-Tan.

These feelings made what he now had to do all the more difficult. But he had no choice in the matter. Ito Yokimah was up to something, of that, he was certain. And he had a feeling Nathan knew what it was, but had not yet shared the true nature of his suspicions. If Yokimah *was* up to something, Makani needed to be in the middle of it, either to ensure its success, or to prevent it, whichever was best for Rakuen.

Makani paused as he entered the main hangar bay, searching for Nathan.

"Looking for Nathan?" Dalen asked as he came out of the door from behind Makani, passing him on his right.

"Yes."

"Far side, with Vlad," Dalen replied, continuing on his way.

"Thank you." Makani continued deeper into the bay, making his way around to the other side of Nathan's Gunyoki fighter, which was still undergoing repairs for the damage sustained in its prior heat.

He found him near the stern of the ship, squatting down alongside his chief engineer, inspecting his repair work. "Captain," he greeted as he approached.

"Master Koku," Nathan replied, standing.

"If I might speak with you a moment."

"What's on your mind?" Nathan wondered.

"Perhaps it would be best, if we spoke alone?"

"Vladimir is like a brother to me," Nathan said. "More so than my real brother was. I trust him with my life. In fact, I trust all the members of my team with my life. So, please..."

"You are lucky to have people whom you can trust so completely, Captain. Take care to remember that, always."

"Is *that* what you wanted to tell me?"

"No." Makani paused for a moment. "I have been selected as Alayna Imai's son bukai kawa no. It means..."

"Honored alternate, I know," Nathan said.

Makani's thoughts stumbled for a moment, surprised by the captain. "I wanted to tell you personally, before the public announcement."

"I appreciate the sentiment, but I've already heard."

"Might I ask how?"

"One of Quory's buddies at Yokimah Racing told him. Not all of that guy's employees think he walks on water."

Master Koku again looked puzzled, particularly by Nathan's turn of phrase.

"I do not wish to be the one who destroys all you have worked for," Makani told him. "Unfortunately, son bukai kawa no is an honor that no Gunyoki can refuse. To do so would bring dishonor on both his ichi *and* his family name."

"It's okay, Master Koku. Yokimah was never going to let me win." Nathan turned to Vladimir. "Vlad, give me your data pad," he asked, reaching out.

Vladimir handed Nathan his data pad as he also stood.

Nathan tapped the pad a few times, and then handed it to Master Koku.

"What am I looking at?" Master Koku wondered.

"A remote power cut-off device," Nathan explained. "One of Yokimah's mechanics installed it. I'm betting he put similar devices on all the ships I faced today, to be sure I'd get to the final round."

"But no ships have lost power," Makani insisted, refusing to believe.

"They're probably all different. And he may not have needed to activate them all. In fact, I think I actually beat my first two opponents fair and square. But Salenger's ship had to have been sabotaged."

"I was wondering why you let him pass you so easily," Makani admitted. "But this doesn't make sense. Such a device would be easily discovered by the incident investigators. Yokimah would lose his accreditation, and he would suffer incredible dishonor. It would literally ruin him."

"Not if my ship wasn't around to investigate," Nathan pointed out.

"I am afraid I do not understand," Makani admitted.

"We believe that Yokimah has made a deal with the Dusahn to protect Rakuen, by handing myself, and the Aurora, over to them."

"The protector of Rakuen," Makani muttered, recalling Ito's words. "I suspected that Ito was up to something. But I assumed he was just trying to increase his popularity and help fund his campaign.

Everyone on Rakuen knows how critical he is of our current president. But to make a deal with the devil himself."

"That's probably the most accurate description I've heard of the Dusahn, yet," Nathan insisted.

"Captain, you cannot allow this to happen. If the Dusahn *are* as bad as you say, surely they will not honor any deal made with Ito Yokimah. There must be some way to stop him."

"It isn't Yokimah I'm worried about," Nathan assured his mentor. "It's the Dusahn."

"How can I help?" Master Koku begged. "You *must* allow me to help."

"I was kind of hoping you'd offer," Nathan replied with a smile.

* * *

"Are you sure about this, Captain?" Loki asked as he walked Nathan to his fighter. "A Gunyoki is a lot to handle for one man, even for someone like Master Koku."

"Koku and I have already made the announcement. The crowd is expecting a *jiyu tori* race," Nathan replied. "What the hell does *jiyu tori* mean, anyway?"

"I think it means ruptured duck, or something," Josh replied as he walked alongside Nathan, as well.

"It means *crippled bird*," Loki corrected. "And it's an insane way to fly a Gunyoki, *especially* in the final round."

"That's why I chose to defend," Nathan told him. "Besides, I need both of you on the Seiiki. The whole plan falls apart without you."

"We've got this, Cap'n," Josh assured him. "And so do you," he added, patting Nathan on the back as he turned toward the Reaper on the other side of the bay.

Nathan walked up to Vladimir and Quory, both of whom were standing by the access ladder to his fighter's cockpit. Quory immediately began checking Nathan's pressure suit, ensuring that all its seals were in order.

"Remember, when you see a sudden, unexplained power drop of at least thirty percent, it means that someone has triggered the device," Vladimir reminded him.

"That's when I play dead," Nathan replied.

"Don't forget to turn *away* from the asteroid field, *first*," Vladimir insisted. "This is most important, Nathan."

"I've got this," Nathan assured his friend. "You just worry about keeping the Aurora in the fight; otherwise, we're all screwed," Nathan added as he headed up the ladder.

Vladimir waited for Nathan to get halfway up, then followed. Nathan climbed up into the front of the Gunyoki cockpit and slid down into his seat. As he pulled on his helmet, Vladimir attached the ship's life-support, comms, and med-sensor umbilicals to Nathan's flight suit. Finally, he checked that Nathan's helmet was properly sealed. "Good luck, my friend," he said, tapping him on the helmet before heading down the ladder.

Nathan started up his reactor and began running through his systems checks. Once he was certain everything was up and running, he reached down and pushed the canopy lever downward, activating the motor. As the canopy swung downward, to seal him inside, he activated the auto-taxi system to take his Gunyoki fighter across the bay and into the transfer airlock.

As his fighter rolled through the doors, he got one

last glimpse of his team as they climbed aboard the Reaper. Now, with only a week's worth of training, he would be facing the greatest Gunyoki pilot on all of Rakuen. The future of the Karuzari, the safety of the world below him, and the freedom of the entire quadrant were riding on one thing...his victory. It was up to Nathan and his team to do what they'd always done. Fly, fight, and win. If they succeeded, all of Rakuen would hail their new champion, Na-Tan, and join them in their fight. And then, the Dusahn would fall.

———————

Vladimir was the last to climb aboard the Reaper, activating the hatch behind him.

"*Everyone aboard?*" Loki called back from the cockpit.

Vladimir glanced around quickly. Marcus, Neli, Dalen, Deliza, Yanni, and Abby were all buckled in and ready to depart. "We're all here!" he shouted back as he took his seat. "I hope Mister Yokimah does not notice we left," he said to the others.

"Don't worry," Deliza assured him. "Quory told his friend at Yokimah Racing that one of us got injured, and that the Reaper is taking them back to the Aurora for medical care."

"That was good thinking."

"It was Nathan's idea."

"Are we going to get out in time?" Abby asked.

"As soon as we land, the Seiiki's crew and I will disembark, and one of the Aurora's Reaper crews will take the rest of you back to the fleet, where it is safe." *I hope*, he thought to himself.

———————

Nathan monitored his systems and flight displays as his auto-flight system guided his Gunyoki fighter into the long, imaginary corridor leading to the asteroid field, through which the final heat would be flown. Three complete checks assured him that his ship was ready for action, although his hands would be full trying to manage the tasks of piloting the ship and managing weapons, shields, and power distribution at the same time. He glanced to his right as Master Koku's fighter pulled up alongside, slowly moving past him to take the position of aggressor.

Nathan switched his comms to ship-to-ship, using a frequency that Master Koku had assured him would not be monitored by Race Control. "Are you ready for this, Master Koku?" he asked in jest.

"I believe you have earned the right to address me by my first name, Nathan. And for the record, I've been ready for this long before you were born."

Nathan smiled. "Which time?"

"Readiness check," the race controller announced.

"Gunyoki Seven Five, ready," Nathan replied.

"Gunyoki Two Four, ready," Master Koku acknowledged.

"Approaching race start in ten seconds. Ka-ahi no su-ido, shinsayi," the controller warned, wishing them both God's speed.

———————

Jessica and Quory sat in the control room beside General Telles, nervously watching the race feeds on the view screen in front of them.

"Koku will go straight between one five seven and one one five," General Telles warned. "He will then dive into the crevice on one one eight."

"How can you be sure?" Nathan asked.

"It is the only logical, opening move." The general glanced at the clock. "Starting in three......two...... one......race on."

Nathan pushed his throttles all the way forward as the auto-flight shut off, giving control of the ship to him. Just as the general had predicted, Master Koku dropped his nose, went to full power, and dove between asteroids one five seven and one one five, below and to the right.

Nathan pitched down to follow, immediately locking his weapons systems onto Koku's ship. But, before he could fire his lasers, the Gunyoki master slipped behind asteroid one one five.

Nathan followed suit, steering his fighter as close to the surface of one one five as he could, paying close attention to any gravitational effects, despite the fact that Master Koku had once told him the mass of the asteroids in the Rogen system was negligible.

As he pulled around the asteroid, he barely caught a glimpse of Koku's fighter as it dove into the trench, again, just as General Telles had predicted.

Automated defenses opened fire on Master Koku's ship as it raced through the trench. But Makani hugged the bottom of the trench so tightly that the weapons had difficulty getting clear lines of fire on him while he streaked past them.

"I'm staying high," Nathan announced. "I'll fire from above." Nathan dipped his nose down slightly below his flight path, keeping his engine nacelles pointed along his course. The angle allowed him to bring all four of his laser turrets, on both the top and bottom of his ship, onto his target. He didn't want to open fire on his mentor, but he had to sell it, and he was quite sure that if their roles were reversed, Makani would not hesitate to do so.

Nathan activated his lasers and opened fire. Bolts struck Koku's aft shields, causing them to glow with each strike. Some bounced off, heading harmlessly into space, while others ricocheted into the walls of the crevice, sending chunks of the asteroid flying in all directions. With each shot, his mentor's shields would be weakened. But lasers, alone, were a difficult way to bring down an opponent's shields.

***

"Reaper has landed," Lieutenant Commander Vidmar reported.

"Remind them to make it quick," Cameron ordered. "We'll only be in Neramese's shadow for eight more minutes. After that, Rakuen will be able to see our ships coming and going."

"Understood."

"Are those stealth drones in place?" she asked the sensor officer.

"Recon drone will be on station in five minutes," Lieutenant Commander Kono replied. "It will have a clear view of the far end of the course. The comm-drone is running cold on its way out of the system. It will be ready when we need it."

"Very good," Cameron said, tapping her comm-set. "CAG, XO. Everyone ready?"

"*Ready birds are manned and in the tubes,*" Commander Verbeek replied. "*Second group is on standby, third group is in the elevators. We'll have twenty-four Eagles in the fight within five minutes of your order.*"

"And the Reapers?"

"*Six is all I can give you, Captain. I've got most of my pilots in Eagles.*"

"Understood." Cameron sighed. "Let's hope it's enough."

***

"I've got the tactical feed from the Aurora now,"

Jessica announced. "Nicely done, Mister Quory. I didn't think you'd be able to pull that off."

"Oh, I'm a man of many talents. Unfortunately, I'll be an *unemployed* man of many talents, after this."

"I'm pretty sure we can put you to good use, as long as you don't mind a little travel and a bit of excitement, now and again."

"Sounds intriguing," Mister Quory replied.

"The signal is much clearer, now, Captain," General Telles told Nathan.

"*Understood*," Nathan replied, understanding the general's inference. "*He's reaching the end of the trench, and I only managed to get his shields down by fifteen percent. He'll have them recharged in no time.*"

"As soon as he comes up, launch a spread of stub-missiles at him," General Telles recommended. "Launch a second spread one kilometer ahead of him. To avoid the first group, he'll have no choice but to fly into the second group."

"*Understood.*"

───────────

"We're off," Josh announced as the Seiiki lifted off the Aurora's aft starboard flight apron. "Get ready to jump."

"Are you sure we have to use these things?" Loki asked nervously.

"There are lots of eyes on Neramese, Lok."

"Yeah, but they don't even *like* the Rakuens."

"We can't take that chance; Nathan's orders."

"*Seiiki, Aurora Flight Ops. Jump now, while you're still shadowed by our sensor image.*"

"Flight Ops, Seiiki, jumping," Loki replied as he closed his eyes and pressed the jump button.

Josh looked out the front windows as the blue-white light poured out across the Seiiki's hull from her new stealth emitters. In a split second, the entire hull was covered with the shimmering jump field. However, even though it did increase in its intensity, the usual jump flash was almost non-existent. "Did it work?" he wondered.

Loki quickly scanned his displays. "The Aurora *is* gone," he concluded as he verified their position. "Holy crap, it worked," he exclaimed, looking at Josh. "We're five light years outside of the Rogen system."

"Hot damn!" Josh exclaimed. "Plot our next jump, quick!"

———————

Four stub-missiles leapt out of the pods on either side of Nathan's cockpit, followed immediately by four more. As soon as the missiles were away, Nathan pitched up, turning to a course that would intercept where he expected Master Koku's fighter to be, ten seconds from now.

Just as General Telles had predicted, Master Koku dropped several countermeasures to spoof the first group of missiles as he pitched up into the path of the second group. But he pitched up much more sharply than Nathan thought possible, and the second group of missiles missed him by more than five meters. "Damn, he's good," Nathan exclaimed as he armed the plasma cannons on the front of his engine nacelles. "These ought to bring his shields down a few points and make the crowds squeal," he said as he pressed the firing trigger.

———————

General Telles looked at the clock, then at Jessica. "He's five minutes from the far end of the course. Time for you to go."

"You're up, Quory," Jessica said, standing. "I'm in your hands."

"I won't let you down," Quory promised, turning to lead her out the door.

Jessica followed Quory, looking at Telles, and rolling her eyes on her way out.

General Telles turned back to his console. "Jessica says you're doing well."

"*Understood,*" Nathan replied, acknowledging the coded message.

"Oh, shit!" Nathan exclaimed as Makani's fighter seemingly stopped in its tracks, forcing Nathan to fly past him in the blink of an eye. "How the fuck did he do that?"

Nathan twisted his flight control stick and leaned it over, sending his fighter into a spiraling dive to starboard as plasma torpedoes, courtesy of Master Koku, streaked past his port side, one by one, following him as he continued spinning down between two closely packed asteroids. He activated the private frequency and called out, "How come you never taught me *that*?"

"*If a master reveals all his tricks, he quickly loses his mastery over others,*" Makani replied in the same sage tone he had used throughout Nathan's training.

"Yeah, well, I can think of a few tricks that you might not know," he replied as he flipped his engine nacelles over, stopped his spin, and fired his engines at full power. His plan was to force his opponent to stop firing and flip his engine nacelles over, as well, in order to decelerate to maintain his advantageous position behind Nathan.

But the plasma torpedoes kept coming, slamming into Nathan's shields and shaking the hell out of him. Two hits, three, five...and his shields were already down to forty percent. The only thing saving him from losing his forward shields was the fact that Makani seemed uninterested in staying behind Nathan, and continued past him.

Unfortunately, Master Koku rotated his engine nacelles as he passed, keeping his plasma torpedo cannons trained on Nathan's ship while he continued to fire. The flashes of red-orange on his shields walked up his nose and across his canopy, filling the inside of his cockpit with their blinding light. By the time the barrage ended, the only shield of Nathan's that wasn't drained below forty percent was on his ventral side.

"That was enjoyable," Makani said. *"Any other tricks you'd like to share?"*

"It's a good thing Master Koku is on our side," General Telles commented.

"Could have fooled me," Nathan grumbled, still shaking off the beating he had just taken.

———

"Stealth jump four, complete," Loki reported. "We're in the launch corridor."

"Get those bad boys ready, old man!" Josh called over his comm-set.

"Let's hope they're right about the target area," Loki commented.

———

"I swear, if that little shit calls me 'old man' one more time," Marcus grumbled as he lowered his helmet visor and sealed it shut. He grabbed the rail to steady himself in the fractional gravity of the Seiiki's cargo bay, and activated the open cycle for the cargo bay door. Before him were two of the Aurora's jump missiles, each of them loaded with the most dense

402

materials possible to maintain their compact size. The weapons themselves were ominous enough, but what really made him nervous were the antimatter mines that had been attached, at the last moment, to the front of them. Either of them had enough antimatter to make the Seiiki cease to exist, along with anything else within one hundred kilometers of them. "You know, that molo farm on Haven is starting to look a lot more attractive right now."

"*But you hate molo,*" Neli reminded him.

"Not as much as I hate antimatter mines."

"Jesus, how does he keep getting behind me like that?" Nathan cursed as more of Master Koku's plasma torpedoes slammed into his aft shields.

"*I'm surprised you haven't figured it out yet,*" General Telles commented.

"You, too?" Nathan replied in frustration as he continued to attempt to shake his attacker.

"*You're approaching the furthest turn,*" General Telles warned.

"I know," Nathan replied as the rain of red-orange fire continued to rattle his teeth and drain his shields. "I think you're overselling it, Makani," he said to himself. Nathan began watching his power levels out of the corner of his eye. If they had anticipated the Dusahn's plan correctly, the operator of the remote power cut-off device installed in his ship would be triggered at any moment. As soon as he entered into that furthest turn, the odds of their plan being successful decreased by leaps and bounds with each passing second.

"Here we go," Nathan announced as he approached the turn. He began to push his flight control stick to the right, when his power levels suddenly dropped by twenty-eight percent. Reacting quickly, he veered slightly left, away from the turn and out into open space, then pulled the remote activator on his main power breaker, interrupting the flow of power from his reactor to the rest of his ship. All his systems went dead, his lights went out, and his life-support system reverted to the pack on his back. Nathan switched to emergency battery power, which was only enough to run his comms and his transponder. "Mayday, mayday, mayday," he called, feigning controlled tension in his voice. "Gunyoki Seven Five has lost all power. Reactor is auto-scram. I'm drifting outbound from asteroid three eight five. Repeat..."

"I'm picking up a control signal from the race platform," Lieutenant Commander Kono reported from the Aurora's sensor station.

"Can you get a fix on the position *within* the platform?" Cameron asked.

"I'm working on it," the lieutenant commander assured her.

"Captain!" the comms officer called. "Distress call from Captain Scott!"

"Put it up," Cameron ordered.

"*...yoki Seven Five has lost all power. Reactor is auto-scram. I'm drifting outbound from asteroid three eight five. Repeat, mayday, mayday, mayday. Gunyoki Seven Five is dead stick and drifting outbound from three eight five, on batteries. Requesting rescue!*"

"That's it," Cameron announced. "That's the code phrase. The trap is set."

"*Repeat, mayday, mayday, mayday. Gunyoki Seven Five is dead stick and drifting outbound from three eight five, on batteries. Requesting rescue!*"

"Roger mayday, Seven Five. I'm notifying Race Control, now," General Telles replied. He punched in a call code, then spoke once he got an answer. "This is the controller for Gunyoki Seven Five. Seven Five is zero power and adrift outbound from asteroid three eight five. Requesting rescue."

"Roger rescue, Seven Five Controller. Help is on the way."

A small smile formed on the general's face. The call code he had used was not that of Race Control.

Makani watched his sensors as he continued on the course. Although he had seen Nathan's ship drifting out into space without power, and he had heard his distress call, the plan required that he keep up appearances. This meant he had to continue on, complete the course, and destroy the final objective, in order to claim victory. Any deviation from that action would alert Yokimah and his Takaran associate, Jorkar Seeley, if in fact he was the Dusahn spy as they suspected.

He only hoped his fellow Gunyoki pilots would come through as promised. He was quite sure of the three who were true Gunyoki, but the independents were all unknown to him. But they were all he had, and trusting them was a risk they had been forced to take.

Nathan sat in his cold, dark Gunyoki fighter, drifting toward deep space at more than a thousand meters per second. It was a turtle's pace compared to the speeds that even the Seiiki could fly. But his speed had been limited by the radical maneuvering required during a Gunyoki combat race. Unfortunately, it made him an easy target. If the Dusahn wanted him dead, he would not be able to get his reactor spun up and his shields raised in time.

Without any power, Nathan had no way to calculate his position. But after looking at his battery-powered time display, and doing a few calculations in his head, he estimated that he would drift past the planned engagement area in just over a minute. The further from the engagement area he drifted, the more adjustments the Seiiki would have to make before launching the antimatter-tipped jump missiles. That meant more time in the Dusahn's crosshairs, which was not a place he cared to be.

———

Vol Kaguchi set his frequency to the one specified by Master Koku, and activated the motor to close the canopy on his Gunyoki fighter. "Six Seven. Who's up?" he called over the secure frequency.

"*Komo, Four Four Two,*" the first pilot replied.

"*Takoda, Three One Eight.*"

"*Kane, Three Two Four.*"

Vol smiled as the replies kept coming in. By the time the last Gunyoki pilot announced his readiness, twenty-six ships had reported in. Nearly every pilot on the platform, other than those flying for Yokimah and the other big teams, had answered Master Koku's call to arms.

———

"Still no contacts," Lieutenant Commander Koko replied.

Cameron was losing her patience. "What's his position now?"

"He's now leaving the planned engagement area," the lieutenant commander answered.

"Gunyoki Race Control has launched rescue ships," the comms officer reported.

"Helm, set a course toward Nathan and accelerate, but keep your rate at normal levels. I want us to look like we're just heading toward our captain, just in case the Rakuens have trouble rescuing him."

"Won't the Rakuens object?" Lieutenant Commander Vidmar wondered.

"Probably," Cameron agreed. "But it will look suspicious if we don't appear concerned."

"Intercept course loaded," Lieutenant Dinev reported. "Accelerating at normal rates."

"Where the hell are they?" Cameron wondered.

"Maybe the Captain's wrong?" Lieutenant Commander Vidmar said.

"I'd be lying if I said the thought had not occurred to me," Cameron replied. "We'll have a hell of a lot of explaining to do, if he is."

———

"What the hell is going on?" Josh wondered.

Loki did not reply. He just looked at Josh, concerned.

"This waiting is killing me!" Josh exclaimed.

"At least you aren't back here, babysitting a pair of antimatter warheads," Marcus grumbled.

"What are you complaining about?" Josh asked. "If one of those things go, we're all fucked." He looked at Loki. "Something is wrong, I can *feel* it."

"Forgive me if I don't put a whole lot of faith in your *feelings*," Loki replied.

"Well, that's just mean, Lok."

———

Nathan was well beyond the planned engagement area and was beginning to wonder if they had been wrong about Yokimah. It was possible that all he wanted was to win the bet, and if he had someone in the race inspector's office, his plan would probably have worked. If that were the case, they had just handed Yokimah his victory, and Nathan had lost one of their biggest assets, the Ranni shuttle plant.

Nathan's doubts were washed away by a sudden flash of blue-white light in the distance. For a split second, he wondered if it was the Aurora coming to his rescue after deciding the plan had failed. But the color and shape of the flash was off.

That's when he noticed the hauntingly familiar silhouette coming toward him. A ship he had not seen in seven years, and one that still haunted his dreams.

It was a Jung battleship.

Nathan played dumb. "Approaching ship, this is Gunyoki Seven Five. I am dead stick, bingo power. Can you offer assistance?"

There was no response.

"Any time now, Cam," Nathan said, resisting the urge to power up and make a run for it as the black and red battleship continued to close on him.

———

Makani's sensor display lit up, warning him of an approaching warship; one that was larger than anything he had ever seen. "Race Control, Gunyoki Two Four. I have sensor contact with an unidentified warship that has just jumped in near Gunyoki Seven Five. Recommend alert one. Repeat, alert one. Scramble all available Gunyoki fighters, and send word to Rakuen Gunyoki Command."

"Gunyoki Two Four, Race Control. Are you sure?"

"You are speaking to a Gunyoki master," Makani replied, his irritation evident. "Activate the alert, or you will taste my blade as it steals your last breath from your lungs."

"Yes, sir," the controller replied in earnest.

"That's what I thought," Makani said to himself as he changed to the secure private frequency. "Six Seven, Two Four. Are you there, Vol?"

"*I am here, Makani,*" Vol replied. "*As are twenty-six of our friends. The alert has just been activated. We should be launching any second. Is the contact confirmed?*"

"It is," Makani replied. "And it is much bigger than I had imagined." Makani watched his sensor display as more contacts appeared. "And they brought friends, as well."

"*Then we will introduce them to the blade of the Gunyoki!*"

———————

"Contact!" Lieutenant Commander Kono announced. "Jung battleship just jumped in. Benta-class."

Kaylah turned to look over her shoulder at Captain Taylor. "It's the same one we exchanged fire with back in the Sol sector, sir."

"Why am I not surprised," Cameron said. "Sound general quarters. Lieutenant, plot an intercept course. Prepare to jump in and engage the target. Tactical! We'll be firing full spreads of plasma torpedoes. Max yields, triplets. We'll fire until the tubes are melting."

"Recon drone just signaled," the comms officer reported. "It stealth-jumped away."

"Send the comm-drone and alert the Strikers," Cameron added.

"More contacts, Captain!" Lieutenant Commander Kono warned. "Considerably smaller. Looks like Dusahn gunboats. They're closing on the captain's position awfully fast, sir."

"It's up to the Seiiki now," Cameron said. "Raise

shields, charge all weapons, and stand by to attack on my command."

"Attention all Gunyoki! Report when ready to launch!" the nervous voice of the controller announced over Vol Kaguchi's comms.

"Control, Gunyoki Six Seven. Check your panel! You have twenty-seven ships ready to launch, you fool!"

"Already?"

"Yes!" Vol yelled. "Now open the doors and release manual control to all Gunyoki, so that we can do our jobs and protect Rakuen!"

"Yes, sir!"

"I am en route to your position!" Makani told Nathan over the secure channel.

"Keep your distance!" Nathan yelled. "That's an order!"

"You forget that I am not under your command."

"Back off on your power, Makani!" Nathan insisted. "And do it gradually! If the Dusahn realize you're purposely slowing, they'll become suspicious and take evasive action. You must trust me on this!"

"They are less than one hundred kilometers from your position, Nathan!" Makani warned. *"They will be on you in less than a minute!"*

"Believe me! I know!"

"Recon drone! Just jumped in!" Loki announced.

"Get ready for release, Pops!" Josh warned.

"Receiving targeting data," Loki added.

"Believe me, kid, I'm fucking ready!" Marcus assured them.

"New course! Two five seven, twenty down. Accelerate to launch velocity."

"Two five seven, twenty down," Josh replied, entering the new course into the auto-flight system. As much as he hated not hand-flying, the precision required for a successful jump-weapon intercept was beyond the capability of a human pilot, and he knew it. "Max power!" Josh announced. "Turning to new heading, now."

"Twenty seconds to deployment point," Loki warned.

"*I've already got the fuckers on the ramp,*" Marcus replied. "*Say the word, and I'll give'm the boot!*"

"Ten seconds!"

"We are at planned release velocity," Josh reported. "On intercept course! Right down the magenta line, baby!"

"Marcus! Release!" Loki barked.

"*Releasing!*" Marcus replied. "*Weapons are free!*"

"Thrusting down and forward," Josh announced. This part, he was able to do manually, as the weapons were now on their final intercept trajectory.

Loki watched as the two mini jump missiles began to drift back and away from the Seiiki's aft cargo ramp, which was currently locked level with the cargo bay's deck.

Josh added more thrust, increasing their rate of separation.

"You're clear to turn away," Loki urged.

Josh wasted no time pulling the Seiiki into a smooth left turn, giving the weapons a clear path to their target, more than two light years away.

"Target line is clear," Loki announced. "Launching weapons."

The press of a button, and two seconds later,

411

both jump missiles accelerated past them to their right, quickly moving ahead of them and out of sight, eventually disappearing behind two flashes of blue-white light.

Josh looked at Loki. "Guess I should set a course for Rakuen, huh?" he said as he entered a new course. "After all, we don't want to miss all the fun, right?"

"I will never understand you, Josh," Loki replied, shaking his head.

———————

Two flashes of blue-white light, in the area of the approaching battleship, warned Nathan to brace himself. Even with his eyes closed, the light from the antimatter detonations was nearly blinding. But before the light had faded, his finger was already on the reactor start button. Unfortunately, it would take nearly two minutes for his systems to come back to life.

Static filled his helmet comms as he watched the antimatter flashes fade out his window and waited for the field of debris to slam into him. But it never came.

"If anyone can hear me, I'm powering back up," he called over the secure channel.

There was still only static.

———————

"...Move immediately to the emergency departure areas. This is an emergency evacuation. This is not a drill. All attendees are to move immediately to the nearest emergency departure areas," the automated message repeated.

Scared and panicked spectators rushed in all directions, while race platform personnel attempted to provide direction and prevent utter chaos. Spectators crowded the nearest emergency departure areas, fighting to be the next to get into the emergency evacuation pods located throughout the race platform.

"Why the fuck is everyone so panicked?" Jessica wondered as she and Quory pushed their way through the crowd toward the entrance to the Yokimah Racing Center.

"Rakuen has not seen a war in over three centuries!" Quory informed her. "Of course, the fact that this race platform is an easy target, and is loaded with fighters, does not help matters."

"Good point," she agreed as they reached the entrance.

The first thing Jessica noticed as they approached the entrance was that now, the guards had weapons.

"I am Quoruson Insimi," Quory announced, holding up his credentials for the first guard to see. "I have important information for Mister Yokimah."

The guard looked at Quory's ID, then at Jessica, who had hidden her credentials after her last failed attempt to get into the Yokimah facilities. "Who are you?" he asked Jessica.

"She is with me," Quory insisted.

"Where is your identification?" the guard asked Jessica, ignoring Quory.

"We don't have time for this," Jessica warned.

"I am a lead engineer for Yokimah Racing..."

"*You* may enter," the guard told Quory. "She must remain outside."

"Wrong answer," Jessica told the guard as she sprang into action. In a fluid-like motion, she caught the first guard's foot with her own, kicking it out from under him as she shoved the butt of her open hand into the base of his nose, pushing him back and toward his, now, unsupported side. As the guard fell over, she pulled his stunner from his holster, and quickly reached around Quory to put two shots into the second guard before he could get his own weapon out of its holster.

"Oh, goodness!" Quory exclaimed in shock. "What are you doing?"

"Improvising," Jessica replied as she bent down and pulled the door card from one of the downed guard's uniform shirt pockets. She stuck the card into the slot, and the door opened. "Let's go," she said, stepping through the doorway as she tucked the stunner into her belt and pulled her jacket down over it.

"What about them?" Quory wondered, looking down at the two unconscious guards as he followed her into the Yokimah facility.

"They'll be taking a little siesta," Jessica replied as she looked about before advancing. "Which way?"

Quory glanced back at the guards on the floor as the door closed behind him.

"Which way?" Jessica repeated.

"Uh, that way," Quory said.

"Perhaps you should lead?" Jessica suggested. "You do have the credentials, after all."

"Yes, of course," Quory agreed, remembering the plan they had discussed. "What's a *siesta*?" he wondered, leading her down the corridor into the Yokimah Racing Center.

"Jump complete!" Ensign Bickle reported from the Aurora's navigation console.

"Target bravo one's starboard, midship shields are down to forty percent!" Lieutenant Commander Kono announced.

"That's it?" Cameron replied in surprise. "Tactical, put everything you have into that shield section, and don't stop firing until you bring it down!"

"Aye, sir!" Lieutenant Commander Vidmar acknowledged as he started his barrage.

Red-orange plasma torpedoes streaked out from under the Aurora's nose, illuminating the bridge's interior with repeated flashes of the ominous color.

"Bravo one is launching fighters!" Lieutenant Commander Kono announced.

"CAG, XO, time to go to work," Cameron called over her comm-set.

"*XO, CAG, on our way!*"

"Where's Nathan?" Cameron demanded.

"Three kilometers ahead of the target, one below, and closing fast," the lieutenant commander replied. "He's powering up now." Kaylah's eyes widened. "Bravo one is targeting the captain!"

Cameron quickly tapped the keys on the right arm of her command chair, adding a new frequency to her comm-set. "Gunyoki Two Four, Aurora Actual! Target bravo one is targeting Seven Five! Can you assist?"

"*Actual, Two Four,*" Master Koku replied calmly. "*I'm already en route.*"

"Targets golf one and golf two have changed positions," Lieutenant Commander Kono warned. "They are now off our port side, and closing. They're locking on to us."

"Port rail guns and plasma cannons on those gunboats," Cameron ordered.

"Targeting the gunboats, now," Lieutenant Commander Vidmar replied.

"Bravo one has locked onto us with their big

guns!" Lieutenant Commander Kono warned. "They're locking missiles, as well!"

"Continue firing!" Cameron insisted. "Ready escape jump, delta seven."

"Escape delta seven, aye," Lieutenant Dinev replied from the helm.

"Escape jump ready!" the navigator added.

"Missile launch!" Kaylah warned. "Ten seconds!"

"Execute delta seven!" Cameron ordered.

Their jump fields were forming before the words left her mouth.

"What are you doing?" Nathan questioned.

"*I am following your executive officer's orders,*" Makani replied over comms.

"You ignore my orders, but follow hers? Is that the Gunyoki way?"

"*It is the way of a man long married,*" Makani replied.

"Your shields won't hold."

"*The tricks I have yet to teach you are many, my young friend. I am merely trying to ensure that you remain alive, long enough for me to show you a few more.*"

"Are all Gunyoki as stubborn as you?" Nathan wondered as his reactor finally began putting out power and his systems started coming alive.

"*Only the ones who are still alive,*" Makani replied. "*How long until you are back in action?*"

"Things are spinning up now," Nathan replied. "Thirty seconds, tops!"

Makani streaked past Nathan's still-drifting Gunyoki fighter, turning toward the approaching battleship and putting his ship directly in between the aggressor and his young friend. Once in position, he flipped his engine nacelles over and went to full thrust, to decelerate sharply and match Nathan's rate of closure with the enemy vessel. "So, this is what a Dusahn warship looks like. Not as menacing as I had imagined."

"*It's not a Dusahn ship, it's a Jung ship,*" Nathan corrected. "*I mean, it is being operated by the Dusahn, but it's of a much older design. Probably one of the original ships they had when they were exiled. It's just painted to look like a Jung ship.*"

"An interesting strategy, this 'false-flag' operation you spoke of," Makani commented as the battleship opened fire on him. A stream of plasma bolts struck his forward shields, immediately draining them, but he angled them just enough to send much of the incoming energy bouncing harmlessly off into space. "Your plan seems to be progressing swimmingly thus far, don't you think?" he commented as he launched a spread of stub-missiles at the battleship.

———

Nathan shook his head as the last of his systems came to life. "You're a real piece of work, old man."

"*I am not familiar with that expression, but I'll assume it is a compliment. Are you ready to get to work, Captain?*"

"I assume I'm flying your wing?"

"*You are not quite ready, but I suppose I will have to make do, given the circumstances.*"

"I'll take *that* as a compliment," Nathan replied as he pushed his throttles forward and lit up his main engines. "Lead the way, Master."

———

Ito stared in disbelief at the massive view screen

on the wall of his office within the Yokimah Racing Center. "This cannot be," he stuttered, his eyes wide.

"It seems that Captain Scott has managed to circumvent your device," Mister Seeley said, his voice seething with disdain.

"But, that is impossible," Ito insisted. "The device is tamper-proof. The only way would be to route power *around* the device. But even then, I'd know, because the power levels on his main trunk would be reduced by fifty percent as it was distributed across…"

"Apparently, you are not as clever as the young captain appears to be," Mister Seeley interrupted, his right hand sliding behind his back. "And not as clever as the Dusahn had hoped." He moved closer to Ito, menace in his eyes. "Such a lovely little civilization your people have created. A pity it has nothing to offer us other than its copious amount of water."

Ito stepped back, noticing the look in Mister Seeley's eyes. "But…" That's when he noticed the flash of Seeley's blade. He tried to call out for his guards, but found no voice at his disposal. For in a swift, highly skilled move, Jorkar Seeley's weapon had taken it from him. In an instant, one of the wealthiest, and most powerful, men on all of Rakuen was on the floor, gasping for air.

Jorkar knelt down beside Ito's body, reaching into his jacket pocket as he spoke. "The Dusahn do not tolerate failure." He removed Ito's access card and slipped it into his own pocket, then wiped the blade of his knife on his victim's jacket before departing.

Ito stared at the ceiling, his hands around the gaping wound on his neck, desperately trying to hold back the gush of blood spurting from his severed carotid artery as the last few beats of his heart ran their course. As his vision faded, he wondered how it had all gone so terribly wrong.

———————

"Jump complete," Ensign Bickle announced as the Aurora's jump flash subsided.

"Come about. Prepare attack pattern beta four," Cameron ordered.

"Beta four, aye," the navigator replied.

"Four jump flashes!" Lieutenant Commander Kono announced. "Cobra gunships."

Cameron changed frequencies again. "Striker One, Aurora Actual. Target bravo one's starboard midship shields, and welcome to the party."

"*Hope we're not late,*" Captain Roselle replied. "*Watch this!*"

"Executing beta four, jump one," Ensign Bickle announced as the Aurora's jump fields formed, and the bridge momentarily filled with its subdued blue-white flash. "Jump complete," he added, two seconds later.

"Turning toward target," Lieutenant Dinev reported as she rolled the Aurora onto its starboard side, and started her turn.

"I'm counting over fifty fighters," Lieutenant Commander Kono reported. "Twenty of them are heavies and are headed toward Gunyoki Seven Five and Two Four."

Cameron switched frequencies again. "Gunyoki Two Four, Aurora Actual. You have twenty heavy fighters pursuing you."

"*We are leading them away from your attack corridor,*" Master Koku explained.

"The heavies are firing," Lieutenant Commander Kono warned.

"*Easy for you to say,*" Nathan added. "*I'm the one in their crosshairs at the moment!*"

"*Consider it evasive training,*" Master Koku told him.

"You *cannot* take on twenty heavy fighters," Cameron warned.

"*Which is why we are leading them toward the race platform,*" Master Koku explained. "*More precisely, toward the flight of twenty-seven Gunyoki who just departed from it.*"

Cameron turned to look at her sensor officer.

"He's right, Captain," Kaylah confirmed. "Twenty-seven Gunyoki just left the platform and are headed Master Koku's way at full power."

"I guess he wasn't as overly optimistic about his fellow Gunyoki pilots as we'd thought," Cameron admitted.

———

"Holy shit," Aiden exclaimed, looking at the threat display at the center of his gunship's console. "I've never seen so many enemy contacts...not even in simulations."

"Let's join the rebellion. It'll be fun. We'll get to hang out with Na-Tan." Kenji chided as incoming fire struck their forward shields and rocked their ship. "Sure, we might get our ASSES BLOWN OFF in the PROCESS......but it'll be fun, trust me."

"Would you let it go, already?" Aiden begged as the gunship continued to shake. "Besides, how many people from our class are attacking a Jung battleship right now?" he asked as he put the gunship on Kenji's selected course. "I'll give you a hint." Aiden turned to look at his copilot. "None. That's how many. They're still flying training exercises back in the Tau Ceti system. *This* is *way* more fun."

"You and I have such different ideas of fun, it's unbelievable," Kenji replied as he charged the plasma torpedo cannons.

Aiden smiled as he pressed the firing trigger on his flight control stick, sending the first wave of plasma torpedoes toward the Jung battleship looming before them.

———

Jessica burst into Yokimah's office, expecting to find both Ito and his friend, Jorkar Seeley, tracking the progress of the battle.

"Do you always leave a collection of unconscious bodies behind you, wherever you go?" Quory asked, looking down at, yet, another pair of unconscious guards outside of his employer's office. He turned around to enter the office, stopping short when he spotted the body on the floor. "Oh, goodness," he exclaimed in shock. "What did you do?"

"*I* didn't do this," Jessica insisted as she knelt down next to Ito Yokimah's pale, lifeless body.

"Oh, my God... I'm definitely going to be out of a job, now."

"I think he's still alive," Jessica said as she bent over him, placing her cheek next to his mouth to check for breathing.

"How do you know?"

"There's still blood gushing out with each beat of his heart," she said, taking off her jacket and placing it on his neck to prevent the last of his blood from leaking out of his body.

"How could there possibly be any left?" Quory exclaimed, gesturing at the enormous pool of blood surrounding Ito's head. "There's *so* much blood!"

"I *know* there's a lot of blood!" Jessica yelled. "I'm

fucking kneeling in it! Now get over here and help me!"

"What do you want me to do?" Quory asked.

"Get over here and hold this against his neck," she instructed.

"Oh, God," Quory said, stepping carefully into the pool of blood and squatting down. "These shoes are going to be ruined," he said as he reached out and held the bundled-up jacket for her.

"Tell me about it," Jessica said, standing up. "That was my only *civilian* jacket." She looked around, surveying the scene. "This must have happened within the last few minutes, otherwise he'd be dead." She reached into her pocket as she stepped over Yokimah's body, pulling out a small single-dose pneumo-ject. "Pull the jacket away for a moment," she instructed as she squatted down on the other side of him.

"Oh, goodness," Quory exclaimed as he removed the bundled-up jacket, and got his first close-up view of the gaping wound in his employer's neck.

"Who the hell says that?" Jessica asked while she sprayed the contents of the pneumo-ject across Yokimah's wound.

"Says what?"

"Goodness. Seriously."

"What is that stuff?" Quory asked.

"Medical nanites," she replied. "*Trauma* nanites, to be more accurate. Put pressure back on that wound."

"What do they do?" Quory wondered as he pressed the bundled-up jacket against Yokimah's wound again.

"Think of them as microscopic mechanics that go straight to the damage and begin repairing it."

Quory's eyes widened. "Will it save him?"

"No, not with only a single dose," she replied. "But it might keep him alive long enough to get him to the Aurora."

"But there are medical teams all over the race platform," Quory told her. "There's even a small hospital."

"Trust me, Quory, he needs to go to the Aurora's medical department, and quickly. If I call them, can you get them in here?"

"Yes, but shouldn't we at least get some of *our* medics in here to help? They may not be able to save him, but they might be able to help your nanites keep him alive a bit longer."

"Good idea," Jessica agreed. "Call them."

"MEDICS!" Quory yelled at the top of his lungs. "HELP! MEDICS!"

"Really?" Jessica asked, dumbfounded. "Quory, think quickly. If you just killed Yokimah, how would you get away?"

"Emergency evacuation areas, just like everyone else."

"No, that would just get you back to Rakuen. I'm talking about *getting away*, as in *out of the system*."

Quory thought for a moment. "Oh! Mister Yokimah has a private shuttle! A Ranni shuttle, ironically. It's in the last bay. It has its own private airlock, and everything."

"Would the killer be able to get it launched?"

"If he had Mister Yokimah's access card and control chip, yes."

Jessica quickly searched Ito's pockets. "What's this?" she asked, pulling a small chip out of Ito's pants pocket.

"It is the control chip for his personal shuttle," Quory replied. "It will not fly without it."

"Is there more than one of them?" she asked.

"I do not believe so."

"Jesus, he can't be *that* dumb," she muttered as a guard and two employees came running into the office.

"What the hell is going on here!" the guard demanded, reaching for his stunner.

Jessica spun around, pulling her knife from the sheath tucked into the small of her back, bringing the blade up against the guard's neck, causing him to instantly freeze.

"Don't!" Quory yelled. "Goodness! You are one dangerous young woman!"

"You'll be executed for this," the guard warned, not moving.

"*She* didn't do this!" Quory yelled, "A surprise, yes, but the truth."

"What do you want from me?" the guard asked, still not moving.

"Just let me go, so I can catch the guy who *did* do this," Jessica said. "It's either that, or you can join old Ito on the floor, there. I wouldn't suggest that, though, because I'm all out of nanites."

"What?" the guard asked, confused.

"She's on our side!" Quory insisted. "Let her go, and help Mister Yokimah! He *is* our employer, after all!"

Jessica stepped back, slowly moving her blade away from the guard's throat, and pulling her comm-unit from her pocket. "I'll call for a medevac from the Aurora. Make sure they are allowed in to see him, *if* you want him to live," she told the guard before she left.

424

"My aft shields are down to twenty percent!" Nathan exclaimed. "I don't think your friends are going to get here in time."

"*Six bandits just jumped in ahead of us,*" Master Koku warned. "*Prepare to break right, I will go left......* *Break now.*"

Nathan yanked his flight control stick to the right and pulled back, rolling the fighter into a tight right turn. He continued to get slammed by enemy energy weapons fire, but, at least, it wasn't on his weakened aft shields.

Suddenly, a familiar sight appeared directly ahead of him, weapons blazing. "Shit!" he exclaimed, reversing his turn and diving to avoid a collision with his own ship. "Where the hell did you come from?" he yelled over comms.

"*Not bad, huh?*" Josh exclaimed. "*The Seiiki's a stealthy bitch now, Captain!*"

"I didn't even see your flash!"

"*That's the idea! Maintain your dive! Four of them are on you, and four are on Koku! I'll deliver the rest of them to the Gunyoki!*"

Nathan continued his dive, pushing his throttles forward to accelerate. At that moment, he decided that going back to Earth to convince Abby to join them had *definitely* been worth the risk.

In the outer portion of the Rogen system, beyond the orbits of both Neramese and Rakuen, as well as the asteroid belt in which the two worlds had once fought a war with one another, two swarms of opposing ships merged in a hail of energy weapons fire and missiles. Jump flashes appeared all about as Dusahn fighters jumped in and out of the engagement, denying the Gunyoki fighters their kill shots, time and again. But even as half their numbers fell to Dusahn guns, the Gunyoki pilots did *not* sway from their commitment. While only a few of them were *true* Gunyoki, those who were not were inspired by the bravery and the unwavering dedication of those who were. It was at *that* moment when every young race pilot became a *true* Gunyoki themselves.

"The Gunyoki are taking a beating," Lieutenant Commander Vidmar warned. "They've lost twelve ships already."

"I thought they were supposed to be some kind of super fighter pilots," Lieutenant Dinev said.

"Without jump drives, they don't stand a chance," Cameron explained. "How long until our fighters reach them?"

"The first eight are jumping into the engagement area now," Lieutenant Commander Vidmar reported. "Reapers are locking jump missiles onto enemy gunships as we speak."

"What about the Gunyoki on the surface of Rakuen?" Lieutenant Commander Kono asked.

"Again, no jump drives. It will be over before they get there," Cameron said. "That's why we knew the Dusahn would make their play at the furthest point on the course from both the race platform *and* Rakuen. They *know* how potent the Gunyoki fighters are, but they *also* know that the lack of jump drives is their weakness." Cameron shook her head. "We need to end this, now."

Nathan pulled his Gunyoki fighter into a dive, then cut his engines, flipped his nacelles in opposite directions, and spun the ship around to the right, to face his pursuers.

"Two more bogeys just jumped in! One five seven, twenty clicks out! Closing fast!" one of the Super Eagle pilots warned.

While he waited for his right engine nacelle to swing back over, Nathan opened fire with the plasma torpedo cannon on the front of the left nacelle, tearing apart the Dusahn heavy fighter following him.

"Fuck! That makes twelve!"

Nathan had no idea who was talking, since he had not yet gotten to know any of the pilots under his command.

"Costa's hit!" a Gunyoki pilot yelled out over comms, his Rakuen accent easy to recognize.

As Nathan's right engine nacelle came back over to point forward, he added it to the barrage, as well, sweeping his nacelles left and right as his fighter sped backwards through the crowded engagement area.

"Shit! Somebody get this asshole off me!" Costa pleaded.

"Where are you, Costa?" Nathan called, recognizing the Gunyoki pilot's name from the race roster.

"I don't know..."

Nathan touched his tactical display as he spun his ship back around to face forward. IDs suddenly popped up on all the targets on his screen, allowing him to locate the distressed Gunyoki pilot. *"Costa! Hang on! I'll have the fucker in ten seconds!"*

———————

The Aurora's bridge was a blurry of activity, voices, and radio chatter as the battle unfolded around them.

"Eagle Four, left! Eagle Six, right! Two targets

each!" Commander Verbeek's voice called over the loudspeakers on the Aurora's bridge. *"Engage at max range!"*

"Forward tubes locked on Bravo," Lieutenant Commander Vidmar reported. "Firing all tubes!"

"Eagle One, fox two," the commander reported, announcing his weapons launch at the twelve Dusahn heavy fighters that had just jumped into range of his flight of Super Eagles.

"I don't have ten seconds!" the Gunyoki pilot cried out over comms.

"Nathan," Makani called. *"You are the closest ship. You must launch a spread of stub-missiles to protect Amon."*

"The targets are out of range," Nathan argued.

"The targets will not know that," Makani insisted. *"Fire them now, all that you have!"*

"The battleship is firing more missiles!" Lieutenant Commander Kono warned from the sensor station. "From her far side! Thirty seconds!"

"Eagle Four, fox two!" the pilot's voice crackled over the loudspeakers.

"Escape pattern echo one," Cameron ordered from her command chair. "On my command."

"Escape echo one, on your command, aye," Lieutenant Dinev acknowledged.

"Amon! Punch out! Punch out!" another Gunyoki pilot urged.

"How many missiles are inbound?" Cameron asked, ignoring the desperate chatter of the Gunyoki pilots. They had their fight, and she had hers.

"Twelve... No; fourteen!"

"Point-defenses can handle them, Captain," Lieutenant Commander Vidmar assured her. "Just give me more guns."

"Helm! Yaw ninety! Roll over, and show the target our topside to bring more point-defenses into play," Cameron ordered.

"Aye, sir," the lieutenant replied as she started the maneuver.

"Eight missiles left!" the lieutenant commander reported. "Ten seconds!"

———

Robert pulled the nose of his Cobra gunship up sharply, after unleashing a barrage of plasma torpedoes into the starboard side of the Jung battleship. Energy weapons and rail gun rounds slammed into his ventral shields, shaking his tiny ship wildly as they passed over the top of the massive vessel.

"*Eagle Six, fox two!*" the Super Eagle pilot's voice announced over Robert's comm-set as he touched the jump button to escape the incoming fire. "You guys might want to try to target some of their point-defenses when we pass over them like that," Robert suggested to his gunners as his jump completed.

"*Eagle Six, fox two!*" the previous call repeated, now that he had jumped five seconds further away from the Super Eagle that had transmitted the call.

———

Nathan watched in desperation as his stub-missiles ran out of thrust and were no longer able to maneuver to track their targets.

"*Fuck! He's coming apart!*" a Gunyoki pilot cried out over comms.

"Damn it!" Nathan cursed. Another explosion went off only a few meters off his port side, the result of an errant missile fired by some unseen foe who had missed his original target.

"*Costa's coming apart!*"

Ryk Brown

"Makani! Where are you?" Nathan called out over comms.

"*Your nine, two kilometers, just above. I'll be passing over you in ten seconds. Be ready to turn to starboard to...*" Makani's transmission was suddenly interrupted.

Nathan glanced to his left, spotting six flashes of light, the color of which was slightly different than those of Alliance ships. "Makani!"

"*Gunyoki Two Four is hit,*" Makani reported, his usual calm surprisingly intact. "*Six heavies just jumped in on my tail. I am attempting to shake them, but I am taking damage.*"

Nathan instinctively turned toward Makani's ship, ready to defend his leader. Four more flashes of light appeared behind Makani's fighter and the Dusahn ships pursuing him. The flashes were the familiar blue-white, and they opened fire on Makani's pursuers a split second after they arrived.

"*Nathan!*" Makani called out in warning. "*Behind you!*"

It was uncommon for the Gunyoki master to raise his voice in alarm in such a way, and it had a startling effect. Nathan's ship shook violently; his back end shifting hard to port as something exploded to his right. Alarms went off all over his cockpit. He glanced out the right side of his canopy as what was left of his starboard engine nacelle came apart in a series of secondary explosions that began working their way through the body of his ship, toward his starboard missile pod and his cockpit.

"*EJECT!*" Makani ordered.

Nathan felt frozen in time, watching in horror as the explosions reached his starboard missile pod. In the blink of an eye, his canopy was gone, and he
430

was rocketing away from his fighter while the mighty Gunyoki ship blew apart below him. He closed his eyes and gritted his teeth, fighting to breathe as he rode his rocket-powered seat into open space, clear of the fireball below.

The funny thing was, he didn't even remember pulling the ejection handle.

Makani watched in horror as Nathan rocketed across his flight path at a slight angle. Makani had ejected once in training, and he knew that it was a bone-jarring experience.

But there were other problems to deal with. Not only were damage alarms sounding in his own cockpit, but the Dusahn gunship that had just destroyed his student's, *his friend's,* fighter was targeting the captain, determined to kill the pilot, as well as the ship. It was at that moment that Master Koku decided the Dusahn truly had no honor, and that was what scared him the most. Men with no honor were the most difficult to defend against. He feared that this did not bode well for his world. "Nathan! Do you read me?"

"Captain!" Lieutenant Commander Kono called out urgently. "Gunyoki Seven Five is down hard! But I'm picking up the captain's transponder, moving away sharply! He must've ejected!"

"Nearest ship capable of rescue?" Cameron demanded.

"The Seiiki!" the lieutenant commander replied. "But the gunship that took him out is pursuing him, and there are at least six other Dusahn fighters in the vicinity!"

"Seiiki! Aurora Actual!" Cameron called over

her comm-set. "Nathan's fighter is down hard! He's accelerating away in his ejection seat, with the Dusahn in pursuit!"

"*Aurora Actual, Seiiki. We're on our way,*" Loki replied.

"*Seiiki! Aurora Actual!*" Captain Taylor's voice crackled over Makani's comms. "*Nathan's fighter is down hard! He's accelerating away in his ejection seat, with the Dusahn in pursuit!*"

"*Aurora Actual, Seiiki. We're on our way.*"

Makani struggled to force his damaged Gunyoki fighter to turn to a heading that would intercept the Dusahn gunship about to lock onto the rescue beacon on Nathan's ejection seat. By now, the seat's propulsion system had run out of propellant, and the captain was drifting out of the engagement area. "Nathan, please, respond," he urged.

"*I'm here,*" Nathan finally replied, his voice sounding dazed and confused.

"*Cap'n! This is Josh! We'll be there in thirty seconds!*"

"Nathan!" Makani called. "Are you injured?"

"*No, I don't think so,*" Nathan replied, still sounding unsteady. "*Negative. I'm good. Jesus!*"

"*Eagle Leader, Aurora Actual!*" Captain Taylor called. "*Engage targets near Captain Scott's transponder signal, and keep those Dusahn ships off of him!*"

"*Eagle One copies. On my way!*" Commander Verbeek replied.

"*Eagle Two copies.*"

"*Eagle Seven copies.*"

"*Eagle four copies.*"

Makani began trying to bypass his damaged

systems in order to regain basic maneuverability, but with marginal success. He looked at his tactical screen. To his left was his student, the man known as Na-Tan, the legend. The man who was Rakuen's best hope for survival. To his right was the Dusahn gunship that meant to steal that hope from his world. After doing the math in his head, he brought his engines up to full power. "Captain, it appears you were correct," he admitted.

"What are you talking about, Master Koku?"

Makani smiled at Nathan's show of respect, especially at such a moment. "The Gunyoki are not capable of defending Rakuen against the Dusahn." Makani swallowed hard as his ship accelerated on an intercept course with the Dusahn gunship closing on his friend. A tear formed in the corner of his eye as the old man spoke. "I am not your master, Nathan. I am not even sure I am your equal."

———————

Nathan tried to turn his head around, hoping to spot Makani's ship. After a few jerks, his seat began to rotate slowly to the right, bringing the Dusahn gunship that was closing on him into view, as well as Makani's Gunyoki fighter, its engines at full power, speeding toward the enemy gunship on a collision course.

"My only hope is that this sacrifice will make me your equal in the eyes of my people."

"Makani, what are you doing?" Nathan asked, fearing that he already knew the answer.

A blue-white flash appeared in the distance, beyond the approaching gunship. *"Eagle One is engaging!"* Commander Verbeek reported as he opened fire on the gunship. But Nathan knew it would take more than a single Super Eagle to take down the Dusahn vessel that was coming to get him.

"*We're right behind you, Cap'n!*" Josh called. "*Half a click! Ten seconds out!*"

"Josh! Forget me!" Nathan ordered. "Target that gunship! Target that gunship!"

———

"Marcus!" Josh called over the Seiiki's intercom. "Get ready for a Palee!"

"Oh, God," Loki muttered.

"Fire on the fucking gunship!" Josh ordered his gunners. "I'm flipping this bitch over to catch the captain!"

"We can take it out with our new plasma cannons, Josh," Loki reminded him.

"Fuck that shit!" Josh insisted. "I didn't spend the last five years babysitting his cloned ass just to let him die now!"

"But he *ordered* us to..."

"NOT happening, Lok!" Josh insisted. "You ready, Pops?"

"*Ready as I'll ever be,*" Marcus replied.

———

"*Eagle Two! Engaging!*"

"Makani! Don't do this, damn it!" Nathan insisted as he disconnected his restraints and pushed himself away from his ejection seat, continuing to drift helplessly through space.

"*Tell my family I died bravely, defending our world,*" Makani pleaded, his voice full of sadness.

"Makani! I'm ordering you to veer away! Do not engage!" Nathan cried out as he watched the crippled Gunyoki fighter open fire with the last of his stub-missiles, hoping to get the gunship's attention off of their prize, long enough for the Seiiki to snatch it away.

Nathan watched in horror, plasma bolts from the Seiiki's gun turrets streaking over his head from behind as Makani closed on the approaching Dusahn gunship. "Makani! God damn you! Listen to me!"

Makani's right hand moved to his reactor control panel, initiating an overload condition as the Dusahn gunship filled his forward canopy. "Save my world, Na-Tan," he begged. "Make your teacher proud."

"NO!" Nathan yelled at the top of his lungs as the Seiiki's cargo bay swallowed him up. The bay suddenly filled with a brilliant flash of light, signaling what Nathan feared most. Then he slammed into something hard, and everything went dark.

"Oh, my God," Cameron gasped, her eyes welling up. She had never met Master Koku, but she could tell by Nathan's voice that the man had meant a lot to him.

"Captain!" Lieutenant Commander Kono cried out in excitement as the pounding from the battleship continued to rock the Aurora and drain her shields. "The battleship's shields have fallen!"

"Pound her!" Cameron demanded. "Everything you've got!"

"Target is moving away," Lieutenant Commander Kono warned.

"Firing all tubes and cannons!" Lieutenant Commander Vidmar announced as more plasma torpedoes leapt forward from under the Aurora's bow.

"They're making a run for it!" Lieutenant Dinev

Ryk Brown

surmised as the battleship began turning and pulling away from them. "She's trying to keep her unprotected side from us!"

"Their fighters are jumping away!" Lieutenant Commander Kono added. "Target bravo is powering up her jump drive!"

The Aurora's main view screen filled with the odd light of the Dusahn jump drive as the battleship made their escape.

"Have the Reapers attempt to track her," Cameron ordered.

"All remaining Dusahn forces have jumped away," Lieutenant Commander Kono announced triumphantly.

"Damn," Cameron cursed to herself. She looked about, realizing that her crew had overheard her. "I really wanted to take that bastard down."

———

Nathan sat on the deck of the Seiiki's cargo bay, his helmet off, resting against the forward bulkhead that he had slammed into upon landing.

"How are you doin', Cap'n?" Marcus asked, noticing the forlorn looked on his friend's face.

Nathan looked at his trusted crew chief, the man who had served as his surrogate father figure for the last five years. "Honestly?" Nathan swallowed hard. "I've had better days," he admitted, his voice cracking.

Marcus put his hand on Nathan's shoulder, squeezing it firmly to show his support. "You wanna get up?"

"I don't know that I can," he admitted.

"Are you injured?"

"Bruises, at the most. I'm just *exhausted*."

Marcus laughed. "Aren't we all."

436

Nathan tapped his comm-set. "Nice catch, Josh."

"Thanks, Cap'n," Josh replied in a melancholy tone. *"Sorry about Koku. But I couldn't let..."*

"It's okay, Josh," Nathan assured him. "Patch me through to the Aurora, will you?"

"Sure thing."

"Go ahead, sir," Loki said a moment later.

"Aurora Actual, Seiiki Actual," Nathan called. "Status?"

"Good to hear your voice, Captain," Cameron replied. *"All Dusahn forces have left the system. The battleship gave up once we got one of her shield sections down; the rest followed. I've got Reapers trying to track them, just to make sure they don't try to double back and surprise us."*

"Good thinking."

"Are you okay?"

"Not really," Nathan admitted. "But I will be. How many Gunyoki survived?"

"Out of the original twenty-seven who launched from the race platform, only eight. But another one hundred and six have launched from Rakuen within the last five minutes and are headed toward the engagement area. That may also have something to do with the Dusahn's retreat."

"Any word from Jess?"

"Negative. Last report from Telles was that she went after Seeley. Seems he slit Yokimah's throat."

"Yokimah's dead?" Nathan asked, feeling like his plan had suddenly unraveled.

"He's still alive... Barely. Jessica pumped a load of Ghatazhak trauma nanites into his wound and called for one of our medical rescue teams. They're landing at the race platform now."

"Understood," Nathan replied. "Tell everyone 'good job'."

"*You just did, Captain,*" Cameron replied.

"Hey, who's the lead Gunyoki at the moment?" Nathan asked.

After a pause, Cameron replied, "*Vol Kaguchi, in Gunyoki Six Seven.*"

"Copy that. Patch me through to him."

Another moment passed. "*Go ahead, sir.*"

"Gunyoki Six Seven, Gunyoki Seven Five," Nathan called. "How do you copy?"

"*Gunyoki Seven Five, Gunyoki Six Seven,*" Nathan's comm-set crackled. "*Is that you, Captain Scott?*"

"Affirmative, this is Scott."

"*It is good to hear your voice, Captain. I am happy to know that my dear friend did not die in vain.*"

Nathan closed his eyes for a moment, the vision of Master Koku's death still fresh in his memory, as he suspected it would be for the rest of his days.

"*What can I do for you, Captain?*" Vol asked.

"I was hoping you could set up a barrier patrol around this system, in case the Dusahn try to sneak back in. Our forces need a chance to regroup and rearm."

"*The Gunyoki stand ready to follow your command, Captain... For as long as you will have us. I believe that* this *was Master Koku's hope.*"

Nathan fought back his tears, struggling for half a minute before he could answer, and even then, his voice was somewhat unsteady. "Thank you, sir."

"*It is my honor, Captain,*" Vol replied. "*Today, we are all of the same ichi.*"

Nathan sniffled. "We always were, my friend," he replied, his voice trembling. "Scott out."

"Seeley?" Jessica called in a lilting tone, hoping to taunt the Dusahn spy. "I know you're in here," she continued, walking slowly about the transfer airlock, where Yokimah's private jump shuttle was located. "But you fucked up, fella. You took Yokimah's access card, which meant it was easy to track your movements by reading the door logs." She moved to her right, peaking under the back end of the shuttle, trying to determine where the man was hiding. "Pretty lousy tradecraft, if you ask me," she continued. "But that wasn't your only mistake. You were in such a hurry, that you *forgot* the security chip for his jump shuttle. I *know*, because *I've* got the chip *right* here in my pretty, little hand, and I'd *love* for you to try to take it away from me."

Jessica stood motionless for a moment, waiting for a response. After a minute passed, she started walking backward toward the open hangar door. "Of course, I could just close the door and vent the bay. Even if you're *inside* that shuttle, you'll run out of air in *there* eventually, as well." She sidestepped to the edge of the hangar door, and activated the door motors, starting the close cycle. "Your call, Seeley, or whatever your name is."

There had been a day when Jessica's emotions would have taken over at times like this. She had grown up a skinny child, and had not blossomed until just before she had enlisted. The fact that she had been so active as a child was mostly due to being surrounded by brothers all her life. That inner rage she had always carried with her had nearly gotten her killed on several occasions.

The Ghatazhak had changed all of that. They taught her to control that rage, and only tap what was needed. She now saw it as a resource; as an energy that she could tap at will. There were still times when it threatened to get away from her, but it was those moments when she managed to go beyond what she knew she was capable of, redefining her own personal boundaries.

This would be one of those times...she could *feel* it.

The hangar doors clanged shut. A moment later, the jump shuttle hatch opened, and Jorkar Seeley climbed down the step ladder that extended out of the lower portion of the ship. He no longer carried himself as the nervous, talkative businessman, hell-bent on selling everything to everyone. This time, he moved with the confidence and swagger of a warrior. More than that, with the look of someone who felt himself superior to all those around him.

That was when she knew. The man was Dusahn.

"Well, well, well," Seeley began. "If it isn't Captain Scott's personal bitch." Seeley smiled as he strolled slowly toward Jessica. "The clone-boy sent you to do his dirty work, again, I see."

"I'm here of my own volition," Jessica stated as she reached for the hatch controls, and locked the doors.

"You can say that all you want, but you and I both know better."

"Are all Dusahn dickheads as talkative as you, or are you just a special case?" Jessica asked.

"How about you just hand me that control chip, and I'll be on my way," Seeley suggested.

"Already trying to bargain," Jessica noted. "A sure sign of a desperate man."

"Not a desperate one," Seeley insisted. "Just one who doesn't like to kill helpless women. It's just not my thing."

Jessica laughed. Once she was done, she let out a sigh. "Well, I can see that you're going to try to stall for as long as possible, so I'm going to force your hand." Jessica reached up to the airlock bay control pad next to the door controls and started the depressurization cycle. A warning horn sounded, and the trim lights around the top and bottom edges of the bay turned red, to warn all those inside that the air was being slowly pumped out of the room. "Perfect lighting for a fight, wouldn't you say?"

A grin came across Seeley's face.

"Just to give you a chance, I set it for a slow depress cycle. Probably take about five minutes to completely depress; even less before we suffocate." A smirk appeared in the corner of Jessica's mouth. "Let's dance."

"This will not take long," Seeley proclaimed as he pulled a short, flat tool from his belt. As he began walking confidently toward her, he pressed a button on the tool, and a blade the length of his forearm extended from it.

Seeley quickened his pace, raising his blade and striking down at Jessica as he charged at her. Jessica stepped aside, spinning away from him with minimal effort, immediately raising her arm to block the next swing of his blade. In a flash, she slid her other arm around his blade arm and twisted it back, knocking the blade from his hand with her now-free hand.

After releasing him, she stepped away, the blade lying on the floor, equidistant from them both. "Go ahead. Pick it up," she said.

Seeley eyed her suspiciously, unsure if she was laying a trap. He took a cautious step forward,

441

keeping his eyes on her as he squatted down to pick up his weapon.

Jessica simply stood there, her arms relaxed at her sides, waiting for his next move. She didn't have to wait long.

As soon as Seeley picked up his blade, he thrust forward and up, hoping to catch her in the abdomen, but Jessica turned sideways and bent just enough for the blade to miss. He immediately moved the blade toward her, but she jumped up, tucking in the air as she dove over the top of the blade as it moved laterally.

Jessica tucked and rolled through her landing, and was back on her feet in an instant, still not trying to attack the man.

Again, Seeley pressed the attack, spinning around as his blade arm came out, slashing at her midsection. Jessica bent at the knees and fell backward, landing with her feet and hands outstretched behind her, sweeping one leg between his, then the other, and twisting her body to pull him over and down. But her opponent was not without skills, himself.

Seeley landed cleanly on his back, and swung his blade parallel to the floor, centimeters above it. Jessica made a snake-like motion with her entire body, lifting it off the floor, and allowing her attacker's blade, and the arm wielding it, to pass under her, coming down with her elbow into his shoulder.

Jessica quickly raised her feet, rolling backward and upright as her opponent scrambled to retrieve his blade, once again. He climbed back to his feet, stumbling for a moment as he pushed back the pain.

Jessica smiled. "I guess you haven't been doing much dancing lately, huh?"

Seeley smiled back at her. "I must admit, I'd forgotten how much I enjoyed it."

"Then, please, don't stop now," Jessica urged.

Seeley lunged, missing again as Jessica deftly dodged his parry. He swung high left, passing over her as she leaned back, then he came back around down low, and she merely jumped over his blade, as if skipping rope.

This time, however, she added a step. A quick boot to his face, sending blood and spit spraying across the floor. "Oops," she mocked in a girlish voice.

Now Seeley was becoming annoyed, and it showed in both his expression and movements. He came at her again, only to find his blade arm locked in hers, and her fist in his chest and then in his face.

Again, Jessica released him, his weapon still in his hand.

Seeley stumbled backward, sweat dripping from his brow, and blood from his mouth.

"Let's make this more interesting," Jessica decided, pulling her own knife from its sheath in the small of her back. "I like blades, too." She spun the knife in her hand, taking it in an overhand grip, and held it ready in front of her.

Seeley charged forth, his blade slashing back and forth across her, but Jessica parried each swipe of his long blade with her own shorter one. The blades clanged repeatedly as he tried everything to get through her defenses, but try as he might, every attempt was successfully thwarted. Every third or fourth attempt, Jessica added a punch to Seeley's face or midsection, once even spinning around and driving her knee into his side.

After nearly a full minute of this, Seeley stumbled backward. His vision was fading, and his breathing had become shallow and gasping. He suddenly realized that he was suffocating. He glared at Jessica, standing there before him, seemingly unaffected by the thinning atmosphere that drained him so.

"Had enough?" she asked, walking toward him. When he did not respond, she punched him square in the face, knocking him to the floor, out cold.

Jessica kicked the blade away from Seeley's unconscious body, then bent over and searched him for any additional weapons. All she found was his wallet. She opened it up, finding all the usual things one carried, including several rectangular Rakuen credit chips. "These should cover my jacket," she said, taking the credit chips and placing them in her pocket. She looked at Seeley. "You're a lousy dancer, you know that?"

Jessica stood up and walked over to the airlock controls, stopping the decompression cycle and reversing it. "By the way," she said to the still unconscious Dusahn spy, "the air on Burgess is a lot thinner than it is in here. But of course, you probably wouldn't know that, since *your* people decided to glass it."

CHAPTER TWELVE

His head hurt, and his hearing felt muffled. He could hear voices, but he did not recognize them. He tried to open his eyes, but they were fighting him, as if they wanted to stay closed.

The voices became louder, a few of them familiar. His eyes finally started to open, but his vision was blurry; slowly it began to focus. A white room. Curtains. Several people, some of them in uniform.

"I think he's waking up," one of the voices said. Then the muffled sounds of movement, and the jiggling of his bed.

"Mister Yokimah?"

It was a woman's voice.

"Mister Yokimah, can you speak?"

"I..." his voice was scratchy, weak.

My neck.

He reached for his neck, the place where the gaping wound had been, but there was nothing but smooth skin.

How can that be?

His vision cleared, and the faces around him became clearer, as did their voices.

"My neck," he said, barely audible

"It's fully healed," the Asian woman told him. "I'm Doctor Chen. How do you feel?"

Ito thought for a moment. "Thirsty."

"Get him some water," Doctor Chen told someone in the distance.

A moment later, someone handed him a glass of water with a straw. He took a sip. It felt wonderful, so he took another.

"Can you speak?" a male voice asked.

"Yes," Ito replied, his voice becoming stronger. He opened his eyes again, spotting Captain Scott standing at his bedside. "You."

"Yes, me," Nathan replied. "If you'll excuse us for a minute," he instructed the others. He waited a moment for them to leave, and for the door to close behind them.

"Where am I?" Ito asked.

"In the medical department on board the Aurora, in orbit over Rakuen," Nathan explained.

"How long?"

"Three and a half days."

"Have the Dusahn..."

"No, they have not returned," Nathan assured him. "Our recon drones have verified that the ships that attacked this system have returned to Takara. Those that made it out, that is."

"My neck?" Ito asked. "How did it heal so quickly?"

"I'm surprised you haven't yet heard of the wonders of Corinairan nanites," Nathan explained.

"I have, I just didn't realize..."

"That they worked so well?"

Ito nodded.

"Yeah, well, that's one of the reasons we kept you unconscious for the last three days. Not everyone finds it pleasant to have those buggers crawling around inside of them. We figured we'd play it safe, considering the depth of your neck wound."

"Then, I will recover?"

"Fully," Nathan promised.

Ito closed his eyes, a wave of relief washing over him. Then reality reared its ugly head. "So, what is to become of me?" he asked, his eyes still closed.

"Well, that depends on you."

Ito tried to make a power play. "People will be asking questions. I am quite well known…"

"They already have," Nathan replied. "Quite a few, in fact."

"What did you tell them?"

"The truth."

Ito closed his eyes again, imagining his imprisonment.

"That you sustained serious injuries while defending yourself against a Dusahn spy and saboteur," Nathan elaborated.

Ito opened one eye, looking suspiciously at the captain. "The truth?"

"None of what I said is a lie," Nathan insisted. "It is just…incomplete. How we let the *truth* be understood, in the eyes of *your* people, depends on you."

"What are my options?"

"Always the businessman, I see." Nathan took a breath before continuing. "Well, we can tell them the truth as you and I, and a few others, who shall remain nameless, know it, or we can tell them a truth that will save your future, and the future of Rakuen. Perhaps even of the entire quadrant."

"I'm not sure you and I share the same *truth*, Captain."

"Let's see. You made a deal with the Dusahn, agreeing to help them capture me and destroy my ship, in exchange for *not* glassing your world and leaving you in charge of Rakuen as their puppet governor."

"An interesting fantasy you've concocted," Ito said, trying to play innocent.

"Trust me, Ito, I have a mountain of evidence to

447

substantiate my claims. I'd be happy to compile it for your review, if you'd like."

By now, Ito was pretty sure Captain Scott was not the type to bluff. "That won't be necessary."

"Would you like to hear the fantasy version?" Nathan asked. "The one where you are the hero?"

"Why not."

"Being eager to open up new markets, you unknowingly allowed a Dusahn spy, posing as a Takaran businessman, into your midst, where he sabotaged several Gunyoki racers, all of which belonged to you, of course, including the one you loaned me. This spy's plan, of course, was to capture me and destroy my ship. When you uncovered the truth, you confronted him, had a struggle in your office, which you lost, obviously, and suffered serious injury. Luckily, your trusted employee, Quory, who had brought Mister Seeley's suspicious activities to your attention in the first place, found you bleeding out and called for help. My people heard the call and offered assistance, knowing what a prominent member of Rakuen society you truly are."

Ito glared at Captain Scott, who was smiling from ear to ear. "You're insufferable, you know that."

"I admit, I have my moments."

"What is it you want from me?"

"I want the support of your world and of your Gunyoki; ships, pilots, and support crews, so that we may drive the Dusahn from this quadrant. I want you to become the savior of Rakuen...a man of vision who realized that the only thing necessary for the triumph of evil was for good men to do nothing."

"Edmund Burke?"

Nathan's eyes widened in surprise.

"I am quite well read," Ito reminded him.

"Ah, yes. The library."

"I'm afraid I do not have the power to grant what you ask, Captain," Ito admitted.

"Ah, but you *do* have the power to stand in the way of your fellow leaders, all of whom are ready to support our rebellion against the Dusahn. You might not be able to stop them, but you could make things very difficult. And trust me, we have enough problems as it is."

Ito sighed. "Did anyone ever tell you that you have a strange way of negotiating?"

"My grandfather once told me that there were two ways to convince a man to see your point of view; through intelligent discourse, or at the point of a gun. In my short life—both of them, that is—I have found that it sometimes requires both. An unfortunate reality, but a reality, nonetheless."

"And I was one who required both," Ito realized.

"Very much so, I'm afraid."

"I was only doing what I thought was best for my world," Ito insisted.

"When men say that, it usually means they were really doing what was best for themselves. However, I'm willing to give you the benefit of the doubt, this time...assuming we have a deal, of course."

"Of course," Ito agreed, closing his eyes.

"Excellent," Nathan exclaimed. "I'll have the galley send you some ice cream for dessert. You'll love it. It will make your scratchy throat feel better."

"What would I have gotten had I chosen not to cooperate?" Ito wondered, trying to keep the mood light in lieu of their new working relationship.

"I don't know, probably molo pie, or something equally unappetizing," Nathan replied. "We'll talk more later."

"I look forward to it," Ito replied, failing to hide his sarcasm.

Nathan stepped out of the room, letting the door close behind him.

"How did it go?" General Telles asked.

"He's going to play ball," Nathan announced as they headed into the corridor.

"I'm assuming that means he will endorse Rakuen's support of our rebellion."

"Wholeheartedly."

"I am impressed," General Telles admitted. "But, be honest, Captain. Was this your plan all along?"

"Of course," Nathan replied, smiling.

General Telles cast him a dubious look. "Where are we headed?"

"The galley. I promised Yokimah some ice cream to seal the deal."

"Another Earth custom that I am not aware of, I assume?"

"Indeed."

* * *

"There are two bedrooms, each with its own bath, as well as a den, master suite, dining room, and full gourmet kitchen," the realtor explained as she led the young man through the top floor apartment. "Since you are single, it may be more space than you need, especially considering the rent."

"The rent will not be a problem, I assure you," the young man promised.

"What was it you said you do?"

"Security," he replied. "For a political lobbying firm."

"Oh, we have plenty of that around here," she laughed as she led him into the living room. "And this is perhaps the best feature, and the reason for the high rent." She pulled back the curtains, revealing a breathtaking view of Winnipeg, including the NAU capital building, less than a kilometer away. "A simply stunning view, you must agree. You can even see the president's office window."

"Stunning, indeed," he agreed. "I'll take it."

"Wonderful," she cooed, already spending her commission in her head. "I'll have my people send the lease agreement to your hotel. Which one did you say you were staying at, Mister..."

"The Excelsior, room three zero seven. And the name is Bornet. Krispin Bornet."

Thank you for reading this story.
(*A review would be greatly appreciated!*)

COMING SOON

Episode 7
of
The Frontiers Saga:
Rogue Castes

Visit us online at
frontierssaga.com
or on Facebook

Want to be notified when
new episodes are published?
Join our mailing list!

frontierssaga.com/mailinglist/

Made in the USA
Columbia, SC
09 July 2020